PLAY FAST

BROOKLYN DAWN BOOK 2

CARI QUINN
TARYN ELLIOTT

RAINBOW
rage
PUBLISHING

Play Fast
© 2020 Cari Quinn & Taryn Elliott
Rainbow Rage Publishing

Cover by LateNite Designs
Photograph by Period Images

First print edition: April 2020
ISBN Print edition: 978-1-940346-63-2

ACKNOWLEDGMENTS

Sometimes we make up fictional places that end up having the same names as actual places. These are our fictional interpretations only. Please grant us leeway if our creative vision isn't true to reality.

FOR THOSE WHO ALWAYS FIND THE SILVER LINING IN THE STORMCLOUDS.

AUTHOR NOTE

We wrote a little bonus scene for people who preordered this book.

FYI—we love all of our readers and super appreciate anyone who trusts us enough to preorder our books!

This is the extra scene that happens juuuust before PLAY FAST begins...

There's enough here that we thought we'd add it to the print copy. And we figure if you love us enough to pay for print, you like all the extras.

We hope you enjoy.

Xoxo,
Taryn & Cari

A LITTLE HELP FROM HIS FRIENDS

Elle

When making out with a sexy, huge, tattooed, bald man—
which weren't pertinent facts other than holy fuck, he was hot—when
you were due on stage in oh, nineteen-point-nine-minutes, one had to
be quick.

And greedy.

"I told you I had a surprise," he panted against my throat, working
hard to shove his hand into my leather pants. They were a new addition
to my wardrobe. I feared a Ross situation from *Friends* when I
overheated on stage, yet here I was wearing them anyway because
someone who wouldn't be named said they made my ass look hot.

And that someone was obviously the one with his tongue curved
around the new shark bite piercings I had in my lower lip or else they
would be dead, because my husband did not do jealousy.

Ever.

I gripped his cock through his jeans and rued that he might like my ass in leather but would never provide me with such eye candy. "Yeah, I love your surprise. Now suit up and slide it in."

His rough chuckle would've had me losing my panties had I come prepared with talcum powder to get me out of these damn pants. As it was, it was going to take an act of God to get them down and back up before the curtain came up onstage.

And Mal would just laugh his ass off at me. His sadistic streak was a mile wide.

"Not the surprise, although I wouldn't mind skipping the suit now and then."

My heart beat just a little faster. We both believed in extra protection, since life had a tendency of having crazy timing. Him even more so than me. He was a reluctant passenger on the baby bus I'd lived on since I was oh, eighteen or so. "Playing with fire, Shawcross?"

His thumb caressed my lower lip as he tilted my head up until our eyes were closer to even. My heeled boots could only do so much. The guy was a freaking giant. "Sometimes the burn feels good."

Yeah, my heart was definitely rocketing now. Was he saying...?

Ah, hell, we'd just have to talk about it later. Now wasn't the time. We were both horny and had a show to play in under twenty minutes and there was some jerk banging on the door.

So, I squeezed my husband's cock that much tighter, either to give him one last moment of pleasure or to punish him for putting thoughts in my head that probably shouldn't be there yet.

"Jesus, woman." He hissed out a breath, but instead of moving back at the rattling door, he just cupped my breast through the equally punishing leather bustier. "I'd have you on my face in a minute. Ignore the fucking door."

It was my turn to laugh, huskily. As if he'd already made me come although we so knew that wouldn't be happening now. "Whomever it is has something important to say."

"Ricki, I know you're in there. And if these red panties on the doorknob mean what I think, I'd be even more horrified if you weren't a properly married woman."

Mal groaned and I threw back my head, swallowing a giggle. My brother—my twin no less—had impeccable timing. "What if I'm in here with someone named Sven?"

"Oh, is that what you're calling Mr. Rough and Ready now? He should be in a tire commercial."

Mal shook his head and glanced down at the grip I still had on his dick through his jeans. "Watch how fast it deflates. Your brother's voice should be put in pill form to kill erections."

"I heard that, and now is not the time for carnal activities. You should be preparing for the stage, not for Wild Times at Nailed High, part three—" My brother Nicky broke off as I flung open the door and cocked my head.

Judging from his raised brows, I needed to tug my bustier back into place, which I did with a toss of my hair. "You intrude on my dressing room, you see what you see, bucko. Also, I am beginning to feel very sorry for Lila if you've now decided a little dressing room nookie is off-limits."

"My wife is never anywhere near my dressing room before shows, or else I would nookie the fuck out of her. Alas, she has a job to do that doesn't have to do with my—"

"I'm out of here," Mal muttered, pulling on the tank top he'd abandoned on the bench near the door we'd had very optimistic plans for. "I know you have sex with her, but I definitely do not need to hear about it."

"Is me having sex with your former stepmother any worse than you banging my sister? My flesh and blood? Then you cause her to make this prune face because you obviously couldn't finish the job." He jerked a thumb at me before crossing his arms.

I simply sighed. Trying to reason with my brother was something very few attempted and even fewer succeeded at. I was convinced my sister-in-law had a pair of platinum wings waiting for her at the pearly gates.

To match the noise-cancelling earplugs she'd probably had surgically welded to her eardrums by this point. Between dealing with my brother and her adorable, slightly demonic kindergarten-aged twins and all the many crazy bands she managed at Ripper—she might be a candidate for sainthood soon.

Mal didn't even address my brother. The fact that he'd still married me even knowing what Nick was like proved he truly did adore me, because no way in hell would anyone join our family voluntarily without deep bonds of love.

"See you in a few?" He brushed his thumb over my lips and was gone before I could do more than let out a long sigh and stare after him a little stupidly.

Probably a lot stupidly. We'd been married the better part of a year and to say we were still in the honeymoon period was probably an insult to honeymoons. The dude was still an ass a good third of the time, but the rest?

Cue the heart eyes and questionably damp panties.

"Jeez, every time I want to flip him off, I see your expression and figure he has to be doing something right." Before I could reply, Nicky held up a hand. "Let's just assume I can fill in the dots and maintain our sibling boundaries, 'kay?"

I had to laugh before I hurtled into his arms and kissed him hard on the side of the head. "You're my favorite person on this planet." I bit my lip. "Okay, second favorite. Have to say Mal is my first now. Since, you know, he put a ring on it."

"Yeah, yeah. I keep waiting for you to say he put a bun in it too. Do they still call babies buns? Weird." He gripped my shoulders and eased me back, apparently not realizing I'd stiffened. "You look good. Happy."

"I am. Very. What are you doing here anyway?" I'd just stall for a minute or two until my heartbeat leveled off and I figured out how to say the potentially most awkward thing ever.

Something I'd sort of been turning around in my head for a while, if unconsciously. If we ever made it over hurdle A—also known as Mal's side-eye tendencies toward the smaller versions of the species—what about hurdle B?

In some ways, it was an even bigger one.

"What, a guy can't swing by to see his sister's show? I told you I'd catch one before we head back to the west coast."

"Yeah, but we had lunch and spent the day with the girls—where are the girls?"

"Probably lighting things on fire in the hotel." He shook his head. "With Stella, their very capable nanny. Why are you so jittery all of a sudden?"

"What? I'm not. Come in here." I yanked him by the arm through the doorway and shut the door, unsure whom exactly I didn't want to hear our upcoming conversation.

Possibly the whole world, since backstage at MSG before a huge-ass double header sold-out show with our tour mates, the incredible Brooklyn Dawn, meant chaos and tons of people.

"Look, we gotta talk—"

"What's the status of things with you and Lila?" I blurted, biting my lip. *Yeah, that was a great segue, Ricki.*

He lifted a brow that nearly disappeared under his shaggy blondish-brown hair, so similar to my own when I wasn't visiting the salon chair. Right now, I was edging closer to platinum, since Mal had a blond fetish, and hey, why not?

"We aren't candidates for that *Divorce Court* show yet, so I'd say pretty good."

"That's not what I meant. I mean, I know you're solid. That you'll always be solid. Everyone knows that."

"Do they? I'm so relieved. Who exactly is this everyone, and why do they care about the status of my marriage?" He pretended to rest his chin on his hand. "Just for curiosity's sake."

"Don't be obtuse."

"I would be happy not to, if I had any clue where this conversation was headed. And quickly, since we gotta talk and you've got a show to get ready for asap. Lila will kick your ass if you're late."

You'd think having your sister-in-law as your band's manager would be basically the ideal situation. Sure, most of the time it was pretty awesome, especially when I was aching for home and we were in some far-flung small town. Mal and I weren't one of those annoying couples that never spent time with anyone else. We both needed our space and that only made the reunions that much better. Especially since we lived and worked together twenty-four/seven.

And hell, Lila *got* it. She was as close to a musician herself as someone could be and not be in a band. She had miles more experience working with them than even I did.

Plus, there was the Nicky thing. They hadn't killed each other in their five-plus years of marriage, so she was definitely savvy to the ways of dealing with temperamental rockstars.

But Lila was also a ball-buster. She did not understand the word *nepotism*. She might tell me tearfully I was her sister in private, but in public, she would happily ream my ass out if I stepped on that stage thirty-two seconds late.

She'd be right to do so too. No one got any *gimmes* in this world. I'd learned that the hard way, and it was a lesson I'd never forget.

"You mentioned a bun, and no, there's no bun, and hell, if there was, you'd probably know before I did because of that freaky twin thing."

"You're saying if you got pregnant, I'd feel..." He looked down at his stomach, currently clad in a skintight Oblivion T-shirt that had enough rips to qualify for the donation bin. "No way. That's fucking creepy. Though I could probably get a song out of it."

I giggled. I couldn't help it. He was such a jackass. "We aren't trying for one. Mal's still not quite on that road."

"Yeah. It's a process. Long as he knows he better start driving before you're too old."

"Ahh, Nicky, you're too sweet to me."

He shrugged. "I'm the same age. Just saying."

"Yeah, I know. Think I'm good for a bit, but thanks for the concern. But if we get to the point where we want to, will it be cool?" I tucked my hair behind my ears and remembered I still hadn't done it up in the braids I'd planned to wear on stage. We had a kickass hair-and-makeup chick available, but I hated sitting in the chair, so I usually threw myself together.

Not so well tonight evidently.

"Uh, sure?"

"Not really with you, I mean, you'll say shit anyway."

He tucked his hands in the pockets of his jeans, looking as if he would've preferred the floor disintegrated under his boots rather than have to finish this conversation. Couldn't say I blamed him. I wasn't loving it either. "You know that I'm just messing with you guys, right? I don't hate the dude. I wouldn't have let him marry you if I didn't think he was decent."

"*Let* me?" I crossed my arms. "Back up."

His golden eyes fired. "You heard me. You're all that's left of my family. My birth family," he corrected immediately. He never forgot about his kids or Li for a second.

"We don't know that. Mama could be out there somewhere."

"Ricki, seriously? You can't honestly believe that. And if she is still alive, she clearly doesn't give fuck all about us. We have our own lives. Good ones. We don't need her anymore."

I hated that my chin wobbled. I was such a tough girl when it came to most things. But mention my mother and I was on the verge of tears. "I thought I saw her at a show last year."

Nicky's gaze shuttered. "You didn't. End of."

"How can you know that? I mean, I came to that conclusion myself, when I chased after her and—"

"You didn't. Why would you drop your pride like that for a woman who didn't care about us?"

"We don't know what happened."

"We sure as fuck do. She left us when we were in second grade. Didn't say goodbye, leave us a note, nothing. My girls aren't far from that age now and do you know what would make me leave them? Not one fucking thing."

I turned away and rubbed a hand over my cheek. I wasn't even crying yet, but I could feel the tears burning into my skin as if I already were. I'd cried so many for her.

I'd fucked up my life because of her, over and over. And now I was arguing with Nicky about her and for what? He was right. She was gone. Probably dead. If not, she might as well have been.

"Ricki, I'm sorry," he said after a moment, coming up behind me. I'd gripped my elbows and hugged my arms to my chest instinctively. "It's not you. You get that, right? I could just fucking kill her for hurting you."

I smiled faintly as I turned back to him, standing there so stoic and proud and defiant. That was my brother, two minutes younger than me but always so determined to save me from the world. "She hurt you too."

He jerked a shoulder. "Don't care anymore. It's finished."

I wanted to toss back that it wasn't. It couldn't be. We only had one mother. She was at the root of everything we were. But maybe he was right and our past with her was over. The only thing left to do was to move on.

It was just that *maybe* that still kept me up some nights.

"I love you. And what I was trying to ask, very clunkily, is if you and Li are still trying for a baby. And if you are," I cleared my throat, "well, Mal and I aren't on any timetable anyway, but we'll just wait. No problem."

His jaw locked. "What? Why would you have to?"

"Because it might hurt—"

"Lila," he finished, raking a hand through his hair. He tipped back his head. "God, you're so fucking sweet. How are you related to me?"

"I've asked that question myself a dozen times. And not just Lila. Maybe you too. I don't know. I just wouldn't want to risk doing anything when we have time, and well, I know how much she wants a baby."

"Don't you worry. She'll get one."

It was my turn to raise a brow. "You know that's not something you can will by brute force, right?"

"No, of course not. But we have time too, and besides, there are options. Stuff we can do. Stuff that could already be—" He blew out a breath, his cheeks reddening under his tan. "Just saying, don't worry about us. One way or another, we'll make it happen if it's meant. In the meantime, our lives are plenty full."

I smiled. "They sure are. Brave guy, wanting more when he has twins." I laughed. "When he has Combat Charlie."

I'd called her that once when I was babysitting. She'd come downstairs with a bucket on her head and the strap under her chin and the name had stuck. The girl was forever getting into trouble.

Just like her daddy. And her aunt for that matter.

"Watch how you talk about your niece." He pulled me in for a hard hug. "Thank you for thinking of us. But just think of you and that big brute of yours. You've spent too much of your life not putting yourself first."

"Why did I have to, when you always did?"

He moved back. "Not always." His brow furrowed. "Look, someone else needs to talk to you. There's no time now, but maybe if you could spare a word for him." He rubbed the back of his neck. "Hell, what do you even say? Just..."

"Spit it out, Nicky."

"Oz. He's having a rough night."

I frowned. "Brooklyn Dawn's bassist?"

"The one and only."

"Rough how? I don't know him that well. I mean, we're on the tour with them, but you know how it is with these things. You see at each other at some of the bigger parties and might jam now and then at a rehearsal or onstage, but we have our separate dance spaces most of the time. Both of our crews are just so big."

Nicky blew out a breath. "I know. I get it. I don't really know the guy much either, except to pass in the halls. But when I saw the fundraiser thing, I knew I had to say something."

"What fundraiser?"

"You didn't know they were doing it?"

"Nicky."

He nodded and locked his hands behind his head in one of his most habitual gestures. Even when he didn't have a guitar in his grip, he couldn't keep his fingers still. "Oz's sister died of an OD five years ago. She was eighteen."

"Oh, shit. I didn't know." At least not consciously. I'd heard scuttlebutt here and there about something difficult in his past, but it had always been referred to in generalities rather than in specifics around me. I wasn't his inner circle. "That's horrible. But you mentioned a fundraiser?"

"Yeah, I saw it on my way in here on the marquee outside. Portion of ticket sales tonight are being donated to a teens against narcotics charity in Kerry Taylor's name. There was a sign outside on a stand and when I was coming in, Oz was ripping it off."

Saying nothing, I lifted my fist to my mouth.

"He was muttering to himself about this not being the place for it. I tried to speak to him, to offer a shoulder, but he said something about 'finding fucking Daisy' and took off."

"Daisy?" I cocked my head. "Hair wizard Daisy?"

"I suppose? Can't claim I know her."

"Yeah, I think I knew they knew each other. Kind of. They don't really speak, but there's tension there."

"Fucking tension?"

I rolled my eyes. "Some things don't involve your pants."

"That definitely doesn't involve my pants, but when a chick and a dude have issues, sometimes it leads to..." He hummed some *boom-chicka-wow* music. "Also, you can't really deny that either."

No, I certainly could not. Mal and I had hated each other on sight. Well, I'd thought I hated him. Turned out I did not. He was my staunchest ally and made me laugh more than anyone. He also made me mad and made me hot and fifty other emotions, sometimes in the course of a single day.

I was very lucky in so many ways. One of them was that I'd

survived nearly overdosing so many times just to get a chance at my own love story.

Kerry Taylor had not.

"No, I can't, and yes, I know you and Li nearly had restraining orders against each other."

"A little extreme, but fair."

"Considering you called her a dragon behind her back, yeah, I'm going with it."

His lips twitched. "Dragon Lady. Vital difference."

"But Oz and Daisy might be different. Sometimes people seem like they don't get along because shocker, they really don't. If they have some past and it involves his sister he lost—that's tough. Not necessarily something they can come back from."

Nicky jerked a shoulder. "Yeah. Maybe. Don't know. But I do know Oz is hurting and you're the best one to talk to him."

"Me?" I couldn't hold back the surprise. Although he'd started this conversation saying that very thing, I was even more confused now that I knew why. "How could I possibly help? I'm practically a stranger."

"We know where's he been."

"You know where he's been, not me. I *put* you there."

"No, thank fuck, you did not." He stepped forward and gripped my arms, almost hard enough to hurt. He didn't mean to. His hands were freakishly strong, and he never quite knew how rough he was. Yet he touched his girls as if they were breakable china, so maybe he knew more than I thought. "You're whole and here and so strong you make me proud of you every minute of every day."

The doorknob turned and Mal stuck his head in. Even this far from the stage, I could hear the stampede of feet and rising voices that meant showtime was officially here. "Lila says you're to get your ass out right now."

"Me?"

"Nope. Him." My husband jerked a thumb at Nicky. "She mentioned a couch."

"I put one in the bedroom." Nicky shrugged with a quick grin before squeezing my forearm and letting me go. "Kick ass. Don't make me get up there and show you how it's done."

His teasing words set off a warm glow in my belly. We'd been razzing each other since we were kids over who was the better player. It was all in good fun, and I fully acknowledged he was the superior one. He'd been practicing hardcore all the years I hadn't even gone near a guitar, never mind been part of a functional band. His was on top of the world and had been for years. Mine was still climbing and reaching milestone after milestone, but we might never reach Oblivion's height.

And that was okay, because Nicky wasn't the only one who was proud every moment of every day.

"I'm going. I'll see you out there." Nicky turned to look at Mal, who stepped back and gestured ahead of him. Mal stepping back didn't make much room though, because he was tall and broad and capable of filling doorways.

Nicky just saluted him and strolled on through.

Mal prowled toward me and hauled me up on my tiptoes for a quick, hungry kiss as if we'd been apart for hours instead of minutes. "Fuck, you in this outfit."

"Mmm." I bit his lower lip. "Please do."

His lips curved against mine. "You like making me crazy."

"Maybe a little." I inched up to run my hand over his bald head. "I can't go back with you. I gotta stop and see Oz. If he's even in his dressing room." Then I bit my own lip, scanning Mal's dark blue eyes as if he could provide me with answers. "Where is it, by the way?"

"Oz," Mal growled. "Why?"

"Because I decided I like hair on a man."

Mal twisted my nipple through my bustier and I laughed. "Funny girl."

"That's a lie. Bald is beautiful. Besides, if you wanted to grow your hair, you certainly could. I vaguely remember when you were a brunette prince yourself."

Mal's look of derision was pure gold. "I never had hair like his. By choice. If it ever hit my shoulders, I was chopping that shit off." He wound his fingers through mine, currently flowing down my back. I'd be grabbing a hair tie and twisting it up before I went onstage. Otherwise, I would sweat to death. "Speaking of hair, yours is a fucking masterpiece."

"Sweet talk will get you a happy ending after the show."

"It got me a happy ending already." He fisted my hair and drew me up for one of those nearly bruising kisses I never tired of.

Knowing he loved me so much that our pleasure veered to just this side of pain was an incredible turn-on. Not everyone would get that, but I did.

Why he was absolutely perfect for me.

"Not sure it was the sweet talk, but yeah, we're definitely on our way to one." I kissed him once more and slid back. "So, walk me to Oz's?"

"What makes you think I know where it is?" He was already leading me out of the dressing room.

"Because you always case every joint we're in. Mr. Silent and Watchful knows all things," I teased, squeezing his hand.

Sure enough, he led me down the maze of hallways. They had a couple of areas sectioned off for dressing rooms and Oz was at the far end, last door on the right. I opened my mouth, about to give Mal a super quick whispered explanation—although he hadn't asked for one —when the door opened, and Oz stepped out.

My husband's a big guy. Massive, really. Oz was similar, plus his flowing hair seemed to give him extra height. It seemed to get longer every time I saw him. Almost like a shield, one he used to block out the world.

Or that was just my self-help textbooks talking.

Before I could say hello and try to explain myself—and gently send Mal packing—Oz's gaze dropped to our joined hands. He knew we were married. Everyone did. But a disgusted expression flashed over his face, the kind those of us who have been single a few too many times on Valentine's Day recognized all too well.

Fucking gross. And I'm fucking jealous.

I cleared my throat and gave Mal another quick finger squeeze before I released him. He just leaned down to brush a kiss over the top of my head, then didn't so much as cock an eyebrow before ambling off. Didn't look back.

That same warmth spread through my chest. I had a good man. One of the best.

"You lose your ball and chain?"

Yeah, I could tell this conversation would go well. And I still didn't know what I was supposed to say.

Thanks, Nicky.

"He's allowed to break the leash now and then, as am I."

Oz grunted and crossed his arms over his barrel chest, currently clad in a leather vest that showed off his many rippling muscles and dense dark tattoos. The funny thing was, I'd been told Oz was a nice guy when we joined the tour. Affable even. Maybe he was around his bandmates, but he sure wasn't checking any friendly boxes tonight.

Then again, he probably smelled a setup.

"I saw the sign," I began, quickly realizing maybe it would've been better to ease in when Oz's jaw locked. "About your sister. The fundraiser. I never realized—I had no idea she had a problem with drugs."

"She just messed up. It happens. Anyone can OD."

"Can they?" I kept my voice even.

"Sure. We see it all the time, especially in this business."

"Was she in this business?"

"Fuck, no, she was a kid. Just a kid." He pinched the bridge of his nose. "She was eighteen and liked to party. The party got out of hand. That's all."

"That isn't all, because she died." I stepped forward and risked losing some fingers by laying a hand on his forearm. It immediately tensed, every distinct muscle going tight. "I'm an addict. I understand."

He didn't so much as blink. "Yeah, we all know your story. So what?"

I did enough blinking for both of us. "You do?"

"Yeah. Famous Crandall twins." He smirked down at me. "You would've soared regardless."

I didn't reel from the jab, because I'd been in enough group therapy sessions to recognize distancing when I saw it. Oz didn't want the spotlight on him or his sister, so why not toss a few hits at me?

"Yeah, you're right. My brother would've carried me on his back if he needed to. He actually did for a while. Which is how I know you aren't nearly as blasé about your sister's death as you're trying to sell to me right now."

The smirk vanished. "Who said I was blasé? I've just got no intention of spilling my guts to a stranger. It's personal. Private."

I dropped my hand from his arm. "Grieving is the furthest thing from that. Those of us who understand, who've been there, want to help."

"Oh, sure you want to help me. You don't even know me, Richelle. As I don't know you."

Even using my full name was another way to shove me away. No one called me that, and Oz knew it.

"I'm not trying to butt into your life. But maybe you need someone to talk to so you can understand a bit more about addiction. Then in time, perhaps you'll start to really believe it wasn't your fault."

His laughter was harsh. "Why would I blame myself?"

Because you loved her, and you couldn't save her. She was the only one with the power to do that.

"I did all kinds of things for drugs." I let the implication hang. "I nearly died half a dozen times for another fix. There are still days when I don't know how I'll make it through. When I'm scared I'm not strong enough to avoid that dealer leering at me on the street corner, or that glass tray being passed around at a party. It's all just fun. One hit. One momentary lapse. But a moment can kill you. When you're an addict— as I will be for the rest of my life—there is no such thing as just 'partying'. Every time you take a pill or a sip or a toke, it could be the one that leads you to a spiral you won't come back from."

Oz let out a long breath and tipped back his head, saying nothing.

"I didn't know your sister, but I know what my brother went through. At least some of it. There are things he'll never tell me. He might tell you. If anyone could understand what you've been through, it's Nicky. And if you think he still doesn't wake up in a cold sweat wondering if one day he'll find me passed out or worse on some bathroom floor, you're wrong." I swallowed hard. "Dead wrong."

Knowing that would make me feel guilty for the rest of my life. I'd put that fear inside my brother, and the only way I could make sure he didn't have to be worried was to do my part.

To keep doing it every freaking minute of every day.

Oz pushed a hand through his hair. "Yeah. I'm sorry. You didn't have to come to talk to me. It's not your problem."

"No, but if I can be a friend, or if Nicky can be, we want to help. Feeling alone and like no one understands is one of the worst parts of addiction." Gently, I touched his arm once more, then stepped back. "We'll be there for you, if and when you're ready. And if you're not, that's fine too." I forced myself to smile. "Just don't call me Richelle. It's Ricki to my friends."

He didn't realize how big of an admission that was for me. For a long time, I'd tried to erase all traces of Ricki from my life. I was Elle now, not that messed up, drugged out girl.

But she was inside me too. I couldn't have become Elle without Ricki taking all the punches and coming out swinging, even if had taken a damn long time for her to regain her footing.

"Got it." Oz gave me a quick smile, so fast I almost missed it. "Ricki, thanks."

"Don't thank me. Talking to you helped me more than it helped you. I remember all over again why my sobriety is so important." I almost said more, but then I turned my head and glimpsed the shadow filling the doorway at the end of the hall, the one that would lead me toward the stage where my band—my family—was waiting for me.

Mal hadn't left me after all. And he never would.

"I'm so lucky," I whispered. "As are you."

"Am I? Some days it's hard to tell. I mean, yeah, I have money, and fame, but Christ, I'm—"

He didn't finish the statement. He didn't have to. I heard the last word as clearly as if he'd spoken it.

Alone.

"I don't know much about your situation, but I know Daisy cares." He jolted at the name, as if I'd tossed a bucket of ice water at his face.

Maybe Nicky was right. Hate and love were such fine lines. I knew that all too well.

"She cares about your sister, or she wouldn't have pushed for funds to be raised in her honor," I pressed when he remained silent.

Again, his jaw tightened. "It wasn't her place."

"Loving someone gives you rights," I said softly as Oz's gaze lasered to mine. "Seems to me you both loved the same person. Maybe you guys should talk about that."

And then I walked down the hall to where Mal was waiting for me, wondering if I'd helped or harmed.

"Okay?" Mal murmured as he slid his big arm around my shoulders, pulling me close.

I smiled up at him. "I'm more than okay. I think you should tell me about that surprise now."

I expected Mal to argue. Or to put me off. Instead, he took out a little replica farmhouse and pressed it into my hand. I frowned, gazing down at it. "Is this made from Legos?"

"No, but it could have been. I used to rock at them."

"Showoff. So, what is this?"

"This is our farm."

I lifted my brows. "Excuse me?"

His low laughter did wonders at evening out the jagged edges inside me from talking to Oz. So many memories wanted to resurface. Most of them were painful.

But Mal made every one of them bearable. Loving and being loved was all I'd ever wanted.

"You like Happy Acres, right? And spending time with my

grandparents. I hope so, because the farm next to theirs came up for sale. Pop almost put an offer on it, but he asked me first if I wanted to."

"If you wanted to what?" I so was not following.

"Buy. The. Farm."

"Oh." My eyes widened. "*Oh.*"

All at once, I could see it. Running across the open fields in the summer, picking apples in the fall, the sound of children's voices...

As if he understood exactly where my thoughts had gone, he ran a fingertip along his collar. "We're seriously fucking late, and we gotta get out there or else Li will string us up, but yeah." He cleared his throat. "Yeah, I get it."

"You get it? Do *I* get it?"

All at once, his nerves seemed to disappear. My strong, tough guy was so rarely anxious that it always endeared me—and sometimes freaked me out—when he was. He grinned and hooked his fingers in my waistband. "We need a place that's ours, away from the city. A place with room to grow. For when the day comes for...important stuff."

"Important stuff," I repeated, feeling more than a little dizzy.

How was this my life? How had I gotten exactly all I'd ever wanted?

"Yeah." He smoothed a kiss over my forehead. "When that day comes. Not saying we'll turn into farmers or some crazy shit, but if we need some time away, it'll be there. It's a good spot for a family." His Adam's apple bobbed. "Once we get there."

I pressed my palms to his chest and stared into his eyes. It wasn't a hardship. Those blue-black depths held all the answers I'd never been brave enough to search for. "I love you."

"You fucking better."

I grinned. "I do. And you fucking love me."

His breath caught. "More than I can say."

"So, let's buy a farm." I leaned up and nipped his chin where stubble was already growing in thick and dark, although it hadn't been that long since he'd shaved. My sexy motherfucking rockstar.

Who wanted to give me a farm, and maybe someday, some babies too.

"Yeah?" I could hear the pleasure in his voice. His days of hiding his reactions from me were long gone.

"Absolutely."

Still leaning against Mal, I glanced back to where Oz was still standing by his dressing room door, his head down.

So stoic. So solitary.

Hurting so much more than even he realized, if he needed so many walls and shields.

"I made it, didn't I?" I whispered, though I understood that I would never truly cross the finish line.

Every day was a new start. A new chance for me to recommit to my goals.

A new opportunity to remember I had so very much to be grateful for.

Mal's lips quirked. "You sure did, little Ricki."

The nickname was a part of our past that had once brought me annoyance and embarrassment. Now, it just reminded me of how far I'd come.

And how much further I would go, with him at my side.

"Hopefully, Oz will too." I sighed. "But reaching out is up to him."

I hoped he made the right choice.

ONE

EVEN ON THE HARDEST NIGHT OF THE YEAR FOR ME, THE SHOW must go on.

Methodically, my fingers moved over Vicki, my bass guitar—complete with the half-naked mermaid I'd sketched on the back when I was seventeen, drunk, and stupid. I played the low, dirty notes that served as part of the intro to "Stripped Away," our surprise new radio single.

This far into the show in the city, our home base, the crowd couldn't get enough. They were screaming, chanting, sweat dripping down the faces of the fans pushing against the barrier. A few of the luckiest ones had been selected to dance in a glowing, revolving cage in a corner of the stage. Some would leave and others would join before the end of the concert. It was something we'd tried on a whim last year, and now the crowd clamored to take part.

Lindsey, our lead singer, kept sliding that cage quick glances as she moved effortlessly across the stage, gliding on her mile-high purple suede boots. She smiled and laughed and sang every fucking high note as if she'd never faced a moment's uncertainty in her life, never mind fear.

But that sparkling, revolving cage was a neon reminder that she'd barely survived the destruction wrought by a man who had danced on our stage last fall.

She could've put her designer heel down and said no. No one would've questioned it. There were other ways to promote, and we all knew what she'd been through. But she never suggested not doing it. She never backed down from a challenge and did what she needed to do to support our fans, just as they supported us.

Hell, they put in almost as much effort as the band, cheering, stamping their feet, singing along to every damn word. Even to the newest songs that had just hit radio, oh, seventy-two hours ago and the streaming services a few days before that.

It was gratifying and humbling as fuck. That bar kept climbing with every sold-out show and every hit record.

We were still touring in support of our last album, yet we were already dropping songs for the next. That was the world we lived in. Churning out music meant for snippets on SnapChat and dances created for TikTok.

Jamie vaulted onto the hovering mini stage that descended from the rafters as wild purple and green lights strobed over each one of us in turn. The lights circled her, illuminating her long dark and streaked blue hair as she took her stance with her purple electric guitar. She flashed the crowd a wicked smile before her fingers raced up and down the frets. The shredded notes from her guitar wailed through the arena and I followed her, a thunderous counterpoint, as Zane joined in from his spot on yet another raised dais. Together, the three of us built up the frenzy while the audience went wild.

Then it was Jamie's moment. She owned the crowd, eating up every bit of their attention as her solo went on and on. She fell to her knees and curled over her guitar, playing so fast her fingers were nothing but a blur. Still playing, never ceasing for a second, she rolled onto her back, her hair streaming behind her, that maniacal smile wreathing her face as she brought down the goddamn house.

While they were still cheering, she leaped down and grabbed Lindsey. They brought their heads together, one dark, one light. Jamie led the next song, our last before the encore, one from our first album we only brought out on certain nights.

"Untrustworthy" was a quiet, acoustic-driven song, at least at the beginning. Lindsey's lyrics were low, mournful, her hands, clad in black lace fingerless gloves, caressing her mic as if she was praying.

Can't trust you
Don't want you back
Can't trust me
My body still craves that
Your touch, your mouth
Your skin up against mine
Your heart, lying every time

The bass came alive in my hands, dragging me through the song although I was unwilling. I didn't want to go there tonight. It wasn't as if I was suffering from some romantic heartbreak—that was rarely a part of my life, and for good reason—but the words still pulled at me. I knew all too well about memories you couldn't force yourself to forget. Thoughts that plagued every time you closed your eyes.

Like right now.

Lindsey let out the piercing war cry that led into the second verse, and my eyes flew open. They caught on the cage, still circling as silver starlight sparkled over the women and men inside. Most wore jeans and a Brooklyn Dawn T-shirt. Some of the guys had ripped off theirs. Lots of glistening abs and tiny stomachs revealed by crop tops were on display.

Only one of the people truly caught my eye. She was stunning.

Her hair shimmered like a shaft of sunshine, reflecting light with every one of her sinuous movements as she stretched her arms far above her head. The man she was dancing with gripped her glittery hip, guiding her against him. Tiny virulent purple boy shorts cleaved to her ass, a match to the half shirt she wore. She glittered everywhere from some kind of body paint or a trick of the lights.

Something was making her fucking *glow*.

My fingers fumbled. I forgot the notes. Fuck, I might've forgotten who I was entirely the instant I realized who she was.

It was fucking *Daisy* dancing in that cage.

How? Why? She wasn't a goddamn fan. She was one of Ripper Records' hair and makeup artists. Not that I ever let her mess with me.

She'd done plenty of that years before.

She'd gone for me again earlier tonight when she'd set up that damn charity thing for teens against narcotics. A good charity, I was sure, but Kerry wasn't a soundbite meant to sell tickets.

Our tragedy wasn't for public consumption. Yeah, I wanted to help people. I knew my sister would too. But it was still too raw. I didn't want to use her death for my profit. Surely Daisy could understand that.

Then again, she'd done it without even asking me. Now she was shimmying in a cage, rubbing up against some dude, some chick, yet another dude. Laughing. Tossing her fistable hair as if she'd never had a care in the world.

Sparkles dripped off her ass. Her half shirt clung to her breasts like a pair of hands. Barely any fabric, just those mirrored bits of glitter that shook every time she gyrated.

"Hey. You okay?" Zane sidestepped to me, still playing, and spoke out of the corner of his mouth. "Did a little too much pre-show partying, did ya?"

The question wasn't from left field. I'd had my nights of getting loaded before a show, although I was careful to put some time between them. Dependency wasn't in my future. Not after all I'd seen.

But it wasn't a few extra drinks that had set me off tonight. I hadn't touched a drop. No, my issues had started with that fundraiser, continued with the little intervention from Ricki from Warning Sign —*if you need anything, I understand, I can offer an ear*—and now had been topped off by Daisy's *Hustlers* routine in the corner of the stage. All she needed was a pole.

Even as I thought it, I wanted to kick my own ass. I had no right to get annoyed. She could do whatever she wanted. Big deal she was dancing. She looked amazing. She was definitely keeping the beat better than I was right now.

When I didn't reply, Zane just shrugged and gave up. He went back to his side of the stage, exchanging a look with Jamie I didn't miss. She'd propped her booted foot on Cooper's drum riser and was making the rest of us look like posers. Lindsey was hitting those notes that made the audience lose their freaking minds, and Jamie was rocking right with her even as she and Zane quietly worried about me.

Screwed up Oz. He can usually play through his misery. Hand him a bottle or give him some equipment to destroy and he'll be fine tomorrow. Room trashing is his antidote. It's all good.

Except it wasn't.

And Daisy was still dancing. Still rocking her ass and shaking her hair and giving the fans a show to go with Lindsey and Jamie's—and hell, Cooper's and Zane's and Teagan's—theatrics.

Everyone was doing their job but me.

Could be I was looking at this all wrong. Kerry had been Daisy's best friend, so maybe she could do whatever she wanted there too. Could be she was just trying to do a nice thing to honor someone she loved.

Take some notes there, asshole.

But what the fuck had she been thinking to not even mention it to me? To not fucking *ask* me how I felt?

You don't matter to her. Why should she care what you think when you haven't said more than a few words to her in the six months she's been on this tour?

We hadn't been touring the whole time, of course. There had been holiday breaks and days off between legs of the tour, but we'd definitely been more on than off. Brooklyn Dawn's tour bus accommodations were swanky enough to be on one of those fancy ass cable shows about rockstar digs, but that didn't mean we never saw each other. Daisy had made friends with my bandmates, because that was who she was.

Friendly. Sweet. *Too* sweet. She'd never quite realized the world wasn't a fucking lollipop land you could just hop your way through, unscathed.

Kerry had gotten hurt enough for all three of us.

The crowd roared, and the cage rotated to a stop with a loud shriek that jarred me out of my head. My hands were clammy, for God's sake. The song was over. The show was too, all but the encore. Lindsey was blowing kisses to the crowd, and Jamie had her arm slung around Zane's neck as she let out a war whoop. Cooper spun his sticks through the air to show off his sick juggling routine before he jumped down.

The fans in the cage spilled out, and the band raced into the back as the crowd's energy ramped up into madness. Feet stomping, cheers echoing, cell phone lights flashing. No one was ready for the night to end.

And I was just standing there like a zombie, barely reacting as one of the techs pried Vicki from my lifeless hands.

"You okay, man?"

I turned my head to find Cooper behind me. He gave a little nod toward the audience, where fans were pushing against the barrier and begging for more. Which we were going to give them after our super short break—as soon as I could get my ass off this stage.

"Yeah, yeah. Sorry. I'm good." I nodded at him and strode into the insanity backstage, heading right for one of the tables set up with food and beverages. I didn't want a soda or a beer. An ice cold water washed the metallic flavor of bitterness out of my throat, and then I reached for the bottle of Glenlivet I'd requested just for tonight.

That was how I toasted my little sister.

To making it through one more year. May it not be the last.

Gotta love my fatalistic Irish side.

I uncapped it and tossed it back, swallowing again and again until the burn raged inside my chest. When I'd finished off a third of the bottle, I slammed it on the table and pivoted to find Lindsey staring me down. She'd just powered through an incredible set, and other than a few curls out of place, you couldn't fucking tell. She barely seemed to sweat. That woman had been made for the stage.

Normally, I reveled in her effortless ability. Tonight? It just pissed me off like so much else.

"Let's talk."

I followed her into the nearest alcove away from the hive of activity and buzz of voices. The thunder of the crowd was reaching ear-splitting levels. We were due back out there basically now.

"What's up?" I asked, as if I didn't already know.

"If you can't do this, we can do the encore without you. It won't be nearly the same, but we can make it work."

Although I knew she was trying to help, that wasn't what it felt like right now. Instead, this was just one more episode of my input not really being needed.

Theme of the evening.

My palm itched, wanting The Glenlivet back again. I needed something to hold on to right now, and for once, it wasn't Vicki. My solace wasn't inside her forgiving curves or her sweet strings.

No, mine would be in getting drunk, alone.

I tucked my hands under my armpits. "You do what you have to do. You're the boss, right?"

She rolled her eyes. "I know you're in a rough spot, so I'm not going to kick your ass for that snide comment."

"You are the boss. You and tall, dark, and deadly over there." I jerked my chin in the general direction of where Jamie was holding court with her latest bunch of groupies.

Men—and women—followed her around as if she was a god in leather and lace. She kept trying to break free, but there was always someone grasping at her.

"I'm offering you an out as your friend. That's all."

"Awful lot of friendship being tossed my way tonight," I muttered.

"Maybe you should take some of it and knock the chip off your shoulder." She patted my arm none too gently. "Free advice, pal." She turned away. "Time to rock," she called to the others, who shouted and followed her back to the stage.

I debated grabbing my bottle but decided against it. I could do a four-song encore.

I hoped.

The flush of the crowd's approval helped to erase the uneasy tension on my bandmates' faces as I took my spot on the left side of the stage.

They were all waiting for me to fuck up, but I made it through. Even adding some of my signature flourishes at the end.

Oz Taylor was no one's afterthought. Especially with Vicki in my hands.

Afterward, I headed backstage. I'd just tucked my bottle of liquid bravery against my hip when Lila Crandall, our manager, tapped my arm with one blood-red fingernail.

"Good show. Glad to see you shook off your stumble right before the finale." She didn't give me time to get out a response. "Quick band meeting in five."

"I'm a little busy. Can it wait?"

She cast a cool look at the bottle I didn't bother to hide. "Your debauchery can wait a few minutes."

Deliberately, I uncapped the bottle and took a long swig. "You know what can't wait? You and Lewis and whatever other flunkies do your bidding deciding to use my sister as a promo chip without asking me."

She arched a brow, cocking her head so that her long blond hair swung perfectly around her shoulders. Another one who was effortlessly cool, when I felt like I was nothing but red-hot anger and ragged edges. "Sorry, our flunkies took the day off, and Daisy actually approached Sabrina about the fundraiser because I was out of the office. Had I been there, I would've agreed as well. Do you have a personal grudge against the Teens Against Narcotics charity?"

"No, I don't. I have a personal grudge against people who aren't part of the family waltzing in like they have a right to make decisions for us."

Lila gave me a thin smile. "Feel free to tell Daisy that yourself, since she's right behind you. But don't break anything you don't intend to pay for and don't be late. You have five."

She turned on her heel and marched off to gather the rest of her troops.

I nearly walked away. Daisy's relentless optimism was the last thing I wanted to deal with when all I craved was a dark corner and some peace. And some alone time with the bottle of whisky, who didn't give me shit.

Then I turned and saw wounded blue eyes looking anywhere but at me and felt even lower than I'd felt all night.

"Look, don't bother yourself." She folded her arms over her bare midsection, glimmering with some sort of sparkly body paint. "I wanted to apologize for how the fundraiser idea came together, but you've obviously decided I deliberately cut you out."

"Why didn't you ask me first before you went to see Lila or Sabrina? Did it ever occur to you how I might feel?"

Shit, I sounded like some emo bastard, all up in his feelings. And I wasn't that guy.

Most of the time, people accused me of not having enough of them. Of shoving everything down into a black box labeled *do not touch*. Tonight, everything was spilling out all over.

Always on this night. No wonder I hated it.

"It did, which is why I didn't ask you."

I frowned. Had I had more to drink than I realized. "Huh?"

But she was just winding up, her pale cheeks reddening. "Besides, when do you ever talk to me? How many conversations have we had since I've been working with your band, hmm?"

"You don't work *with* us. You brush on blush and do braids and shit. Not exactly a collaborative effort."

Dick.

Even as the hurt bloomed across her face, I wanted to bite off my tongue. I had to get out of here before I caused permanent damage.

I wasn't fit for anyone's company tonight. Not even my own.

And definitely not sweet little Daisy Flannigan's.

TWO

I DIDN'T THINK. I JUST ESCAPED.

Like a coward.

God only knows what Oz would think of me now. Although judging by what he said, it was hard to imagine him thinking anything worse of me than he did already.

I sprinted down the hall, not even sure where I was going. I wasn't familiar with this massive building, and I didn't belong back here in any case. After all, I was just the girl who did blush and braids. Nothing complicated.

Dashing away a stupid tear, I turned down the next hallway. I wasn't capable enough to play a bass guitar, or hit four octaves like Lindsey, or break the sonic barrier like Cooper.

I was just a hairstylist who had some talent with a mascara wand. End of story.

And I didn't even know where I was headed right now, other than away from him. I needed a couple of minutes to regroup. Then I'd be fine. I would shore up my defenses, put my game face back on, and join the afterparty.

Because there was always an afterparty, especially at the end of an MSG show. Home base meant rocking extra hard, onstage and off.

I'd started my partying tonight as part of the fan experience. Had Oz even noticed? I thought he'd looked our way a few times while I was dancing, but he hadn't mentioned it. Hadn't seemed to even notice my outfit. It was an eye-catcher, which was how I'd even ended up in that cage. It wasn't my laminated hairstyle and makeup credentials, that was for sure. Nope, I'd been granted a trip onstage thanks to my skill at shaking my ass.

Kerry and I had honed our talents in that department years ago. To this day, I thought of her when I danced. I remembered her endless energy and that fifty kilowatt smile that could brighten the darkest room.

Oz had the same smile, if he would ever use it. I so rarely saw him do anything but glower these days. Although he seemed to save most of those sneering expressions for me.

When and if he bothered to look my way at all.

The doors on the first two rooms I tried were locked with a keypad. But there was another set of them down the hall, and one of those was open, according to the keypad flashing with an error.

I cast a quick look around. Other than hanging backstage with the others—or getting the hell out of Dodge—I didn't really have my own space. I wasn't going to cry in a bathroom stall like some teenager.

No, you're going to cry in an empty meeting room like a pathetic twenty-three-year-old.

Whatever.

If no one saw me sniffle, it totally didn't count.

I reached for the doorknob, then recoiled and grabbed the hem of my boy shorts to try to fumble the door open. Not ideal but it got the job done. I slipped into the room and flipped on the light switch with my elbow. It looked like it was mainly a storage space, connected to the room beside it with a door between them, currently closed.

Good enough for my use.

I'd no sooner sagged into an old chair when voices next door caught my attention, growing in volume as if the people were just arriving. Laughter and the hum of conversation had me rising again. I supposed it was just as well. I wasn't going to eavesdrop, and it looked like I wouldn't be giving in to my emotions either.

Minus a swipe or two under my burning eyes anyway.

Then Oz's voice boomed across the small space I was in as if he was standing right in front of me.

"What the fuck is this about? Does anyone know? We never have band meetings after a show. We got shit to do."

"Oh, you mean chicks to do?" Jamie's sly laughter had my cheeks flaming to go with the sting in my eyes.

"Hey, if that's how you plan to spend your night, I won't judge," he tossed back. I could picture him lifting his hands, palms out, all innocence.

Yeah, right. Oz Taylor hadn't been innocent even when we were back in school. Far from it. Not that Kerry and I had been in high school at the same time he was attending. He'd been a freshman in college when we were freshmen in high school, so we'd only seen him at the occasional party. Until the end of our freshman year when those parties had become more frequent, and Oz had been home on summer break so he'd come around more often. Always lurking.

Waiting for us to mess up.

"Not me, jackwit, you. You're the one who bangs anything that moves."

"Not sure that's even necessary," Cooper chimed in, his voice thick with amusement. "Long as they have a pulse and pretty hair, good enough for old Ozzy."

"Maybe it's the name." This time, it was Zane. "Instead of Prince of Darkness, ours is just Prince of Pussy."

I shut my eyes. I knew how the band was with each other. Their banter included lots of teasing and inside jokes and a friendly bit of rivalry. Mostly all in good fun. They got along so well most of the time that an outsider could get jealous.

Someone such as myself, for example. Who wanted more than anything to fit in somewhere.

Anywhere.

"You're all hilarious, but no, I'm not looking to hookup tonight."

That last word sounded so final. The room grew quiet, as if everyone understood what it meant. Because they all most likely did.

Today was a day far too important for something as trivial as casual sex. As for that bottle of Glenlivet I'd seen him toting around? That was a different story.

Sweaty Oz, with his shirt wide open to bare his damp chest and that small silver cross he always wore, along with some other pendant on a black cord. The cross had been Kerry's. I remembered him taking it off her body and pocketing it while I yelled at him that it was hers and she needed it with her in the—

I choked and brought up my hands to cup my mouth. God, I still couldn't think of that word. Or that Kerry had ended up in one when she was just a kid.

He'd ignored my shouts then. Pretended not to see my tears. Just as he would now if I cried. I'd always envied him that stoicism, because heaven knows I couldn't ever be that emotionless. I wore my heart on my sleeve for everyone to see.

And stomp on.

Kerry had given me something that last night. I hadn't understood why. She loved the necklace so much, but she'd told me she wanted me to have it when she was gone.

I'd always assumed she meant to California. She was so happy and excited. So optimistic about the future.

Everything will be better now, Flanny. It's going to be so good.

Worst of all, I couldn't even wear the necklace. Kerry's essence was so ingrained in it that putting it on felt as if I was wearing clothes that were too big. Ones that would never fit, no matter how much comfort they gave me.

There was no comfort to be found here tonight.

From next door, someone spoke too quietly for me to make out the words. Lindsey, maybe. Then a scrape of chairs and more muffled talking before Jamie chimed in again. "Dude, just tell us to shut the fuck up. You know we're morons. Hey, if you want, we can go find you a chick. I suggest a big-breasted one."

Lindsey laughed. "Right. So you can get jealous?"

"Hardly. My tits are magnificent."

Despite the uncomfortable tickle in my throat at thinking about Oz cruising for some faceless curvy woman, I had to smile at their efforts to make him feel better. They were closer than it seemed on the surface. Their joking around was just a way to unwind.

Oz wasn't one to talk much—at least I assumed, based on how he'd always been with me—but obviously, at some point he had told them the story. Maybe even when I arrived.

That Daisy chick killed my sister. Be careful around her.

Another voice joined the fray. Lila's. She said a few things I couldn't discern, and then she mentioned Noah, my second cousin through marriage. Indirectly, he was how I'd gotten this job. At least he'd vouched for me when Ripper was scouring my past to see if I was really a serial killer in training.

Their security was far more intense than I would've guessed for a record label, but Noah had told me a few difficult things had occurred in recent years that made Donovan Lewis, Ripper's head shark, "wary".

Of course Noah was about as talkative as Oz. Were all men so close-lipped or did I just bring it out in them?

"What the hell do you mean we need more security? We're a rock band, not a police state."

Even if I hadn't recognized the voice, there was no mistaking Jamie's level of irritation. I had to agree with her. How could they possibly need more? Even with the crazy stuff that had gone on before —the full extent of which I didn't even know—the sheer amount of bodyguards and barriers at their shows was crazy. The stage was literally ringed with guards, a few of them the size of The Rock. I couldn't even imagine where they would include more. At the rate they were going, they'd have to infiltrate the tech crew or stand right on stage.

Lila spoke for a couple minutes, her voice measured and low. So low I couldn't make out more than a few choice phrases here and there.

"Recent concerns have led to..."

"We're bumping up the alert level..."

"More than the usual kind of crowd control issues..."

And scariest of all to me:

"This is probably just the beginning."

The beginning of what? I couldn't even fathom. Neither could the members of Brooklyn Dawn.

Lila did her best to settle the troops. But her method didn't have the intended effect.

"I understand that this is disturbing. It's better than the alternative of cancelling shows. And if we can't get these security concerns dealt with, that may become necessary."

Whoa, hitting them in the bottom line. They weren't messing around.

"Look, Lila, we get that you have a need for discretion. You still have to see our point of view. We worked hard to get where we are." As always, Zane was the calm, clear voice of reason. The guy had practically turned meditation into an Olympic sport, and it showed. "Cancelling sold-out shows will hurt the fans most of all, and we can't turn our backs on them."

"We aren't turning anything. It's our last resort." Lila's voice dropped even lower. "Safety is paramount."

"Well, then, if we're in so much fucking danger, why can't we find out what's going on? Has there been a specific threat?"

Again, the voices became muffled, and I strained to hear things more clearly. At the same time, I didn't want to. Goosebumps popped up and down my arms, and a cold chill danced along my spine. My lack of much clothing didn't help.

I needed to get my stuff and get the hell out of here. A warm shower was waiting for me back at my temporary place. Cramped as it was.

Last thing I wanted was to get caught spying on the band, although that had never been my intention. But Oz would never believe anything but the worst about me, that much was clear.

So, you need to make him. You can't just give up. Isn't that part of why you wanted this job? To get closer to Oz again?

Again as if we'd been close before. Yeah, right.

There was more squabbling, punctuated by Jamie's usual curses and colorful complaints, but the meeting soon ended. I waited until the commotion from their leaving died down, and then I quickly exited the room. I was still the newbie. The last thing I needed was for anyone to start questioning my actions.

I really wanted to be here. For once, I wanted someplace to belong. One I'd created for myself.

Sure, that's why you went chasing after Oz.

As if I'd conjured him up, I glanced into the room as I tiptoed past. Oz sat with his big shoulders slumped, his long legs spread wide, his head in his hands. He grasped handfuls of his hair as if he had a headache—or was frustrated enough to pull them out. I started to speak, amazed he hadn't noticed me yet, when he mumbled a word I had no trouble making out. That name had haunted me all night tonight, along with too many others.

Kerry.

Suddenly, there was a flurry of motion. He stood and kicked back the chair, the wheels rolling over the floor.

I hurried away.

He hadn't seen me, I was almost sure. He was too lost in his own thoughts to worry about pesky Daisy. But now that I'd seen more proof of the torment he was in, there was no way I could let him be alone right now.

No one understood what we had gone through. Just us. We were alone in our grief. I knew all he wanted was to push me away and bury his bad memories, but I knew he needed me more than he realized.

Maybe even more than *I* realized.

We were the sole survivors of a tragedy. What had happened to Kerry could have happened to Oz—or me, if things had been different.

But Oz was still in that lifestyle. Most of the band didn't party all that hard, which surprised me. Sure, they drank and a few of them smoked joints now and then, but I'd never seen anything more hardcore. That was probably part of the reason they were so successful. They were actually aware of the music they were writing and playing.

At the end of the hall, I turned right and stopped to suck in a breath. Now what?

I couldn't just follow Oz home, if he even still had one in the city. I didn't have one here anymore, but I was crashing with my younger sister Everleigh. Which sucked giant balls because she lived in an apartment with three other young aspiring artist types who made about ten dollars between them. There was barely enough room for all of them, never mind me.

I hadn't slept on such a lumpy couch...well, ever. It wasn't something I wanted to endure for long, which was why I was saving every penny for my own crash pad when we weren't on tour.

And speaking of crashing, my ass was about to hit the ground if those heavy footsteps were Oz. Who else could they be? No one was as big as he was. I shivered. Based on what I'd seen at sixteen, that was definitely true all over.

Not going there right now.

I went with instinct and rushed down the hallway, turning at the end to hurry down the next. Soon, I was near the dressing rooms. I found Oz's and tried the door without remembering to use my shorts to grab the knob. Maybe I didn't mind touching where Oz had.

Miraculously, the keypad flashed green. Somehow the door was unlocked.

Lucky break? Maybe.

Unless all these little supposed wins were going to add up to the biggest fail of all.

Inside the room, I pressed my back against the wall and took a deep breath. Seemed to be something I was doing a lot today. Oz had left on a small light on the dressing table, casting most of the small, unremarkable room in shadow. My heart was beating like a trapped hummingbird's wings. He was going to flip when he discovered me in here. What the hell was I thinking?

I still couldn't hear him in the hall. Maybe he'd left directly without stopping by here, although I could see his backpack tipped over on a chair.

I might live to see another day.

Stiffening my shoulders, I yanked open the door, gasping at the tall, broad wall of man filling the doorway.

Too slow, Flannigan.

"Lost, little Daisy?"

Though the words were mocking, his tone was not. He sounded so exhausted. Deep lines furrowed around his beautiful dark eyes, currently bloodshot with fatigue. How long had it been since he'd had a nice home-cooked meal and a good night's sleep?

If I had to guess, he probably hadn't slept well in five years. Just as I hadn't.

"We have to talk." The quaver in my voice seriously pissed me off, almost as much as my confidence collapsing in front of him backstage.

I was not a woman who didn't know her own worth. Not anymore.

He crossed his arms and shifted enough to let me see the bottle poking out of the pocket of his jeans. "If you're here to demand an apology about what I said, don't bother." He lifted his gaze toward the ceiling. "I know I was a dick. I probably didn't mean it. Now can you leave?"

I'd already gotten more than I expected from him. What a sad statement that was. But it wasn't nearly enough.

"No."

"No?" He didn't seem mad so much as puzzled. "Why the hell not? You're missing the afterparty."

I rolled my eyes. "Like I care about that."

His gaze drifted all too quickly over my ensemble. I was proud of my body. Sure, I had some flaws. Who didn't? But normally, a hot guy checking me out didn't make me want to look for the nearest fluffy bathrobe.

Everything was different with Oz. *I* was different. If he said something derogatory about how I dressed, I wasn't sure I'd be able to look at him the same way. He had always been slotted into the older brother role in my life because of Kerry, but I was a grown woman now and he had no right to judge my choice of attire.

"You'd shut it down for any other woman, coming in there like that."

I nearly choked. Had he just said I was attractive? Or at least insinuated it?

I had to practically do a high jump to reach his forehead. I laid the back of my wrist against it while he frowned at me, causing the dent in his chin to turn into a furrow. "What the hell are you doing?"

"That almost sounded like a vague compliment. I'm checking to see if you're ill."

He grabbed my wrist, holding on a second too long with his far too pleasurable grip. If someone had asked me, oh, eleven seconds ago, if I enjoyed any sort of rough play, I probably would've said no. I liked being in control—now. But between his implacable hold and the steely glint in his eyes, I was putty in his hands.

"Oh, yeah, I'm ill, all right. Obviously. What are you doing in my room?"

"Your dressing room, you mean? You don't own it."

He dropped my arm. "Yeah, well, you're right about that. Only thing left for me to do now is clear the fuck out." He quickly scanned the room, a long exhale leaving him as his gaze alighted on something clearly very valuable. "There she is."

My back prickled with jealousy. Had I missed some memento of a woman in this room? There certainly hadn't been some female secreted away in a shadowy corner.

I pivoted to watch Oz. Oh, how wrong I was.

He stalked to a blue-black acoustic guitar on a chair, lifting and cradling it as if he'd just discovered a newborn. No, he was far more sensual with it than that. His long, surprisingly artistic fingers skimmed the strings, filling the room with achingly sweet sound. It was the start to a campfire song, so familiar I could've sworn I'd heard it before although I knew I hadn't. His mouth opened, and he was about to sing when he snapped up his head and seemed to remember I existed.

And from his frown, that fact displeased him.

"I'm gonna ask again. Why are you here?"

Impulse seized me. It had been a while since my reckless side had popped out her head, but apparently, tonight was the night for bad decisions. "You need a friend."

His laughter was not inviting in the slightest. "Dude, I must, since people are practically throwing themselves at me tonight to hold my hand and sing Kumba-the-fuck-ya."

"Did it ever occur to you that maybe they see something you don't?"

"No, it occurred to me that you going around begging for change has put my business front and center."

If he'd slapped me, I couldn't have reared back any harder. "That's not—I didn't—"

"What you did wasn't for you," he said simply. "Period."

Once again, I didn't belong. Other than with my sister—and now that she was a bratty eighteen-year-old, we fought like feral cats—I didn't have a spot. I'd thought I was forging one here with the band, but Oz wanted me to understand that I was an outsider. Sure, he didn't mean within the band, but wasn't that true too? If I didn't have a right to raise funds in honor of a girl who'd been as close as blood to me, where else could I possibly fit?

I nodded and turned away. I had my pride. That was one thing I'd never let go of.

A set of keys sat on the chair beside the door. Tossed carelessly by a person who was used to not even needing them. He was rich and famous, the kind of guy who was used to doors opening as soon as he arrived.

And me? I sneaked in places. I followed people. I pressed my face up against windows that would never show me a life I could picture myself in.

Some part of me knew I was playing with fire. The rest just wanted to annoy the piss out of him. Like the kid he would always see me as, I had to settle for any reaction I could get from him. I couldn't hurt him as he did so easily with me. I didn't even want to try. But he didn't want my friendship. Or my love for his sister. Or even my love for—

He didn't want anything from me. So, I would be a fucking brat. He didn't realize I'd received a master class from my perennially PMS-ing baby sister.

I snagged the keys and sailed out the door. He didn't call after me, didn't say a damn thing. Just kept strumming his gorgeous guitar.

Probably the closest he'd ever come to loving a woman. Of course his acoustic was a she.

I went to Cooper's dressing room and knocked sharply. Most likely, he was already gone. Everyone probably was. But Oz wasn't going off to sulk alone, even if I'd probably live to regret my impulsive action.

Coop stuck his head out. From his crown of spiky, wet dark hair, he'd just had a shower. He wiped droplets from the side of his cheek. "Daze? What's up?"

Unexpectedly, my heart lurched. A nickname meant inclusion, didn't it? It was a start.

"Sorry to bother you." I gave him a quick smile and held up Oz's keys, dangling them from his ancient Mötley Crüe "Girls, Girls, Girls" keychain. It was practically a relic. "Can you just tell me where Oz's car is parked? He told me to get it started while he grabs a shower, but he forgot to tell me where it is."

Coop's dark brows lifted. "His truck, you mean."

My winsome smile could charm anyone who wasn't Oz Taylor. "Right. Where's it parked?"

"He didn't tell you it's on the trucks? I'm assuming it's down by now."

I had no clue what he meant. So, I motioned for him to continue.

After Coop explained it would be with the rest of the gear and tech rigs, I smiled and waved and thanked him profusely. Pretty sure he knew I was lying, but I didn't care.

Oz and I were having it out tonight, once and for all. No matter the cost.

THREE

I kept strumming Annette until Daisy and her insanely tight ass left.

No, it wasn't appropriate for me to notice it. Had that stopped me? Nope. It hadn't helped that she wore rainbow sparkles that made her look like a pornographic Rainbow Sprite.

For a hot second, I'd had her curvy body pressed against me while she checked me for fever. She was built in ways I'd probably never get out of my head. When I jacked my own dick in the shower tonight, I'd be thinking of her full tits and worse, so much worse, those pleading blue eyes that had always asked me for far too much.

"Fuck." I dropped Annette on the chair and immediately regretted it. As if she was a sentient being, I picked her up again and rubbed my hand over the battered midnight blue painted wood, circling my thumb over the pinprick yellow stars and sliver of a canyon moon.

This guitar was the embodiment of the times I felt most at peace—out alone in the woods in the dark, sitting by a campfire, woodsmoke stinging my eyes while crickets chirped and cicadas buzzed. Off in the distance, a lone coyote howled or an owl hooted while I played my guitar and pretended I loved having no one to share my happiest moments with.

I loved the solitude. I also hated it with a passion. Sometimes I didn't want to be alone with my thoughts. Sometimes I wished someone was there to sing bad songs with me and roast marshmallows and sleep in my too small sleeping bag when I roughed it in a tent.

Somehow the loneliness wasn't as obvious in my cabin. The King-sized bed didn't feel too big for me because I was a huge motherfucker. Out on the wraparound deck with a beer and Annette, I could pretend my party of one was all I'd ever wanted.

It wasn't as if I didn't have friends. Or hell, my bandmates. I could've made some calls and had the place filled in a few hours, not counting travel time. But loneliness wasn't only about bodies filling a space. Only the right ones—*one*—made any difference.

And I wasn't dwelling on any of this tonight.

Still carrying Annette, I pushed aside my backpack and searched around for my keys. I'd tossed them here, I was sure of it. A search behind the chair didn't help. Then I remembered Daisy jingling as she left. With my keys.

"Fucking Daisy," I muttered, grabbing for my phone.

Except I didn't have her number. Of course I didn't. What kind of game was she playing?

I hit the speed dial for Lila. She answered on the second ring. "Osmond?"

I winced. Only Lila, man. I hadn't even told her my full name. She must've snagged it off my tax documents or something, for fuck's sake. "Yeah. I need Daisy's number."

"Daisy Flannigan?"

I yanked the bottle of whisky out of my pocket and zipped it into my backpack for later needs. "Do we have another Daisy I missed?"

"No. If a lady wants you to have her number, she will provide it. Have a good night." She clicked off before I even had time to curse.

Even so, I had to grin. That was Lila for you. I couldn't even say I blamed her. It was probably a good policy, but maybe I should've mentioned I was pretty sure the little wench had stolen my keys.

I still couldn't figure out why.

I was mean as hell to her most of the time. The rest I ignored her. For good reason. She looked at me a lot, as if she was trying to figure out what was going on in my head, or worse, analyzing my behavior.

Like that whole friend comment. I must be giving off a vibe.

Then again, I'd just been thinking about being isolated and shit in the woods, but who could blame me? When a hot as fuck chick wiggled against me, of course I was going to start thinking about not wanting to spend the night alone. She was sexy. It wasn't because she was Daisy, or because we had a past. Definitely not because I'd had to practically tape my hands to my own ass to keep from touching her when she'd been barely jailbait.

She was off-limits. She had been when Kerry was alive, and nothing had changed now that my sister was gone.

It was just as well I couldn't contact her, especially not in my current mood. But I still had that pesky little issue of not having my keys. I'd intended to head up to the cabin tonight, and I had a long ride ahead of me as it was when I was already exhausted. We had another show in town next week. Time was wasting. I didn't have the patience to play games with my mischievous sprite.

I rubbed my forehead. Fuck, her shorts should be banned. That woman was *not* mine.

Had never been. Would never be.

Regardless, I wasn't going to find my keys standing around. I had to find Daisy.

Obviously, that was what she wanted. Unless she just enjoyed messing with me. Could be either one.

Besides, how hard could it be to find one 5'5 blond covered in sparkles?

As it turned out, actually pretty hard.

I searched all over the damn venue. High, low, and a dozen spots in between. I ran into fans who squealed and hung off me as if I was their own personal funhouse attraction. I signed posters and posed for selfies and was offered alcohol, baggies of pills, and breasts in equal measure.

Big shot rocker, anything was in reach, right?

Everything but Daisy and the chance to escape to privacy by the lake. Surrounded by the forest without even the capability to get a Wi-Fi signal.

For all I knew, she'd taken off in my truck and used the map on the front seat as a guidebook. I'd been going up to my cabin for years now, but since I usually only made the trip a few times a year due to our touring schedule, I still got lost. Also, I kinda sucked at directions, even with GPS. So, I used a paper map as a backup, just in case. It never needed to be charged or depended on a good signal.

Also, my "maneptitude", as Jamie called it, with directions was a fact I did not want Daisy to have about me in her arsenal.

I waited around a bit longer for the crush of fans to disperse. Why not? I had nothing but time.

Once the coast was finally closer to clear, I pulled on a hoodie, yanked up the hood, and ducked out of a side entrance.

My truck was parked near where the band rigs were stationed. At least it was supposed to be there. The space I'd expected it to be in was empty.

The bellow I let out scared crows out of the nearby trees.

I dropped my bag and set Annette against my leg so I could shove back my hood and fist my hands in my hair. The pain centered me. Besides, I knew a surefire way to find my damn truck.

Pulling out my phone, I stabbed the buttons for 911.

The screech of tires made me hold down the 9 until the screen wavered. I gritted my teeth. I did not look up. If she was hanging out of that window, I was going to kill her.

If she *wasn't* hanging out of that window, I was going to kill her twice.

The hand crank window squeaked as she rolled it down. I knew that squeak. I also knew that quick intake of breath before she spoke. Did she even realize she did that?

Bolstering herself to drive me insane.

"I had no choice."

10-9-8-7.

"You drove me to it."

6-5-4-3-2.

"You know you aren't really that mad."

1.

Fuck it, I was starting over from 100, because a set of ten numbers wasn't nearly enough to keep from reaming her out.

100-99-98-97.

"Think of it this way, no one likes to go on a road trip alone."

1000-999-998-997.

"Ugh, Oz, stop being a jerk and talk to me."

I pocketed my now probably crushed phone and grabbed my bag and Annette. Saying nothing, I walked around to the back of the truck and lifted the hard-shell camper, stowing my stuff inside. I slammed it with more effort than needed, since it was better than kicking the tires.

Marginally.

After climbing into the truck, I locked my jaw as I shoved the passenger seat back. I hadn't moved it in a damn long time. This wasn't a vehicle I used to tote around other people. It was for trips to the cabin, period.

"I can't believe you still have this."

"I can't believe you don't have a record."

She clucked her tongue and it took all my will to not look her way. "Who says I don't?"

Before I could reply, she gunned the engine and shot across the lot.

"Easy. What the actual fuck? You don't drive a classic like that."

"A classic?" Her giggle was surprisingly musical. Like windchimes or something, when they didn't make my head hurt. "You had this truck in high school. How is it even still on the road? God, remember that time Kerry puked—" She gripped the wheel in tense fingers. "Never mind."

Her name made my hackles rise. Nothing new there. Any mention of my sister and about fifty shields went up. But this time, I was more curious than annoyed.

I never had anyone to talk about her with. A blessing most of the time.

"Tell me."

On the verge of exiting the lot, she braked and let out a long breath. "We drank until we got sick. Both of us. And then we climbed in the back to sleep it off, but—"

"In the back of what?" My eyebrows rose. "Not my truck?"

She jerked a shoulder. "It was a good place to crash without being disturbed, and you had taken the Fiesta to school. Why, I don't know. That car sucked."

"According to you, this truck sucks too. No taste. Keep going."

"She woke up and got sick again. We cleaned it up. We did," she insisted when I glared.

On the inside, I wasn't pissed. I was greedy for snatches of my sister's life. In a way, it kept her alive.

Yet I didn't want Daisy collecting money for a charity in her name.

You don't want people looking at you. Pitying you.

Caring, so you have no choice except to allow yourself to care back.

"I'm going to get out and we can switch seats."

"Why? So you can drop me off here and speed away?" She shook her head, her stubborn chin lifting. "Nope."

"This is my vehicle," I said calmly. "I could have you arrested."

"Want to see me in cuffs? Is that your kink, Osmond?"

More *Osmond* crap. I shut my eyes, and it wasn't to keep my reaction to her question from telegraphing across my face. Entirely. "Ker told you my name."

"Of course she did. We used to make fun of you with it. 'Oh, Osmond won't let me go out tonight. Mom's sick, so he's playing Daddy.'"

Again, her words were creating images in my head that didn't belong there and had absolutely nothing to do with my sister.

Topic change time.

"I'm going three hours out of the city. Guarantee you won't be able to handle the accommodations."

"Is that so? What, too swanky for me?" She slapped her bare thigh and sparkles shimmered. "Surprise, I can clean up pretty well."

I didn't doubt it.

"Yeah, that's it. Too swanky for you. Bet you don't have any formal wear with you. Give me the keys."

She turned off the truck. For a second, I thought she might actually do the adult thing and stop this forced hostage situation. Only it was my truck being held against her will, not me.

Instead, she yanked out the keys and deposited them inside her top. Between her fucking breasts. Tilting her head, she smiled sweetly. "Come and get them."

"You are such a child."

Those were the words my lips formed. Inside my head, there was a completely different dialogue taking place.

I wanted to call her bluff.

"Right. It's super adult of you to be pissed at me for what, five years now? And to refuse to talk to me even though we spent years together."

"We knew each other. We were not together in any sense."

"Fine, Mr. Specific. We have a history. Kerry would hate what this has done to us."

"Don't," I warned. "Do not use her as a chip."

Her chin trembled. "I'm not. I wouldn't. But that's a fact, and you know it. She always used to joke I was as much your sister as she was."

I rubbed my temple. "*Flowers of the Attic* style?" I muttered.

"What?"

"Never mind. Just give me the keys. If you're so all fired up to talk, we'll do it when I get back."

After I'd jerked off enough to barely notice she had firm, perfect tits. My right hand would probably be in a cast, and I wouldn't be able to play for a week, but it would be worth it to get this ache out of my damn system. One that had been there since last fall when she sashayed into our band meeting and wrecked my world.

Again.

"No. It has to be now. If you walk away, you'll probably get an order of protection against me so I can't bother you again."

I scratched my chin. "Thanks for the idea."

"Oz." She dragged her hands over her face. "This is fucking me up. Seriously. I get that it's nothing to you. Probably less than. But I don't have anyone, not like her. She was so much of my life, and there's no one I can talk to about it. The one person I could talk about it with hates me. And I get it. I blame me too. I hate—"

"No. Christ, don't do this." I gripped her wrist and yanked her hand away from her face. "Whatever you were going to say, just end it right there."

Her lower lip quivered until she stilled it between her teeth. She wasn't crying, which was a minor fucking miracle. Tears would've killed me. I couldn't stand Kerry's, and I couldn't have withstood Daisy's either.

Especially if I was partially—or entirely—responsible for causing them.

"I don't want to be alone, okay? Not tonight. Any other night, you could send me off, and I'd go. I'd probably be hurt as hell, but I'd deal. You have every right to handle this any way you want. It's just...I need..."

I didn't interrupt. Maybe I was a sucker or a fool, because the idea of her saying she needed me was far too dangerous.

But I wanted it.

I wanted someone to still need me.

I wanted *her* to need me.

"It's been five years." I shoved a hand through my hair, then snapped a band off my wrist and tied it back. I could feel Daisy watching me with the kind of interest that meant we should not be alone in a cabin. Even if I was basically her brother.

Fuck me running.

"I know. But I'm not past it. Holding your best friend while she..." She shuddered. "I wanted to die too."

Hearing her say aloud what I'd fought to never think was a release somehow. I'd always known it was the grief talking. It would solve nothing. I didn't want to die. I just wanted my sister back. To get a chance to make a different choice. I wished like hell I'd been a better brother, one who'd had a clue how to handle his grieving sister. She'd skated close to too many edges after we lost our mom, and rather than actually talk to her, I'd buried myself in anything I could to avoid my emotions. And her emotions. I'd tried to blunt the pain in any way possible.

I hadn't guessed it would get so much worse before it got better. That by the end of that year, I'd be the only member of my family left.

I yanked my seatbelt into place. "Drive," I gritted out, lacing my fingers together to keep from reaching for her. To remind her and maybe myself that we were still alive. We'd made it for five years, just by putting one foot in front of the other.

The sun always came out eventually. Tomorrow or next week or next month. Bravery was hanging on long enough to see it.

"You're not going to tell me where to go?"

"Don't tell me you didn't study the map." I glanced around the front seat, finally noticing it was tucked under her thigh on her seat. "Uh huh, you sure did. And I remember you could find your way out of the woods without even a handful of breadcrumbs, so I bet you have those first turns memorized."

"I remember you were shit with directions."

"You were supposed to have forgotten that."

Again, that giggle. Low and soft and a little rusty, as if she rarely let loose anymore. I wondered if that was true in more ways than one.

In the months since she'd joined the crew, I'd rarely seen her make appearances at the afterparties. Of course before tonight, she'd never shown up in the cage on stage either. First time for everything. And when I had seen her at a party, she was always sipping ice water or soda, not anything harder.

Maybe she'd changed. For her sake, I hope she had. It was too dangerous to use substances to escape. To have a good time, okay, fine. But to avoid living your life? Hello, asking for trouble.

I should know.

She didn't reply, and I didn't force it. Traffic was definitely slower this time of night, but in the city, it never truly stopped. She seemed to be concentrating on the road, so I let her do her thing.

We'd probably get there faster with her at the wheel than if I was driving anyway.

"You don't have anyone waiting on you?"

Her gaze veered toward me just long enough for someone to lay on the horn behind us when she hesitated at a yellow light. She scrunched up her shoulders and gassed it, making me growl. Her lips twitched and she eased up a little.

"No. No one waiting on me but Ever."

"Oh, Jesus, you live together? There's trouble squared."

She smiled fully, although it was gone too soon. "See, that's the kind of thing I miss. It's nice to be known. To have in jokes and shared experiences."

"You don't have anyone like that now?"

"Not really."

"Surely you must have someone who—"

"If you want to know if I have a boyfriend, just ask."

I didn't.

She signaled around a hulking delivery truck moving at the speed of a turtle and sighed. "I like being on the road because dating isn't really a thing. No one knows you're not seeing someone, because we're in different cities every week. But eventually, the tour ends."

"Tell me about it."

She pursed her lips, the red wash of lights from the car stopping ahead of us playing over her far too beautiful face. As a teen, she'd been cheerleader cute. As a woman, she was stunning, with an intelligence and sense of perception in her eyes that made me uneasy. I didn't want her figuring me out. I hadn't managed it yet, so I damn sure didn't want her to get there first.

"What about you? You have a girl?"

"I've had many girls." The flippant answer was one I'd give to a music journalist. Good for a soundbite without saying much.

The wild rocker image was a pair of leather pants I put on easily. Sometimes it wasn't even an act. I could party as hard as just about anyone.

And crash even harder when I was alone.

Daisy didn't acknowledge my response. I almost apologized, but something held me back. There was no point in pretending to be someone else. I wasn't trying to charm her. She knew me in a way few others did. No matter how much I'd changed in five years, deep down I was mostly the same. The path to get there was just scarred over and brittle.

Other than a few quick questions about the route—which I could barely answer without access to the map currently growing hot under her thigh—we didn't speak for a good hour or longer. By then, my stomach was growling and I was thirsty as fuck.

I motioned to a sign for an upcoming rest stop. "Stop there."

"Please," she said primly.

I grinned.

She must've sensed it because she turned her head toward me. "Wow, you do know how to smile. I'm surprised."

"I used to smile plenty."

"You did. So did I. We should fix that, don't you think?"

"Got any ideas?"

Bad question to ask. I knew it as soon as she leaned forward in her seat. "There's no one on this road right now."

"There will be in a second. Do you know how many people travel the Thruway every day?"

But she wasn't paying attention to me, because she'd slammed her probably tiny ass foot on the gas and sent us bulleting forward.

"What the hell are you doing? Do you want to get a ticket?"

"Not particularly, but I want to go fast." She cranked down the driver's side window all the way and let out a screech as the wind blew her ponytail straight back from her head. The next gust pulled pieces free and teased them around her face. She laughed as she unexpectedly switched lanes, making the old truck sway. "We need music," she shouted over the wind. "Give me something good."

I could've said no to her. In fact, I should have. Then again, I didn't much like this role reversal. I was the crazy rockstar. Right now, she was out-maneuvering me by a mile.

So, what did I do? I gave her some good music.

I scanned to the hair metal channel and turned up the volume as high as it would go. Daisy let out a whoop and stomped on the gas.

Fuck, I was never getting to my cabin. We were going to be spending the night in lockup somewhere.

But some part of me didn't care. I was having fun with Daisy. Sort of. In between looking for the cops and formulating what I would tell Lila when we got arrested for going—I leaned over to look at the speedometer and let out a low whistle—over one hundred miles per hour.

"I love Whitesnake," she yelled. "David Coverdale's hair was so fuckable."

My jaw tensed. Went well with the hand clutching my denim-clad thigh for dear life. "He had a perm."

"He did not." Her voice was indignant.

Without warning, she signaled for the rest stop I'd forgotten all about in my jealousy over eighties' hair gods and shot down the exit ramp.

We slid into a space, and she leaned over the wheel dramatically. "What a rush."

"Yeah, so's stop and frisk."

"I think you're mad because David had better hair than you do."

I nearly said *he so did not* before I retained hold of my man card. Narrowly. "What do you want to eat?"

She didn't hesitate. "Roy Rogers. Two chicken sandwiches with extra pickles."

I unsnapped my seatbelt and cocked a brow. "For you and who else?"

She rolled her eyes and undid her own belt before climbing down from the driver's seat. "Whatever."

I climbed out of the truck and stopped to retrieve my wallet from my backpack in the back before meeting her on the sidewalk outside the rest stop's main building. "You coming in?"

She shook her head and started walking toward one of the round tables a few feet away. "You can get dinner this time. I'll get it next time."

For a second, I just stared. I was so used to women just expecting I'd pay, because hey, I was a rockstar with tons of money. That it didn't even occur to Daisy to do the same floored me. Not that I minded paying, but it was nice she didn't have any expectations.

At least about food. Otherwise? I had no clue.

Shaking my head, I went inside to use the facilities and grab Daisy's chicken. I also picked up a couple of Big Macs and some french fries, along with two supersize Cokes. Juggling was definitely necessary.

I came back outside and glanced around, my heart racing.

Daisy wasn't in sight.

Juggling bags and drinks, I jogged around to the back of the rest stop where there were more tables. Daisy was dancing beside one, lost in the music coming from the mounted speaker nearby. She lifted her arms over her head, swaying in slow circles that made her rainbow sparkles shimmer in the low light.

My breath caught. If I'd had a free hand, I would've rubbed it over my chest to get my heart going again. She had the power to stop it dead.

She always had.

Quiet as a cat, I strolled to the table behind where she was dancing in a beam of light near the flagpole. I set down our meal and then lurched toward her, catching her off-guard. She squealed and laughed as I shoved a hand in the waistband of her boy shorts where she'd tucked my keychain, leaving the keys dangling free. I plucked them out and dangled them over her head, enjoying her attempts to leap at them.

"Too bad, sprite. You dance, you lose." I smacked her ass—fuck, it felt good under my hand—and absorbed the surprise that flared across her face.

Not displeasure. Not even close. She just hadn't been expecting it.

Neither had I.

I moved back to the table and straddled a bench to dig into my burgers and fries. She joined me after a moment, stealing a fry and chewing it thoughtfully. Even without looking at her directly, I could feel the weight of her stare.

"Do you have to do that all the time?" I asked between bites.

"What?"

"Stare at me."

"Yeah. You're pretty."

I literally choked. She cracked up, offering me a napkin when I sputtered lettuce. I was too shocked to laugh as I cleaned up.

"Pretty? I'm a motherfucking badass bassist. You just made me a kitten. All I need is a bow."

"Or could tie a bow..." She trailed off and caught her tongue between her teeth.

Okay, that was a sexual innuendo. This woman was asking me to tie her up.

Wasn't she?

I kept eating. I had no idea what was happening right now.

She unwrapped one of her chicken sandwiches and started eating, keeping pace with me. We didn't talk, but she continued that watching thing. I couldn't decide if it made me uneasy or hot.

Probably both.

"Why are you headed so far out?"

I snagged the last pickle abandoned on her wrapper before she balled up the paper. "Got a place."

"Rented?"

"Own it."

"In Lake George? Why?"

I took out my second Big Mac while she worked on her fries. I'd already demolished mine. "Because I like it there."

"I didn't see where the final destination was. Is it in town proper? A cute little condo? Or a townhouse? Or maybe—"

"Daisy."

She clamped her lips together. "Shutting up now."

My mouth twitched. "You remember."

"That I used to drive you crazy with my incessant questions? Yeah. Kerry used to goad me to do it more."

"She liked seeing me lose it?"

"No, she liked seeing you relax, and you always did once I got done badgering you."

"That makes no sense."

"Sure it does. You'd get annoyed but eventually, I always made you laugh. And Kerry enjoyed watching the show." Daisy took a long pull on her soda. "She made me promise I wouldn't hit on you once she went to Cal State."

Choking again would've been ridiculous. Yet guess what happened? Her eyes crinkled at the corners as she went back to sucking on her straw, waiting for me to man up and reply.

"Hit on—what?"

Yeah, that had been worth waiting for. Definitely.

She nodded and pulled back from her drink with a sigh. "We had so many plans. '*Gonna take on the world, aren't we, Flanny?*' I didn't know how to tell her I didn't want to go to college, but when I finally got up the nerve, she just nodded as if she'd known all along."

I set down the last of my burger, my appetite gone. Apparently, so was Daisy's, because she tucked the second chicken sandwich back in the bag.

"Sorry. I can't stop thinking about her. And there's no one I can talk to about her who knew her the way we did. I mean, Ever listens, but she always feels sorry for me. She thinks I should talk to someone, like professionally. But I don't know what I'd say."

"I don't think you've ever had a problem with talking."

"True enough." I hadn't meant it as a joke, but she gave me a small smile anyway.

It disappeared as I reached across the table to cover her hand with mine. "Even if I growl, you can always talk to me about Kerry."

Her throat bobbled and she turned over her hand to clasp mine. Holding tight, generating a heat between us that made my breath stumble all over again.

All at once, how small she was struck me. How breakable. But in her eyes shone only strength. Much more than I had.

"What about other things?" she asked softly.

"Like what?"

The moment hummed between us. Then she smiled slyly. "David's hair."

Abruptly, I yanked my hand back and stood to collect our garbage. "Find another ride, sprite."

FOUR

Daisy

Oz decided he was going to speed too, while doing air drums on the wheel to a variety of hair metal classics. Dokken. Poison. Cinderella. Great White. There was even some Bon Jovi in there, which he punctuated with some hair banging worthy of a Brooklyn Dawn stage.

I laughed and sang along, surprised by how many of the lyrics I remembered.

Even more surprised when he wrenched off the radio and cut me a look as I finished off the end of "Every Rose Has Its Thorn" without the radio accompaniment. My voice wobbled but I made myself complete the song. Talk about nerve wracking. Me and my bedroom warbling on display before a bona fide rockstar. One who had rocked on stages across the world while I was doing prom updos and party makeup at a small salon in Queens.

When I finished, he switched into the fast lane again and hit the gas. He didn't say anything for so long that my face went from warm to agonizingly hot.

So what if he didn't think I could sing? I did hair and makeup for a living. I rocked at those things, and I was learning more all the time.

Singing and dancing were just what I did for fun. I didn't party anymore, so now I found freedom in forms of expression that didn't make me pass out at the end of the night.

I shifted on my seat, uncomfortable with the silence. I didn't know if he'd grown tired of the music or what. I was also freezing. The early May night was warm, but inside the truck in my painfully brief outfit, I was on the verge of shivering. So, I fiddled with the heat, half expecting him to bark at me to leave it alone. Most males seemed to be perennially overheated.

We went another couple of miles, and then he jerked over to the side of the road and flipped on his hazards. I didn't have a clue why until he pulled off his seatbelt and hauled off his hoodie from behind his head, swearing under his breath when his hand hit the ceiling. I smothered a giggle that disappeared entirely when he dropped it in my lap. The material was warm from his body and smelled like him— balsam and woodsmoke and sweat, an oddly alluring combination. I wanted to bury my face in the fabric before I wrapped myself in its warmth.

Instead, I stared at it as if he'd tossed a python in my lap.

"Put it on," he commanded.

"You're too big."

"So I've been told."

I was *not* touching that one. But I was also cold and the gray hoodie was so soft. I undid my belt and pulled it on, letting out a sigh of pure pleasure as the warm fabric slid against my skin. As I'd suspected, the thing was about five sizes too big, but I wrapped it around me and snuggled in.

"Better? Can I turn this down before my nuts roast?" He was already doing it, his big arm stretching toward the dials and buttons on the dashboard and absolutely dominating the space.

The leather vest he wore from the stage only accentuated his size. In the shadows of the front seat, I couldn't see much clearly, but I remembered how he'd looked in it earlier. He'd nearly busted out of the damn thing. The sides were held together in the front with just a couple of small hooks that stretched and gapped when he played. His long hair had streamed behind him, making him look like a demon sent to earth to drive women crazy before they became his willing sacrifice.

"Yes, please, don't want to be responsible for you being out of commission for any length of time. Your many admirers would be brokenhearted. I half expected you to show up with one or two hanging off you when you came looking for your keys."

He didn't say anything as he turned off the hazards and shifted back on the road. Then he turned up the music again.

So much for conversation.

Then again, what had I expected from that little fishing expedition? It was a damn miracle he hadn't left me at the rest stop and called Lila to have a car come pick me up. He hadn't wanted me on this trip to his swanky digs, and he'd made that clear enough. I'd just tagged along like the pesky kid sister he probably saw me as.

God knows he'd never given much indication he'd even noticed I was a woman, other than the occasional quick comment or lingering look. He'd even nicknamed me "sprite" tonight.

A nickname, always the surest way to my foolishly lonely heart. Even if it was akin to a gnome or a troll. Something little and adorable.

Yay me.

"To anyone who isn't a giant, I'm actually a bit over average height for a woman, you know."

He didn't appear to hear me, just stomped on the gas. We rocketed forward, although we weren't anywhere near my earlier speeds. Just enough that the wind slicing through the sliver of window I'd left open streaked through my hair and made me shiver again. But now I had his hoodie to drag even tighter around me.

"Belt," he snapped out.

"So bossy. Is that why you don't have a girlfriend?"

I didn't expect an answer to my question, and I didn't get it. I had no explanation for why I kept circling around his love life. In the little over six months I'd been doing hair and makeup for the band, he'd never let me touch him. Technically, he wasn't supposed to refuse those services, since everyone was supposed to be stage ready at all times. But Oz did what he wanted, whether it was going onstage sans any makeup but his own or tossing a guitar into a hot tub at a hotel party. I'd only heard about that secondhand from Teagan, who'd tried to smooth over my hurt feelings the first time he'd pitched a fit about sitting in my chair.

"He has issues," Teagan whispered conspiratorially. "It's not you."

Except it *was* me. The couple of nights I'd been off with the flu in December, he'd let the woman who filled in for me do his hair. She'd gone on and on about how she'd buried her hands in it and just let herself pretend they were in a much different scenario. He'd been nothing but charming to her, which I knew because I'd asked.

I'd needed to know, even if now I wished I didn't.

At some point, I started singing with the music again. Low at first, then losing myself in the songs that Kerry and I had listened to so often in high school. She'd been all about the retro hair bands, and I'd learned to love them too. Oz had been doing his share of rocking back then himself, and he'd always had longer hair—the kind a budding hairstylist would've loved to get her hands on. Even back then, he'd acted as if my hands were poison.

Now they were radioactive.

Again, he wrenched off the radio with no warning. This time, I stopped singing. "Sorry," I said automatically. "It's habit."

"Why are you apologizing?" His voice was pure grit. "I turned it off so I could hear you better."

"I—what?"

"Why are you doing hair when you could be on a stage somewhere and not just shaking your fine ass?"

There was so much more to unpack than I could in the space of a few seconds. Then he started speaking again.

"You can do more, you know. You don't have to settle."

"Who's settling?"

He didn't answer, but it was clear he thought I was.

"I love my job. Do you think what I do isn't important? That it's not a skill? If you'd let me touch you, you'd see I could even do wonders with you."

He slid me a long glance in the darkness of the front seat. Even without being able to decipher his expression, the heat from it enfolded me from head to toe. He was pissed.

Good. I was tired of being mad alone.

"You were going to college to get a degree. What happened there? Too much partying?"

His censure stung. "It's none of your business."

"You made it my business when you stole my keys and my truck."

"I didn't steal your truck. You're sitting in it, aren't you? And I wouldn't have needed to if you hadn't acted like such a self-important, immature jackass. Instead of just dealing with our past, you try to pretend it doesn't exist. Sticking your tongue down any woman's throat who wanders past at the afterparties any time I started walking your way, or picking nonsense fights with me when all I wanted to do was to remind the world she existed." The backs of my eyes burned hot. "She matters and I still care, even if you don't."

"If you think I stuck my tongue down any woman's throat because of you, you're the one who's self-important and immature." He made a sound that was part amusement and part derision. "As if you're even in my sphere."

"Oh, right. Stupid little hair and makeup girl can't even talk to the big rockstar. You know what? Just let me off at the next rest station. I'll find my way back."

"Fuck that."

"No, fuck you." I yanked at my seatbelt and grabbed the door handle. I didn't even know what I was doing right now. I couldn't exactly jump from a moving vehicle at eighty miles an hour.

I also couldn't sit in this confined space with him another moment longer.

"Goddammit, Daisy, if you open that door—"

Blind with frustration and pain, I opened it.

I reared back as his big arm shot in front of my chest, somehow yanking the door closed while we careened across the road. The truck rocked so wildly that the trees beyond the guardrail swerved frighteningly close. Brakes screeched as I shut my eyes and braced for the crash, every part of me clenched in preparation.

And then...nothing.

I opened my eyes as we swerved, regaining our forward momentum although I would've never been able to say how. The truck bounced around before finally stabilizing, a long breath whooshing out of me as I touched Oz's arm, still banded across my chest. Holding me safe even though I'd nearly killed us both.

"I'm sorry." The words sobbed out of me. "I'm so sorry."

He was breathing hard, his features set like granite. He didn't speak. Didn't look at me. Just signaled into the texting pull off station we were passing and wrenched off the truck.

Then he unsnapped his belt and turned toward me, snapping out his hand to grasp my chin. "Don't you ever try a stupid trick like that again, understand me?"

I wanted to rail at him, but fear had struck me mute. Or maybe it was the sheer panic coming from him, as potent as the seductive scent of him surrounding us. Making everything seem so hazy and secluded and...hot.

Suddenly, I was on fire. I pushed at his hand so I could get the hoodie off. I was burning up. Shaking with it.

And then he was dragging at it too, but not just to help me with my overheating problem. He didn't stop once the hoodie was pooled on the truck floor. He yanked at the thin straps on my top, pulling them down my arms until I was exposed, my flesh overflowing the flimsy cups of my strapless bra. I blinked, my brain sluggish between what had just happened and what was happening now.

What was happening?

Our gazes locked and clung, his deep, dark pupils dragging me down. I couldn't stop the pull into his force field. Couldn't remember why this was a bad idea. Why I'd regret it in the morning or in an hour. My heart pounded in my ears, throbbed between my breasts.

His eyes never left mine as he gripped my chin again, this time yanking my mouth to his.

Hunger poured from him into me, as tangible as his hot rush of breath against my parted lips. He fused our mouths together, kissing me without a hint of finesse or caution. He didn't wait to see if I could keep up, just trusted that I would. His hands delved into my hair, wrecking my ponytail, driving into it to turn my head just where he wanted me. Our tongues tangled, and some part of my brain cataloged that he tasted like expensive liquor and frustration, the most erotic combination I'd tasted in my life.

I drew back sharply enough that I bumped my head on the ceiling. "You've been drinking—and you drove—"

He started laughing so hard that he wheezed. "Are you fucking kidding me? You're the one who almost killed us, and you're fucking sober."

I didn't laugh. "You would've just driven up all those hours alone?"

"I do everything alone."

The bald statement combined with the smear of lipstick that had somehow gotten on his cheek hit me square in the chest. I reached for him, framing his face in my hands before I leaned in and nipped his lower lip. Sucking on it hard while he watched me, his chest rising and falling so fast that I could see it even in the near dark. The tip of my tongue touched his and then he was on me, feasting on my mouth as if it was a banquet and he was starving to death.

One hand cupped my cheek and the other squeezed my breast. I gasped, but he didn't gentle his touch. If anything, he grew rougher. Bolder. His hand slid up between my breasts to my throat, his big thumb pushing against my pulse. Trapping it while his lips and tongue devoured me until I was grasping at his big arms, trying to find purchase. My head was spinning, my breath leaving me in staccato bursts, and he wasn't even breathing heavily anymore.

He'd entered some zone where he could control me masterfully while he stood back and watched me shatter.

I'd been on a collision course with this night for so very long.

Probably since the very first time I'd walked into Kerry's basement and seen her older brother bent over an old acoustic bass guitar, carefully restringing it with hands more suited to catching a football than to making love to an instrument.

Or making love to me.

I slid my hands up his bare chest, slipping underneath the vest to touch the ridges and planes that had been off-limits to me. Nibbling at his mouth while I caressed him and absorbed the sensation of his heart stampeding under my palm, along with those shallow intakes of breaths he probably didn't think I heard. Ones that grew deeper and shakier as I reached up to undo his hair. His eyes stayed dark and steady on mine when it tumbled out of the band I yanked free.

Then I was pushing him back into the seat to straddle him, fighting to make room in the tight confines of the front seat. He hit a lever and the seat jolted backward, sending me flying forward on top of him, pressing my bare breasts to his skin and those narrow panels of leather.

His groan was pure torment. "Get those shorts off before I fuck you through them."

The words had me shifting back so that his very large, very aroused cock settled against my achy center. This time, the groans were mutual.

I shut my eyes, wondering if I had a concussion from nearly dying. This couldn't be happening. His thick fingers couldn't be pushing aside my shorts and panties so he could find my pussy, already wet and hot and craving him.

"Goddamn, you're ready already. I knew you'd be like this."

I couldn't puzzle out what he meant, especially since I was never ready when things progressed to this point. My engine had started and stalled so many times that I'd given up even trying to slip in the key. Or trying to wedge it in the lock that was not built to Oz's dimensions, thank you very much.

But from the way I was rubbing and rutting against him as his fingers made themselves at home between my legs, I was ready to try.

"I want to pull you up here," he panted into my mouth between long, drugging kisses and short, heady ones. "Put you right on my face."

I was blushing. My scalp was blazing hot, and it wasn't just because his free hand was massaging my scalp while we kissed. Every part of me was lit up, especially where his thumb was circling my clit, spreading my wetness around, teasing me with pressure before sliding away and wiping it on my thigh. As if he wanted me to know how wet I was, in case I'd somehow missed that fact.

"More," I begged. "Please more."

He didn't leave me hanging. Two fingers slipped down, sliding in the proof of my desire for him. Spearing into me without hesitation, making me moan and arch so that my breasts were close enough for him to suck and lick and...bite.

The first one caused me to jerk, unintentionally driving his wide fingers deeper. So deep that I couldn't breathe for a second until his thumb found my clit again and eased the sting. He rubbed me harder than I would've guessed I could handle, fingerfucking me so wildly that my body made obscene noises.

So embarrassing. So hot.

The windows were so foggy I couldn't see anything but clouds of condensation. I could barely make out the glow of his eyes in the low light, focused on me like beacons. Trained on me to see every nuance. Waiting for me to crumble literally into his hands.

I bit my lip, dropping back my head as the pleasure climbed inside me, twining with the pain of knowing it would be over soon. That peak meant the drop would hurt even more.

His teeth scraped over my nipple, and the jolt snapped me back into my body. I couldn't find distance. There was no way to cushion my landing. To do anything but to take every bit of his hand flexing against me, demanding all I'd held back for my own safety.

We didn't need words. We just needed *this*.

I shook and cried out as I came, moaning into his mouth. Somehow it was there to meet mine, his lips gentle instead of punishing, his fingers coaxing instead of relentless. Nursing me through the moment, extending it, rather than forcing me to give him everything. He was taking it all.

I dropped my head to his shoulder to catch my breath, burying my face in the thick ropes of his hair. Smoke and sweat and destruction, surrounding me. Centering me as his big hand rubbed up and down my back.

"It's okay," he whispered, and the thickness of his voice made me want to cry. I didn't know if they were happy tears or leftover from nearly dying or because I knew this moment would probably never happen again.

I didn't know how it had happened now.

The silence grew between us, but it wasn't uncomfortable. My heartbeat fell back into an easier rhythm and the gentle movement of his hand could've lulled me to sleep if he hadn't let out a groan and shifted, reminding me exactly how big he was and how small the space.

"Sorry. Sorry," I repeated, backing up too fast again and hitting my head for what, the third time? I'd lost track.

He shook his head and reached up to rub my scalp, soothing me yet again. "You can drive."

It made me giggle—and cry. The tears would've embarrassed me if he hadn't reached up to cup my cheek and smoothed them away, one by one.

Sniffling, I rubbed my nose with the back of my hand. "I haven't come in a really long time."

"Okay."

It made me giggle again. "You're wondering if you just had your hand in the panties of a crazy person, aren't you?"

"No."

"Don't be so effusive, Osmond." When I would've eased back in a futile attempt to collect myself, he just wrapped his arms around me and cuddled me close.

Even surrounded by his heat, my eyes widened. As stupid as it seemed, I didn't know he knew how to hold someone. That he could feel so good, so right, holding *me*.

"Stop thinking so loud. Just take a minute." He rubbed his chin against the crown of my head. "Give me one."

I gave it to both of us because I couldn't do anything else.

"Daisy."

Gently, he shook my shoulder. I blinked and lifted my head, taking in his slow smile with confusion.

"You fell asleep," he said, wincing as he shifted beneath me. "And so did my ass and my left hip. Holy Christ, these seats suck."

I grinned and yanked up my top. "I'm moving."

His quick frown was a bolster to my ego I hadn't realized I needed. "I really liked that view."

"Good to know."

"Daisy." He gripped my hip. "Thank you."

"For driving? You're welcome. I'm eager to sleep in a real bed too." Not wanting anything to bring back the tension that had nearly killed us, I flashed him a smile and shifted back into the passenger seat. And happened to slide a glance at his groin.

"That has to be a trick of the light," I muttered.

"What light?" He pulled his seat back into an upright position and seemed to gather the direction of my gaze. And smirked in full Oz mode. "Nope. That's a trick of genetics. One good thing I can thank my worthless pop for."

"How do you know it's not from your mother?"

"Are you really asking how I know I didn't get my big cock from my mother?"

I rubbed my forehead. "I think I'm concussed."

"Or desperately in need of a good fuck."

Yep, blushing again. "If you only knew the half," I said under my breath as I reached for my seatbelt.

"You're driving, remember?" His hand closed around mine on the belt buckle and squeezed.

I shut my eyes and let myself pretend this was real life. Us joking around and getting naked and not hating each other.

It was real, at least for this moment. And it felt pretty damn good.

I squeezed his fingers back and opened my door. I jumped down like I normally would've, and my legs actually folded under me.

Oz leaned across his seat and peered down at me, his brows knitted together. "What the fuck?"

That was probably the best way to sum up this whole night.

From where I was kneeling on the cold ground, I clutched the door handle and laughed.

FIVE

Daisy slept for the rest of the trip up north.

After she'd collapsed to the pavement—why I still wasn't sure, although my ego enjoyed thinking it was due to the orgasm I'd given her—I'd decided the passenger seat was the best place for her. She hadn't argued. Nor had she tried to kill us or bewitch me or any other of her little tricks.

Mercifully, she'd just dozed. She let out these little snuffling snores now and then that shouldn't have made me grin but did just the same.

I even followed the damn map to a T and didn't make any wrong turns.

Just when I thought I was going to have to wake her up, she lifted her head and fumbled out for the dash. "Is it time to get up?"

"Unless you want me to drag you in by the hair, yep."

In truth, I'd planned on carrying her. It wasn't as if she was heavy. I'd had her on top of me—fuck, I couldn't start thinking about that or the pike in my jeans was sure to return—and she'd barely weighed anything. If it hadn't been for these seats not being built for a guy my size, I could've held her forever.

Something I had no intention of analyzing, now or ever.

She rubbed her eyes and let out a moan as she straightened her back. "Ouch. Think I'm broken. Thank God you have a cushy place, because I need a fancy shower. The one at Ever's place sucks. The hot water tank is like the size of a thimble and—" She broke off as I continued up the winding drive that was surrounded by trees and more trees. "Oh, nice and secluded. That's good."

I tried not to smirk. Truly, I did. "There is a shower."

"With lots of hot water. Lots and lots. And I hope there's a big bed. Or two," she added hastily. "Not saying we'd share a bed, but if there's only one, then I can..." She trailed off and braced her hands on the dashboard as the truck rumbled over the ruts in the earth. "Where the hell are we going?"

"To my humble abode, of course." There was no hiding my smirk now as we finally reached the crest of the road and came into a clearing that ended with my cabin. "Your waterfront awaits." I gestured broadly to my left, indicating the expanse of lake that was just a rippling blur in the darkness.

Daisy wrenched open the door and jumped out, managing to keep upright this time. She slammed the door and ran toward the cabin, ascending the three steps that led to the wraparound porch. That was pretty much the biggest amenity it boasted.

She propped her hands on her hips as she studied the broken sign leaning against one side of the porch proclaiming the property was Fisher's Rest, then turned toward where I was pulling the truck into the slip.

The second I opened the door, she shouted, "You're an asshole."

I hadn't laughed so hard since... Damn, I had no idea.

Yes, I did. I hadn't laughed that hard since my sister and my mom had been alive. Back when I'd still had hope.

"C'mon, tell the truth. You're just messing with me." She came down the steps. "This isn't the real place. It was hard enough to believe you kept that relic," she jerked her thumb at my truck, "but there's no way an actual millionaire would have a place like this."

Before I could respond, she pressed her hands to her cheeks. "Oh my God, no. No wonder you're such a sourpuss all the time. You lost all your money. Gambled it away? Drank it away? Wine, women, and song?"

"You listen to too much country music."

She flipped me the bird. "Obviously not, because I didn't mention your dead dog."

I laughed again, gripping the door to keep from doubling over. God, this was fun. "You haven't even been inside yet. It could be a palace."

She yanked open the rickety screen door and turned the knob, only to find the inside door locked. "I thought we were going to Lake George."

"We're near the town proper, just on one of the surrounding lakes that feeds into it. Allow me." I climbed the steps and nudged her out of the way to unlock the door. I flipped on the lights, then stepped back and gestured. "After you."

She shot me a look full of malice and crossed the threshold. I didn't immediately follow, enjoying her gasp too much to spoil it by laughing my ass off.

Which I did as soon as I walked inside and found her examining the old fireplace.

"It works," I said proudly, shutting the door.

"You do not live here."

"Not most of the year, no. I have a few places, but I definitely do own this one."

"A few places? Any near here that actually merit a tour?"

"First, you offer to pick up the tab for our next meal. Then you pitch a fit worthy of a trophy girlfriend that my place isn't a showpiece. Pick a personality, sprite."

"Uh uh. You calling me by a cutesy nickname isn't going to keep me from being pissed. You lied to me."

I crossed my arms and watched her study my space. "Did I now?"

She picked up a tattered throw pillow from the sofa that had seen better days and tossed it at me. I didn't bother to duck. "You made me come to soften the blow."

"No, I made you come because you're hot as fuck and it was better than you killing us."

She stopped stalking around the small space and pointed at me. "Flattery will get you nowhere."

"Noted."

"Seriously, this doesn't make sense. Surely this is more of a liability than a write-off. If someone broke in here, they could get hurt and sue." She rubbed the toe of her heeled sandal over a floorboard that tilted up at an odd angle. I'd have to fix that when I got time. "This is a death trap."

"It's actually not, but thank you for the compliment."

"I don't understand." She sank on the couch, and then made a face and rubbed her ass. She'd obviously hit the flat spot. "First, the old truck—"

"Don't insult Jenny. She's not old, she's vintage."

"Jenny?" She shook her head. "Wasn't her name Betty before?"

"No, it was always Jenny. Kerry called it Betty because she thought I'd named it that to get into Jenny MacCorkindale's pants."

"Did you?"

I shrugged and turned to go back to the truck to retrieve my backpack and Annette. "Didn't have to. I'd already gotten in her pants before I got the Bronco." The screen door slapped shut behind me, nearly drowning out Daisy's sigh.

But not quite.

If I was a better man, I probably wouldn't answer such questions. Or even refer to other women at all, considering what had occurred in the front seat a couple of hours ago. I was honest to a fault, which didn't always serve me well.

Besides, what, I'd gotten her off, so now we were going steady? No. I shouldn't have even fucking touched her, but after she'd nearly jumped from my speeding truck, the adrenaline had been coursing too hard. Add in a healthy dose of lust and that sexy as hell outfit and shit happened.

I wouldn't soon forget how her pussy felt convulsing around my fingers. Problem was, that taste hadn't been nearly enough. I wanted to *actually* taste her. Put my mouth between her legs and—

I crossed the few feet to the truck and slammed my fist against the side. Immediately, I rubbed it out and murmured an apology. It wasn't Jenny's fault I couldn't control myself. It had been too long since I'd been with anyone, that was all.

After hauling out my backpack and Annette, I came around to the passenger side to see if Daisy had brought some kind of bag with her. All I found was a tiny purse the size of a napkin, my hoodie, and the Roy Rogers bag, neatly folded up with her leftover sandwich inside.

My stomach growled, and I debated eating it before I went back in. She owed it to me for pain and suffering due to this whole crazy trip. Plus, additional mental anguish for fingerfucking her.

It wasn't as if she was just a hot girl. She worked with my band, and she lived in my memories. That wasn't even mentioning how she drove me mad every single day she was in my realm.

My saving grace was that I hadn't fucked her. It had been a close thing. Granted, this was pretty bad, and it wasn't easy to be platonic once you'd gotten in a chick's panties, but we were adults. It wasn't as if either of us were virgins. We could just chalk the moment up to an instance of near-death insanity and move on.

Then I walked back inside and found Daisy curled up on the couch, fast asleep once again, and my heart rolled over.

Her sunny hair tumbled over her face, making her appear impossibly young. She'd tucked up her legs and made a pillow out of her hands beneath her head. Jesus, she was cute.

Who was I kidding? She was beautiful.

Before I could talk myself out of it, I set down our belongings and went to pick her up, cradling her against my chest as she stirred. She said something unintelligible, and I mumbled the typical sweet nothings back so she didn't wake while I carried her down the short hall to the master bedroom.

The *only* bedroom, which was problematic on several levels.

I set her down on the bed that dominated the room, looking at it critically for the first time since I'd purchased the place. The thin cotton that barely covered the windows when I didn't pull the heavy blackout curtains on my rare weekends recovering by the lake in between nights on tour. The rickety bookshelf of old books I'd brought with me from my room at home with my mom and Kerry. The small TV on the wall that more than covered my needs.

That was about the sum of the room's furniture, not counting the hinged trunk at the foot of the bed that held the small amount of clothes I kept there. There was only one closet in the entire place, and I used it to store rain gear and fishing poles and outdoor equipment for the times I tackled the shrubbery and weeds.

Swallowing hard, I stepped back from the bed. Even the navy comforter seemed entirely too dull for her. This cabin was intended for a single male and decorated with his tastes in mind. No room for rainbows and glitter and sunshine. Yet here she was, brightening up the room already just by existing.

I tugged the comforter over her and she muttered something before falling asleep again.

God, I envied her that. I hadn't slept that easily in I didn't know how many years. Only the pure exhaustion that came from performing a two-hour plus set could effectively knock me out.

Tonight, even that wasn't working.

I was too edgy to sleep, so after a quick pit stop in the bathroom, I went into the kitchen and made a pot of coffee. I still hadn't shaken off the terror I'd felt when Daisy had opened that door on the highway. Some part of me had seen her broken and bloody on that road. Another light extinguished at my hands. Or if not because of me, because I wasn't strong enough, smart enough, quick enough to save them.

The jury was still out if I'd even be able to save myself.

I poured the steaming coffee into a cracked moose mug and moved back into the living room. Settling into the couch, as shitty as it was, made me sigh. This was the closest thing I had to a real home despite the couple of other places I owned. No one else came here. There were no pretensions. Nothing I'd decorated to impress someone. I wouldn't be inviting any photographers or journalists in here to do a spread as I had a couple years ago with my place in LA. It was a showplace with no soul that fit my persona and nothing else.

Certainly not the real me.

I tossed back half the coffee and pulled out a pad and pen from the side table before reaching for Annette. Already words were coming to me, boiling in my brain as if they'd been waiting for the match to be struck. Inspiration in the form of destruction.

Save yourself for me
That candle I couldn't hold
Flame too hot to touch
Burned through my skin
Beneath the bone and ash
Blood that courses for you

You're not the angel to my devil
I'm not the Satan of your nightmares
Wish I was
Wish I could be the dark you'd never want
Because then I wouldn't ache
Wouldn't want to take the pieces
To twist and turn
Into something you could use

Save yourself instead of me
Can't do both
No favor to be had
I had my chance
Earned my spot
In the inferno of my mind

I pushed aside the pad and rose to start the small gas fireplace in the corner. It was midway through spring, and the warm evening had given way to the crispness of night in the woods. I didn't want Daisy to wake up cold. Or afraid. I'd left a light on for her in the hall so she wouldn't be in the dark.

Like I was.

After tying my hair back again, I went back to my guitar and laid it across my lap. If Daisy wasn't here, I'd go out back and start a fire in the woods where I could hear the lap of the water and the rustling of animals scurrying between the trees. But I didn't want to leave her alone, so the fire here would be enough.

That and the work of making the chaos in my brain into something worthwhile.

I messed with the words for hours, adding them to the melody that wouldn't come together. I drank coffee and debated going back to the whisky. Every time I reached for it, I heard Daisy's shock that I'd consumed part of the bottle and gotten behind the wheel.

The alcohol had barely touched me. Sometimes when I drank, it was as if I bypassed the buzz for the hangover. The part where everything hurt and I hated everyone and everything.

Her misfortune had been intercepting that.

Eventually, daylight began bleeding into the room, creeping in at the edges like a savior no one wanted. My safety was the night.

Gone now.

When the shadow crossed the floor, I was bent over the guitar, my hair falling in my face, my fingers cramping from playing the same notes over and over to match them to the words I wasn't happy with. I glanced up and swiftly remembered the other reason I'd been so edgy —extreme sexual frustration. One look at Daisy, all sleepy and morning soft with her watchful bluebird eyes, and I went as hard as stone.

She didn't speak, just came to sit on the coffee table. Her bare legs touched mine as she cupped her hands around my mug. I'd kept a steady stream of brew coming, so I was probably on my fifth cup by now. She drank the coffee greedily before spitting it back into my mug and dropping it on the table as if it was toxic.

"No sugar? What kind of heathen are you?"

Oh, there was a question. Judging from the direction of my thoughts as I followed the long line of her legs right up to the hem of her tiny shorts, I'd say I was a pretty depraved one.

I ignored the question. "Sleep well?"

"No. Weird dreams. I heard you singing sometimes. Why don't you do it more?"

"I'm the bassist," I said simply. "We have a singer far better than I'll ever be."

"So, you do harmonies and that's it."

"Playing the bass isn't exactly delivering the mail. Not that there's anything wrong with that."

She snatched my pad, paging through it as if she had the right to anything on those pages. Even odder, I didn't yank it back. My yearning for approval from her surprised and humbled me. I couldn't remember the last time I'd put myself in that position.

Asshole, you put yourself in that position every night on the road.

But not with her. Although she could judge me every damn show if she wanted to. She probably had. God knows she'd never told me she was proud of where I'd ended up. I'd made good yet her only commentary so far had been to inquire about my mansion and to compare my hair negatively to Coverdale.

"You used to sing more," she said instead of mentioning the song. Words that revealed so much of what was in my head about her. She might as well have just read a grocery list.

Did she really not get I was writing about her? Trying to anyway?

She probably didn't care.

Brother, remember?

One she'd let get her off in the front seat of a truck older than she was.

Man, we were both fucked up.

"Again, in a band with a quite capable singer. Are you hungry?"

"Why, you offering to make breakfast?"

I set aside Annette. I was eager to get out of Daisy's sphere for a few minutes for more reasons than one. "You can call it that."

In the kitchen, I turned on the microwave and picked off the pickles on her sandwich before depositing it on a paper plate. After some microwave magic, I cut it in half and put the pickles back on. Then I made some more coffee and dumped in three pink packets left on the counter probably from the last owners. They definitely weren't mine.

I carried the makeshift meal back into the living room, only to find her with Annette on her lap and my pen between her teeth. She strummed a couple times before setting the guitar aside and removing the pen. "This song isn't working," she announced.

Rather than offending me, it made me laugh. "No shit, Sherlock. Though what do you know about it?"

"I have a pair of ears and a working brain. It's not coming together yet. Probably because it's so woe kitten."

"Excuse me?" I bristled. No part of me was like a kitten. Maybe a lion. That was manly.

I shook my head and remembered I had my hair in a bun. At least I had the mane of one.

Daisy spotted the plate in my hand and forgot all about her criticism. She snatched the sandwich and offered me a quick, fervent, "thank you" before digging in. When she'd finished half, she must have noticed it was cut in half because she held it out to me. "You can have this half. I'm stuffed."

Somehow I laughed again. She didn't put on airs, that was for sure. She was authentically Daisy, just as confusing as fuck as she'd been when we were kids.

Difference was, she still wasn't much more than one and I felt ancient.

I traded the plate for the mug of coffee. She eyed it with trepidation, smiling at the deer wearing a moose hat on the side. "Am I going to spit this out?"

"Dunno. You seem pretty good at spitting." Speaking of that, I needed to dump out my mug and get a fresh cup.

It was impossible to miss the twinkle in her eyes. "I'm good at swallowing too."

I picked up my mug and went back into the kitchen.

She called after me, "Wuss."

She wasn't wrong.

I made more coffee and debated hiding out in there the rest of the day. I had the weekend—we had the weekend—before I had to be back in the city for a fan club show on Tuesday. Monday we were due for rehearsals and God only knows, probably another bullshit meeting where Lila would hint at security concerns that amounted to nothing more than a few petty thefts and overzealous fans. As usual.

You'd figure after so many years in the business, she and Lewis and the rest of the Ripper team would have more chill. Instead, they seemed to be getting more amped up about every little thing.

I came back out to find Daisy gone. But my half of the sandwich was still there, so I ate it in two bites before I went looking for her.

And soon wished I hadn't.

A few feet outside my door, she was sitting on a rock in her bra and panties. Which was actually an optimistic name for them considering the amount of material they'd been constructed from.

"What the hell are you doing?"

"Right now? Getting some sun." She braced her hands behind her on the rock. "I'm so pale."

I couldn't argue. Her skin was like moonlight sprinkled with fairy dust. I knew that was probably just leftover glitter from the night before, but out here, she glinted like a damn beam of light.

"I'll just leave you to it." I turned to head back inside.

"Coward," she muttered, but I didn't rise to her bait. "Also, that coffee had way too much sugar. Don't you have any balance?"

There was a loaded question. I let the slamming screen door answer for me.

I dumped out the paper plate and drank my coffee in a few gulps before rinsing out both mugs. She'd barely touched hers. Couldn't please some people.

She was probably naked by now. God forbid she have any lines.

Why had I allowed her to come along? This couldn't end well. A man only had so much endurance.

How long had it been since I'd had sex? I didn't even know. Far too long when presented with Daisy Flannigan and her obviously wicked intentions toward me.

To drive me insane if nothing else.

Probably because she'd seen the outline of my dick. I couldn't blame her there. That part of me was impressive.

My songwriting skills after a sleepless night? Not so much.

Five hours down was what I needed. If she disappeared in the interim, I'd consider myself lucky.

I stripped down and got into bed. It smelled like her maple-fucking-syrup scent and was still warm from her curvy body. I'd probably wake up with a hard-on after a dream about diving headfirst into a plate of sticky pancakes.

No euphemism intended.

I expected to toss and turn, but apparently, being surrounded by Daisy both inside and out was sedative enough. But I didn't dream of pancakes.

Instead, it was screams. My sister's, replayed over and over. Bouncing off the walls while I stumbled around in a fair attraction, one with mirrors that distorted shapes and turned hallways into a maze. I slammed my fists on doors that wouldn't open, kicked at hinges that wouldn't give way. My knuckles dripped with blood and pain sang through my exposed toes as the leather of my boots split. I couldn't reach her no matter how I tried, and her screams wouldn't stop.

"Oz." I could feel hands pulling at me, dragging me back from the abyss. "Oz, dammit, wake up."

I fought them. I couldn't leave Kerry again, not like I had that night. She was depending on me, and I'd already let her down once.

Let her die.

"Oz, you better wake up. Oz! Dammit, come back to me."

I shoved at the voice. I recognized it, but I couldn't make her stop either. She was hammering at me, forcing me. Too soon. I wasn't ready. Couldn't she see?

My arm swung out, and her cry of pain had my eyes flying open. They locked on Daisy crumpled on the floor, her hand clutching her cheek.

Horror flooded through me as I clambered out of bed to kneel at her side. I expected her to cringe back, to beg me not to touch her, but she held up her arms.

The forming bruise on her delicate skin made my stomach twist and heave. It was a miracle I didn't lose the half of sandwich I'd gotten down earlier.

I'd done that to her. Hurt her in my agony, as I surely would again if I didn't put some distance between us. Fast.

"I'm sorry," I choked out, backing up without touching her.

I couldn't touch her again.

The kindest thing I could do for her would be to stay the fuck away.

SIX

Daisy

I DIDN'T KNOW HOW LONG I STAYED CRUMPLED ON THE FLOOR. Like a broken doll.

Physically, I wasn't. The shock of Oz striking out had sent me tumbling backward, and my cheek ached like a bitch. I imagined it looked worse than it felt, but I was good with makeup. I didn't have much with me, because I'd forgotten my stuff at the venue in my hurry to steal Oz's truck.

And look how that had turned out. But I didn't regret doing it.

My only regret was that I'd let him suffer for all these years alone.

Hearing his cracked voice saying Kerry's name over and over in his sleep had torn something open in me. I'd stitched over so many parts of myself to make a facsimile of a whole. Good enough to pass, strong enough to fake. But he'd opened me up as surely as he'd bled in front of me. Just because the wounds weren't physical didn't make them any less real.

When I was almost certain my legs wouldn't buckle like they'd done the night before, I crawled over to the bed and pulled myself up. I didn't have my purse in here. I had no clue if Oz had remembered to bring it in. I needed to call my sister, something I should have done the night before.

Ever knew that show nights tended to run late, but it was now the following afternoon. Even if she'd been out last night—which I didn't want to think about overmuch—by now, she'd be stumbling home and wondering where the hell her sister "who didn't know how to have fun anymore" could be.

Pretty sure she'd never guess where I was. I still couldn't believe it myself.

I also needed to call Lila to see if they could get my stuff back for me. I hadn't brought many personal belongings to the venue, and I could count on my cart to be collected by the crew and stowed with the rest of our gear. But I had some of my own makeup I didn't want to replace, along with my favorite denim jacket with the patches I'd collected over the years. Including the side-eye daisy on the pocket that I'd bought on a night out with him and Kerry a million years ago. He would never remember that.

Then again, maybe he remembered far more than I gave him credit for.

I sat on the bed for a minute to gather my wits. It had already been a while since I'd awakened Oz—note to self, think twice about doing that next time—and I'd heard the door slam a bit ago. He might've taken off with his truck and my purse. For all I knew, he wouldn't even come back. He might just send up an Uber for me and consider his duty done.

My stomach growled, and I let out a long breath. Even with all the sleep I'd gotten, I was just so tired. My grief for Kerry still felt fresh, especially at this time of year.

Especially since Oz and I were epically bad at acknowledging our emotions.

I looked down at myself and suddenly couldn't stand to look at these fucking rainbows any longer. Oz's clothes wouldn't fit me, as I'd seen last night with the hoodie.

Hell, was that still on the floor of his front seat?

I buried my face in my hands and forced myself back in line. Not important right now. Surely he had something I could wear around here. It didn't have to look good. It just had to cover me in some fashion.

Before that, I'd take a shower. I felt beyond grimy and disgusting, and besides that, now I had a headache, probably due to hunger and stress. I'd given up hoping this shower would be much larger than the one in my sister's apartment, but I didn't care anymore as long as it had hot water.

I rose and glanced around for a closet. I didn't see one. What kind of bedroom didn't have a closet? No one would guess Oz was even a moderately successful musician, never mind an internationally famous rockstar with homes featured in architectural magazines.

A torn-out four-color spread that may or may not have been tucked into the pocket of my suitcase, shoved under the couch in Ever's apartment.

Spying the trunk at the foot of the bed, I opened it and let out a long sigh of relief at the neat stacks of clothes. Not that there were many of them. How often did he come here? Or did he just parade around naked all day? Considering how the man looked naked—and how close to naked he liked to get onstage—I would not have been surprised.

I shivered, remembering how he'd looked rolling out of bed. Even after he'd clocked me in the face and I was dizzy and heartsick, I'd still had to swallow hard at the full sight of him.

He was a living wet dream, especially nude. I'd never had one before, but now I probably could just from the memory.

That was for later, assuming I ever managed to sleep again without hearing his tormented sounds as he thrashed on the bed.

I dug through his clothes, finally settling on a pair of gray sweat shorts with a drawstring waist and a navy blue sweatshirt and tank top. The sweatshirt wasn't needed now, but I really didn't want to dig through all of his belongings again. As it was, I couldn't help lifting them to my nose and taking a long sniff. They smelled of generic detergent but beyond that, I could still catch a hint of that woodsmoke and forest scent of his. I was tempted to curl up with his clothes on the bed and cuddle them close like a giant-sized security blanket, but that was the last way I wanted him to find me.

If he even came back. But if he did, at least I would be presentable.

I carried the clothes into the utilitarian bathroom and checked out the shower more closely than I had while doing my business. I was pleasantly surprised that the shower was indeed bigger than the one in Ever's apartment. Inside it, he had blue and green bottles of combo body wash and shampoo that matched his scents. I'd just use those. They couldn't be any worse than my current straw-like hair, still crinkly with yesterday's products.

A quick glance in the mirror revealed my shiner was a bit bigger than I'd thought. Ever would think I'd gotten mugged.

Ever. I needed my phone. I needed a shower.

Personal vanity won out. I slipped into the stall, letting out a low moan as the prickles of hot water hit my scalp, quickly followed by a douse from Oz's outdoorsy body wash combo. I soaped and shampooed quickly, hitting all the important spots, my ears trained outside the room for any sound of him returning. Any telltale squeaks or screeches from that noisy screen door opening—

And then came that creak. Hurriedly, I shut off the water and realized I didn't have a towel handy. Who didn't keep towels by the shower?

A man not expecting company who lived as he pleased.

I grabbed for the clothes I'd stacked on the sink, dragging on the sweat shorts and tank. They were huge, as I'd expected, so I tightened the drawstring waistband as much as possible and did a quick knot along my ribcage with the tails of the tank. My hair fell in my face so I tied it up in a quick knot with the band on my wrist. I didn't look at my face again. More than anything, I wished I could hide the evidence of what had happened, even though my cheek was currently throbbing. But I had been the one who'd climbed in bed with him. I'd been the one willing to do anything to wake him up.

I was the one who'd tagged along on a trip not meant for me. And I'd do it again.

Taking a deep breath, I crossed the bathroom, stepped into the hallway, and stumbled to a stop. A thin, lanky man stood in the living room, but it wasn't Oz—and when he turned to face me, I glimpsed the silvery sheen of the knife he gripped.

I didn't think. Didn't make a sound.

Whirling around, I lurched back into the bathroom to slam the door shut, but I wasn't fast enough. The guy was there before I could get it closed, sliding the hand with the knife through the gap in the door. I put all my strength into closing it, but I couldn't combat his strength. Too many hours in dance classes, not enough in strength training.

His arm swung out as he wedged the door open, and the knife jaggedly sliced down my arm.

I cried out in shock and surprise. And terror. So much terror as my blood dripped down my arm and onto Oz's cracked blue and white Mediterranean tiled floor.

He was going to be mad. I hadn't even been invited, and now I was bleeding all over his floor...

The roar outside the door had me stumbling backward. I bumped my hip hard on the corner of the sink, but the pain didn't stop me from reaching for the small bucket beside the faucet that held a fancy toothbrush, toothpaste, and a washcloth. I couldn't make sense of the commotion outside until Oz's shout spurred me to move.

I yanked the door open with only my makeshift weapon in hand. The two men were a blur of fists and legs, but Oz was clearly on top. He hit the intruder again and again, and my head reeled at the blood pouring out of the other man's mouth.

Somehow I marshaled the forces to run past them—practically leaping over them—to grab the knife that had slid across the hardwood floor. As I turned back to them with the weapon outstretched, the other man managed to scramble up and run for the still wide open door, leaving a few drops of blood in his wake.

He didn't look back, and Oz didn't give chase. He was too busy staring at me holding a knife and bleeding on my bare feet.

"Oh, baby." His voice was a rumble of emotion as he picked me up off my feet and cradled me against him. I might as well have been weightless for all the effort he'd shown in lifting me. His thundering heartbeat beat clear through the walls of my chest and restarted my own.

"You're hurt." He cupped my sore cheek for a moment before he gently pried the knife out of my grip and tossed it onto the couch. It stuck straight up, handle first, between the cushions, which struck me as strangely funny.

And now I was bleeding on his gray thermal shirt.

"Sorry," I gasped, pushing against him until he let me go.

He shifted toward the small dining table where a large paper grocery bag was tipped on its side, with a package of cold cuts and a pint of ice cream peeking out. My stomach grumbled, but neither of us acknowledged the sound while he grabbed a sheaf of napkins and pressed them to the wound. He kept the pressure steady, his brown eyes searching mine.

For what, I didn't know. I was still dizzy and probably in shock and I really wanted that ice cream, even without knowing what flavor it was. I didn't care. I'd sit down and eat the whole thing.

"Your cheek," he murmured, tipping his head down until our foreheads touched.

In my head, I wanted to question his priorities. I'd been stabbed. I was bleeding. And the dude was worried about a pesky bruise?

That hurt like a bitch, I acknowledged. Just like the shallow slice in my arm. I was now the walking wounded on multiple levels.

"Not gonna steal any more trucks," I muttered, and he shocked the hell out of me by laughing.

Until he drew back, and I glimpsed a sheen to his eyes that froze me straight to the core.

"Oz, don't. I'm fine. I handled myself." I frowned down at my arm. "All right, not well. I need more strength classes. I hate the stupid machines, but I'll use them. But I wouldn't have stopped fighting. I would have hit him with the pail."

"What pail?"

I frowned again. "The one in the bathroom. Think I dropped it when I saw you two rolling on the floor and you pounding the shit out of him. You probably broke half his bones."

"Not nearly enough," he growled, removing the napkin and cursing at the amount of blood—*my* blood—staining the white material.

Even in my woozy state, I could tell it was slowing down. Finally.

"We should get you to the hospital."

"I don't need a hospital."

"Daisy—"

"Don't 'Daisy' me. I've done almost as bad to myself on a hot curling iron. I mean, that's a burn, but whatever. We should call the police. Call someone."

"We're going to do both. I need to tell Lila what happened here."

"What? Why? She's going to think we're—that something is up, us being out here alone."

The look he gave me was two parts annoyed and one part frustrated. "What she thinks is irrelevant. You were stabbed. And you also have a nice shiner from some asshole clocking you."

"Wanna talk about irrelevant? That definitely qualifies. It was an accident. Completely. You know it. I know it. And you brought me sandwich fixings and ice cream, and I could probably marry you. So, don't be a dick about it, all right?"

His lips twitched and the pressure on my arm faded as he gently turned it toward the sunshine streaming in the window. Already the bleeding was down to a trickle. "You might need stitches. You need your arm."

"Yeah, no kidding. I'll be okay. If I start to get gangrene, I'll make you drive me to the ER, okay?"

"You aren't funny."

"Not trying to be. Just we need to get the cops out here and call

Lila, I guess." I made a face. "If you insist. I gotta call my sister too. Is my phone—where's my purse?"

He gestured vaguely in the direction of the couch. "I brought it in last night, but you can't use it in here."

"What? Why?"

"No service. I have a satellite phone for emergencies." He tugged it out of his jeans. Before I could take the phone, he pulled it back. "Let's get a bandage on you first. I have a first aid kit."

I nodded. "Fine. Whatever. Let's do it." I glanced back over my shoulder at the groceries. "Can we put that stuff away first? If that ice cream melts, someone may get hurt."

Again, his lips twitched, a minor miracle considering the events of the day so far. He grabbed the bag and motioned ahead of him to the kitchen. "Go on in and I'll fix you up quick after I take care of these."

His idea of a quick dressing was far different than mine. He washed the cut with warm water and soap for about ten minutes, or so it felt like. Then came the round of antibacterial cream and the actual bandage application. When that wasn't adequate to his liking, he removed it and put another on before nodding in satisfaction and finally producing his phone—once he'd called the cops and they were on their way.

"Keep it brief," he instructed before leaving me alone in the tiny kitchen. Not that his leaving offered any privacy. The entire cabin was the size of a large box.

"Don't go in the bathroom yet," I called out. "I made a mess."

Then it occurred to me he'd likely gotten the first aid kit from there and shook my head. Someday I'd replace the brain cells I'd lost on his tile floor. Maybe.

Quickly, I called my sister's number. She answered on the second ring.

"Ever, it's me."

"Daisy Louise Flannigan, you are in so much trouble. The orgasms better have been worth making your sister worried sick."

I flushed. Someday I'd get used to my baby sister talking so much more casually about sex than I ever could. "Just one, and it was, until I was stabbed."

"Um, what?"

"Never mind. I'm okay. Everything is fine now. Just a little bit of insanity. You know, your average crazy weekend." With added blows and blood and breaking and entering.

"Where are you? You better have been kidding about being stabbed."

"Uh, not exactly, but don't worry, the police are on their way."

"What?" Ever's screech nearly busted my eardrum to go with the rest of the infirmities I'd collected so far this weekend. "You better start talking."

The sound of wheels rolling over gravel outside meant it was time to talk to the cops. "I can't right now, but I'll call you back later, promise. We should be back tomorrow night." At least I was pretty sure. "But if I'm late, don't freak. It's okay. I'm safe."

"Oh, yeah, did you meet a hot guy?"

"No, I'm with Oz."

I wanted to clarify the hot thing. Was there any male hotter than the one I was with? Not hardly. But I wasn't going to say that when he was in earshot.

His head—both of them—was big enough already.

Exactly why I hadn't praised his songwriting—fucking amazing—or his hair—glorious—or the sound of his sexy, raspy voice singing me awake this morning. I would happily be awakened just like that for the rest of my life.

Good luck there, Daze.

"Not Croly Street Oz. What the fuck are you doing?"

I rolled my eyes. 'Croly Street Oz' was always how she referred to him, a nod to the street Kerry and Oz had grown up on. She'd always seen Oz as untouchable. Like he thought he was too good for me or something. I'd never said anything to give her that vibe, but she'd always accused me of being in love with him, even back in the old days.

Which was crazy. I'd never been in love with anyone. Certainly not

Oz. And so what that I'd rarely been able to come when it came to any hand but my own? He'd just gotten lucky. Add in an adrenaline spike from the near crash and it was completely explainable. It wasn't as if him touching me was the fulfillment of a dream more than five years in the making.

I'd just keep telling myself that.

"It was the anniversary," I said quietly, picking at the edge of the bandage Oz had carefully applied to my arm. His big fingers so tender, his brow furrowed with concentration. He hadn't rushed or fussed or been anything but kind and patient. As if his entire being was focused on that one task.

My heart sometimes felt too big to be contained in my chest when it came to him. Sure, I probably had some hero worship in his direction that hadn't faded with the intervening years. He was so big and strong and beautiful to boot, especially when he had his bass in his hands.

Who could blame me for falling into that typical role of having a crush on my best friend's older brother?

Except my best friend was gone. I hadn't seen Oz in years until last fall. But I'd never forgotten him. I'd never stopped thinking of him. When the chance to apply for a spot on the band's hair and makeup crew had opened up, I'd jumped at the great opportunity. Not because of Oz.

I wouldn't allow myself to believe it.

A couple of male voices joined Oz's in the living room. "Look, I really gotta go. We'll talk later. Everything's fine. Love you to the moon." After giving her our standard goodbye, I hung up before she could argue.

Because she would have. That was my Ever.

I tucked the phone in the pocket of Oz's shorts and threw back my shoulders. I could do this. Talking to the cops was no big deal. So what if the last time had been after Kerry's overdose? This wasn't then. I wasn't a shaking eighteen-year-old girl who couldn't decide if I wanted to throw up or sob.

In the end, I'd done both.

But I was stronger now. I still did stupid, crazy, overemotional things—this whole weekend and our near accident last night was proof enough of that—but I also got my head back on straight pretty fast. I'd taken some punches, literally and figuratively, and I wasn't on the floor, weeping.

At least not yet.

Bolstered by my self pep talk, I took two steps and came to a halt as Oz's voice boomed out.

"You can talk to me. I know what happened. Give her a break. She's already dealt with enough today."

He sounded so defensive. So absolutely ready to do battle with anyone who dared to try to hurt me, even if their few questions were just routine.

My throat tightened. I could take care of myself, but God, it had been so long since anyone had even tried to protect me.

My mom definitely didn't relish the role, which is why Ever and I had kind of parented ourselves. She'd been too busy worrying about her love life and her designer wardrobe and about never growing old. I could trace my skills with a curling brush and a mascara wand directly to her planting the essentials in my head early.

"Never let them see you cry, baby girl—or without good makeup."

Here I was, on the verge of doing exactly that. My face was bare. I'd left all my warpaint behind, and my vulnerability was on display.

That was just how it had to be.

I stepped into the living room and stiffened my spine at the sight of the two uniformed cops standing beside Oz. His arms were crossed, and he wore a glower scary enough to make just about anyone take a step back.

My protector was in full intimidation mode.

"Oz, I'm okay." I moved to his side and laid a hand on his arm. His muscles tensed under my fingers, and I swallowed hard at his stiff posture. This was as hard for him as it was for me. If not harder.

Seeing you hurt caused him pain, dummy. Can't you see that?

"Miss—"

"Flannigan," I quickly supplied. "Call me Daisy."

Oz shot me a sidelong look I didn't acknowledge. And I left my hand on his arm, adding a little thumb rub that was meant to soothe him. If anything, his arm tensed even more.

The cops exchanged glances before the shorter one spoke first. "I'm sorry to bother you, Daisy. Truly, I am. But if you can tell us what exactly happened before Mr. Taylor arrived home, that would be a big help."

"I already told you—"

"Oz. You weren't here," I reminded him gently. "Let me just run through it quickly for them. It's fine, I swear."

Oz set his mouth in a grim line and nodded.

"Let's sit down," the other cop said, gesturing to the couch.

"I could make coffee? Or—" Then I shut the hell up, because this wasn't my home. Oz and I weren't a couple, and we definitely weren't playing house.

The shorter cop smiled. "We're good, thank you. We'll make this as fast and painless on you as possible."

I returned his smile and glanced at Oz, who was looking anywhere but at me. I barely resisted a sigh.

This was going to be a long afternoon.

SEVEN

THE QUESTIONING WASN'T FAST OR PAINLESS. IT LASTED OVER AN hour and included such side trips as, "Did he give you that shiner too?"

Of course I couldn't blame them for asking. The bruise on her cheek was becoming more colorful with every passing minute. I went back and forth between wanting to give her ice to put on it and wanting to get the hell out of there so I couldn't see the reality of what I'd done on her skin.

Daisy didn't falter as she explained what had occurred with her cheek. One of the cops had given me a sidelong look, but the other hadn't looked away from her as she spoke. He was probably wondering why she was hanging around with a brute like me.

I couldn't answer that question.

They finally left after promising to call if they nabbed the suspect or had any further information.

Feeling at loose ends, I went in the kitchen to make Daisy a sandwich. I nabbed a piece of the ham but didn't bother making one for myself. Not yet. Seeing Daisy bleeding had taken several years off my life. Add in the bruise on her cheek, and my appetite had vanished. I was a big guy though, so I knew it wouldn't stay away forever.

I came out and she wasn't in the living room. I found her in the bathroom on her hands and knees, scrubbing at minuscule spots I'd already cleaned up.

"Seriously? The floor is fine."

She huffed a hank of blond hair that had escaped her topknot out of her face. "Gives me something to do anyway."

"Right, with your injured arm. I still wish we'd gone to the ER."

"Yeah, well, I wish you'd realize this morning was an accident and stop beating yourself up about it. We all want things we can never have."

"I made you a sandwich." How that related to what she said, I wasn't sure. Except that I'd probably be trying to make up for what I'd done for twenty years.

Right, because she's going to be in your life for twenty years? Not likely. It's a miracle she hasn't taken off already.

She sat back on her heels and tossed the sodden hunk of paper towels in the trash. "Guilt-induced food preparation?"

"I figured you have to be hungry."

"What about you?"

I shrugged. "I'll eat later."

She rose and rinsed off her hands, then dried them on a towel she'd pulled out from beneath the sink. "You're still set on calling Lila?"

"She always finds out anyway when shit goes down. I'd rather she hear it from me."

"As if you're responsible for me somehow."

"This is my cabin. You came here in my truck. I left you alone. You're also one of her people. Yeah, I'm responsible."

"Right, because you control the universe, Superman." She rolled her eyes and brushed past me to go back into the living room.

I rubbed the growing ache in my forehead and followed her. She sat at the small square dining table, eating the sandwich as if she was on the verge of starvation. I'd loaded it up with pickles and she shot me a look as she picked each one off and ate it. But I didn't miss how she winced a couple times, probably due to her nicely swollen cheek.

Jesus, I was an asshole. Who the hell swung like a boxer when they were coming out of a dream?

Just fucking me.

"Soon as I finish, we'll call."

I nodded and moved to the couch. Neither of us spoke for what felt like an eternity.

She finally rose to clear away her dish, ignoring me when I told her to leave it. Then she returned to sit beside me on the sofa, producing the satellite phone from where she'd tucked it in the pocket of her shorts.

My shorts, drooping off her curvy frame. They barely stayed on her sexy ass and hips. And my tank top was the same, huge and baggy except around her tits, where the material stretched just a bit tighter. The knot at her hip kept coming loose, and every time she fixed it, I glimpsed a slice of her perfect belly and the slash of her navel.

I couldn't swallow from the dryness of my throat, and it wasn't just because I couldn't stop looking at her bruise or the bandage on her arm.

She was stunning. And completely off-limits.

She held out the phone. "You want to talk to Lila, you call."

I nodded and did the honors, unsurprised when Lila answered on the second ring despite it being mid-afternoon back in California. I knew she usually took a red eye out after our shows on the rare times Lewis's jet wasn't available so she could get home to her kids and her husband as quickly as possible. That domestic life had always seemed crazy to me. I couldn't imagine being that eager to get back home when the stage had always been my draw. The only time I wanted to be exactly where I was.

In twenty-four hours, so much had changed for me. I hadn't become a family man, but I was certainly looking at a lot of stuff differently.

Such as the woman sitting beside me, her chin held high and her hands steady in her lap. Her strength staggered me.

More than anything, being with her reminded me exactly why my sister had loved her so much.

"Osmond?" Lila asked. "To what do I owe the pleasure of this call?"

Behind her, the sounds of children's laughter and a lower, more even voice I recognized as Nick's made me grimace. "Sorry if I'm interrupting."

"We're at Disneyland, about to eat giant Mickey Mouse ice cream heads. Interrupt all you want." I hit the speaker on the phone so Daisy could hear too just as Lila added, "No, I'm still not giving you Daisy's number."

Daisy coughed into her fist.

"About that. I don't need her number. We're together at my place near Lake George." At the silence that suddenly descended over the line, I cleared my throat. "Look, we go way back and—"

"Whatever you're thinking, it's not that," Daisy interjected. "We're just friends."

For probably the first time in my life, I wanted to argue that we *were* something more. And remind her that I'd had my hand in her panties last night. I could still feel her warmth on my fingers as she shook and cried out.

Was that what it meant to be just friends in Daisy's world? If so, did I really want to think about it?

Hell no, I did not. Now was not the time and definitely not the place.

Before she could elaborate—or worse, before I corrected her—I got to the point. "There was an incident. Well, two."

Daisy pinched my thigh and rapidly shook her head. Guess she didn't want me bringing up my dream-induced swing. Too bad. People would ask questions, and I would rather be embarrassed about my actions than pretend the fucker who had broken in had done it to her. I wasn't going to deny my actions.

I'd denied far too much over the years.

All at once, the sounds around Lila lessened, and I imagined her shooing away her family so she could go into full business mode in some alcove at Disneyland. Although I had no clue where that might be.

"What happened?" Her voice was sharp.

Briefly, I ran through the break-in. Daisy filled in the parts before I'd arrived. Before Lila could reply, I added, "Something else happened too, earlier today. I was having a bad dream. Daisy woke me up, and I clocked her."

"Excuse me?" Lila's tone dripped frost.

"It was an accident." Daisy narrowed her eyes at me. "He freaked out and apologized and ran off, but it was totally an accident. He even bought me ice cream and cold cuts, so you know he feels guilty."

"Not ice cream and cold cuts. Why, that's practically a diamond. Are you okay, Daisy?"

"I'm fine. Just a small bruise. He didn't even have to mention it. That's completely irrelevant to the break-in."

Small bruise, my ass. The thing encompassed her cheek. Thank fuck I hadn't hit her eye.

I shut mine and let out a long breath. I didn't know when I'd be falling asleep again. Probably not anytime soon. If I had another one of those dreams, there was no telling what I'd do. And after the shit that had gone down with the would-be robber, I wasn't exactly relishing closing my eyes and imagining Daisy on the other end of a knife.

"Have you seen a physician?"

"No, it's not needed," Daisy said before I could answer. "The wound isn't large. It was more of a swipe than a cut. Oz bandaged me up."

"Oh, does he have a medical degree and I missed it?"

"She's as stubborn as a mule, so she won't go. I told her I'd take her, but she refused. She'll be fine, trust me. I'll be watching her, so if she isn't, she'll go to the damn hospital."

"Excuse me? You'll be watching me? What am I, six?"

I could tell Daisy was glowering at me, but I didn't give her the satisfaction of looking her way. On this point, I wasn't backing down. If she thought I wouldn't do everything possible to ensure her safety after what had occurred today, she was sorely mistaken.

"Whatever age you are, Daisy, I'm glad Osmond is there with you, although I don't doubt you are quite capable yourself."

Daisy's lips twitched, no doubt at my full name. Punchline: me. As usual lately. Whatever. I didn't give a shit. Let her get her kicks at my mother's bad taste.

"That said, he won't be the only one watching you. I'm sending up a member of the team. You're returning tomorrow?"

"Sending up who for what reason? My cabin is small. There's no fucking room for a party."

Daisy groaned and buried her face in her hands. I understood the sentiment.

"Don't open the door for anyone but someone from our team. They'll have a badge with a number on it. If anything strikes you as off, call me immediately."

I snorted. "A badge? Like rent-a-cops? Also, what about the actual police? Or are we supposed to duck and run when we see them too?"

"Lila, what's going on?" Daisy frowned. "Don't you think that's a bit much for a little break-in? Even the local police figured it was just someone trying to take advantage of an empty cabin out-of-season. Tourism doesn't really start here for a few weeks yet."

"No offense to the police, but we take our own precautions. We'll have someone out to you by nightfall. Daisy, take care of yourself. If you're hurting, go to the ER. It's not worth putting yourself at risk. And Osmond?"

I braced.

"Thank you for taking care of our Daisy. And yourself. You're both very needed."

It was my turn to frown. "It wasn't a big deal."

"Yes, it was," Daisy murmured. "Lila, since you're sending someone up here anyway—which isn't necessary, but I know you don't believe us —can you have them bring me a couple of outfits and some pajamas and underwear? Oh, and my makeup case. If they can get with my sister, Ever, that would be great. Stupid me left all my stuff at MSG. I meant to call earlier, but I'm assuming now it's probably too late."

While she and Lila discussed essentials, I wandered into the bedroom.

My backpack sat on the chair by the door, and my gaze dropped to the zippered pocket where I'd stashed the bottle of whisky. Finishing off the rest seemed like a great alternative to a late lunch.

But I didn't do it. I sat on the edge of the bed and cracked my knuckles, only now noticing they were bruised too.

It was so easy for me to ignore pain. To pretend it didn't exist and roll it into some other emotion. Except right now I couldn't. I kept seeing Daisy's panicked eyes. Kept picturing her lying dead in my arms like my sister.

No do-overs. No second chances. No opportunity for me to tell her I was a fucking asshole who'd blamed her for too much, but mostly blamed myself.

When she appeared in the doorway, I swallowed hard. She appeared so small and fragile right now with that bruise discoloring her face, but not breakable. Her strength somehow shone through the tiny cracks in her armor, shoring up the spots tested by stress. Daisy wouldn't collapse.

She also wasn't the person I'd accused her of being. It was so much easier to point the finger at her rather than look at myself in the mirror.

If she wasn't to blame, I must be. Someone had to be responsible for me losing my sister.

"All these years, I wanted to blame you for Kerry's death."

She reached up to grip her throat, turning her arm so my gaze zeroed in on the bandage. I wanted to go to her and wrap her up tight. Keep her safe, when I'd never been able to do the same for my sister.

"You think I didn't know that?"

Okay, hadn't expected that one. Leave it to Daisy, man. She wasn't what I'd anticipated on so many levels.

"You both were pushing the boundaries so hard, but you were the level-headed one. I always trusted you to bring her back down to earth."

Daisy tipped back her head. "I nearly jumped out of a moving vehicle last night because you pissed me off, and I'm the level-headed one?"

"Maybe I'm not the best judge of character." Except I was, at least when I was being honest with myself.

Something I hadn't done enough of for a very long time.

"Or maybe you just really fucking piss me off."

"There's that too."

She came to sit beside me on the bed. Close, but not too close, the shoulder strap of my tank top dipping enough for me to see her bra situation. She had on that same strapless one as she'd had on the night before—of course, because she had nothing else with her—and the tops of her full breasts made my throat ache.

As well as other parts of me.

All of a sudden, I didn't care that she was younger than me, or that she'd practically been as much of a sister to me as my own growing up. Nor did I want to picture her clutching Kerry's lifeless body and crying, begging me to help her.

"It was a mistake. An accident. It can't end this way."

Right now, it was the good times I wanted to remember. The way Daisy always laughed with her whole body. How she'd asked me to teach her the bass, and we went out on the roof to practice until Kerry awakened from a nap and found us. The time she'd made me a triple decker sandwich using an entire package of cheese.

Silly, happy things. Back when we'd been too young to realize what lay ahead. Even I had been young then, though I'd felt beyond jaded.

I hadn't had a damn clue.

Now I just wanted to stop looking back, at least as a reason to get lost in a bottle. Besides, Daisy was part of our world now. She worked on the tour, and she was doing a damn good job. She'd probably be around for a while.

Fuck, it scared me how much I hoped she would be.

I didn't want to expend more energy blaming her for stuff that wasn't her load to carry. Even if it was mine.

"I pretty much stopped partying after she died. Drugs, I definitely stopped." She let out a little laugh. "I actually swung the other way. I kind of turned into a germaphobe. So much for passing around cups or joints at parties."

"No way."

"Yeah. I sprayed hand sanitizer on your steering wheel." She smiled sheepishly. "I'm amazed you didn't smell it when you got in."

I frowned and leaned closer to her. She didn't smell like maple any longer. Now she smelled like the outdoors, just like the shampoo and body wash in my bathroom. Her hair was still wet, and the few strands that had escaped from her messy knot were curling at the ends.

Christ, she was a damn picture. All big blue eyes and temptation.

"Is it maple?"

She frowned. "What?"

"Your hand sanitizer."

"No, it's pumpkin pie scented." She blushed. "I stocked up last fall."

Not laughing simply wasn't possible.

Best of all, she joined in. Then she lifted her hand to my cheek, stroking the stubble quickly turning into a beard. I hadn't shaved for a bit, and clearly, I needed to.

"I like it," she said quietly, as if she could hear my thoughts. "Wild man Oz. Goes with the long hair." She reached behind my head to tug on my ponytail, her wince telling me her arm still hurt.

Carefully, I took hold of her arm and lifted it to my mouth so I could press a kiss to her bandage. "I'm sorry. I should have been here, not run off like a coward."

It was a bad habit of mine. One I wasn't sure I would ever be able to break.

"You're not a coward. You fought a guy with a knife without a weapon other than your wit and your fists."

"He hurt you. I wanted to kill him."

She eased her arm away from me. "See, you're a defender. You want to protect. That's who you are."

"No, it's because it was *you*. Just you."

She lowered her head. "You feel responsible."

"You aren't my charge. You're definitely not a child."

Her chin came up. "So, I'm not just your kid sister's friend in your mind?"

"Would I have touched you last night if that was all it was?"

"I don't know. Everything was so chaotic. I nearly killed us. Add in that I was half naked, and I danced in a cage last night onstage, with all that concert energy bouncing between us... Maybe stuff got muddled." Her gaze dropped to her clothes.

My clothes. I liked seeing her in them. Probably too much.

When I didn't speak, she continued. "I'm not much more than naked now."

"Yeah, you're having some trouble keeping my clothes on." Which I couldn't say I minded.

"And you were naked earlier." Her chest rose and fell with her quick breaths. "Impressively so."

"So, you think all it takes is some nudity and sex happens?"

She rubbed the corner of her mouth. "*Is* sex happening?"

Good question. God knows I shouldn't go there. It wasn't smart. Wanting to ease the cold war between us—mostly from my side—was one thing. Throwing aside all caution and sense as if she wasn't someone on the crew and as if we didn't have a fucking complicated past was another.

She was my baby sister's best friend. Off-limits. But Kerry was gone now. I didn't know how she'd feel about *this*.

Daisy had mentioned Kerry not wanting her to hit on me. Was the reverse also true?

I would never know.

However Kerry would feel, we were just burning off steam. We'd had a hell of a weekend so far, and it was only Saturday. Maybe if we got rid of this crazy tension between us, things could go back to normal. Whatever that was.

"I want to protect you, even from me."

"I don't need protection. Especially from you. You're not dangerous. I'm a big girl, Osmond."

Her faintly mocking tone didn't make me back down. "You got hurt because I was all churned up. Like I have been for the past six months since you joined the tour."

Her lower lip trembled once before she controlled it. "Because you hate me. You think it's my fault Kerry is gone."

"No, because I want you so much I can't fucking breathe."

She swallowed so loudly I could hear it and leaned back on the bed, bracing her arms behind her on the mattress. The move made her breasts jut out, and her nipples were rock-hard. Christ, it was a miracle I didn't whimper.

Wetting her lips, she cocked her head. "Then take me."

EIGHT

Daisy

He didn't laugh. Thank God.

Had I really said "take me" like a virginal rom-com heroine?

Oh, yes, I really had.

Well, part of that description was true. Embarrassingly so. I did not relish having *that* conversation.

Then again, if I really acted the part, maybe he'd never guess. Applying makeup could be like putting on a costume, and I was good at stepping into a role when the real unvarnished you wasn't quite enough.

His caramel-brown eyes heated. "If you add 'to McDonalds' or something when I lean in to kiss you, I'm not responsible for my actions."

I giggled. "You already fed me, remember?"

That melting expression in his gaze turned up about a million degrees. "Not done satisfying you by a long shot."

Hmm, yeah, okay, I could work with that.

Before I chickened out, I straightened and pulled off the tank top. His expression bolstered me to continue, so I quickly undid my bra.

"Hair," he gritted out when I would've gone for the shorts. "Take it down."

"Like Rapunzel?"

He didn't smile, so I complied. The still damp strands fell heavy against my bare skin and curled around my breasts like a protective shield. He brushed it back, his knuckles skimming my nipples and making me arch. God, if just his eyes and the lightest of touches could arouse me this much, how would I survive actual sex with him?

Spoiler—I probably wouldn't.

Physically, yes, although his wand of destruction unnerved me more than a little. But emotionally, there was no doubt some part of me would be irrevocably changed after having sex with Oz Taylor.

I still wasn't backing away. I'd been dreaming of this moment since the days when I thought sex meant promises and forever love. Not just a few sweaty minutes with the late afternoon sun pouring in the window, making him look both older and younger at the same time. His eyes were haunted, the grooves around them cut deep. But his mouth was so soft as he gazed at me. Unguarded. Almost as vulnerable as I felt sitting here topless under his perusal.

"You're so beautiful. If I could sketch, I'd want to fucking paint you in watercolor."

Okay, now we were getting into deeper water. "You're mixing mediums. Besides, yours is music."

His jaw worked. "Yeah, it is. Thanks for reminding me."

I wasn't exactly sure if he was being a smart ass, but I wasn't about to engage him when it meant the keeper of my orgasms might just toss away the key.

I reached for the drawstring on the shorts, but his big hand closed over mine. "What's your hurry," he murmured an instant before his mouth met mine.

Whereas last night had been all hunger and need, today was something else. Oh, the desire was still there, but there was more. A gentleness that showed up at the oddest times with him and probably wasn't surprising considering the way his other hand cupped my sore cheek. His thumb feathered across the swelling, and his kiss turned even sweeter somehow. We were both breathing hard, moving against each other in a simulation of what was to come, and all I could do was beg for more.

Over and over, like a mantra.

"You'll get more," he said between kisses, a smile in his voice as he grasped my hip to pull me over his lap. I straddled him as I had the night before, but it was so much different now because I knew we wouldn't be stopping.

God, this was really happening.

I framed his face in my hands and moved back to search his eyes. They were heavy and so, so dark, with flecks of gold in the brown. I smoothed my fingers over his growing-in beard, reveling in the feeling of the burn against my chin and around my mouth.

And against my breasts as he lowered his head to worship them, licking my nipples with a delicacy I'd never have expected from huge, strong Oz. The guy who tossed guitars in hot tubs and broke amps on stage and had earned every bit of his crazy rep. Here and now, he was thorough and tender, his teeth a welcome pressure against the tight tips.

I gasped and he bit down harder, laving his tongue over the sting he'd left behind. His big hands, rough with calluses from playing guitar, slid up my back, adding more sensation. Overloading me while he made love to my breasts. I squirmed against his hard cock, already impatient.

His low chuckle rumbled against my skin. "Slow down, Flannigan. This is gonna take a while."

"It's taken long enough. Let's pick up the pace."

He skimmed his mouth up between my breasts to a particularly sensitive spot at the base of my throat. Sucking softly, he toyed with the drawstring on my shorts, heightening my anticipation until I was ready to shove them down myself.

So much for playing it cool.

"You sure you're ready for that?"

"What?"

"For me to put my mouth on you. Because that's what's going to happen when those shorts come off."

I took a shuddery breath. I should probably tell him I'd never experienced that yet. Some fumbling finger bangs? Yeah, definitely. Once or twice I'd even had an orgasm from them, but they were far rarer than when I touched myself.

But I'd never let anyone go down on me. Not that any of the guys I'd made out with had offered or seemed particularly interested.

Oz was different in every way from those men.

He didn't wait to see what I'd do. He just rolled with me until my back hit the mattress and loomed over me, his hair coming loose from his ponytail, his mouth so close to mine. He kissed me hard and deep, occupying my attention so completely that I almost didn't feel him easing down the shorts. Almost didn't notice when he found me bare beneath them and made that seductive little growl in his throat that signaled my virginity was swiftly coming to an end.

Hallelujah.

Coasting down my body, he made sure to pay attention to my breasts again, taking his time to cup and kiss and lick them. He watched me all the while. I wanted to shy away from his penetrating gaze, but I knew he'd never allow it. Those long-lashed brown eyes held me captive.

I stretched my arms over my head as he peeled the shorts down my legs, following the material with his mouth. He nicely bypassed my slit to roll his tongue high up my inner thigh, making it clear from his hum of approval that he could taste me there.

I was soaked for him. How could I not be? He was the embodiment of sin.

Another stretch of my arms made the cut on my arm throb. But it wasn't the only part of me throbbing now as he pressed his palms to my inner thighs and pried them apart, opening me up for him.

He licked his lips like the dirty rockstar he was before he dove deep.

I arched, coming straight off the bed at the first swipe of his tongue. He didn't ease me in, didn't take his time as he had with my breasts. He devoured me without shame.

After the first couple of licks, he lifted his head to study me as I shifted and squirmed. So intense. Then he added a finger to the mix, and I couldn't keep from crying out.

Instead of slowing down, he redoubled his efforts. One finger became two and he focused on my clit, sealing his lips to suck and tease. Inside me, his fingers didn't stop. Sliding, twisting, filling me in a paltry way that just made me yearn that much more.

"I want your cock," I whispered, my cheeks flaming hot when he turned his head to bite my thigh.

"And you'll get it, but not before you drench my fingers." He narrowed his eyes. "And my tongue."

Oz slipped out his fingers and I squeezed around air, hating that empty feeling. I wanted him inside me with a fierceness that made me tremble. As if he understood, he licked his fingers, sliding his tongue up between them in a pantomime of what he'd done—what he would do again—to my pussy before bending his head to his work.

He pushed inside me again, this time widening me with three instead of two. The quick flash of pain soon turned into a deep, churning ache, way down low. His thumb brushed my clit as he licked me again and again, backing off every time I was on the verge of coming.

I clutched the sheets and swore at him, and he chuckled darkly without giving me a respite. He liked my torment. Loved looking up to pin me with his volcanic eyes while I thrashed and moaned and wished like hell he'd saved his sadistic streak for another day.

Yet I was secretly glad he hadn't.

The sounds my body was making for him would've been embarrassing if I had rational thought left. I didn't. I was just a feeling creature, wild and crazed.

I reared up from the bed, grasping his hair in my hands, finally pulling it all the way free from its tail. Holding him against me as his mouth and fingers drew out my orgasm, and then made it last so long that I slumped on my side and weakly kicked at him after it was over.

He just opened up my legs again and started anew. Growling as he lapped at what I'd given him and demanded more.

My body was his to command. And God, did he.

When I could stand no more, I nudged at his shoulder. He finally gave way, yanking off his T-shirt and then moving up the bed to lay down and pull me on top of him. He hadn't given me time to properly appreciate his chest, but God, there was so much of him to learn.

So many intriguing reactions I wanted to draw from him.

My hair fell down around us, a curtain that seemed to close the waning sun in around our faces. His expression was lighter now, his mouth soft and used and tasting of me as I kissed him. Lightly at first, sliding deeper as I fisted my hands in his long, thick dark hair, spread out on the pillows beneath us. My breasts pressed to his bare chest, and the sensation of skin on skin overwhelmed my senses.

Finally, it was really happening.

He groaned into my mouth, nipping at my tongue. Distracting me again while his calloused hands grasped my ass. His fingers delved between my cheeks and slid downward, proving how ready I was for him.

For us, and what this could be.

I rocked over the steely length in his jeans, and he cupped the base of my head, turning me so he could devour my mouth the same way he'd done with my pussy. I reached between us to fumble with the button and zipper keeping him from me, soon finding that he didn't have on underwear either.

"We don't have to do this."

His breathless statement caused me to lift my head. "We don't?"

He smoothed his ridged fingertips down my arms. "You're shaking."

Was I? How incredibly mortifying. "I'm turned on." And also shaking. Now that he'd mentioned it, I was covered in goosebumps—and the room wasn't cold. "But you're intimidating."

He didn't chuckle or preen. So much for taking his mind off of my spectacular fail. "We're moving kind of fast."

"*Fast?* I've been wanting you to take my virginity since I was seventeen. Maybe sixteen."

Possibly fifteen, but I wasn't admitting it.

When he didn't speak, I looked up at his face and wanted to cry or laugh at the sheer shock that resided there. "There's no way."

I tried to recover. "I spied on you in the shower one time while I was waiting for Kerry. You were my first example that cold water doesn't make *everything* shrink."

He reached up to take my sore cheek in his palm, his eyes searching mine wordlessly. I expected him to say something incredibly humiliating and shut this down, but he just drew my mouth back to his. He shifted us on the bed, changing our positions until I was half underneath him and his long hair fell down around us.

So dense and dark and sexy as fuck. Just like the man himself.

His lips touched mine while he stroked my breasts. His caresses were soft and easy, and my rocketing heartbeat slowed even as the heat between my legs bloomed once more.

His kisses were endless and unhurried. Eventually, he moved them to my shoulders and back to my breasts.

Methodically driving me wild.

He turned me on my side so that my back was to his front and kept right on brushing kisses over whatever spots he could reach. I was getting impatient, but whenever I tried to lift my leg so he'd get the hint, he just kept kissing and touching me as leisurely as if we had all the time in the world.

Maybe we did.

He shifted behind me and then the hot, hard column of him skimmed my ass. Instead of freezing up, I rubbed against it, needing the friction. Wanting to *know*. He still didn't hurry, just lifted my leg over both of his, opening me up so that the ceiling fan paddling overhead streamed cool air over my warm flesh. Then his fingers were there, working their magic. Stretching me open again with seductive purpose.

"I don't have condoms here," he said in a guttural voice I scarcely recognized. "I've never needed them. I should have some in my wallet, but I haven't needed those in a while either."

Inside, I did a mental cheer. Oz—the most gorgeous rockstar in the entire history of them as far as I was concerned—didn't carry condoms in his wallet. Not because he was riding every groupie bareback, but because somehow. He. Did. Not. Need. Them.

Sure, he might've been feeding me a line, but I trusted Oz. If I hadn't, we never would've been in this situation.

Until I realized exactly what his lack of latex meant for the destruction of my virginity. "Are you clean?"

"Yes, but I don't want to risk you like that."

"What's the risk? I mean, I know what they are, but if you're clean and you pull out—"

"As if I'll ever want to leave that sweet pussy."

I swallowed hard. "Consider this the practice round. We'll refine the dance card later."

"More mixed metaphors." His low laughter flowed out with the brush of his lips over my shoulder. "Nothing is practice with you. It's game on."

I shimmied against him and reached back to slide my hand around the back of his neck. This time when our mouths met, the head of his cock slid against my pussy. Just one testing push. I would've tensed if he hadn't made me so goddamn needy. But he knew. His thumb rolled over my clit as he adjusted his placement between my legs and drove forward. One long, slow thrust that left him buried inside me.

I didn't cry out because I bit my lip. Which was now bleeding.

Holy fuck, he was *huge*.

"Sorry. Did I hurt you?" He turned my chin toward his and kissed me, saying nothing about the blood.

Somehow it fit everything about all of our interactions this weekend. Between us lay wreckage and disaster and a tragic, perfect beauty that could only come from the ashes.

He drew out, swearing, before anchoring my leg over both of his and sliding home once again. The sting almost seemed worse the second time, but his long exhale as if he'd found a slice of heaven distracted me from the pain.

"Fuck, Daisy," he said against my ear as we moved together.

He was doing most of the work, but we were finding a rhythm. Ours, meant for just us alone.

"Pretty sure you already are," I whispered back, grasping his hand against my belly when his fingers would've wandered. I wanted them between my thighs again, but more than anything, I needed to hold on to him. He was my anchor in the center of insanity.

God help us both.

He let me have that hand and then slid his other arm beneath my body, sliding up so he could stroke my clit. I was half on top of his body now, lying down draped over him, and I couldn't reach the parts of him I wanted to. I felt filled and surrounded and so fucking hot, as if I was burning up from the inside out. His teeth grasped my earlobe as he lifted me with his strong thighs, powering in and out of me like we'd been made for this.

Even if I knew I'd be walking funny tomorrow. Hell, tonight.

He brought our joined hands to my breast. "Touch your nipples. Let me watch."

While I did what he asked, I looked down at us, me sprawled over him so languidly in the last of the sun's rays. So much of what had happened the last couple of minutes seemed beyond my comprehension. His hands were everywhere, and he fucked me so masterfully I wasn't even sure if I was helping. I wished there was a mirror overhead so I could see every detail, but what I *could* see was beyond erotic.

His cock, slick with me, sliding in and out of my pussy would live in my memory forever. Along with our restless fingers plucking at my nipples together, knowing he was studying every movement over my shoulder, his darker fingers tangling with my lighter ones.

"That's it," he breathed as I squeezed him. "More."

I did it again and he groaned, twisting my nipples so hard that the ache inside me turned into desperation. He pulled his hand away and found my clit, rubbing it in frantic circles that matched the drumbeat rising to a fever pitch inside my head. Between my legs.

Everywhere.

"I can't."

"You can." He drew his fingers away for a moment before bringing them back, moving them that much faster. I gasped, but he didn't stop. He braced his feet on the edge of the bed and drove into me so deeply that I knew I screamed. Not from pain, but sheer, mindless pleasure. I'd never imagined being taken over this ruthlessly could feel so powerful.

"Come on me."

As if I had any choice.

The orgasm ripped through me, shocking in its force. His hand came up to cover my mouth as he rolled us one more time, pinning me beneath him so he could surge into me, driving me into the mattress. I was completely enveloped by him, my cells screaming from lack of oxygen and the massive heat of him holding me in place.

And I liked it. I loved it. The pressure of his body and his hand and his cock kept me coming and coming, my cries trapped behind his palm.

He was so thick inside me, I didn't think he could pull out. I didn't want him to. I knew what it meant, and I didn't care. It was my first time. What were the chances?

All of a sudden, he yanked free of my body. His shout came an instant before the warm wetness that streamed over my back and my ass.

Another form of deliciously dirty possession.

I couldn't lift my head. Could barely move. But before he did, I reached back to touch what he'd left on me, bringing my fingers to my lips for one forbidden taste.

Salty sweet, just like Oz.

"Dirty girl," he murmured, sounding proud as he brushed my hair aside to kiss my neck.

Warmth suffused my cheeks. Only for him. He was the one who'd brought this side out of me. With every other man I'd been with—or tried to be with—I'd almost always stiffened up and gone cold. I'd always suspected I hadn't met the right man yet.

Except I already had, and deep down, I'd always known it.

He slid out of bed, the frame creaking at his heft moving across it. I shifted to press my legs together, wanting to keep his heat inside me a little longer. Along with heat, pain flashed through my pleasurably used muscles, but even that felt like a badge of pride.

I'd done it.

Well, he'd done it, but I'd helped. In time, I'd help more. Assuming he didn't kick me out of his bed after this.

Maybe once was all I'd ever get out of him. If that was the case, I wouldn't be sorry. This moment had been meant. Even after all the heartache and the years and the bullshit between us, we'd found our way back to each other.

"Don't move," he said an instant later, placing his knee behind me on the bed. Before I could even look, a warm, damp washcloth moved over my back, and I moaned, more than a little disappointed.

"Did I hurt you?"

"No, I wasn't ready to lose that part of you yet."

"Jesus, you're criminal."

"I don't actually have a record. Just so you know." I managed not to moan again as the washcloth slipped between my legs. He didn't miss a spot. I couldn't help flexing against his hand, and he bit my shoulder.

"Good goddamn, you could go again, couldn't you?"

"I have a lot of time to make up for."

"Me too." Proving it, he tossed the washcloth aside and eased down my body to open up my legs. His teeth raked gently over my still oversensitive clit, making me jump—and turn my head just enough to see the faint pink tinge on the washcloth.

It wasn't much. Hardly anything. And he'd kissed my sore lip, but that was different.

My arm shot out to grab the washcloth, and the cut on my arm throbbed its way into my consciousness. A couple of times, pain had tried to interrupt, but Oz had been my world.

That's an ongoing issue of yours, isn't it?

"What's wrong?"

I didn't have time to answer before he turned me to check me over from head to toe. His worrying would have been cute if he hadn't taken one look at my arm and cursed a blue streak even Ever would've appreciated. She had a fouler vocabulary than anyone I'd ever known —until now.

"Fuck, you're bleeding. I'll change the bandage. God, I'm sorry, baby. I wasn't paying attention."

"We were a little busy." My voice sounded distant. Dizziness rolled over me, and I dipped back my head, breathing in and out through my nose as I knew to do when I panicked.

"You good?" He framed my face in his hands, his gaze far too probing. "If I hurt you—"

"No. I'm just a little woozy. You know, like I was last night. I've never heard of orgasm-induced fainting spells or panic attacks, but it might be a thing."

Then again, I'd also nearly caused an insanely stupid car crash last night, gotten smacked in the face today, and had my shower ended by an intruder who'd tried to slice and dice me, so I supposed I could grant myself a little grace.

And that wasn't even mentioning losing my virginity to my best friend in the world's older brother.

He glanced down at my arm, and evidently, he decided I wouldn't bleed out for another minute or two. He shifted behind me in bed, pulling me against his chest so I could catch my breath. His lips brushed my hair, as softly as a wish I'd never known to make.

"Next time you want to follow me someplace, think twice, huh?" His voice was thick with amusement.

"I'd do it all over again."

"Got a death wish, Flannigan?"

"Call it a life one. I'm tired of living in the past. I've been stuck for

so long. It was as if I stopped growing when Kerry passed. I didn't think
it was fair if I had fun when she couldn't." I glanced over my shoulder
and wanted to carve out my tongue at the deep creases beside his eyes
and mouth.

Good job. You are the worst ever at pillow talk.

"What do you think she'd think of...this?" He gestured at us. Legs
tangled. Bodies so close. Sweat cooling between us.

I squeezed the damp washcloth in my fist. I wanted to tell him what
Kerry had said the day before she died, but I didn't want him to think I
was making shit up considering what had just occurred.

And I hated myself for thinking it, even for a second, but I wanted
this moment to be only ours. We'd had so few of them, and I was
greedy.

A knock sounded on the front door, staccato and sharp.

We exchanged a look before Oz stood to drag on his jeans and shirt.
He took the washcloth from me, and I crawled to the end of the bed,
grimacing at the soreness between my legs. I'd expected to ache a little
at being plowed by the equivalent of a dick dump truck, but this was
excessive.

"You okay?"

I gave him a grim smile. "I'll just limit walking for a bit."

He stepped closer and brushed his hand down my face, a slow
caress that made my heart turn over. "Let me see who this is and then
we'll take a shower and get you bandaged up."

We. Was there any better word in the English language? I didn't
think so. The whole taking a shower together thing had possibilities
too.

I glanced down at my arm. The splotch beneath the bandage was
no longer growing, so I'd probably live. I wouldn't mention that it
currently hurt like a bitch. My fault for stretching it so much in bed.
Then again, would I ever regret that?

Not likely.

Oz moved away, his steps quick and clipped as another knock
rattled the front door. Hopefully, he didn't think I'd avoided answering

him on purpose. I was still kind of in shock about this weekend's events. Every one of them had been crazier than the last.

I sincerely hoped that trend would not continue.

All I wanted was to bask in what had just happened—and cross my fingers it would happen again very soon. And this time, I would be a much more active participant. Oz had barely even let me touch him. He hadn't expressly told me not to, but he'd so fully taken my attention with what he was doing to me, I hadn't even realized how one-sided it had been until now.

I mean, yay me. For a first time full sexual experience, I had no complaints. Just next time, I wanted to get some of my own back.

He had such a sexy body. All those miles of muscles I craved to explore with my hands...and my mouth. He'd surprised me by having just one shadowy dark tattoo on his left pec, tucked near his arm so it was easily covered by the leather vests he liked to wear onstage. I'd had a glimpse of a rounded shape within a frame and some roman numerals, but it was as hazy as a lot of the last hour. I intended to learn every detail about it next time.

Such potent words. The future was so scary—and filled with so much promise. Especially now.

Oz's voice rang out, louder than usual. I frowned and bent to grab my clothes—*his* clothes, which was even hotter now that he'd been inside me—and hurriedly tugged them on. I'd just shoved my head through the tank top when the lower, more controlled male voice finally registered in my head.

Good God, was that Noah Jordan? Aka my cousin?

Dear Lord, why?

Okay, so he wasn't exactly my cousin. His family had married into mine somehow about a decade ago, and he and his brother, Hunter, had just started showing up at the occasional family gathering. Not that we attended many of those anymore since my mother had started using her passport like a bingo card, but back in the day, we'd spent time with extended family more than at holidays and funerals and weddings.

Hunter had never paid me much mind. Probably because he was

mister big rockstar now, and in the early days of our acquaintance, he'd been on his way up. He had larger concerns than negligibly related family. As did Noah, who had been an Army Ranger and now was part of some super secret security operation run by the Roth brothers. I only knew that because they'd vetted me before I was hired by Ripper Records.

My nefarious past as a teenage shoplifter of gummy bears from the local Shop Mart had nearly sunk my battleship.

I pushed my hands through my wild hair and tried to tie it up into a respectable bun. Gee, too bad we couldn't have my mom parading through while I was still flushed after being thoroughly rammed.

I should probably quit with the descriptive adjectives in my head before one slipped out and gave Oz enough fodder for his ego for a lifetime.

"Daisy?" Oz called, his voice clearly strained. "Can you come out here for a moment, please?"

If Oz was saying *please,* things were serious. He wasn't one for pleasantries.

I glanced at the disordered bed, figuring I should yank the sheets into place in case "Leave No Bedsheet Unturned" Noah came in here to look for boogeymen under the bed. Then I noticed the tiny, almost invisible spot of blood on the white sheets. Of course he'd had to go plain and traditional with them.

God.

"Just a second," I called back, rushing around the bed to gather up the sheets. I'd just added the pillowcases to the pile in my arms and made it to the doorway when Noah came clomping down the hall in his heavy military-style boots—and halted at the sight of me clutching bedsheets with a probably guilty look on my face.

"Noah, what a surprise." I cleared my throat. "What's new?"

NINE

Daisy looked thoroughly fucked.

She'd clearly tried to do something with her hair, but it stuck up in odd tufts. Running out of the bedroom with her arms full of sheets didn't exactly diminish the look. Then she lowered her arms and it was even worse—at least for Noah.

Her neck and the skin above her cleavage was reddened with scruff burn and a hickey or two. Or three.

So much for being circumspect.

My chest swelled with pride and possession as if I'd just planted a flag on the astroturf. "He insisted," I said when no one spoke.

"I was told you were injured." Noah's voice snapped out without inflection. "That you might need medical assistance."

"I gave her all the assistance she needed."

Yeah, that was bad even for me.

When Noah shot me a baleful glance, I cleared my throat. "I mean, I bandaged her wound."

"Hmm."

I stared hard at the back of Noah's head and his close-cropped cut. His hair was as curly as mine was straight, which I bet pissed him the fuck off. He didn't seem like a guy who tolerated errant hair behavior. Never mind such base activities as late afternoon fucking.

There was a reason I'd never enlisted. I was far too self-indulgent.

"He did a really good job," Daisy offered.

"I just bet."

Behind Noah, I smirked. Which good job she was referring to, I wasn't sure. I was a multi-talented sort.

Also, I wouldn't be crowing about this particular victory for long. I knew myself well enough that when the last of the endorphins faded and I was alone with my thoughts, I would kick my own ass. My eyes would close and my baby sister would be there, and then I'd see Daisy with denim cutoffs and her unlined face and entirely too sweet long blond ponytails.

I'd stripped away the last part of her innocence. Bully for me. But some part of me would grieve for what she'd lost—what we both had.

Neither of us had been truly innocent for a damn long time.

"And that bruise?" Noah crossed his arms. "Looks like he did a really good job with that too."

I raked my fingers through my hair and turned. Looked like my self-inflicted ass-kicking would be starting earlier than I thought. *Thanks, Noah.* "I'll leave you two alone. I'll be out back."

"I need you too, Osmond. I need the most complete account possible of what occurred."

More Osmond. Who had I pissed off lately? I'd heard that name more often this weekend than in the last decade.

With a short nod, I led the way into the living room. "I'll make coffee." Which I would liberally lace with whisky in my case.

So different from your sister, huh?

"Black," Mr. Chuckles commanded.

"Of course. I live to be of service."

I thought I heard Daisy snort behind me, but I wasn't sure.

I aimed for the kitchen and grabbed the box of sugar packets and fresh bottle of creamer I'd picked up at the store, then set the coffee to brew.

Damn, how long had Daisy and I been in bed? Obviously, a lot longer than I'd realized or else Chucklefest had broken some land speed records to get up here. Which seemed unlikely. He'd probably lock himself away for a lifetime of eternal solitude in penance for going one mile over the posted limit.

While the coffeemaker hummed, I moved to the laundry alcove to dig through the dryer to see if I had another set of sheets in there. Same place I'd found the jeans and shirt I was currently wearing. Earlier, I'd stomped out of the bedroom naked, and the dryer was the only source of clothes in this place outside of the trunk at the foot of the bed.

Yeah, I wasn't exactly a stellar housekeeper. So sue me.

And I didn't have any other sheets. Fabulous.

I stepped outside the kitchen and grabbed the pile of sheets Daisy had dumped beside the doorway. She probably suspected my washer was full. It wasn't, but the dryer surely was. I grabbed them and set the washer going.

The low buzz of voices in the living room made me itchy between the shoulder blades, so I was happy when the washer drowned them out.

I wasn't used to having people here. Ever.

Daisy was one thing. But Noah and his judgmental expressions were not welcome. Especially since I didn't have a fucking clue what was going on back home that required this level of intensity.

Lila was going to have to show some of her damn cards soon. I was not going to keep dancing to her tune without some idea of what the band was facing. And clearly, not *only* the band. Daisy too. I might tolerate some level of cloak and dagger when my bandmates and I were on the hot seat, but not for her.

And that bore more examination than I had any intention of doing.

I dumped the coffee into three mugs and added creamer and a couple packets to Daisy's cup. Because I didn't want to be anything like Chuckles, I added more creamer than usual and winced as I took the first swallow.

Yeah, I should've gone with whisky instead.

I brought in the mugs and sat them down on the side table.

"I'm not going to the hospital."

I passed Daisy her cup and she murmured her thanks.

Chucklefest didn't even glance my way as I handed him his cup.

"Are you up to date on your shots?" he demanded.

He was asking Daisy, I assumed. Or did he think I was handing out STDs like party favors? I could only imagine his view of most rockstars. Daisy claimed to be the germaphobe, but it wouldn't have surprised me if Noah used Lysol on the places any of us contaminated sorts had been recently.

"Noah, I'm fine. It was a shallow slice."

"Does your mother know about this?"

She pinched the bridge of her nose. "You do realize you aren't actually related to any of us, right?"

"I'm here in an official capacity, Daisy. But that doesn't mean I can't be concerned about your welfare."

Heavily, I sat beside her on the couch. Chuckles was seated in the chair off to the side. "I already tried it, she's not going, can we just move on?"

Preferably to this official capacity business.

No one answered me. I wasn't surprised.

"This happens every year," I said tiredly, deliberately burning my mouth on the coffee so I didn't follow the urge to kick something.

Daisy had just lost her freaking virginity—plot twist of the century. But this was not the afterglow period that anyone had ever ordered. Not me either.

"You engage in hand to hand combat out here every year? Consider selling."

Daisy gestured around us. "Hello, it's a freaking palace."

I poked her in the side. "You know it's charming in its own way."

She leaned her head on my shoulder. "Is that how you refer to yourself too?"

"I'm an acquired taste." It took everything in me not to sling my arm around her shoulders. What the hell was my problem?

I wasn't the virgin here. So, why was I so hellbent on showing my possession of her? As if anyone could. She was like a hurricane. No one could tame her. Exactly why she'd always drawn me.

Among other reasons.

She smiled up at me, her blue eyes still so soft and sleepy. That the look I'd put on her face could still be there in the middle of all this crap was amazing. Especially considering the purple edging across her cheek. "Yeah, so's this place."

"Lila neglected to inform me that you two are involved."

"Who says we are?" Daisy asked.

My fingers tensed on the mug handle. Right. That was the answer when she still couldn't walk straight. "Is it any of your business?"

"Everything is my business right now if it affects Ripper Records." Chucklefest set aside his mug without touching it. "Explain what you meant when you said this happens every year."

Still smarting from Daisy's comment—even if it was logical—I gave him a short, terse answer.

Cabins were broken into out of season every year. It hadn't happened to me before, but so what? We'd told the police and detailed the situation to them.

Apparently, that was not enough, because we had to run through everything again, including why Daisy had a purple cheek.

When we were finished, Noah went to get some stuff from his vehicle, and I dumped out the coffee he and I hadn't drank. Daisy had finished hers and gone back for more.

While she was in the kitchen, I paced around the coffee table, stabbing my fingers through my hair to try to quiet the riot inside me.

"Oz?" Her soft tentative question had my back going straight. "Are you okay?"

"What the fuck is going on?" The question exploded out of me, but her stricken expression made me want to haul the words back.

"What do you mean?"

"With all this Ripper shit. Something is up. You weren't part of the security meeting we had after the show, but—"

She re-anchored the knot in my tank top at her hip. "Um, I kind of heard. I needed a minute alone, so I ended up in the room next to yours. I overheard most of the meeting. Not on purpose."

"Uh huh." I shook my head. "You're a little spy *and* a thief. I had no idea of all your talents."

"It started with the gummy bears," she said soberly as Noah marched inside, letting the screen door slap shut behind him.

"You requested clothes." He passed Daisy a purple sack emblazoned with the Powder Puff girls on the side. At least that was what I think it said.

"Oh, thank fuck. I need some of my own. Did you find—" She set the bag on the sofa and frowned as she yanked out a woolly-looking turtleneck. "I didn't even know I still owned this. What the heck?" She started digging through the bag, tossing things to and fro. I was pretty sure I saw thermal pajamas and underwear twice as big as Daisy's ass.

"My sister did this," she announced before Noah could speak. "Why would you have Ever pack my clothes?"

Noah propped his hands on his waist. "Who would you have suggested pack them? Me?"

"She's trying to wrap me in eighteen feet of material." Demonstrating her point, she held up a dress with a high, frilly collar. The thing seemed to go to Daisy's ankles.

"Why would you even own that?"

"I used to go thrifting and snag stuff that I could make into different stuff later. You know, like *Pretty in Pink?*"

"Sorry, that's still on my watchlist."

She flipped me the middle finger.

"Well, at least she wants you to be warm. Although it's spring. Soon to be summer."

"What she wants is for me to never get any."

I slid a look to Noah, whose expression revealed nothing.

"Too late," I said cheerfully before I left the room. And the entire cabin. I'd had enough of family time.

Although they weren't actually related. Whatever. I needed space.

If I was a better man, I would've stayed and made nicey-nice. But I wasn't one. I was the guy who'd ignored Daisy for half a year and then taken her virginity within a day of spending time with her.

Oh, look, self-recrimination right on cue.

I picked my way over the rocky ground out back that led down to the lake, the biggest selling feature of this place—if it had any. My paddle boat was tied up at the dock, rocking gently in the fading light of dusk. This whole day had alternatively dragged and sped by. Now it was nighttime and my already small cabin would contain not only Daisy, but a humorless man standing guard.

For what, was my question.

Seemed a tad excessive for a minor league hold-up. Not that it was minor league in my head. The intruder hurting Daisy was a great addition to the range of nightmare images I'd already collected. But it wasn't the level of thing that should require an armed guard.

I wasn't exactly a lightweight when it came to kicking ass. I could protect Daisy. I would with my fucking life if I had to.

Besides, this was just a random event. What else could it be? The police would find him and that would be that.

Instead of dragging out a chair from the storage shed, I went to sit in my boat. On the side, it had a shamrock for my sister and was about as rundown as the cabin itself. I didn't take it out on the water, although I'd gone on many solo night trips—probably far more than wise, despite this water being not all that deep. Still, shit could happen, especially when you were alone.

Except I wasn't alone right now.

I still didn't go out. I didn't want Daisy to think I was sailing away from her, as dumb as that sounded. My phone was still inside so I couldn't write anything, even if the murky sky going dark at the edges with twilight, stars just starting to twinkle, and gentle lap of the water against the boat was making my fingers twitchy to tap out some lyrics. I didn't write all the time, but when I got the urge, I usually went on a spree until the need to expel whatever was in my head passed.

Right now? The need was huge.

I didn't know how long I sat there, staring up at the sky, my fingers linked over my belly. There wasn't much room to spread out, and I was a big guy, so no matter how much I shifted, I was always fighting off leg cramps. Maybe it was time to upgrade the boat. Maybe even go for a two-seater.

There was a road to perdition.

Loneliness fucked with your head. I knew that all too well. Despite my life with the band, I spent many hours alone, usually by choice. It had taken some years for me to get that having the wrong person in your bed was just as lonely as being by yourself.

Sometimes even worse.

Hours passed, perhaps even lifetimes while I sat in that boat. The sky changed, deepening, darkening, the colors changing with the onslaught of night. I trailed my fingers through the water and cursed. Fucking cold. So much for my fleeting idea of going skinny dipping.

Not if I wanted a working unit afterward.

I frowned, remembering something Daisy had said. She'd spied on me in the shower years ago? When? Why?

Well, I could probably fill in the why. Curiosity maybe. She must've had a lot if she'd held on to her virginity this long.

I still couldn't wrap my head around that one. She was gorgeous and funny and smart and sweet. What asshole men hadn't been good enough for her to get the job done?

But I was glad it was me. Even if it shouldn't have been for half a dozen reasons.

"You know, you'll get farther if you use oars instead of your fingers."

Her voice shot through me like The Glenlivet had, streaking warmth in its wake. "Would get farther if the boat wasn't tethered too."

"Oh. Missed that." She stepped closer and I took her in, wrapped in the giant comforter from my bed. Beneath, she wore thick socks that climbed up her calves and sandals. "Yes, I'm a fashion victim. Doing the best I can with what my sister provided."

"She shouldn't have bothered. I'm ridiculously turned on by you in wool, cotton, and Birkenstocks."

Even in the darkness, I saw the quick gleam of her teeth as she smiled. Then she produced my phone from inside the folds of the comforter. "Lila called. She talked to Noah and wanted to speak to you too. I told her you'd call her back."

I sat up straighter. "What now?"

"Something happened at the venue. Minor vandalism. She said to come back Tuesday morning instead, since clean-up will be happening tomorrow night and no one can rehearse there."

When I didn't speak, she cleared her throat. "I can call an Uber and go back on my own tomorrow. Or maybe Noah can drive me. You can salvage some of your weekend—"

I shot out my hand and snagged the edge of the comforter, dragging her closer. She squealed as she nearly tripped on the uneven ground, and then I made sure she tripped—right into my arms, nearly capsizing the boat. My sudden move would've dumped us into the water if it hadn't been properly secured.

Daisy was not amused, but I was. At least until she winced and grabbed her arm.

"Shit, did I hurt you?" When would I stop doing stuff like that?

"I'm fine." She gave me a quick smile. "It's just a flesh wound, baby."

I wanted to believe her, so I let it go.

"What do you have under here?" I tugged up her comforter and she batted halfheartedly at my hands while still maintaining her grip on my phone. I plucked it out of her hand and stuffed it in my pocket. "There, now you can fight me more effectively."

"You really think I'm parading around naked with cousin Noah there?"

"Cousin Noah sounds like the kind of show I wouldn't watch on TV."

She sighed. "He's a good guy. Too good most of the time. He has no idea how to have fun. He asked if you had a deck of cards. I told him I had a mini deck of oracle cards in my purse, but not exactly what he meant."

I had to laugh. "Cards? What am I, a ninety-year-old man?"

"He's not ninety either."

"Yeah, but he does a good imitation. What are oracle cards? Woo-woo shit?"

She jabbed her finger into my chest. "Harnessing your intuition is not woo-woo, Osmond."

"Oh, Christ on a cracker." I dipped my head back far enough that the ends of my hair trailed in the water. "Can we outlaw that name?"

"Sure, if you'll let me see your tattoo."

I lifted my head. "There's an unusual bargain. Besides, we were very naked. You got to see all of me already, so that isn't much of a deal for you."

"You barely let me look. I definitely didn't touch." She shifted on my lap and my cock roused. She didn't act as if she noticed while she felt around under the comforter.

"If you wanted to grope me, sprite, you could've just asked."

Although I seriously doubted I would've given her free rein over me. That was something I rarely gave anyone.

"Give me your phone."

I handed it over and she turned on the torch, nearly blinding me. She giggled and redirected the light while spots danced in front of my eyes, then yanked down the collar of my shirt to get at my tattoo.

"Don't wreck the neckline. Jesus, woman, don't you know anything?" I eased back enough that I could haul the shirt off from behind my head. It wasn't easy with the lack of space in the boat and the avaricious expression she wore, visible now that my vision had mostly returned. I tossed the shirt beside me in the boat and resettled her on my lap so she was straddling me.

Our favorite position these days.

The boat rocked precipitously, but she balanced herself with one hand on my shoulder as she trained the torch from the phone on my tattoo. "An hourglass," she whispered. "Sand's running out. I thought I saw Roman numerals."

Wordlessly, I nodded. While she was studying me, I studied her right back.

The comforter shrouded her shoulders, but her sunny hair spilled out and framed her face. She wore no makeup, no artifice whatsoever—not even jewelry. Yet she was the prettiest woman I'd ever seen.

"When did you get this?"

"Before." I knew what she was getting at.

"Before your mom too?"

"When she was sick."

She combed her fingers through my hair, pushing it away from my face. The wind kicked it right back, so she did it again.

I grabbed her wrist and kissed it. "Do you have any tattoos?"

"No. There was nothing I ever loved enough to put it permanently on my body. Except maybe something for Ker, but I don't know what would be right."

"When it is, you'll know."

"Is that right?"

"Yes. Your gut is never wrong. It's just a matter of choosing whether or not to listen."

Exactly why I'd been avoiding this woman for months. And for years before that, though I would've sworn I hadn't thought of her in forever before she showed up in that conference room last fall.

Lies.

I was the king of them.

"My gut always chose you," she said, her voice barely audible over the breeze, the rocking water, and the thunk of the ropes against the side of the boat. "Why I followed you even knowing you might hate me for it."

I slid my arms around her waist, bringing her flush against my chest. My teeth caught her lower lip. "See this? This is me hating you."

The phone buzzed in her hand and she sighed. Heavily. She flicked off the torch and turned the cell screen toward me.

Lila. Guess she wasn't waiting for me to call her back.

"Yeah?"

"Sorry to interrupt your evening. I'll be brief. I trust Noah or Daisy conveyed the message about the venue."

"Yeah. What's going on?"

"Just some minor destruction, graffiti and the like. Some of the equipment was tampered with. I let the others know, but you were the only one left."

"Tampered with?" I repeated, my gaze connecting with Daisy's in the moonlit dark.

Out here, we were in the center of tranquility. But back in the city, shit was going crazy.

Or was it? Maybe Lila and Noah were just being overly paranoid. People had died before at a Ripper show. I supposed that would make anyone overly wary.

Yet that whole gut thing I'd just mentioned to Daisy was working overtime.

"Minor tampering." Lila's voice never so much as rippled. She could've been discussing a summer day. "I know you all wanted to rehearse at the venue the night before rather than simply doing soundcheck, and sadly, that won't be possible."

"Which Daisy told me. Did you not trust her or Chuckles to relay the message?"

Daisy stiffened in my arms.

"I trust them both implicitly, or they wouldn't be in our employ."

I knew Daisy heard her because she bit her lip and turned her face away.

More than anything, I wanted to ask Lila if she believed there was a connection between the situation at the venue and what had happened at my cabin. As much as I had believed the dude with the knife was just a random guy who figured the place was deserted—or had even seen me drive away—maybe Lila knew more than she was saying. Perhaps she wasn't just being paranoid because of previous events.

From all I knew of her, she normally wasn't someone who overreacted. So, what exactly did she know? And what did Chuckles know that was making him keep watch at my place when he doubtlessly had tons of other stuff on his plate? I wanted to demand answers.

Then I glanced at Daisy. A ton of shit had gone down this weekend already. She needed a break. *I* needed a break.

We were going to take one. Together.

"We'll see you Tuesday," I said rather than what I wanted to most.

Daisy's shoulders immediately softened. She'd been prepared for me to rail at Lila too. Nice to know I had a MO.

Well, maybe not always.

"You'll watch over Daisy too?" Lila asked, and that question more than any other made my fingers clench around my phone. She'd said something to that effect earlier, but it seemed even more poignant now. "You'll watch over each other."

I swallowed hard. "We will."

TEN

Daisy

We didn't have sex in the boat.

I was not happy about that fact, but after Oz's call with Lila, I couldn't really press the issue. The timing wasn't really on our side, since Noah came out looking for me shortly thereafter, claiming he found some cards and he needed someone to play with.

That was how the three of us ended up playing gin rummy until late, though Oz repeatedly denied the cards were his. Oz even chilled out a little in Noah's direction, and Noah almost smiled a time or two.

When he finally went off to sleep, I was sure the sexy times bell was about to ring again, but then I fell asleep the minute we hit the now freshly made bed.

Sex, strike two. But I couldn't say I minded falling asleep in Oz's arms.

Another first. I'd never slept with a man before for an entire night. Well, mostly entire. He crept off before dawn to do who knows what, and I fell asleep again. I was exhausted. It was as if I'd been running on a deficit for so long, and being with Oz had demanded repayment on the sleep debt right now, no ifs, ands, or buts.

I dragged myself into the shower near lunchtime and got out to gasp at the sight of my naked body in the mirror.

Irritated pink marks striped over my flesh, some areas more than others. Like my breasts and my neck. And my thighs. His stubble had done a number on my fair skin.

Then there were the hickeys. I had one right above my left nipple, for heaven's sake.

I searched through my purse for the travel-sized bottle of lotion I carried with me and slathered every spot I could reach before pulling on some yoga pants and a shapeless sweater courtesy of my sister. Quickly, I tried to scrunch some life into my hair before declaring it hopeless and tying it back in a thick braid.

I stepped into the living room to see if Noah wanted something to eat, only to find him doing pull-ups using the ceiling's crisscrossing beams. And he wasn't alone.

It wasn't an exaggeration to say my breath stopped at the sight of Oz's toned back muscles bunching and rippling every time he pulled himself up and down.

Lordy.

I sat cross-legged on the floor and tugged my phone out of my purse. It was quite handy I'd carried it into the living room, because I wouldn't have wanted to miss proof of this very important moment.

I'd snapped half a dozen pictures of Oz's very fine ass in navy sweat shorts, squeezing and releasing, squeezing and releasing, along with that buffet of long, lean back muscles, when he dropped down to mop at the sweat dripping off his face with his arm. I was a little slow with lowering my camera, so I accidentally caught a shot of Noah mid pull-up, his own banquet of muscles on full display. Then I clicked again and caught Oz's photo-worthy scowl in the frame.

"Seriously, sprite? How would you feel if we took photos of you working out?"

"If I looked like you two, I'd figure it was my due. But you're welcome to take pictures of me doing my Kegels if you want." I snorted as the two men exchanged puzzled looks.

Yeah, I wouldn't bother explaining that one.

I flipped through my photos while Oz wiped off his chest with a towel, then refastened his hair into a tail. Noah was still methodically doing his pull-ups, and I couldn't imagine what number he was on now. But mercy, he had the body to show for it.

Oz growled and stepped directly in front of me. I lifted the phone and aimed—until he snatched it and turned the camera around to face me. Rather than freak out, I leaned back on my hands and grinned.

He grinned back and took picture after picture.

Noah jumped down from his last pull-up. He wasn't even winded. "If you two are done playing, let's go get some lunch."

"Go?" I echoed, snatching back my phone when Oz glanced over his shoulder.

"Yes. We can't stay locked up in here forever."

"You haven't even been here a day," Oz muttered before snagging my hand and dragging me down the hall. "Time for that shower."

"I'm already clean," I protested.

The bathroom door shut behind us, and I realized Oz's idea of cleansing involved a whole lot of getting dirty.

Which I would've been wholeheartedly onboard with, if not for the buzz of his even thicker scruff along my already sensitive neckline.

"Hang on, Osmond." I used his full name deliberately, just for the joy of seeing him move back to scowl down at me.

"You promised." He pointed at me. "Now you must die."

I let out a squeal as he tossed me over his shoulder in a fireman's carry.

Instantly, a knock sounded at the door. "Everything okay in there?"

My skin flushed scarlet. I didn't have to see myself to know it, because my cheeks were literally on fire. "We're fine. Sorry, I'm ticklish."

"She's fine, Dad," Oz yelled.

Noah's footsteps beat a hasty retreat as I slid down Oz's large, deliciously sweaty body and buried my face in his chest. "Oh, God, I can't have sex with him here. I can't have sex with you again anyway, not like this."

He grabbed a fistful of my topknot and gently lifted my head. "Virgin's remorse?"

"No. Sensitive skin." I pulled down the collar of my top and he lifted his brows at my reddened flesh. "So, either we give it a rest or you have to shave." My eyes widened. "Oh, yes, let me shave you."

He backed into the door so fast he almost stumbled. "Nuh uh."

I advanced on him. "C'mon. I'm good at it. Do you know how many shaves I've given?"

He narrowed his eyes. "You get paid to shave men? I want names and numbers so I can kick all of their asses."

His teasing tone made me wiggle my fingers. "I'll give you a freebie."

"I'm quite capable of shaving myself, you know."

"So, do it." I tilted my head. "I was going to give you a topless shave, but if you'd rather do it yourself, be my guest."

He tugged me closer, but he didn't kiss me. He wasn't nearly as gruff and inconsiderate as he seemed at first glance. "How much for bottomless too?"

"Better idea. I want to taste you."

He rubbed his thumb over my lower lip. "Your deals never quite benefit you."

"Says who?" I licked my lips, deliberately running my tongue over his fingertip. His low groan made my nipples tighten. "I've imagined peeling off your pants ever since—"

"Since you spied on my manhood in the shower, you little pervert?" He filled his hands with my ass and tugged me up against him, demonstrating he was also a pervert who'd gotten hard at the mention of me creeping on him.

"I'd never seen one before, and I was curious. Can you blame me for wanting to start at the top?"

Something dangerously soft crossed his face, followed by a look of possession I'd never seen directed at me by a man before. "First dick you saw. First dick inside you. I want all your firsts." His thumbs met over the crack of my ass through my yoga pants, and I swallowed deeply.

"Um, let's not shoot for the sexual Olympics when I'm still riding around with training wheels, okay?"

"Give me time," he said against my temple.

I didn't know whether to slug him or shiver at his presumptuousness. So, I did both.

He held my fist against his hard abs and cocked a brow. "You've given me some firsts too."

"Oh, really."

"Yes. First woman I've ever had here."

"Clarify had."

He didn't smile. "First woman who has ever even been inside these four walls."

I swallowed hard again for a whole new reason. "Why?"

"Because this place is just for me. There was no one I ever wanted to share it with." He brushed a loose strand of hair away from my cheek. "Until now."

My heart kicked hard behind my breast, and I whirled away to fumble blindly across his small, sparse counter. "So, I'm pretty sure I saw shaving cream here."

"Daisy." He cupped my shoulders. "We're cool, right?"

"Sure. Uh huh. So, do you have a straight razor, or do you have one of those electric deals? Knowing you, I'd imagine a razor. Low-tech to match your vintage-y man cave. Does it count as a man cave if you don't even have a big TV? Which boggles my mind, I'm sorry. Poor Noah was bored senseless. And no Wi-Fi is just crazy."

"'Poor Noah' was not invited here, in case you've forgotten. And I have a small TV in the bedroom, as you saw. He could've watched that." As calm as could be, Oz opened the cabinet beneath the sink and pulled out a basket with shaving cream and a drugstore variety razor. He handed both items to me without a word.

He knew I was freaking out. I could see it all over his face. Did he think I was freaking out because I just wanted to use him like a bouncy house? Or worse, did he think I was freaking out because any sign of genuine feelings from him would make me try on wedding dresses and start selecting good dates in June?

The truth was somewhere in the middle.

"Oh, nice. And your shaving cream smells like—" I popped off the cap to take a sniff, "nothing. Well, that's good. No conflicting notes with your outdoorsy mountain man body wash and shampoo."

"It says fresh, clean scent, and also, my body wash is called alpine, smart ass."

"Fresh, clean scent must mean nondescript. I love the body wash though. It reminds me of doing a striptease by a bonfire in the darkness. Towel? Soft washcloth? Oh, and I can't imagine you'd have a badger brush?"

"Say what?"

I sighed. "You're lucky you have good bones."

"I thought we were talking about my hair." He opened the same cabinet again and pulled out a nearly threadbare hand towel and a surprisingly soft washcloth. One out of two wasn't bad.

"A stool would be better, of course." I sighed again as I glanced around the small, bare bones bathroom. It wasn't much nicer than Ever's, but at least the shower was an improvement. "Okay, sit on the can then."

"And people accuse me of being unromantic," Oz muttered, flipping down the lid and doing as I asked. "Are you sure you know what you're doing?"

"It's my actual job, remember? Someday maybe you'll let me give you a trim." I knew it was as unlikely as harnessing the power of lightning with my mind, but I was still rattled enough that I lifted his ponytail to study his ends. "Yeah, you could use one. You have breakage. I'm going to recommend a different shampoo. Do you have pen and paper in here?"

"This is the damn john. Also, did you miss that I have a pair of nuts? I'm not gonna go buy special shit at the store."

"No, you aren't," I said cheerfully as I dropped his ponytail. "This has to be special-ordered."

He just rolled his eyes.

"I'll order it for you and have it shipped to Ripper. We can try it there first before you use it at home. Oh, right, no, we can't, because you won't let me touch your hair, although I'm skilled at what I do and could make you look so much better." A little peeved, I tugged on his scruff.

"Correct me if I'm wrong, but chin hair still counts as hair."

I huffed, but he wasn't finished yet.

"Besides, if I looked any better, you'd probably start peeping on me in the shower again, except at work. And we can't have that, can we? Since we aren't involved even though you're covered with marks from my beard and my lips and my damn dick."

Guess I wasn't the only one who was unnerved. Or pissed. Or whatever that peevish tone and furrowed brow implied.

My lips twitched. "Your dick didn't mark me."

"It surely did mark you. Missing a hymen, aren't you?"

"My hymenity is yesterday's news. Now shut up and let me shave you, Osmond."

He reached up to twist my nipple, and I smothered my giggle. I moved to the sink and ran the washcloth under the hot water before turning back to lay it over his jaw. His eyes practically rolled back in his head. "How's that feel?"

"Mmm."

Fighting a smile, I moved the washcloth over his jaw, stroking gently. His eyelashes were fluttering, and they were far too long for a man. As usual. All men got the gifts we women had to fight for.

"Most women like my scruff."

"I do too. Especially certain places." I cleared my throat when he opened one eye. "Friction, you know?"

"Mmm."

"But you saw my skin. Guess I have to build up my tolerance for whiskers. I probably should've had you take a shower first," I mused, stroking the washcloth down his throat.

"If we get under water, I'm gonna be inside you before you raise that razor. And most accidents in the home happen in the bathtub."

I grinned. "Still no condoms. Still Noah down the hall."

"We'll be getting some while we're out. And Chuckles is not keeping me from having you again."

"*Shh.* Don't call him that."

"I'm letting you shave me like a poodle. Don't think you can call the shots, sprite."

I gave him one last rub with the hot washcloth, letting it drift down his neck to his chest. That was purely for me, however. His body was ridiculous. "You'll need a shower anyway. So, if you want to give me a show, be my guest."

"Wouldn't be the first time, would it?"

"Nope." My voice was cheerful. "But you'll be showering alone, and I'll be shaving you after—"

"We're leaving in twenty," Noah called through the door.

"Says who?" Oz roared back, knocking the washcloth off his jaw.

I picked it up. "He is supposed to go with us."

"Why? I'm pretty sure we can handle an afternoon in a lakeside town alone. And if he wants to pretend to be human and semi-friendly, he doesn't get to call the shots."

"It's just his way. He has his reasons for wanting to keep us safe."

"No kidding. The question is why don't *we* know them? We're fucking adults." He cracked his knuckles. "We'll save the shower for later. Don't want to be late for lunch."

"You'll have time for a quick shower once I'm done. I'll do the fast version."

"Oh, will I now?"

Since I knew there was no appeasing him now, I looked under the cabinet for his aftershave until he lifted his brows and pointed at the cabinet above the sink. I took it out and took a sniff, hurtling headfirst into memories of our teen years. He'd always smelled like pure sex, and this scent was part of that. The familiar sandalwood and smoky notes made me take a long breath before I set it aside and grabbed the shaving cream.

"Since you don't have a brush, I'll be using my hands."

"Not until you fulfill your end of this bargain." He nodded at my top. "Shirt off."

"Seriously?"

He waited.

"Fine." I hauled off my top and set it aside. The bra was super modest, and from his hand gesture, he clearly had no intention of allowing that to pass. I flicked open the clasp and let it drop. "Better now?"

"Almost." I let out another unfortunate squeal as he dragged me forward to straddle his lap. "Now lather me up."

His face was practically between my breasts. "How am I supposed to work at this angle?"

His smirk from that position was devilish. "You're the professional, right?"

"Hand me the can."

He extended his long arm and grabbed the shaving cream, but he pressed a kiss to my nipple on the way back. They were already so hard, just from the heat in his gaze. "Here, let me open this." He popped the top on the can, which was wholly unnecessary—especially considering the backs of his knuckles brushed over my breast.

"Thanks." I took the can from him and tried not to pant.

I wasn't entirely successful.

My chest rising and falling was just what he wanted, considering the slow lick of his lips while I sprayed the shaving cream into my hand. I nearly bobbled the can three times and errantly sprayed some into his hair. He just calmly wiped it away and took the opportunity to suck on my nipple, his big dark eyes innocent.

Ha, there was a joke.

"You're incorrigible. You want me to wear your marks all over."

"I can't say that's untrue." He slid his fingers down my arms to my wrists. "I wouldn't mind seeing some here either. Velvet ropes attaching you to my bed."

My heartbeat stuttered. "Um, okay."

His laughter was rich and deep. "Chapter two. We have a lot more left in this one first. Since you won't even let me take a shower with you."

I rubbed the shaving cream over his jaw, lathering it with absolutely zero finesse. The next time I sprayed it, he ended up with some on his nose.

"Sorry, sorry." I cleaned him up with the washcloth, and then let out a long, slow breath as I reached for the razor.

"I'm not feeling too confident about you coming at my face with a blade."

"Then stop feeling me up," I muttered, reluctantly dodging the hand currently curved around my breast. I hopped off his lap and rolled my shoulders. "Okay, let's do this."

"I think we discussed bottomless too."

"Dream on, perv." I pulled the skin taut on his cheek and set to work on his sideburns.

It took longer than I anticipated—and we were interrupted by Noah one more time, who insisted there was "no time for hijinks". Oz was as wiggly as a kindergartener after a snack break, but finally, I finished him up.

And nearly let out a moan when I got a look at his gorgeous face on full display.

I hadn't seen him clean-shaven in a long time. As hot as he looked with the scruffy beard, he was somehow just as arresting without it. Those expressive dark brown eyes and perfectly soft lips, paired with surprisingly high cheekbones and an impressive jawline, could've been on the cover of magazines, not hidden behind miles of hair as he rocked out on stage.

Sucking in a breath, I turned to clean off the razor one last time. "Antiperspirant?"

"Getting sweaty, baby?"

"You have a bleeder." I kept my voice prim, which was a task and a half since my nipples were on high alert.

Why had I agreed to this crazy idea?

Absently, he touched the side of his neck and pointed with his other hand to the cabinet above the sink again. "Top shelf. If you can reach it, sprite."

I grabbed it and dabbed a little on my fingertip to put on the cut. He let me, then released a long sigh of pleasure as I placed the washcloth—now dripping with cool water—against his newly shaven face. "Your touch is magical."

I had to snort. "When you aren't afraid for your life?"

"I was never afraid for my life. Just concerned about a little maiming." His quick grin dazzled me, setting off a whole new swarm of buzzing in my belly.

Once I finished wiping him down, he managed to stay still as I applied his aftershave in as businesslike a manner as possible. Not being distracted by Oz Taylor was a feat.

But before I could step back, he slid his arm around my waist and yanked me against him. "Fucking finally," he growled, nipping my nipple.

The flash of pain shot straight to my clit, humming there as he licked and sucked. He did the same to my other breast before pulling me up higher. "Let me between your legs."

Damn this man. *Let* him? I wanted to give him a permanent engraved invitation.

"After lunch," I said breathlessly, framing his newly shorn cheeks in my hands. "We'll get condoms."

"Not my dick. Want my mouth on you. Fuck. You're so goddamn hot, Daze." He reached down to cup my ass through my yoga pants. "We should be spending the day in bed, not wandering around looking for tofu cups for Mister 3-percent-body-fat."

"He eats red meat. I've seen it." I couldn't help laughing as I wound my fingers through Oz's hair. I was probably developing a fetish.

Ah, heck, that fetish had been a part of my life for a long time.

"Yippee. What kind of panties have you got on under here?" I didn't have a chance to bat away his curious hands before he tugged down my pants. His expression of disappointment was priceless. "Your sister was birthed by demons."

Giggling, I brushed a kiss over the top of his head. "I'll buy something new while we're out."

"Promise?"

Those sexy brown eyes could get me in a whole heap of trouble. "You ask for a lot, Osmond."

"One of these times, I won't ask. I'll just take."

I couldn't stop my shiver. "I'm going to hold you to that."

ELEVEN

We went to a steakhouse for lunch.

Noah made sure we were seated in the very back so as not to cause attention. Lake George wasn't exactly the city, but I was known enough places that I'd wrapped my hair up under a ball cap and gone with the shades and hoodie look. Small bonus was that it wasn't too warm out yet, because if it had been, I would've lost the sweatshirt. Fans be damned.

Normally, I didn't mind doing the pictures and signatures thing. With Daisy, though, stuff was different. She wasn't used to any of that, and I didn't want to overwhelm her. Even working with the band wasn't the same as strolling the streets with one of us.

Or riding in a car with our lawless bodyguard, who drove a goddamn sports car. Long, low, and lean—the kind that barely had a backseat. Good thing sprite didn't mind crawling in back, although I'd offered to let her sit on my lap.

Chuckles did not approve.

Turned out Noah did not drive like a grandma, prior indications aside. I'd assumed he must have some propensity for speed in light of how quickly he'd arrived at the cabin yesterday, but all this drama llama nonsense was making me paranoid. For all I knew, he'd been tailing us all along.

Fuck it, I was going to ask. See what I could pry out of him. I'd prefer if Daisy was elsewhere, but short of waiting until she left for the ladies' room, I wasn't about to ask her to leave. Besides, she had every right to hear whatever the answer was.

Even if I wished I could shelter her from what was happening—and I wasn't about to dissect that gut instinct, thanks—she was a grown woman. Smart, capable.

Skilled enough at using a razor she could lop off my balls if she found out I'd excluded her.

Hey, self-preservation was important.

I waited until we'd placed our orders—steaks for all three of us—before turning to Noah.

"We want to know what's going on here."

Daisy sighed and set her napkin in her lap. "He didn't tell me he intended to ask."

"When I'm at liberty to say—"

"Don't give me that bullshit." My voice whipped out louder than I'd intended. I immediately lowered it. This was not the conversation to be had at top volume. "I did some research this morning, and I read about what happened with that crazy fucker Snake, and how he'd roped in one of the Ripper sales reps to do his bidding. There was talk of the mob pulling strings behind some of the shit that went down and—"

"What?" Daisy's eyes widened. "The mob? Are you serious?"

"Enough," Noah snapped. "If you can't sleep, let me suggest some Tolkien for next time. It's no more fiction than what you apparently found on those conspiracy theory sites."

"What do you mean, he couldn't sleep?" She frowned and glanced at me. "But you were in bed—I mean," she flushed delicately and glanced at her plate, "I thought you were with me."

God, she was so beautiful and sweet. And here I was, ruining lunch with talk about stuff I didn't know squat about. How could I? No one came forward with anything concrete. We were one of the biggest jewels in Ripper Records' crown, but by damn, they weren't going to tell us what was at risk.

"I got up early," I said in lieu of everything else I could have said.

Like...

That hour or two I slept beside you was some of the best sleep I've gotten in years.

We'd stayed out on the boat for a couple of hours last night. Talking sometimes, just sitting for the rest. Not groping each other, not making out. Just...quiet. Peace wasn't something I found often in my world, yet with her I had. It had continued when Noah came out to make sure we hadn't been kidnapped, and we'd gone in to play cards before bed.

Sex hadn't even been on the table. We were both tired, and I was well aware of the condom issue. I used to always carry them, because hey, rockstar necessity, right? Until I'd discovered in the past year that I'd rather face myself in the morning than a stranger.

So, we'd slept. I'd been wary about holding her in case of more lashing out, not to mention spooning kind of blurred the boundaries. But what the fuck were they anymore? We'd had sex. I'd taken her virginity. And all the lines were wavering.

Including mine.

Especially mine.

Turned out spooning wasn't all that bad.

Until I dragged myself awake, still caught in a dream—this one of Daisy fighting off a deranged man with his hands around her throat and nearly kicked out of the sheets.

Maybe someday I'd be able to just sleep like a normal person again. But obviously, not this weekend. Not when everything was so close to the surface. Add what had happened to Daisy, and I was on edge.

Rather than wake her, I'd just rolled out of bed and found Noah already up doing planks while listening to NPR.

A rocking morning indeed.

"So, I had some time," I said when no one spoke.

Daisy sat up straight. "And just how did you do this without internet?"

"Sat phones have come a long way. Especially if you throw enough money at coverage plans." Noah answered for me. "Or work for a tech giant like I do."

Daisy crossed her arms. "Well, aren't you two fancy."

I'd smooth her feathers later. "I decided to do a little digging. I knew some of it before, but everything is such a huge freaking secret. Clearly, I didn't know enough."

"I understand it's frustrating, but the less you know, the safer you'll be." Noah steepled his fingertips over his plate of fresh bread. He'd surprised me first by driving far beyond the speed limit, and now he was inhaling carbs.

Nothing about the world made sense anymore. The least of which was Noah's appreciation for red meat and grains.

I glanced around and lowered my voice even further. "Is the band a target for something or someone? Are we in real danger?"

My answer was the momentary flash of Noah's eyes. He probably regretted removing his mirrored aviators upon coming into the low lit steakhouse. If I hadn't been studying him so closely, I would've missed it. The guy was like a vault surrounded by steel. Nothing getting in. Definitely nothing getting out.

"If you follow protocol and don't do anything reckless, then no, you won't be in danger." His attention slid to Daisy, who was rubbing at the edge of her bandage. We'd changed it after she finished my shave, since she'd gotten it all wet. She claimed she wasn't hurting, but from the way she was worrying it right now, I didn't know if I believed her.

Maybe she just wanted to check out on this conversation. I couldn't say I blamed her. I just didn't like feeling as if I wasn't privy to something that affected me.

Like you shut Daisy out of your feelings about her and Kerry for how many years?

I'd also wanted to keep her physically at arm's length, because I was a dickish male who wasn't the best at avoiding my impulses unless I stayed far, far away. My impulses toward Daisy had always veered toward disaster.

She'd insisted we stop at a nearby drugstore before coming in here. After buying a shit ton of makeup, she'd slipped into the restroom here and covered most of her shiner. I could still see some purple peeking through in the right light, but she'd left her hair down, and it covered that side of her face.

We all had our shields. Some worked better than others.

While at the store, I'd picked up condoms—the largest size and quantity in stock. Noah had looked as amused as if I'd filled him with buckshot and left him to roast in the sun.

"What happened at the venue?" I asked into the silence.

Noah leaned back in his chair and arched a brow. "Are you under the mistaken impression that I'm going to ease your fears? That's not my job. My job is to keep you safe."

"Telling us what to watch out for isn't easing fears. It's called treating people like adults."

"Also not my job. I'm not the band's social director. If you have questions, I suggest you present them to Lila. She'll direct you as necessary."

"What about Daisy?" I demanded.

Daisy's head jerked up. "What about me?"

"Don't you care if she's safe? Isn't she your family? Somehow."

Noah's nostrils flared. "I'm here, aren't I?"

"Yes, but denying her information—"

"Hey, oaf, sitting right here. I'd appreciate you not using me as bait. If I wanted information, I'd ask for it."

Noah looked smug as he tore apart his bread and slathered on butter, and that annoyed me almost as much as being kept in the dark. "You know you're curious. You said so last night."

"Not in so many words. But I also trust Noah. If he's not telling us, there's probably a good reason. Besides, we're only barely related and it's through marriage."

"Aren't most relations through marriage?" Noah asked mildly.

I couldn't fault the guy there.

Conversation stalled about twenty times during lunch. Once or twice, people came too close to the table, and I hunched my shoulders in a futile attempt to seem smaller. At my size, it was hard not to attract attention. But my new clean-shaven look was definitely a decent disguise. I didn't think I'd shaved it all off since college. I was just too lazy most of the time, so my scruff usually went from manageable to verging on forestation.

I rubbed my jaw. I couldn't decide if I liked it or not. Mostly, I appreciated that being as smooth as a baby's bum meant I'd be getting another taste of Daisy tonight.

Assuming my conscience stopped knocking at the base of my skull every time I got a look at that bruise peeking through her carefully applied makeup.

After lunch, Noah said he needed to make some calls so he offered to meet us in an hour at a nearby ice cream stand. It felt a bit like dear old dad pretending to do something while the kids went on their first date, but whatever. At the very least, I knew Noah wasn't a guy to waste time on trivial things. If he was tailing us, he probably had a good reason—or a good suspicion.

I just didn't like knowing we were basically sitting ducks, requiring security to watch us at all times.

We weren't a political band. Jamie especially had enough opinions for ten people, but she and Lindsey had decided early on that we didn't want to go that route. We were about the music. Politics and opinions about world events belonged to other realms, and we weren't about to wade into those waters. At the shows, we wanted to have a big ass party, not talk about shit that weighed everyone down. Every band made their own choice in that arena, and we respected it. But our lack of controversy was yet another reason it didn't make sense we were in the crosshairs.

It had to be something to do with Lewis. That was the only possibility that made sense. Sure, Brooklyn Dawn grabbed attention, and fans could veer toward the unstable side if their love grew too obsessive. By and large, most fans were sweet and adored us. Which made the threat of physical violence aimed our way even more disturbing.

"Hey." Daisy squeezed my hand before pointing at a lingerie shop. "Let's go in."

The whole Noah situation had me so messed up that it took me a minute to get why she wanted to go in there. Must be bad off if even my dick wasn't getting any play.

"Sure."

She smiled and hurried in ahead of me, but the moment she was inside, she popped behind a rack and craned her neck to peer out the window.

"What are you doing?"

"Huh? Oh, nothing." She gave me an insincere smile and darted another glance at the window. "Just making sure Noah didn't decide to tail us. He's not a liar though. But—shit." She fumbled her purse and it fell on the ground with a jingle of keys. Hurriedly, she yanked it off the carpet, making a face. "Gross. I knew I should've brought my travel sanitizer."

I stepped closer to the window and glanced around. Lots of shoppers were strolling the streets of the quaint lakeside town in the sunny Sunday warmth. "I don't see Noah."

"No, I know, that was just silly talk. He wouldn't pretend to take off." She ran a hand over her hair and took a deep breath, a move I already recognized as her way of trying to calm herself down.

I just couldn't figure out why she was so rattled. It was a busy day, with lots of people all around. Safe enough.

Except we kept getting reminders that our world wasn't nearly as safe as we'd been led to think. And Daisy had just stared down a knife-wielding robber, so of course she'd be uneasy.

I was an idiot.

"Hey. Come here." I opened my arms to her and she bit her lip, looking as if she was arguing with herself.

Then she moved forward and linked her arms around my waist,

pressing her cheek to my chest. I rubbed her back and let out a deep breath of my own. Some of the raggedness inside me eased, just from having her in my arms.

Fleeting perfection.

Almost immediately, the memory of the last time she'd approached me with such trepidation in her eyes filled my head.

Kerry's funeral. Standing at the front of the church. Talking to the long line of mourners—her many friends, the worthless punk who'd been her on and off again boyfriend, a scatter of relatives we hadn't spent much time with in years. And finally, Daisy. Dressed in mourning black, her hair tucked away under one of those modest hats. I remembered there had been a fucking feather in front. I'd laughed at her, making her big eyes fill with pain and fear.

Of me and what I'd say.

Even after this long, I remembered almost every word of our conversation.

Who the fuck are you pretending to be? Some society matron? Newsflash, Daze, we came from the gutter. Pretty polish doesn't change shit.

She'd given me a tight smile and started with some clearly rehearsed speech.

I'm so sorry for your loss. Kerry was a wonderful girl—woman. She was a woman now. Almost.

She'd looked up at me as if she were waiting for confirmation I saw her as something other than a girl. A child. I'd laughed at her again, because the gaping hole inside me felt like an open grave caving in on itself. Dirt filling up all the spaces inside me that had once held room for love and happiness and friendship. All capacity for caring, gone in an instant.

Buried with my sister.

She was a kid. You're a kid. Playing with fire. She didn't learn fast enough, and God knows you weren't her savior.

I'd held myself responsible. I knew Kerry partied. That Daisy partied. Hell, I'd partied *with* them on more than one occasion. I was going to do it anyway, and if I was there, I could keep an eye on stuff.

Sure I could.

Except the night Kerry died, I'd argued with her. She was getting back together with her boyfriend, and I was sure he was bad news. When she was with him, she lived on a rollercoaster of emotions. All I wanted was my happy, carefree sister back. It was too soon for her to be in love. What was love anyway? Just a chance for someone you cared about to fuck you over.

I'd been full of wisdom from my own failed college relationship. And Kerry had cried when I yelled at her.

That night, she and Daisy had gone out, and I hadn't been with them.

I'm sorry.

Daisy's last words a whisper before she'd escaped.

"How can you stand to touch me?" I closed my eyes, then opened them to find her staring up at me with more understanding in her gaze that I expected—or deserved. "You were hurting, and I just made it worse."

She didn't offer platitudes or say I hadn't hurt her. We both knew I had. She didn't let me off the hook either, just held on to me.

God, she was shivering.

"Hey." I stroked a hand down her hair and around her cheek to grip her chin. "What is it?" I racked my brain, trying to remember what she'd said about the germaphobe thing. I knew she had some kind of anxiety issues, and this weekend's events hadn't exactly alleviated them. "Do you want to get out of here?"

"No. It's okay. I'm okay. Just I swear someone was following us out there. I looked over my shoulder twice, because I wanted to go in that stupid wax museum—"

"We'll go in there." Anything she wanted. I couldn't stand the fright in her eyes. Whatever it took to eradicate it, I'd do it.

Speaking of saviors, who's trying to be one now?

You can't make up for the past.

Can't erase what happened with Kerry.

"Oz, I don't care about the stupid wax museum now. Someone was trailing us. Maybe we should tell Noah. You brought your phone, right?"

She knew I had, because she'd insisted I bring it.

"Do you really think he can protect you in a way I can't?"

She rolled her eyes. "It's not about protecting me. It's about us. What if they want to mess with you? You heard what Noah said."

"I heard a lot of nothing from Noah. Don't worry. I got it." I wrapped my arm around her shoulders and turned her toward the wall of lingerie before us. "So, what did you have in mind?"

I didn't have to look at her face to get that she was frustrated with me. I knew I was being a pigheaded male, but the day I deferred to Noah Jordan when it came to looking after Daisy was the day I no longer had a damn dick.

She huffed out a breath. "I'm not feeling super sexy right now."

Deliberately, I let my gaze drift down her body. Her yoga pants and top were the opposite of revealing, but it didn't matter. Checking her out made me think of her naked on my lap, shaving me with her gorgeous breasts an inch away from my mouth.

"I want to fuck you right here."

"Oz," she gasped as an older woman nearby shot me a disgusted look and hurried away.

I shrugged. "I should have cleared the store while we shopped. In fact, I'll do just that." I turned and gestured to a pair of salespeople clustered by one of the checkout counters.

They exchanged a glance before a brunette with a high ponytail scurried toward us. "Yes, sir? May I help you?"

"Yes, you may." The smirk I gave her made Daisy step not-so-discreetly away. "We want to shop in peace. What do we have to do to make that happen?"

The brunette salesclerk glanced over her shoulder at the other woman before nervously tugging on the end of her ponytail. "I'm sorry, sir, was someone bothering you? If your lady would like to select some items, we could bring companion pieces to the dressing room while she tries on her choices."

"No one bothered us, and I want to keep it that way." I pulled my wallet out of my pocket, making sure to flash the wad of bills stuffed inside. Daisy let out a startled sound beside me as I withdrew my gold credit card. "We want privacy. We're willing to pay for it."

"This is not necessary," Daisy said under her breath.

"I think it is. What do you need for this to happen?" I asked the brunette.

She smiled. "Come with me, sir. I'm sure we can accommodate you."

Within ten minutes, the shoppers inside the store had been hustled out. A *closed* sign now hung on the door. We were given carte blanche and told to take our time shopping. Out of the back emerged a shopping assistant referred to as our concierge, toting a bottle of champagne that I waved off and Daisy stared at as if she was in a foreign country and didn't speak the language.

"It's three o'clock."

"You wanted proof I hadn't blown all my money, right?" I shrugged and gestured toward the champagne. "Drink up."

She didn't touch the glass they'd poured for her. "I saw your house in that magazine. That's why I said what I did. I don't care about your stupid money. Is that what you think I'm here for?"

I shrugged again. Something dangerous was brewing inside me. The past was too close, and the future was uncertain as fuck. I didn't like Noah lurking around. Didn't know what to make of the vandalism at the venue and the undercurrents around the band.

Never mind what the hell this was with Daisy and I.

But this was something I could do. I could buy out a store and remind myself that I wasn't at anyone's mercy anymore. I'd fought my way out of my past.

Outrun it.

"What do you like?" I indicated the racks surrounding us. "What's your favorite color?"

Despite obviously not liking any of this, she couldn't help the interest flaring in her eyes as she looked around. She was a wizard with hair and makeup, and for all I knew, she was already selecting ensembles.

Good. If she was thinking of lace and frilly underthings, she couldn't tremble at the possibility we were being followed.

She moved to a rack of nightgowns and robes—peignoirs, I heard the saleswoman call them—and started flipping through different styles. My spine itched at standing around, but I wanted her occupied.

Some of her anxiety issues might have to do with me. I'd nearly knocked her out yesterday even before the guy with the knife had appeared. I certainly hadn't taken the time to see how she was after Kerry died. Even knowing I should, that Kerry would want me to watch out for her too. I'd tried to ensure she would be looked after, but caring by proxy didn't count.

I'd been too self-absorbed to think about much more than fucking my way through life. Drinking myself into oblivion and on the nights that wasn't enough to kill the memories, taking whatever came to hand. Until I woke up full of sickness and self-loathing. Dragging myself onto stages that grew bigger with the passing years, playing for crowds that grew to match the stage. The music as much of a tonic as the drugs I eventually started staying away from.

Not soon enough.

"What do you think?"

Daisy has emerged from the dressing room in the palest lilac lace. The robe was modest, the nightgown a column of silk meant to hint at curves rather than reveal them.

It was pretty, but my mood was too fucking raw for sweetness.

"Nice." I stalked to a rack with a lot of tiny red contraptions with more cut-outs and straps than material. I grabbed one, not even knowing what her size was, and shoved it in her direction. "What about something like this?"

She frowned and checked the tag. "Sorry to break your heart, but I'm not a size 2."

The concierge hurried forward to find her size on the rack. "Here you go," she said, offering the lacy thing to Daisy.

She accepted it and went back into the dressing room without a word.

I was pissing her off, but what was the big deal? I'd paid for the private shopping session, and I'd be ponying up for whatever she wanted too. She could get her purple-whatever thing, but I liked the idea of her tits practically hanging out. Easy access. So what?

Daisy didn't have any qualms about her body, which was sexy as fuck. She walked out wearing the piece I'd selected with a pair of heels she'd gotten from somewhere with her makeup freshly applied—and a lot smokier. Her blue eyes glimmered with the sweep of dark wings at the corners and her lips were a soft raspberry pink that made me think of her pussy.

Probably on purpose, damn her.

I had to crack my knuckles to keep from picking her up and setting her on the nearest marble table. I wondered how much discretion from the staff my money would buy.

She didn't ask me what I thought of this one. She knew how she looked. Tits up high and proud, framed by lace, her nipples covered with tiny satin triangles. Her cinched-in waist was the perfect counterpoint to her full hips.

She walked in front of the mirror, her long hair swaying with every step, brushing the top of her ass. That part of her was barely concealed by the red lace and a satin strip that disappeared between her legs. Pity. I'd have to find another one that was crotchless.

Raising her arm, she lifted her hair, letting it fall as she turned back toward me. I literally could not breathe.

"All I need is a sports car and I can spread out on the hood like that girl in the Whitesnake video."

I spoke without thinking. "We can borrow Noah's."

Too late, I realized she wasn't saying it as something she wanted to do. Blame it on all the blood rerouting beneath my waist.

"Oh, goodie. Why dance in a cage at the show when I can do it for your entertainment?" She gave me a shallow smile. "Hope you have your dollar bills ready." She whirled around to head back into the dressing room.

"Daisy," I began, taking two steps toward her. Christ, I was being a colossal ass. "Daze, I'm sorry—" I broke off at a quick tapping sound against the front window.

Turning, I stared in shock at the asshole crouched near the side of the big plate glass window fronting the shop. He was far enough down that he was disguised by some of the racks between us and the windows, but he'd had a clear view between them at the dressing area and mirrors where Daisy had just been.

Fucker.

I took off running, ignoring the calls and admonitions from the concierge and her team. I yanked open the door just as the guy realized he'd been spotted. He smiled wide as I burst onto the sidewalk, and dimly, I realized there were more of his kind congregating around him. Guess I shouldn't have skipped the sunglasses while I was in the store.

Stupid. I was stupid in so many ways.

I held out my hand to the photographer. "Give me the camera. Now."

His smile stretched across his face. "You're fucking joking, right? I'm not giving you my equipment."

"Hey, Oz, pretty girl you got with you. Daisy works with you, doesn't she?"

"Daisy Flannigan's a hairdresser, isn't she? Do you give her extra tips?"

"You've known Daisy a long time. Have you been seeing her in secret all this time?"

More questions pelted me as I flexed my fists and tried to lock down my rage. I hated, absolutely hated, that they knew her name. Her face. That she'd become a soundbite as I was. I'd chosen that life. Chose it every day. She'd had no say.

"Give me your camera. Those pictures are private."

His smile turned lecherous at the edges. "She's a hot piece. You should add her to your collection of band babes. Gotta tell you, I always figured you were fucking that wild guitarist—what's her name? A dude's name, right? James? Jamie? She's gorgeous."

Out of the corner of my eye, I saw Noah crossing the street toward the congregation of photogs and paps. I was surrounded by them, but I didn't feel overwhelmed. Their questions and shouts fueled me like a tornado gathering strength. I'd been on edge all weekend, and I didn't have an amp to kick to shreds.

As a rule, I would've said I wasn't violent with people. Today was going to prove me wrong.

Some of the questions were tamer. Almost polite. I ignored those. Through all of it was the relentless *click-click-click* of flashes going off.

One.

Two.

Three.

Building the fire inside me to an inferno.

"Yeah, yeah, Jamie," another of them called out. "Guess you aren't as much of a bad ass as you think if you haven't tapped that. Or did—"

He didn't get the rest of the sentence out because Noah picked him up as if he was a plastic doll and clamped his arms at an awkward angle behind him. The photog's camera clattered to the pavement with a crash. He howled as Noah did something behind his back and spoke low into his ear.

The photographer paled and shut the fuck up.

"Give me the camera," I said to the dude in front of me. I hadn't missed how he'd started snapping me again while my attention had briefly been diverted by Noah. "This is your last fucking chance."

More questions flew at me. I heard my sister's name, then Daisy's and mine. Tangled up. The word *druggie* stampeded through my brain as if someone had express sent it right to all my pressure centers. I could practically feel my blood boiling in my veins.

Fuck it. I was almost begging now for someone to push me over the edge.

"Tell us what happened yesterday. News just hit the blotter."

Oh, shit, was the police report what had brought them out on us? I knew better.

Handle it privately. How many times had Lewis impressed that upon us? *Call us first, then the police.*

But with Daisy involved, I'd forgotten for a freaking second I was a public commodity. I'd just been a guy trying to protect his girl.

Behind me, the shop door opened.

"Oz." Daisy's voice cut through the din, clear as a wind chime through the buzzsaw of voices closing me in.

She was pleading with me to slow down. Back off. Think it through.

She knew me. Far too well.

And she was about to get a demonstration why Noah was right not to want us anywhere near each other.

"Held up? Heard your little blond confronted the dude? Bad timing." The photog who'd been snapping Daisy licked his lips as he glanced over my shoulder, probably right at her. A fucking doe surrounded by wolves. "From what I see, she looks like she's doing just fine."

That was it.

I didn't think. Didn't try to temper my reaction.

I slammed into the guy with the full force of my body. He flew backward and I leaped on him, pounding his camera into the ground before my hands locked around his neck. Noah's shout dented my consciousness as I lifted my fist above the photog's terrified face—and brought it down.

Again and again.

TWELVE

Daisy

I spent the evening at the police station. This time, the charge was more serious than gummy bear larceny.

So much worse.

I closed my eyes against the memory of the photographer's damaged face. Oz hadn't killed him, thank God, probably because Noah had acted fast and jumped in to stop the carnage.

Oz had been edgy all day, and even when we were kids, that had meant bad things. He'd always had too much energy, most of it the physical kind. Back in the day, he'd expended some of it by skateboarding off low walls and other daredevil stunts. Then he'd joined a rock band and become consumed with practicing six hours a day. And of course I'd heard the stories around the neighborhood from the girls he'd been with.

Words like *insatiable* weren't used that often for high school or college boys—at least in our acquaintance. Kerry had heard more about her brother's appetites than she'd ever wanted. I had too.

Part of me knew what he needed. He was all out of sorts, too many things out of his control, and for someone like him, only physically getting it out would allow him to breathe. As much as he was able.

Until the next storm.

The next amp tossed off stage.

The next shredded bass.

Even before I joined the band's crew, I'd heard the stories. I'd followed his life because he was a link to my best friend, and also, because I wanted him to make it. He'd said the day of the funeral that we'd come from the gutter. We hadn't, but our families had skated closer to the filth than the rarefied air on the upper West side, that was for sure.

Now he was one of those people. He could buy whatever he wanted, as he'd shown so readily this afternoon.

Except peace. That had no price tag and came in no store or VIP lounge.

The sound of the screen door opening made me spin around. Immediately, my shoulders drooped.

Not Oz.

Noah's mouth was grim, his eyes flat. His mood was obviously as bleak as mine.

Understandably.

We'd gotten back from the police station about an hour ago, and Oz had gone straight to his bedroom without a word. Lila had pulled some strings from a distance, getting him some fancy lawyer from the city who'd shown up in a Mercedes with an Italian briefcase and loafers and cool condescension dripping from his silvery-blond hair. In no time, Oz had been out with a ticket to appear before the judge in a few weeks. The lawyer had assured him it wouldn't "stick". He'd probably have to pay some restitution and that would be that.

Toss some money at a problem, watch it disappear. Must be a fine way to live your life.

"Are you okay?" Noah sat down beside me on the creaky porch swing I'd missed the night we arrived. It bobbled enough for me to grab the metal links attaching it to the ceiling in case the thing crashed to the floor. Somehow it held.

"I'm fine."

"You're hardly fine. You don't belong in a police station."

I sighed. "I know you and Oz don't believe it, but I'm a grown woman who can handle..." I faltered. "Life."

Like I had much choice.

"Oz is the one who put you in that situation. As he'll keep putting you in them, because he's a hothead who can't control his temper."

"Seriously? This is what you came out here to tell me? Let's skip the lecture." I started to stand.

"Daisy, wait."

I sat back down, yet again rocking the swing.

"Your sister asked me to look out for you when I picked up the bag. She's concerned."

"She's still a teenager. What does she know?"

Plenty, actually. My sister had more street smarts than I did, not that I would ever tell her that. But as far as Oz, she'd always just seen his bad side. The one that was brusque and rough and made me bleed—metaphorically speaking—so very easily.

But I wasn't falling in love with him.

I wasn't.

She didn't have to worry. I got who Oz was. Who I was. Which parts of us mixed well, and which ones didn't.

"She knows he's hurt you before. She told me about Kerry. I knew some of it, but she filled in the details."

I rubbed my forehead. "You do realize you're only a few years older than me, right? This whole benevolent uncle vibe you have going on is fairly creepy."

"I'm thirty-six. I have underwear older than you."

"Really? You've stayed the same size all that time? It must make it hard to get dates."

He flicked my nose, and I laughed. Oz would be surprised to see Noah had another side. Not that he ever laughed much, or even understood the meaning of downtime, but he wasn't nearly the hard ass every minute of the day Oz figured he was.

Just most of them.

"I care about him. You know about Kerry, so you get he went through a lot. Their mother died too not long before Kerry's...accident."

I still couldn't say the word *overdose* out loud. Especially when it tended to lead to questions about whether or not it was intentional.

I didn't think so. Kerry hadn't seemed suicidal, and even if she had been, she probably wouldn't have chosen a high school party to do it. But there were all kinds of ways to harm yourself. You didn't always need to spell out the words for the intention to be behind them.

But I didn't like thinking that. She'd had a rocky relationship with her boyfriend, but that weekend, they were back on. He'd even mentioned proposing. She'd been so excited about their life together, despite how young we were.

And then she'd talked to Oz and he'd deflated her dreams the way only he could. With a pin and a snarl and reckless abandon.

Beyond that, she'd been dealing with grief from her mother's death and trying to figure out what she wanted to do. Cal State and her dream of being a teacher had been a constant. A new life on the west coast, sun and fun. But with marriage possibly on the horizon, along with blending her wishes with her boyfriend's needs, she hadn't been sure which step to take.

Being in a relationship was hard at any age. Add in excess hormones and a desire to escape... Yeah, I'd almost gone down a path I couldn't have come back from either.

Oz had been right the day of the funeral. Kerry and I had been driving down the same road. The only difference was what had happened to her had scared me straight.

In a very real way, I owed my life to her. That made me immeasurably sad, as well as grateful for the second chance I'd been granted.

"We've all lost people we care about. Sometimes we blame ourselves, rightfully or not. That isn't an excuse to act like an entitled prick."

My head whipped toward Noah's. "Gee, tell me how you really feel."

Also, who had *he* lost? I mean, totally not my business, but the tight set to his jaw told me there was a story there.

It was so hard to imagine him seeing someone. He was definitely handsome, in a remote, dangerous, I'm-armed-right-now sort of way. But the guy had so little bend to him most of the time and had made work his god. His single-minded focus was admirable, especially since he kept people safe for a living. But what woman would be enough to make him want more?

Or what woman already had?

I studied my knuckles and pictured Oz's, torn up, bruised, and bloody. He hadn't allowed me to see to them before he strode off to his room. He was an expert at shutting people out—especially me.

Someday I'd learn to stop chasing after an unavailable man, but this wasn't that day.

"You haven't seen the other side of him."

"Have you?"

I squeezed my hand into a fist. Oz's had to be hurting, which would make playing at the fan club secret show a trial and a half for him. Yet again, he was alone with that pain. Stewing in it.

I just wanted to help carry his load, even if I didn't understand all of it. The Kerry stuff, the self-blame, lashing out when the thoughts got to be too much...absolutely. But his boundless, often destructive energy and desire to isolate himself weren't like me. I craved contact. I just hadn't figured out how to have friends my age who understood my boundaries when it came to partying.

Dancing I was up for. I could dance all night.

Or I could do other things all night, with Oz. Channel that crazy energy between us in a healthy, *dirty* manner.

Maybe that was the answer.

He didn't want to talk. Right now, I didn't either. So, we could communicate in other ways.

"I appreciate you're worried. You don't need to be. He would never hurt me physically."

"I'm not worried about that. I know he wouldn't. If he did, he'd be zipped up in a body bag before they could identify the remains."

Noah's flat answer made me hug him tight. He didn't yield for half a minute before he finally linked his arms around me and hugged me back.

"I'm glad we're cousins of undetermined means," I told him seriously as I eased back.

His mouth quirked. "They're determined, you're just too impatient to trace the lines of our family tree."

"Maybe someday. When I'm old and *thirty-six* like you." I hopped to my feet, then turned back and bit my lip. I really did not want to ask this question, but I had no choice. "Do you have AirPods with you? Preferably the noise-canceling kind?"

"Yes, why?" Then he winced and held up a hand. "Say no more. Just make sure he deserves you."

"We'll see. Thanks, Noah."

I headed inside. Now that I had a plan in mind, I needed to go for my supplies.

Also known as the bag from the lingerie shop I'd hustled outside with, only to find Oz boxed in by a fleet of paparazzi. I'd purchased both the lilac set and the red lace video girl outfit that Oz had nearly drooled over, along with the slingback red heels even though I sucked at walking in them. I'd paid for everything with my own credit card. He might be rich enough to buy whatever he fancied, but I wasn't bought and paid for.

He hurt your feelings by wanting you to dress like a video vixen yet you're wearing the same getup to seduce him?

Oz might've been riding on fury to begin with, but I also knew he'd been trying to protect my honor. I had no doubt of that. The photographer had given me a lascivious look and said some truly shitty stuff, and Oz was a possessive man. I still hadn't worked my way around to understanding how he'd come to be possessive of *me* in such a short time, but I also wasn't adept at this whole sex thing. Maybe it was a natural consequence of being that close to someone. Sometimes the feelings lasted, sometimes they didn't.

Looked like I'd be learning how all of this worked.

I took off my makeup and my bandage and took a quick shower, bracing my hands on the tile wall while I tried to get my bearings. My shoulders ached from tension. I'd slathered my hands with sanitizer at the police station until my palms were itchy and dry. I'd forgotten to bring my travel bottle to lunch, so I'd had to buy a bottle at the store down the block from the station.

When I felt out of control, the more I did stuff like that. Just like Oz pounded on things.

Or people.

A couple of tears slipped out, washed away in the warm water. If I hadn't followed him this weekend, none of this would have happened. He wouldn't have accidentally hit me coming out of his dream. He wouldn't have had to kick a would-be robber's ass, which would naturally be included in coverage of today's unfortunate event, because they had to make the story as salacious as possible to sell copies. And he wouldn't have felt compelled to attack the guy who'd probably seen me with my tits one breath from lingerie explosion.

Ugh.

Too late now. I had come here. Mistakes had been made, yes, but we'd also made a little magic too. We couldn't go back. So, we had to go forward.

I climbed out and dried off, then did my hair as best as I could with no hair dryer, curling wand or paddle brush. I should've bought some of those things at the store, but I'd been obsessed with makeup.

And later on, hand sanitizer.

First, I put a new, smaller bandage on my arm along with some Neosporin. Already, the cut hurt less. Small steps.

I dressed in the lacy red getup and tried not to wince at the big bruise on my cheek now that I'd scrubbed down. It wasn't as horrific as I'd feared it would be, but it definitely required more than a little concealer.

I added some lipstick and went au naturel otherwise. He'd seen me naked. He'd also seen me when I was a kid with no visible eyelashes to speak of—thanks, blond hair and fair skin—and problem skin and pigtails. I wasn't going to pretend to be anyone else with him than who I was.

And tonight, who I was was a chick in red lace and red heels with lime green toenails.

I felt exposed without a layer of gloss over my imperfections, and I would've preferred the purple set over this one. I was getting a serious chill. But I wanted to help Oz forget, just as he'd helped me last night by holding me while I fell asleep. For a guy like him who avoided emotions, he'd jumped in with both feet.

So was I.

After a quick look up and down the hallway, I left the bathroom. The coast was clear, but I could've sworn I heard some tinny country music playing down the hall. It had to be Noah's choice, because no way in hell would Oz ever listen to that.

I smiled. Good ol' Johnny Cash. Though I really hoped Noah had those AirPods handy.

Just in case.

"One Part at a Time" was my soundtrack as I approached Oz's closed bedroom door. Wasn't exactly a club banger made for seduction, but I would make it work.

Three knocks later, Oz finally opened the door. He didn't look at me, just stared off into space above my head. "I'm not hungry."

"Glad to hear it, because I don't have any food for you. Is the word *woman* synonymous with food provider in your male-sized brain or what?"

He still didn't look at me. "Just assumed. I made food for you."

That he had, and he'd also just made me a fat guilt sandwich. "Yeah, I didn't think of it. Sorry. I haven't eaten tonight either. Wasn't really in the mood."

Surprise, surprise there.

"Look, I'm not really in the mood to talk."

"Funny, me either." I braced a hand on the doorjamb. "Oz."

He finally glanced my way. The quick bob of his Adam's apple said everything his mouth didn't. "I don't think this is a good idea."

"Noah has noise-cancelling headphones. Hopefully, he'll use them. But if you'd rather go outside, I bet that swing on the porch might be fun." I wasn't sure it would hold both of us, especially if we were at all vigorous.

Oz didn't reply, just gripped the edge of the door. "Seriously, you don't want to go there."

I stepped forward, wedging open the door that much farther. He blew out a breath and stepped back. "What if I do?"

He pivoted to go to the window and braced his hands above his head on the frame.

Quietly, I shut the door behind me. He wore the same faded jeans and T-shirt he'd had on earlier, but he'd long ago ditched the hoodie.

I bit my lip as I studied the tensed muscles in his back, visible even through his tight shirt. I hoped I was doing the right thing.

I moved forward and touched him, letting out a sound at the warmth pumping from his skin.

"Daisy—"

"Don't 'Daisy' me. Did it ever occur to you I know what you need?"

He turned his head, his jaw locked. "You think you know."

I stepped even closer and slid my hand under the material, lightly dragging my nails over his taut skin. His hiss of breath made me keep going downward and around to the front, where I cupped his hard shaft through the denim. If anything, he seemed to grow in my grip. "Show me."

His fingers clamped around my wrist, almost bruising in their intensity. It was my turn to hiss. "There isn't a lot of gentleness in me." He sounded as if his vocal cords had been scraped raw with shards of glass. "I used up my store with you yesterday. What's left...isn't that."

"Do you see me running away?"

"You have no idea what you're playing with, virgin. Quit while you're ahead."

The derisiveness in his tone would've wounded me if I hadn't recognized it for the distancing tactic it was. He wanted me to run away. To save myself from him.

Little did he know that only drew me more.

"I'm not a virgin anymore." I shook off his grip until he finally relented and let me go. "You saw to that."

"The rest of what I'd 'see to' would scandalize the fuck out of you. Do us both a favor, and don't give me a chance."

I moved around him, wedging myself into the small space between him and the window. I slid my palms up his chest, registering the feel of him under my touch. Hard as granite. Completely unyielding. So hot that I was amazed he didn't burn me.

He didn't look down at me, just kept staring out the window at the lake, flat and still under the light of the rising moon.

If this was a battle of wills, he was about to learn just how determined I could be.

THIRTEEN

Tʜɪs ᴡᴏᴍᴀɴ ʜᴀᴅ ɴᴏ sᴇɴsᴇ.

She also had no self-respecting fear of the unknown. *Me.* I was unknown to her. She thought I was still safe Ozzy, Kerry's older brother. I might growl some, but ultimately, I wasn't dangerous.

Shit had changed in the years we weren't in each other's sphere. *I'd* changed. Whatever she thought she knew about me was just surface, and she was itching to explore.

Whether or not she could handle it.

"Last warning," I gritted out as she touched me, her skin so unbearably soft even through my T-shirt. "Walk out of here while you still can."

Staring up at me, the smudge across her cheek as plain as a thundercloud about to break, she dropped to her knees.

I tried to speak. I wasn't only afraid for her safety, but my own. I couldn't control myself when I was riding this edge. If I took things too far and she never forgave me, I would let down my sister.

Again.

Fucking again.

Daisy reached for the button of my jeans. She flicked it open with her tongue caught between her teeth, her gaze steady on mine. The sound of her lowering the zipper echoed in the silence. The cabin might as well have been a tomb. Nothing else existed beyond what was occurring within these four walls.

What *would* occur, for good or bad.

She didn't bother with teasing. Instead, she simply yanked down my boxers and my jeans, pulling them off with my socks and boots.

Then she licked her lips and murmured, "I do have some experience with this," and slid her mouth over the head of my cock.

Fuck.

Slowly, she drew me into her wet warmth. Surrounding me in her heat and suction and wrapping her delicate hand around me with so much more strength than I could've given her credit for.

All the while, her deep blue eyes dragged me into someplace unfamiliar. A place where she asked for my trust, when I didn't deserve the question.

I would destroy her faith in me. It was inevitable.

Sometimes it was better to steer into the crash than to try to avoid it. Cleaner. More expedient.

Fisting a hand in her damp hair, I hauled her off me as she struggled to catch her breath. Before she could, I pulled her right back.

She opened as if she'd been waiting for the demand. Aching for it.

Sucking me down, she reached beneath my shaft and cupped my sac, her crazily strong fingers doing things that shouldn't have felt good yet turned my brain inside out.

She couldn't breathe and neither could I.

Both of us dying for more.

Threading my fingers through her hair to cup her head was the only thing keeping me on my feet. I gripped her too hard. I knew it, but I didn't stop. I forced her down my length, testing her, testing myself.

Her velvety blue eyes watered as she complied. Never hesitating. She made a sound that veered on pain, and tears gathered on her cheeks, making the bruise that much more pronounced.

Open a vein, make it bleed.

She grabbed my thigh, her short nails digging in. Leaving welts. Her cheeks flushed, and a droplet of sweat wound down the side of her face while the muscles in my legs tensed.

Already, I was so close. With every suck of her mouth, every twist of her wrist, the pulse of blood pounding in my temple and inside my dick grew to the point of bursting.

At the last second, I ripped her back by a handful of her hair, holding her still while she panted and sobbed for air. Her swollen lips were smeared with me, and I dragged her halfway up my body to ravage her mouth.

We went at each other like feral animals, teeth crashing together, tongues dueling. She scraped her nails down my lower belly, inches above my painfully hard cock, and my balls throbbed.

So close.

I wanted to spill inside her mouth. All over her brand new red lace and her gorgeous tits barely hidden beneath it. But more than anything, I wanted to come inside her with nothing between us.

Not because I didn't have a condom. I did. I had plenty. But I was so fucking tired of holding back. Of pretending I had good inside me when it felt as if I was nothing but darkness, cold and empty and unforgiving.

Want me? Take every fucking drop.

But I didn't get to make the choice. Not this time. She dove down even while her eyes were still streaming. Her throat and jaw had to ache. She had to be in agony, because I was a brutal man who didn't care if I made pretty, sweet girls cry.

And my pretty, sweet girl wasn't even allowing me the option to break her. She was breaking herself first.

On her own terms.

She drew on me relentlessly, hollowing her cheeks, drawing my gaze to the bruise like a warning sign before I couldn't take it a second longer and fisted my hands in my own hair. She reached up and grasped a handful of my T-shirt, pulling on it until I realized she wanted my hands back on her head. Directing her. Forcing her to swallow me until the pain between us vibrated like energy in the air.

Lungs straining, chest heaving, I yanked on my own roots as I stared her down, willing her to stop. To move away. She didn't. She took more, longer between breaths, her hand squeezing my shaft in between to stop the pleasure so close to overtaking me. It would drown out the ache, and I didn't want that either.

I wanted it over. Wanted it to last forever.

I drove my hands into her hair and she moaned as if I'd given her a benediction. I wrapped it around my wrists, silken ropes binding us together, as she did something with her tongue and pulled me over the precipice.

Tugging me down with her into the salvation of her blue eyes and her giving, yielding throat.

I dropped my head back to try to get oxygen. To breathe through this madness. But right away, I had to seek her eyes again. I couldn't tear my gaze from hers. She didn't close her eyes, and I couldn't close mine. She was the center of my universe as I drained everything I could no longer carry into her.

And she took it. Every bit of me. No hesitation. No judgment.

She finally released my spent shaft and lowered her head to inhale long, shaky breaths. Her shoulders shuddered, only going still when I reached down and cupped her elbows, drawing her up against my body. Her mouth was used and wet, messy from her lip gloss and what I'd left behind. I kissed her again, tasting myself on her tongue. Sucking on it while she swayed in my hold and clung to me as if her knees wouldn't hold her.

God knows mine were barely keeping me upright.

I picked her up, tossing her over my shoulder in a standard fireman's carry. The Daisy who'd walked in this room would've fought me. Slammed her not-so-fragile fists into my back and driven her knee into whatever parts of me she could reach.

This one went limp.

I threw her on the bed and she didn't move from the spot where she landed. Her hair splayed around her. Her arms and legs fell wide. The lace hugged her sexy body obscenely, showing me every delicious inch I wanted to violate.

To mark as mine even though she wasn't.

Would never be, except here and now.

I reached behind my head to pull off my shirt. The whole time she watched me, no part of her moving but her eyes and her chest, rising and falling. Leaning forward, I snagged the little bow between her breasts, meant to adorn them. I used it to pull her toward me, tossing it aside when it came off in my hand. She didn't blink when I loomed over her, planting my hands on either side of her shoulders.

The tentative brush of her fingers over my tattoo had me rearing back. I didn't question myself. I couldn't do this if she was going to keep touching me. It was enough I couldn't cover her eyes. Because I wanted her to see who I was in living Technicolor, so she wouldn't keep lying to herself that I could be worthy of someone like her.

I grabbed the sheet, yanking it out from underneath her. Her eyes went wide as I ripped it apart and moved to secure her wrists to the bedposts. I had to drag her up the bed to do so, but she didn't fight me. Didn't speak at all as she watched me destroying us.

We didn't have an *us*. For very good reason.

Once her wrists were secured, I slipped my finger into the crude cuffs I'd made. It was far from the safest or most comfortable, but this wouldn't last long. "Do they hurt?"

"No."

"Would you tell me if they did?"

"If you didn't want me to touch you, you could've just said." Her voice sounded rusty. Breathless. Raw like I bet I'd made her throat.

There were lots of things I should have said.

I walked to the end of the bed and shoved the trunk out of the way before I drew her legs wide. The red lacy thing had a strategically placed snap. I undid it and her bare pussy gleamed up at me, so wet I had to swallow hard.

She's turned on. Not scared. Guess you calculated wrong.

I leaned down and opened her up for my mouth. Ruthlessly, I devoured her, tasting every bit of what she'd made for me. Using lips, tongue, teeth, and fingers, I tore her apart as surely as I'd ripped the sheet. She writhed against my face, her legs trembling, her face flushed and her temples dotted with sweat. I stopped and drew my mouth away, my fingers still busy, my thumb working her clit. Keeping her system humming without giving her the relief she craved.

Then when she started to calm, her wrists relaxing against the sheets that held her fast, I started again.

Over and over, I drove her up. Wanting to break her as completely as she'd done to me.

In a weekend. Half a year. The lifetime since my sister had brought her into my world.

I slid my mouth up her leg and over her quivering belly, opening snaps so I could sample her skin. Salt and nerves, sweetness and Daisy. Moving higher to tug down the lace cups so that her full breasts stood proud, the tight tips beaded for my kiss. But I was rough with her, nipping where I could've sucked, twisting where she might've craved a tender touch.

Her back arched and the sounds she made nearly undid me. Like she was dying or being reborn, both at the same time. Her beautiful body straining toward me, asking wordlessly for whatever I would give her.

Hard and fast, I shoved two fingers inside her. Three. Widening them so she'd never forget where I'd been and how I'd used her.

She only widened her thighs and stretched toward me for more.

I flexed against the footboard, grinding my already painful cock into the wood. Not to make it stop. I wanted to ache like she did. Making her crazy was doing the same to me.

"Oz." My name left her puffy lips on a gasp as I rocked my hand. She'd soaked me to the knuckle, but it wasn't enough. Not nearly. "Now I do think you hate me."

I pulled my hand away and pushed my drenched fingers between her lips. Her pupils flared wide for a second before she started to suck. Hard. Biting at me so that my cock lurched against her belly.

Wanting in. Bare. Fuck the rules.

It was as if she knew.

As soon as I drew back, she whispered, "Do it."

Her words unleashed something in me. I yanked the sheet cuffs loose from her wrists, unwilling to acknowledge her noise of protest. Like she didn't want to be free. I rubbed the redness away from them, getting the circulation going again, and then I laid down on the bed, hauling her on top of me. She flailed, still off-balance, but I didn't give her time to get acclimated. I picked her up and set her down on my face, making her fall forward and slam her hands against the wall while I licked her. Relentlessly. Sucking her clit, swallowing her flavor, inhaling her delicious scent.

Distantly, her cries echoed in my head. Not enough.

I'd tossed the lengths of torn sheet on the bed, and I fumbled for one blindly, unwilling to divert from my task for even a second. From my awkward position, I seized her jittery hands, tugging them behind her back while she jockeyed to stay upright on me. I bound her wrists in a sloppy tie and went back to the meal I'd made of her, loving that she was a mess for me. Flushed and drenched and pulsing against my tongue. Her thighs shook and I knew she was close, even more so because I'd taken some of her choices away.

Somehow that was a trigger for her. So much for repelling her.

Fuck me.

Right on the brink, I lifted her away and set her on my thighs. She wobbled, nearly falling without the use of her hands for balance, but I steadied her with my hands on her hips. And I reached over to open the drawer beside the bed.

"Why?" she asked the question with a whimper. "Why?"

Her disappointment carved through me. She was a match for my recklessness. Encouraging mine. I had to be the smart one.

God, I'd already been so very stupid.

I withdrew a condom and tore the packet with my teeth. She

looked thoroughly ravaged—hair wild, makeup smeared, her lacy lingerie all askew, snaps open and showing off the parts of her I couldn't get enough of. I sheathed my cock and gripped her hip, knowing this would be the last time I'd allow this.

Even an alcoholic knew when he needed rehab.

Lining myself up with her slit, I drove forward, burying myself to the hilt. No gentleness. She wasn't a virgin anymore, as she'd been so quick to remind me.

She clamped her lip between her teeth to stifle her moan as my hand cupped her breast, pinching her nipple. "Ride me," I demanded, drawing back and slamming home once more before she could.

Unsteadily, she tried to do just that. She faltered a few times before she found a rhythm, sliding her hips forward and back, her heavy lashes falling down to shield her eyes. She moved faster and faster, digging her knees in beside my hips, bearing down to grind her clit against the base of my shaft.

I gritted my teeth, guiding her with my grip on her heaving breasts. Squeezing them, twisting her nipples to get her to speed up.

Not that she needed my help. She'd found her pace all on her own.

Her hair bounced over her shoulders, falling down over her tits. Covering part of her face so I couldn't see the rapture overtaking her, but I heard it in the little gasps and moans she couldn't hide from me.

Not my name. Not anymore. Now I was just the object she was using to get off.

The way I wanted it.

The way it had to be.

She rode me with growing speed, losing herself. Taking me with her. She was so tight and perfect, clenching me with every pass before she lifted herself off me and took the bliss away.

Then it was back, churning deeper, darker. A maelstrom she controlled. She lost the beat and fell forward onto me, letting out a surprised cry. Her eyes popped open and she found my mouth, kissing me with every bit of the frantic need climbing higher inside me.

It took everything inside me not to take over. To command her body so she couldn't rule me all over again.

She was the one tied up, but I was the one in chains.

Her teeth scored my lip, one hard bite. Bringing me back as she rubbed her taut nipples against my chest and bucked her hips impatiently, not liking the angle.

I could help with that.

Fuck, I had to.

I reversed our positions, rolling her onto her belly. I grabbed hold of the tie around her wrist, and her shoulders slumped, as if she was anticipating me freeing her. But I only used it to haul her up on her knees. She buried her face in the pillow, pushing her ass high.

Daring me.

Tempting me.

I gave it a quick slap and her body went still for an instant. Two. Then she turned her head on the pillow and huffed her tangled hair out of her face. "Is that all you've got?"

Slipping two fingers inside her, I leaned over her and nipped the back of her neck. She moaned and squeezed my fingers. I knew what she wanted. What she was begging for with every drip.

Moving back, I snapped my hips forward and filled her, driving her hard into the bed. Even the pillow couldn't muffle her scream.

The taut ring above where I was embedded deep in her body taunted me, so I wet my fingers with the moisture coating my cock before I filled her there too. She gasped, wriggling against me, wanting more.

I didn't spare her, fucking her hard and deep. Long strokes, shorter, more chaotic ones, making her back tense and her thighs quake. She liked my finger in her ass, so I twisted it, using my other hand to drag her up off the bed by the tie around her wrist. The angle change ripped a cry from her throat as I held her upright to fuck her.

She sagged forward, her head drooping, her body mine to enjoy.

And I did.

"Oz," she begged. "Let me come. Please. Please."

Her desperate cries fueled me. Instead of giving her what she thought she wanted, I let her go without warning, a shocked, panicked cry leaving her as she hit the mattress. I pushed into her twice as fast, as hard, shoving her up the bed until she could only pant and sob into the bedding as her body hovered on the edge.

I pulled the finger out of her ass and she whimpered until I gave it to her again, along with a slow thrust meant to make her shatter.

She didn't disappoint me.

Her pussy clamped down hard on me and I gritted my teeth against my own orgasm. But I couldn't stop it. It was like a freight train, bearing down on both of us. Drowning out the light as her body twisted and spun out under mine.

Letting out a roar, I poured myself into the condom, despising the thin latex separating us. Wanting to fill her up and watch it spill out around me onto the sheets where I'd torn us apart.

Panting while I loathed myself and loved her in measures I'd never known I was capable of.

It took everything inside me to yank myself free of her and remove the condom. Then I headed into the bathroom to dispose of it and clean up.

Back in the bedroom again, I tied my wild hair back from my face with one of the ragged strips of sheet.

And I allowed myself to look. Just *look*.

In the center of the bed, she laid completely still, wrecked beyond words.

I'd done that to her. Just as she'd done her own version of it to me.

The difference was she would recover.

She would wake up from her sex coma and hate me for using her and dumping her. When, in truth, I was doing her a favor.

I wouldn't bind her to me with anything but cotton and desperation.

She deserved so much more than that. I lo—

I forced myself to breathe through it as I sucked down one last glance. Her bandage had come half off. I'd been rough with her. Not even thinking of how she would hurt.

Taking what I needed without a fucking care. But this—*this* was what I could give her.

Freedom.

Swiftly, I undid the tie around her wrists. She didn't stir as I rubbed them, my dick growing stiff again at the faint abrasions on her delicate flesh.

Bastard.

I'd already caused her so much embarrassment and unwittingly pulled her into the spotlight. What had happened earlier was just the beginning. Next, someone would see her cheek and combined with my rage tonight, they would start to speculate. The stuff with Kerry would be tossed around like confetti. Private details of our past and present would become fodder.

I'd signed up for that life. Daisy had not.

She didn't deserve to be collateral damage when I let my hotheadedness get the best of me. As I tended to do with disturbing regularity.

This was the kindest thing I could do for her.

For me? It was just one more wound to add to the collection, most of them self-inflicted. But at least I would know I'd limited how long this went on. With every hour we spent together, it would only become worse.

I shut my eyes. My sister would hate me for what I'd done. And she would be right.

I picked up my clothes and shut the door behind me.

FOURTEEN

Daisy

THE ROOM WAS PITCH BLACK WHEN I WOKE.

Rather than panicking at being in a strange place, calm enveloped me. I had to grin. I'd been fucked unconscious.

I lifted my head and realized my arms were free and curled around the pillow beneath me. I turned over my wrists and rubbed at the slight sting on each of them. Stupid to be disappointed it wasn't more.

Had to say I didn't mind Oz's already slightly growing-in stubble. Hopefully, it had done less of a number on my skin than his full beard. My pussy and my nipples definitely missed his more grown in facial hair. Maybe in time my flesh would toughen up.

A girl could dream.

I didn't know how long I'd been asleep. Enough that when I stretched, every part of me hummed pleasantly—even the ones that were sore in delicious ways.

Sex had so many benefits I'd never realized. It was a workout and a sedative in one.

I rolled over, extending my arms over my head. The bandage on my forearm flapped with the movement, and I frowned as I smoothed it back down. The part of me that was still healing didn't appreciate such...energetic activities.

The rest of me though? I squeezed my thighs together with a happy sigh. Freaking glorious.

My stomach growled, and I sat up. The sheets were cool, so Oz hadn't stretched out with me. I couldn't say I was shocked. He was restless at the best of times. This afternoon had been hard, but maybe he was feeling more smoothed out now.

At least I hoped. If he wasn't, I was totally up for another round. Including those very interesting wrist securements and maybe even some of that back door fingering action.

I flushed. Who knew that would feel so good? Probably everyone other than me. I was a late bloomer.

And I wanted to bloom a lot more, after I got something to eat.

I climbed out of bed and noted my knees weren't wobbly. Progress. Must've slept off my usual post-orgasm unsteadiness. It certainly wasn't because Oz hadn't rocked my world. He'd rocked it so hard I was tempted to curl my toes into the bare floor even now, hours later.

A quick glance at the bedside clock made me do a doubletake. Five a.m.? How was that possible?

We'd gotten back later in the evening after spending hours at the police department, and Oz and I had been...occupied for a while, but still. I couldn't believe I'd slept that long.

Frowning, I looked over my shoulder at the other side of the bed. Well, in theory anyway, since I'd awakened sprawled in the middle. I patted the sheets. That side of the mattress was cool.

Now Oz not sleeping with me loomed a lot larger. Had he just stayed up all night? Where? Noah had taken the couch to sleep, so short of camping out in the not-so-comfortable chair, he didn't have many options in the small cabin.

My chest tightened at the knock on the door. Not Oz. He didn't knock. Not in his own place, and not with me.

Especially not now.

I took a deep breath and started to go to the door, before I remembered my current state of undress. Pretty sure Noah didn't want to see me in half undone lingerie. I glanced around and saw Oz's hoodie on top of the trunk that had been shoved away from the foot of the bed.

After tugging it on—and pulling it down like a damn dress—I opened the door.

With one look at Noah's face, I backed up. My calf hit the solid wood bed frame, but I barely noticed the flash of pain.

"He left, didn't he?" My voice was dull. Hollow. I scarcely recognized it.

I didn't give him time to answer before I turned toward the bag of my clothes Oz had set in the corner. My gaze tripped over the mangled bedding and ripped sheet, hanging somehow obscenely off the edge of the bed.

He tied you up to let you go.

I wasn't sure how that made sense to me, but this was Oz we were talking about. I had always understood him under the bullshit.

Or so I'd believed, because I'd never really thought he would do this to me. Not after what had just happened between us.

Noah didn't speak as I rooted through the bag of clothes Ever had put together for me. Turned out my little sister was the smart one.

I slept with him anyway. And it was amazing, which really sucks.

I drew out a green sweater with Rudolph the red-nose reindeer on the front. My sister really did not want me getting any—ever.

It made me laugh, the sound twisting into a sob as I clutched the sweater to my chest.

Noah moved closer, and I straightened, clinging to the ugly Christmas sweater I'd bought for a salon party one year and was now using as a fuzzy tear-collector.

"I'm okay."

"Of course you are." His brisk assurance bolstered me, and I threw back my shoulders.

"Yes, of course I am. Because boys are stupid."

He cleared his throat. "Often."

"Especially that one."

"From where I'm standing, he's a fucking moron right now."

I smiled through my annoying tears. "How come you're still single? Or is being married to your job truly a life choice?"

That's right, Daze. He's nice to you, so ask inappropriately prying questions.

Noah gripped the back of his neck. "You aren't going to ask about him?"

"What's to ask? He's not here. He's a prick."

"I can't argue with any of those things."

"It's classic *Dr. Phil* stuff. He's not ready to have an adult relationship. Especially not with me. I didn't save his sister." I rubbed the back of my hand under my nose to stop it from dripping. "For all I know, this was some big ass revenge plot. But hey, my fault, because I forced the issue. He didn't speak to me for six months. I probably should've left well enough alone."

"No."

"No?"

"No," Noah repeated. "You didn't see his face when he left here. He looked desolate."

"Desolate?" That didn't compute. Also, it was possible this bedroom had an echo chamber. "We'd just had an amazing fu—sexual congress," I amended. "He had no reason to be desolate. I thought you male types crowed after such moments."

"I can't say I've ever crowed after any moment."

"I'm sorry," I said sincerely. "But believe me, he should have. *I* should have. If he was woe-face when he left here, he's an even bigger prick than I thought because no one made him go except himself."

Noah scrubbed his hands over his eyes. "I haven't had coffee yet."

"That doesn't really compare to my heartbreak, but okay."

His rough chuckle surprised me. "I'm just saying, I'm not really prepared for this."

"No shit, Sherlock. Me either. But fuck it. I'm wearing a Christmas sweater even though it's May, and it's so ugly it shouldn't even be worn in December. And I'm gonna plait my hair and do kickass mascara wings and rock the shit out of all of it." I sat down heavily on the bed. "He really left you to drive me back like cattle?"

"What he did was run away. End of story."

I reached out for his hand and gave it a quick squeeze. "He really hated that you could do more pull-ups than he could."

"He'll have plenty of time to do them while he's getting his head out of his ass." He squeezed mine back.

I shook my head and dropped my hand into my lap. "No. We're finished."

"So, he's not the only stubborn one then. Good to know."

"He had his chance."

"He did, and he was an idiot to waste it. But if he's lucky, he'll get another." Noah's Adam's apple rose and fell in the dim light coming from the hall. "Some of us don't."

My eyes stung, so I shut them. "His sister didn't."

"No. So, maybe think about that, huh?" He walked to the door. "And for the love of God, put on some pants before breakfast. I'm making waffles before we head back."

I perked. Or rather, my knotted belly did. "Frozen?"

He shuddered. "Good God, no. I made Osmond get ingredients for real ones before he ran for the hills. He even brought back whipped cream without me requesting it." This he said with an arched brow, as if I understood the gravity of this gesture.

"So?"

"Never doubt the importance of whipped cream."

"You're a weirdo sometimes, Jordan."

I didn't let another tear fall until he shut the door behind him.

FIFTEEN

I drove back to the city in a haze. I had a place there, a showpiece apartment. The kind of apartment Daisy would've believed was more fitting for my status as a rock god.

Today, I felt like a poser. A pretender. Hiding out under a hood and dark glasses on a cloudy day wasn't helping my mental state either.

Your fault. You made all of this worse.

A block away, I got a glimpse of the encampment out front. Tons of people, cameras, equipment trucks. Great.

In times like this, it wasn't hard to see why I didn't spend much time there.

I veered into the next lane and turned off without a signal to a chorus of horns.

Shit, was Daisy dealing with this? Had I run off and consigned her to facing that alone?

Not alone. Noah was there. He would protect her. Far better than I could. He had a hell of a lot more control than I did, that was for certain.

My left hand tightened around the wheel. The right was in my lap, because it hurt like a bitch after the dual battles of fighting with a photographer and making love to Daisy.

Fucking. We'd fucked. End of story.

I circled around for a while, finally giving in to the urge to call Lila. She could check in with Noah for me if nothing else.

"Hello, Osmond. I'm going to assume you aren't in jail again."

I was in such a funk that I didn't even care she'd called me my given name. "Not yet, but it might happen. My place is infested."

"I know. We have someone on their way over, since you left your security guard with Daisy."

"He's her cousin. Or something. Besides, she might need security, but I don't."

"Right. You can clearly handle large crowds of paparazzi, since you did so well yesterday."

I slammed my horn as someone cut me off, swearing a blue streak.

"I can tell you're much calmer now," she continued. "So, the security guard will meet you around the corner. Let me give you exact coordinates. Please hold."

Coordinates. Only Lila, man. Sometimes I wondered how she'd ended up corralling crazy rockstars instead of working in air traffic control or something that dealt with life and death on a daily basis.

Then again, with all this security secretiveness, maybe she had more to do with such things than I fully realized.

"Li, wait. You talked to Noah. Is it a mess at the cabin?"

"Define mess." Her voice cooled, telling me Noah had informed her what had gone down. I couldn't even call him a traitor, since his allegiance was clearly to Daisy, not me.

It wasn't as if I thought I'd bought his silence with premium sausage links. Bad enough he'd sent me on a grocery store run as if I was an errand boy when I was making my dramatic exit. I'd been foiled by him doing his ridiculous ab crunches in my living room.

"Look, you've probably figured out Daisy and I had a thing."

"A thing." Considering Lila's frosty tone, I almost expected to see icicles dripping from my in-dash screen.

"It's nothing to concern yourself with. It's over."

"Oh, thank God. I'd hate to have anything else to be concerned about."

"You know, your husband offered to be my friend. Does he know you have such a disdain for me?"

She didn't hesitate. "If I truly had a disdain for you—which I do not —that would not influence Nicholas in the slightest. Because he's an adult, as I am. We choose our own friends without checking in."

"This is why I don't do relationships," I muttered.

"No, you don't do relationships because you have to risk more than your hair."

I skidded into a space a block from where I was supposed to meet my sanctioned lackey. "How come women all stick together and men don't?"

"A question for your therapist, not me."

"Which one of you came up with the therapist thing, you or Nick? He said something similar."

"Sometimes the audience dictates the message."

I frowned. Yeah, that was an insult.

"As for the *mess* at the cabin, there isn't one, because Noah got her out of there as a crowd was starting to form. You had to know your hidden spot wouldn't stay hidden for long when you create a public spectacle."

Right. Because I'd thought it all out so coherently. I still hadn't realized all the repercussions yet.

"What was I supposed to do? He was saying shit about her. Looking at her. Treating her like a piece of meat."

"Newsflash: looking at people is not a crime. Luckily, your attorney is a very capable individual, and you won't face lasting repercussions. Still, I would advise you to work on getting your temper under control. We're going to be under enough media scrutiny for a while due to our recent security lapses without you going off half cocked."

"Which is why I can't wipe my own ass without security?"

"Unless you're planning on doing that when you step out on the sidewalk, that doesn't apply here. Sarah is just accompanying you into the building for ease of transport. She's worked out an alternate route."

"You did not just say *Sarah*. You gave me a female bodyguard? I'm six-foot-four. What exactly is she going to do to protect me?"

"Keep your ass out of jail, for one. Band meeting before rehearsal tomorrow afternoon. Don't be late." She clicked off.

"Bye to you too."

The passenger door of my truck opened, and a blond wearing jeans and a cap climbed in. Fuck. Just what I needed—fan service this early when I was in a bear of a mood.

"Hi, look, I'll sign whatever you want me to if you'll make it quick. I'm in the middle of something." I tacked on a smile, the kind that had resulted in more than a few pairs of bare breasts being presented to me. And bare other things. "Sorry, sweetheart."

"I'm not your sweetheart." She gave me a bland look. "I'm Sarah. I do not want your autograph unless it's on a check, and I doubt you could compensate me as well as Ripper Records is already. We can't stay here. We need to move. Drive."

I frowned as I took her in. "You're the bodyguard? You look utterly harmless. I could toss you over my shoulder."

"Try it. I've been authorized to use whatever force is necessary."

"On me? Aren't I the client?"

She sniffed. "Hardly. You're the equivalent of a society princess who can't stop partying. In your case, you can't resist trouble. Same difference." She pulled out her phone and typed at max speed. "Now move."

I moved. Under duress, but I did it.

We circled the block for half an hour. When that didn't give us "clearance" according to Sarah, we went to a diner in Brooklyn and ate eggs and burnt hash browns and said virtually nothing to each other.

The next time we stepped outside, I wasn't sure if I really did hear the sound of shutters flashing or if I was imagining them.

We finally made it back to my apartment by late morning. By then, I was bleary-eyed from lack of sleep and personal disgust, which I was wearing like a cloak at this point. I needed a shower and a few hours of unconsciousness while silent Sarah stood guard and protected me from the big, bad tabloid types circling outside.

She had gotten me into the building with a minimum of fuss, so I supposed I couldn't bitch. Much.

I showered and dragged a hand over my rapidly growing scruff. Daisy shaving me seemed like a lifetime ago, and it had only been a day.

My phone was blowing up with texts and calls. Several of the ringtones I recognized as belonging to my bandmates. I was sure they were curious what had possessed me to attack a tabloid reporter. It had been a long time since I'd laid hands on anything but some equipment or the occasional piece of hotel room furniture.

It wasn't a trend I was looking to continue.

For the first time in forever, I took a melatonin to sleep. I was already having crazy dreams, so how much worse could it get?

When I woke up ten hours later after being chased by zombies with high blond ponytails, I decided I didn't know shit.

A quick look outside told me I hadn't slept long enough. They were still all there. If anything, there was more of them. Was it a slow news day or something? How was I such a huge topic right now?

I'd fucked up a fake journalist. Big deal. He was still breathing. He didn't even have any broken bones.

I shook out my hand and winced. I wasn't sure I could say the same for myself.

Sarah was sitting in the kitchen in the dark, cleaning her gun.

Okay, then.

Careful not to make any sudden moves, I went to the refrigerator to put together a sandwich and found I only had bologna nearly expired and a heel of bread. I really needed to hire an assistant.

Or better yet, I needed to stop firing them.

"How do you stay alive?" Sarah asked as I slapped the meat between two thin slices of bread.

"Why, are you planning on using that on me?"

She just spun the chamber. I would've been lying if I didn't admit it creeped me out a little.

"I mean the contents of your refrigerator."

"I tour a lot."

"You might want to have it checked for mold."

I would've flipped her off if she hadn't been armed. Even so, I couldn't really argue with her assessment. I was living rough right now.

After I forced down the sandwich with my last remaining beer, I went to grab my phone to place a grocery order for the next day. And got a slew of notifications about the rockstar gone wild who liked to beat up on poor guys just trying to make a living...and maybe even sweet hairstylists from his past who were dumb enough to date him.

Served me right for setting up a Google alert on myself. I should've known better.

I flicked the notifications away and decided to take a bottle from my cupboard back to bed with me as my version of a teddy bear.

Sarah didn't comment.

Nor did she say anything when I emerged in the same state the next day, just in time to pour coffee down my throat before I dragged myself to the venue for rehearsal. She came with me, because she was my new judgmental buddy who didn't talk much but liked to fondle her weaponry. She even managed to laugh when I took the opportunity to swap Jenny for the red Porsche Spyder I kept stored in the garage down the block.

The Spyder's name was Priscilla. She was a fussy female, but she sure was pretty.

"This is how you try to be inconspicuous?"

"Yeah, since they already made the truck, didn't they? I haven't taken Priscilla out in a long time."

"Men who personify their vehicles as women are usually crying out for love."

I smirked because somehow that hit a little too close to home. "Or what passes for it after a show at two a.m."

"You could let me drive. In fact, I should. I'll be able to lose any tails on the way to Brooklyn."

Staring at her across the roof of my car, I laughed out loud. "You actually think you'd be better at losing some creep?"

All at once, I remembered sitting beside Daisy as she drove my truck at top speed, laughing maniacally. All the humor drained out of me.

"No," I said before Sarah could answer, sliding inside the car. "No one drives my vehicles but me."

Silence reigned on the ride over to the unusual venue we'd chosen for our secret fan club show. It was tucked away on a side street, which allowed me to notice the fuckwad who'd slipped into traffic behind me and now stayed a discreet distance back, no matter how many times I turned off.

"Told you I should've driven."

Sarah's smug voice had me gassing it to swerve around a postal truck. Horns blasted, and I got more than a few middle fingers raised in my direction as I cruised down another side street. I did an illegal U-turn, coming back up the same street in time to pass the fucker on my ass.

I gave Sarah a tight smile. "Got it handled."

She didn't reply. I wouldn't have been surprised if she was plotting where to bury my remains.

When we finally strolled into the converted bowling alley-slash-concert venue where we were holding the show, Sarah was muttering about poor security set-ups and improper clearances. I didn't respond. I had bigger issues.

Like trying to look for Daisy without making it obvious.

I'd been on edge all morning. I didn't know how to handle this. Normally, I'd freeze her out. I'd done that for the better part of six months. But every time I envisioned her smile and heard her laughter in my head and imagined her squeezing my cock while she gasped my name...

Yeah, cold was not what I felt.

"Nice of you to show up. Think you can answer a goddamn text?" Jamie strolled toward us in her towering boots, her long dark hair swinging from some cone thing on top of her head. Then she stopped dead. "Jesus, you shaved. Without the chin pubes, you lost a decade."

I set down my guitar case between my feet. "Thanks, Jame. Always full of the compliments."

"And look at your new hottie." Jamie eyed Sarah, propping her hands on her hips. "You've got a rotation of blonds lately, huh? Shouldn't shit where you eat." Jamie shook her head in not-so-mock disapproval. "You know better."

"This way," Sarah instructed me as if Jamie hadn't even spoken.

I wished she hadn't.

Any other day, Jamie's razzing wouldn't have fazed me. But it wasn't any other day. Along with all the crap with Daisy, heavy black drop cloths were scattered on the floor, and there were stepladders and other signs of work-in-progress all over the place.

"What happened here?"

Jamie shifted her gaze from mine. I recognized her evasive look all too well. "Someone broke in and messed some stuff up. Damaged the bowling lanes, screwed with the equipment, made a mess. Then there was the graffiti—"

"We should go," Sarah said.

"Wow, a bossy one. Isn't it a little soon in your relationship for that, sunshine?"

Sarah's eyes narrowed. "I'm his bodyguard."

Jamie's loud snort nearly caused the guy on the nearest ladder—who was painting the wall in quick, efficient strokes—to lose his footing. He scrambled to hold on while Jamie clapped a hand over her mouth. "Damn. That's pretty sweet. How come I don't get a hot one?"

The door opened. Noah strode in, and I stilled, already primed to see Daisy.

She stepped in behind him, with a giant canvas bag over one shoulder and her hair in some intricate updo, and my heart forgot to beat.

Our gazes clashed. The breath stalled out in my throat. I started to speak.

To fucking beg her to forgive me.

She looked through me as if I was a ghost before marching past us, her head held high.

No more than what I deserved.

"Ohhhh," Jamie said in a low voice. "Ouch. Not an amicable parting. TMZ said you were hot and heavy, but nothing lasts long with our bass boy."

Daisy came to a halt and turned back. "Mind your own business for a change, DuCaine."

I didn't laugh, mainly because I was too shocked. Sweet Daisy had enough backbone to tell off someone who wasn't me? Damn.

Jamie held up her hands. "Shutting up now."

As soon as Daisy was out of earshot, she whistled. "She could've sterilized you with her eyes. Hope you're wearing a cup."

My attention diverted to the door and the reporters outside it. Noah had herded Daisy past them, doing his job without creating more of a scene or causing blood loss.

Thinking of her first, not his own battered ego. Probably because Chuckles didn't *have* a battered ego. He seemed at peace with his lot in life.

As was I. Minus not having my family with me and being alone. By choice mostly, until Daisy had slammed back into my world and reminded me I didn't have to be.

That some memories didn't have to hurt. At least the better ones from the distant past.

The current ones? Hurt like a damn bitch.

"Look, I know you guys had a rough time this weekend." Jamie rubbed a hand over her jaw. "That guy who broke in, he hurt Daisy, didn't he?"

"He stabbed her."

"It would've been so much worse if you hadn't been there. If you hadn't pummeled the shit out of him." She lightly punched my shoulder. "Good job, slugger. Just save it for the bad guys and not the tabloids. Those dudes are cockroaches, but we aren't allowed to stomp on them."

"I didn't do enough. She shouldn't have been alone in the first place."

"Oh, because you're Batman, right? And psychic to boot? Must be a burden, having so many superhero qualifications."

I flexed my busted-up hand—twice busted in one weekend, although somehow I hadn't registered much from the first fight in my concern about Daisy. The flash of pain centered me as I looked away from Jamie, narrowing my eyes at the ghosted words still coming through the paint. The painter had already done a coat, but the graffiti had clearly been done with spray paint so the words weren't fully obliterated.

Slut.

Bitch.

Cunt.

"Kids, huh? Seem pretty fucking nasty. Sure something bigger isn't going on here?" I stared hard at Sarah. "We all have bodyguards now, but what about the crew? What about the ones who work with us? What if one of these so-called pranks gets someone seriously hurt? Like Daisy already was?"

"So, you really think that's part of this?"

"I think sometimes people are collateral damage." And I'd be damned if Daisy got hurt any more because of me.

Maybe staying away from her was the wisest thing I could do for more reasons than one. If members of my band were being targeted, the further away from me Daisy was, the better.

For a second, Jamie looked uncharacteristically worried. "Lila mentioned a band meeting, but she got called away for something. I'm assuming we'll have it later in the week."

"Right, so she can tell us more about nothing." I glanced at Sarah. "The people she hires are much the same. Even if Daisy could use the protection more than me. They didn't catch the supposed kids who did this?"

Both women remained silent.

"They also didn't nab the guy who broke into my place yet. If this is really some big conspiracy, shouldn't she be guarded?"

Sarah pursed her lips. From her expression, I had a feeling that had already been discussed. "Noah will keep an eye on her."

Lindsey clapped her hands, summoning us.

Jamie's gaze sharpened. "Yes, all the big, strong men must protect our Daisy."

The unusual show of jealousy from Jamie had me raising a brow as I picked up my guitar case. "I'm going to get ready for rehearsal. Tell Lindz I'll be back in five."

Sarah led the way to the dressing room.

"Seriously? Am I going to be allowed to take a piss alone?"

"Absolutely." She tapped a series of numbers on the door's keypad before opening the door. Then she stepped in first, making me roll my eyes.

She moved right to the dressing table. There was an assortment of girl crap spread over the surface, along with a few denim and leather items slung over the back of the sofa. A pair of huge boots I recognized as Cooper's stood beside it. We didn't often have to share dressing rooms nowadays due to the bigger venues on our arena tour, but this place was kitschy and different, the perfect space for an intimate fan club show.

Minus the fuckery from whomever wanted to screw with us.

Sarah picked up a folded piece of white paper from the dressing table and something fell out on the desk, a flash of brown and gold. There was a note with it. She read it quickly before pushing it in my direction, along with the item that had fallen out.

"Sorry, this is yours." She cleared her throat. "I'll check in with Noah and catch up with you soon."

She was gone before I could make a smart remark.

I set aside my guitar case and unfolded the paper first, my throat tightening at Daisy's looping handwriting.

Notes from years ago popped in my head.

We're going to the field party. Pick us up at 11? Ker says pretty please.

I'd kept that particular note. I hadn't known why, even back then. It was folded up at the bottom of my sock drawer, buried under socks that were best suited for the trash bin.

This note wasn't nearly as entreating.

Kerry gave me this the last night. I've had it all these years. You need it more now.

It wasn't strictly a goodbye, but I knew that it might as well have been. I couldn't fault her, since I hadn't given her the courtesy of even that.

The last night. Had there even been three more painful words?

I pulled out the chain from beneath the paper, the knot in my throat growing at the sight of the arrowhead edged in fake gold. I didn't know why Kerry had loved this necklace so much, but she'd found it one day when we were kids. Our mom had given her a metal detector for Christmas one year, and the three of us had gone out to Long Island to the beach. Kerry had searched for something cool for a while before she'd unearthed the arrowed necklace with its faux gold over sterling and inlaid turquoise stone. The stone was gone now, leaving just an empty casing.

She'd worn that necklace for years. Then, the turquoise had been intact. When had it fallen out? Before she'd given it to Daisy? After?

I closed my fingers around the arrowhead, picturing Kerry wearing it. Her bright smile, her expressive green eyes.

"Look, Ozzy, I found my own buried treasure."

I fumbled with the lobster clasp. I hooked it around my neck after a couple of tries, swallowing deeply as it settled over my chest. The arrowhead felt warm. Whether the sensation came from Daisy's hand or mine or just my imagination, it didn't matter. The heat against my skin brought so much rushing back, none of it pleasant.

My sister was gone. Forever. The me I'd been then was too.

All I could do now was regret.

I folded the note and tucked it in the small pocket on Vicki's guitar case. Then I sat down on the couch and opened the mini fridge, hoping like hell someone had stocked alcohol. I didn't care what. I just didn't want to think anymore.

A bottle came to hand and I popped the top, drinking it down in a long gulp.

The knock at the door made me growl.

"I'll be ready in a minute." As soon as the words were out, I jumped to my feet to throw open the door in case it was Daisy.

I might know I had to stay away from her, but my stupid reflexes did not.

The hall was empty.

I pressed my forehead against the doorjamb and gripped the necklace against my chest.

Help me, Ker. Help me get through this.

SIXTEEN

Lindsey

"I DON'T LIKE IT."

"Noted. Still gotta sing." I drank deeply from my box of water. Right now, I kinda wished it was a box of those individual white wines I'd been stashing in my overnight bag.

Between Nash and the team of security that was following me around like I'd suddenly become part of British royalty, I was ready to take up day drinking.

I finished off the water and reached into my bag. Handily, it wasn't daytime anymore. I didn't even have to feel guilty. I found the last of my stash and my glittery tumbler I'd bought in SoHo during one of my afternoon shopping trips with Jamie.

She had a purple one. I, of course, had a pink one. I never had anything stronger than wine in mine. I could not say the same for Jamie.

I popped the top and splashed half the box in.

Alex gave me a dark look. He was a little touchy about drinking—recovering alcoholic and all. But he never minded if I had a glass. Usually.

And today, I definitely needed it.

I set the tumbler down before taking a drink. "Look, I get it. Lila is making all of us a little on edge with the security, but I think she's mostly doing it as a preventative measure."

God, I hoped so. What had happened last fall with Kyle was still on my mind far too often. The current situation was not helping.

"I don't trust any of them. Donovan is dodging my calls."

I crossed the living room of my tour bus and shimmied my skirt up a little to sit astride my man. His hands went to my ass immediately and pulled me tighter to the perpetually ready shaft of his cock. The temptation to lose myself in some quick and dirty sex was overwhelming.

It might even chill him the hell out.

Me too—win, win.

I toyed with his shaggy hair. His inky hair was nearly to his shoulders and I couldn't say I was mad about it. His winter blue eyes were serious and direct. Strain lines bracketed his lush mouth.

He was intense in the best of circumstances, and I loved him more than I thought was possible. However, when he got like this I wanted to toss him onto his exceptional backside.

"You don't need to do meet and greets. You're beyond that."

"First of all, I'll never be beyond that. Our fans are why we have jobs in this fickle music environment. You, of all people, know time with the ones who support us is important."

His eyebrows furrowed and his jaw went as stony as his eyes.

"You know it's true."

"I don't fucking care. I'm not chancing you—ever. There is no discussion."

I climbed off of him, letting my knee apply enough pressure on his dick that he grunted. "You're not my keeper, Alex. I understand that you're worried, but we have it under control."

That sounded credible...*ish.*

"What, because you have a few tossers in black T-shirts and cargo pants clustered around you and the band?"

"You know the Roth people are way more than that. Noah and his team protect far more important people than us."

He stood. "No one is more important than you."

I rushed back over to him, pressing my hand to his chest. His heart was racing, and the telltale glint of his obsessive side was peeking out. It was warranted. We'd seen more trauma and drama than anyone should endure in the short time we'd been together.

His childhood friend had tried to lead us into his path of destruction. Nash had almost lost me. It had taken a good long while for either of us to be comfortable without hourly check-ins.

But dammit, we'd been doing so well. I was not going to let him spiral again. Work-life balance was new for both of us, but we were making it work.

"I'm not saying that." I cupped his scruffy jaw with both hands and smoothed my thumbs over his cheeks. "What I mean is that we're in good hands."

The little lines between his brows eased.

"Noah's team is as professional as it gets. He won't let anything happen to us—to me."

The last bit was to reassure me as much as it was for him. Watching the security guards flank us like we were the boys from One Direction was messing with all of us. The more isolation we endured, the more ramped up all of us were getting.

Jamie was dangerously close to getting locked in a storage locker by Noah between cities. She kept disappearing from her security detail only to show up five minutes before soundcheck with a flask and a smile.

Cooper, Teagan, and Zane were turning to workouts and yoga to keep sane. Master Zen—aka Zane—was responsible for the yoga. I'd even been joining them for their sessions. It helped calm my nerves, and my abs were phenomenal because of it.

Oz had been retreating with a notebook and his guitar instead of hanging out with the band during down times. He'd been on auto pilot the last few shows. We usually gave him space this time of year. Grief didn't always have a timetable, but his sister's anniversary was like a hard reset.

He usually went away to his cabin and came back a little more hollow, but a lot more himself. This year was not going the same way. He was being even more of a prick than usual, and as an added bonus, he'd decided to punch a photog and get his stupid ass arrested. Even Daisy had gotten caught up in Oz's undertow.

The paps had run with it, splashing our names all over the damn tabloid blogs. Dredging up the shit Nash and I had dealt with months ago. Oz's sister's overdose years ago.

Were Brooklyn Dawn cursed?

How many times did I have to read that in a notification?

How was I supposed to convince Nash we were safe when I didn't really believe it? The law of averages could not account for all the bullshit that had happened the last few days. Not with the vandalism at the fan club secret show venue and a break-in at Oz's off-the-grid cabin.

Lila was trying to keep all of us in line, but instead of easing our fears, she was locking us out, and I didn't like it.

I was exhausted, and Nash was picking up on it, damn him. I could only handle one volatile personality at a time, and my band had a couple of them. Between them and the love of my life, only one of them could be soothed with sex.

I went onto my toes so Nash and I were eye to eye. "I know you don't like it, but you believe in me and trust me, so trust my team."

"That's a big ask, duchess."

"Please."

His gaze dropped to my mouth then came back up to meet mine. "I'll be in the crowd."

My eyebrows shot up. "Really?"

"Backstage isn't close enough. Not when I'm tripping over your fucking crew. And I don't want to hear shit when I'm standing near you during the meet and greet."

I rolled my eyes. "At least the fans will get a show. They like when you growl."

"Then they'll be thrilled tonight."

"Goodie."

He gripped my ass and dragged me even closer. His kiss was a little wild and very hungry. Enough that I dragged at the tails of his black button-down shirt.

The discreet knock on my door was easy enough to ignore. Especially when Alex did that thing with his tongue. Jesus, he had some crazy key to my damn lock. Even when he wasn't between my thighs. Still worked damn well.

"Miss York?"

"Fuck off, mate."

I laughed into his mouth. "I have to go to work."

"In a minute." He dragged my skirt up enough that he could wedge his wicked fingers between my thighs.

"Alex," I moaned into his mouth. The sexual side of me that Nash had unearthed wanted to say to hell with schedules and professionalism. Unfortunately, my life had been ruled by my work ethic for too long. Our fans had given us their time, and tonight's show was particularly special.

The fan club had members in it since the beginning. Our roots in Brooklyn gave a little more meaning to everything. While I might be considered the little rich girl of the band, we all had a special bond with Brooklyn.

And playing here to the fan club was one of our favorite parts of touring. No matter how big the venues got, we found a way to have little intimate shows here where it all started.

I couldn't let them down—even for Alex's exceptional talent at giving me orgasms. But boy, could I use one.

I tore my mouth away and stepped back.

"Duchess." He caught the back of my neck and dragged me back to him.

"Later."

"Now." The word was guttural and flavored with Ireland.

"No, now I have to work."

"Why do you have to be so fucking professional?"

I laughed into his neck. "To make up for your rudeness."

He grunted and pulled my skirt down. "Later, you'll be screaming my name."

I swallowed. "Promise?"

"Good thing you don't have to sing tomorrow night, love." He teased his way up my hip to find my hand, lacing our fingers together.

"Cocky bastard."

He pulled me toward the door. "The bastard part is right."

I crowded behind him at the door to cup him. "And you do have an exceptional cock."

He glanced over his shoulder. "Keep it up and I'll lock this door and keep you busy until the meet and greet is over. I sure as fuck don't need to share you with five-hundred people."

I nipped his ear. "More like six."

"For fuck's sake." He opened the door and growled at the duo of black-garbed security personnel.

"Sorry, Pete." He was one of my usual guys.

His face didn't betray any emotion. I was fairly sure Noah trained them not to. "No problem, Miss York. Mrs. Crandall is looking for you."

"Great." I tried to pull my hand from Nash, but he held tighter.

"We'll go together."

"Awesome."

The Brooklyn Bowl was a smaller venue. It had always been one of my favorites when I'd still been a nobody soaking up every concert I could find with Jamie.

We cut through the alleyway and met up with Jamie and her disgruntled trio of guards. Noah wasn't messing around tonight. We didn't actually need three guards—things weren't that bad. At least I was pretty sure they weren't. But Jamie was very adept at losing her detail.

She spotted me and perked up. "Yo, bitch."

I shook my head. "Hey, Jame."

Jamie gave Nash a long, slow perusal. "Looking like a snack tonight, Al."

Nash stiffened. He still wasn't sure what to make of Jamie's confrontational sexuality. I knew she did it just to push his buttons—she enjoyed making everyone uncomfortable, but especially Alex as of late. Oh, and Noah. Couldn't forget that bit of insanity brewing.

Ever since the three of us had gone through our experience with Kyle and the rooftop, Jamie had been even more abrasive. Watching her go off that ledge had sliced me to the bone. That Alex had made the ultimate sacrifice to save me and mine lived in my nightmares to this day.

Nash cleared his throat and slid an arm around me. "Always a pleasure, Jamie."

She patted his chest none too lightly. "Liar." She lifted her arms and did a slow turn. "Like?"

Her bronze skin was on full display with the barely there sparkly handkerchief she called a shirt. It literally covered her breasts—and that was about it. It was backless save for a string that kept her small breasts from swinging free. Jamie was all sinewy muscle and interesting tattoos. They were scattered over her back and arms, made up of symbols and lyrics with a few music notes. From the waist down, she was completely covered in skintight black leather and motorcycle boots.

"Aren't you chilly?"

"Nah. You know me, always hot." She snapped her teeth at her security guy. The fourth new one this month. They kept begging to be reassigned. This one just stared straight ahead without flinching. I wondered how long he would last.

She hooked her arm through mine and dragged me down the alley toward the venue. "Let's surprise the people in line. I love watching them lose their shit."

"Lila is looking for us."

"Don't be lame. It'll just take a minute."

I sighed and waved at Nash, who simply shook his head.

As we came around the corner, a hoard of fans were lined up.

Velvet ropes were still a staple along the brick building, and everyone was in an orderly line.

Well, they had been.

"Hey guys!"

Jamie, who usually went out of her way to avoid fans, was wading in like she was trying out for a reality show. Jesus. She dragged me with her, and we were lost in a sea of people. Arms, books, playbills for the show tonight, scraps of paper, CDs—all of them were shoved in our face.

The security ran after us and tried to wade in after us.

Jamie just dug in deeper, dragging me into the middle of the line.

Laughter, screams, crying—the noise was deafening. The excitement, a reminder of the first days when we'd exploded on the scene, emboldened me as well. To actually enjoy the fans again, to steep myself in their fever activated the Lindsey I'd been a few years ago.

When the fans weren't scary.

When I actually could connect with people.

I didn't know how much I needed it until just now.

Jamie was leaning back into a cluster of girls, taking selfies. Her flask was out and being passed around to people.

I might've been cool with a bit of jostling and people loving on me, but I wasn't swapping spit with anyone except Alex.

"All right, back it up." Noah's deep, no nonsense voice cut through the din. "You've had your fun."

A chorus of whines and shouts for one more minute rose from the crowd.

"Back off, Mr. Boring. We're having fun." Jamie held out her long arm to take a few more selfies. Passing phones all around to those who kept shoving them at her.

Noah shoulder-blocked a few women and gently shuffled a half dozen more aside to get to us.

I looked around, suddenly aware of just how many people were surrounding us. The fizz of excitement abated. The small group was now a few hundred deep. Alex's voice was gruff and impatient along the fringes.

"Duchess."

I braced myself against the jostling. More people pressed in to get to us, and I got an elbow to the ribs for my trouble.

Two of the security guys pushed through and flanked us, and then an arm slid securely around my waist. I stilled, my muscles seizing tight.

"Duchess, relax. I've got you."

I sagged against Nash and turned into his arms. His hand came up to cup the back of my head as he hauled me out of there.

"Put me down." Jamie's husky voice boomed.

I glanced toward her and found her slung over Noah's shoulder. Her shirt—lack of shirt—was twisted around her neck.

"If you wanted to get me naked, all you had to do was ask."

The crowd laughed, and flashes went off.

Jamie lifted her head, her waterfall of near black hair tipped in ultraviolet falling forward around her face. She lifted her arm and flashed devil rocker horns. "We'll see you in an hour."

The security detail had tripled, and now they were playing sentry to make an aisle to get us out of the crowd.

"Thanks, everyone. We're looking forward to the show." I waved, adding a smile so people would know we didn't want to leave. Even though that was very much a falsehood. I was more than done.

"Ever the frontwoman," Alex muttered in my ear. "What the fuck were you thinking?"

I didn't answer him. Obviously, I hadn't been thinking, but the quick high of the fan adoration had melted damn fast. It had been awhile since Jamie had led me into temptation. And I was going to pay for it.

Great.

We made it inside the side door of the venue where security was far tighter. Nash's hand was securely clamped around mine as we were herded inside.

"You can put me down now, Master Sergeant."

"You're fucking naked." Noah's voice was flat and cold.

"So? Who hasn't seen a pair of tits? It's no big."

If I wasn't being manhandled by my own man, I'd have facepalmed. "Jamie, shut up."

She wiggled against Noah. "Or maybe you're enjoying my tits."

Noah just kept walking.

"They're spectacular tits." She kept wiggling to get free.

"Jamie," I snapped.

"What? Pretty sure you've seen them."

The line of fans hadn't been allowed into the main level yet. There were a few VIP fans clustered around the stage where Cooper and Zane were answering questions.

The Brooklyn Bowl wasn't a large venue. The stage was intimate and shallow, leaving barely enough room for Cooper's abbreviated kit. A trio of stools were set on the side for our acoustic set. Teagan's dual keyboards were set up on a dais on the right side of the stage. Amps lined the edges like wings with colorful plumage in the form of guitars.

Our techs and stage crew were running around, and microphones were being tested.

The crash of pins on the side of the room caught my attention. Oz was standing in between two lanes with a bowling ball in each hand. One was a strike, one was very much a gutter ball.

"Balls." He lifted a bottle sitting beside his boot.

I really wished it was beer.

He took a swig from the bottle of Jack and sauntered over to us. "'Bout time you two showed up."

Noah stopped in front of one of half a dozen leather couches lined up just outside the bowling alley half of the room. He dropped Jamie onto the sofa. "Cover the fuck up."

She swung her long leg over the arm of the couch and grinned up at him, her breasts on display. "Everyone here has seen them."

"Some of us prefer to remain professional." Noah's tone was clipped.

She glanced down at his black jeans. "Sure about that?"

"Miss DuCaine, please find some decorum. I'm aware it's not your natural state, but we have guests in the establishment." Lila's heels snapped as she walked across the hardwood floor. She was dressed in a petal pink suit and had her ever-present iPad tucked in the crook of her arm. "We'll be discussing this later. Right now, we have a show to get ready for."

My gut unclenched. I really didn't mind passing the buck on getting yelled at right now.

Jamie rolled down her shirt and tucked her breasts under the slinky material, her smug smile still in place as she kept eye contact with Noah.

Good grief, that probably wasn't wise. Jamie lived to push buttons, and Noah was a prime target. I'd never seen him ruffled in the few years I'd known him. The Ripper Records family was like one big twisty tree. We'd worked with Hammered before—and their lead singer was Noah's little brother.

Oz gave Jamie a little side-eye, but he sprawled on the couch beside her before sharing his bottle.

She accepted and took a good belt before finally settling her gaze on me. My unamused face must have finally dented her bubble of narcissism.

"If you're all finished?" Lila's no-nonsense tone kept the rest of us in line. As always. "Zane and Cooper stepped up to speak with the fans." She shot a derisive look at Oz.

He was on the schedule to do the same, but since he'd gotten back from the trip to his cabin, he'd been even more growly.

Oz simply shrugged and took a longer pull from his bottle. It was already half empty and we hadn't even started the show. Wonderful.

I marched over and took the bottle from him.

"Hey."

I took my own sip because...well, because I could use a little fire. As far as swapping spit went, my band didn't count.

His eyebrow shot up, and he crossed his arms over his ripped to shit shirt. "Since when did our resident princess drink anything other than white wine?"

"Fuck off, Oz. Get that burr lodged up your ass out before we start the show. Let's not have a repeat of the last show, shall we?" When his jaw clenched, I had to tamp down the urge to soothe. It wasn't what he needed right now. He needed to get his head in the game. And if that meant I had to be the bitch—well, it wasn't the first time I'd worn those pair of shoes.

"Look, I know things have been crazy. We all have been on edge with the security," I paused to look at Noah and Lila, "and our lack of answers as to why things are changing with alarming irregularity. So, it falls on all of us to keep our shit together on stage at the very least. The fans don't deserve anything less than us at our best. In fact, we need to make sure it's better than our best. They are already wondering what's going on. We don't want anyone else talking about Brooklyn Dawn's stupid curse."

I handed the bottle to Noah, who tucked it into his crossed arms. His pose mirrored Oz's belligerent stance. Just wonderful. All the men around me were varying levels of posturing jackasses these days.

I could feel Nash behind me, and he probably had the same damn crossed-arm action going on.

Jamie threw her arm over the back of the couch. "Is that a directive, Lindz?"

I resisted the urge to sigh. I knew Jamie had been out of sorts for months. I'd hoped that she would settle down after some distance from the rooftop night, but she seemed to only be more sarcastic—actually bordering on rude. She was pushing everyone away.

And I needed to get that shit under control. Regardless of her best friend status, I was also the leader of this band. They looked to me to keep my head clear, and I'd been falling down on the job too. That was going to change tonight.

"If I was in that line outside, that's what I'd expect from us—a top of the line, incredibly kickass show. Especially since these are our super fans. The ones who care enough to join our fan club and have traveled to see us here in Brooklyn. They deserve it, regardless of how pissy you want to be." I glanced at Oz. He had the good graces to actually look away.

"So, let's play like we used to in the clubs. You want to throw an audible tonight—throw it. There's no rules."

Jamie sat up straighter. "Really?"

"No light show we have to follow, no setlist that needs to be programmed ahead of time. Tonight's just us. Cover songs, old songs—I don't care. I'm game."

Instantly, I knew I'd hit on the right way to play this. The excitement I'd been trying to find curled in my gut.

Zane, Cooper, and Teagan walked over to us. "Are we having a band meeting?" Zane flipped a bamboo pick through his fingers.

Jamie stood up. "Nope, this is actually something I care about."

Lila said nothing. She seemed more consumed with whatever she was typing on her iPad.

Teagan smothered a grin. "So, what's going on?"

"Queen Bee gave us carte blanche on the setlist tonight."

I cocked my hip. "Fuck off, Jame."

She crossed to me and threw an arm around my shoulders. "Come on, you love playing queen to all the honeybees. You know it." She blew a kiss over my shoulder. "Besides, it makes Snack get all unruly. Then you get a doubly good fuck. Win win for all of us, right?"

Cooper barked out a laugh. "Well, that means we're definitely doing some 'Dear Agony' if I've got a vote."

"Sounds like a plan to me." Oz stood. "I'm singing duet."

Everyone went silent.

My mouth dropped open. "What?"

He shook his hair back. "I'm feeling a little wild tonight."

Oz hadn't sung with me in ages. He used to do it all the time when we did the club tours, but it had been damn rare for the last few years.

My grin spread. "Tonight is going to be amazing."

"Damn right." Jamie flashed a grin. "You know I'm going to have to have some Pat or Joan."

"As if that was a question."

"Just checking." She gave a war whoop and ran over to the little cluster of fans who were waiting. "Who wants a picture?"

I finally relaxed, some of the tension in my shoulders loosening. It was going to be an interesting night.

SEVENTEEN

ALL I HAD TO DO WAS TO GET THROUGH TONIGHT. THE STAGE WAS
my favorite place in the world to be, even if nothing seemed the same
after the days I'd spent with—

I shoved it down. There was only this right now.

My skin was dripping with sweat. I'd lost my shirt around the third
song. The Brooklyn Bowl was an interesting venue, one we hadn't
played even when we were younger. The acoustics were surprisingly
good, and the bowling alleys along the side made for a crazy crash of
sound to compete with.

Everything was a throwback to a simpler time.

Even the costumes we generally relied on had been stripped away.
Jamie had changed out of her scrap of glitter into a concert T-shirt she'd
attacked with a pair of scissors. It was still little more than a bra by the
time she was done with it, but at least I didn't have to worry about
leaning on her and flashing the crowd.

As the last notes for "Judgement" faded out into the screams from
the crowd, Jamie suddenly spotted something. She twisted her Warlock
around her back and climbed on one of the amps along the side of the
stage. "Excuse me. Yo!"

The crowd went quiet. Mostly. The crash of a bowling ball and pins colliding made her crane her neck toward the lanes. "Hey! You too!"

The guy in the last lane turned around and held up his arms. "Strike!"

"Awesome! Now shut the fuck up!"

"Come over here and make me," the dude shot back.

Jamie climbed up one more level of speakers and swung out as far as she could with one arm. "We shall work on your fucking manners—after we play a song." She focused on a girl in the middle of the pack of fans. "You. Is that a goddamn Madonna shirt on you?"

A blond woman—who looked far too much like Daisy for my peace of mind—screeched. She jumped up and down, doing a damn good simulation of a breakdown.

"Is that a yes?"

The girl shrieked back in the affirmative.

"Fuck, yeah." Jamie sat down cross-legged on the speaker before settling her guitar back around in front of her.

She started and stopped a few times, but finally found the notes for "Like a Virgin." It was a rockier version—more like the Mötley Crüe cover than the original pop song.

Memories battered me. Daisy breaking under me. Daisy kneeling before me with those innocent eyes.

A virgin I'd defiled.

I didn't realize my bass line had become so overpowering. That I'd instinctively followed Jamie as I did most nights. She and Cooper were my usual compass. I was the beat—the heartbeat of a song most of the time.

It was more of a pulse now. It matched the throb of my sore knuckles, reminding me of all the chaos and mayhem I'd experienced along with the sweet heaven of Daisy's body. It was all churned up inside of me. My music, the memory of her heart beating so fast against mine. The way she vised around me. Innocence and innate sexuality. She matched my depraved side in every way.

I stalked back to the drums and found my bottle. I couldn't think about that night—nights. They twisted and twined around my sternum, strangling me.

Somehow I had to get out of my head.

I brought the bottle to the edge of the stage and sat down with my bass. A crush of fans moved forward, so I offered up my bottle with a laugh and watched people pass it around until it finally came back to me.

Lindsey's powerhouse vocals were sweet, tinged with sandpaper rockstar.

Zane climbed the stairs adjacent to the stage until he matched Jamie in height. They were for the lighting people and rickety as fuck. I was fairly sure Lila was backstage having an apoplexy beside Chuckles. He was probably sending one of his minions to hover under Zane to catch him, just in case. I snickered, picturing Zane splatting some poor idiot into the hardwood.

I stood up, slapped a few hands before I made my way behind Cooper and swung my bass around behind me. I stole his backup sticks and fucked with his cymbals. Being on tour with the same people for a major part of my life left lots of room for nights of learning multiple instruments.

I could drum in a pinch.

However, touching Coop's rig was asking for retribution, but my restless mood was begging for trouble. I grabbed the extra mic set up for him. He rarely used it, but when the band was bantering back and forth between songs, he usually came up with a good one-liner.

"Hey. Stop fucking with my shit."

"Bored. I'm heading into the crowd."

"Oh, shit," Coop muttered, bouncing one of his sticks high into the air.

I caught it and tossed it into the crowd.

"Fucker."

I handed him the pair I'd stolen.

I *was* a fucker. No point in denying it. And if I didn't get this mood under control, I was going to do something stupid.

More stupid than you've already done? Doubtful.

I jumped down into the small space between the bowling lanes and the stage.

"Where the hell are you going?"

I ignored Zane's question and threw one long leg over the barricade. The audience grew rowdier, extending the song as Lindsey encouraged the crowd to sing with her. I moved through the crush of bodies that suddenly gathered around me. I was aware I was asking for trouble, but I just didn't care.

I had one goal—to smash some pins.

I headed for the guy who had been bitching at Jamie and lifted his ball as it came out of the return carriage. "Can I?"

"Holy shit." The guy stumbled back.

I handed him the mic. "Be right back."

I could hear him singing to "Like a Virgin" in an off-key, pitchy voice.

I'd pay for that too, but the pins were my focus. The new paint gleamed along the back of the lanes. The vandals had scrawled their rude comments in a garish red here. I could still kind of see it. My misspent youth spent tagging the metal reinforcements of the Brooklyn Bridge back in the day gave me a little knowledge. You couldn't hide spray paint with just anything, and in their rush to get the place ready for our show, they hadn't done enough layers of primer. I'd hoped earlier that they would slap on enough layers to make the words disappear, but there hadn't been time for that either.

I didn't want to read any more of what the so-called kids had written, but it was impossible not to.

Typical crap like *Brooklyn Dawn sucks* was reinforced with slurs about Jamie and Lindsey. Even an inventive one including Teagan in a disgusting trio of threats against them. As if the girls were just meat.

The crash of pins helped with the rage burning inside my head.

I moved to the next lane and threw another ball, then another when

I missed. I didn't even wait for the guard to lift before I sent another ball down the lane.

Fuck, I was so sick of this shit. Sick of the secrecy and the drama and all of it.

Sick of worrying about Daisy. I'd only been fully back on the job for a few days, but it seemed like I couldn't quit.

Old habits died hard. There had been a time when watching out for her and my sister had been like breathing.

Now it felt like futility. There were too many potential threats, and I couldn't be everywhere. Noah certainly couldn't.

I frowned. Maybe I knew someone who could help. I'd run it by Lila, make sure he was up to her very high snuff.

I had to do something with all this frustration inside me. Calling Sean qualified.

As long as she was safe. That was all that mattered.

I stalked back to retrieve the mic from the guy who was screeching like a dying cat, and then I crashed through the mob of people who had moved to the lanes. I climbed onto the couch and leaped over the back to bob and weave around the fans. My long stride gave me the advantage in getting to the barricade quickly.

Lindsey was trying to bring the crowd back to her. She'd even lowered the shields on her rocker Barbie self and shouted for the girl with the T-shirt inspiration to come forward so they could swap shirts. Both women wore skintight tanks under their tops.

I was pretty sure most of the dudes in the room were hoping for a pair of tits to ogle.

Once upon a time, I'd have been the same. Now I could only picture the the perfect pink-tipped mouthful of a certain woman.

I waded into the crush of fans in the center of the general admission pit. Bodies slammed into me, nails scraped down my arms, along my belly. Leaving marks.

Would Daisy care?

Would she notice?

She'd stared right through me just hours ago. And still, every time I closed my eyes, she was there waiting for me in the night. I felt her under me as I used her body like a vessel to pour my rage into. She didn't deserve me. Didn't deserve what I'd done to her.

And I'd loved every moment.

Craved more of it. Her silky skin, her voice screaming my name, her shattered eyes.

The worst part was that I was pretty damn sure she'd loved it too. She was meant for me.

Except she *wasn't*. She couldn't be.

The rage started building again. I was so tired of fighting, myself most of all.

I spotted Jamie monkeying her way down the stacked speakers and amps to the stage once more. I made my way over to her and turned to give her my shoulders. I shoved the microphone into my jeans pocket and got as close to the stage as I could. Music had always saved me. And it would again. It had to, or I'd slide back down into the cesspool of my thoughts.

Jamie grinned and handed her guitar to Lindz, and then hooked a leg over my shoulder. I braced for her surprisingly solid body. She might be whip lean, but Jamie was tall.

When the fans swarmed around us, I clutched her by the thighs to steady her. She rode my shoulders as I slogged my way through the shocked audience. Lindsey crooned a little impromptu "Papa Don't Preach" to keep with the Madonna theme.

"Couch?" I asked.

"Hell, yeah."

I grabbed my bottle on its way by. There was little more than a swig left, but it was enough to clear out the war wounds and echoes of Daisy's voice.

People parted for us, as if they knew we needed the space.

Jamie jammed her long, bony fingers into my shoulder and vaulted herself up and off me onto the leather. A guy caught her as she wobbled back since the cushions were not made for that kind of bouncing. He curled his arms around her to help straighten her out. The dude's hand slid over her taut middle. Jamie grinned back at him. "Careful."

The dude immediately unhanded her.

She sat down cross-legged on the sofa. "I wasn't complaining, but I gotta make sure you're cute before you get to cop a feel." She gave him a feral smile. "You'll do." She jerked him down by the T-shirt and planted a hot kiss on him before pushing him aside. "Now I gotta work."

The bark of a low, rumbling voice behind me demanding people move out of the way made me look over my shoulder. "Just in time, Chuckles."

Jamie peered around me, her eyes narrowing as she spotted Noah. "Great. He always ruins the fun."

I sat down next to Jamie and pulled the microphone from my jeans pocket. "Mind if we do a little 'Dear Agony' from over here?" I glanced at Jamie. "Duet."

"Shit. We haven't done that in years."

I flexed my sore hand before curling my fingers around the microphone. "Scared?"

She gathered her hair over her shoulder. "Fuck no."

"This is not a secure area." Noah's voice was firm and loud over the boos of the crowd.

"We're just hanging with our friends, right?" Jamie leaned back against the guy she'd kissed. He was more muscle than brains, and I was pretty sure he had a death wish.

Noah crossed his arms and nodded toward three other members of his security force to make a semi-circle perimeter around us.

I twisted enough to see the stage. Lindsey had pulled out her acoustic. "Mind if we give you a break, Lindz?"

She settled on the stool we'd be using for the acoustic set. "Go for it."

Evidently, we'd be starting the session early. Phones were up and recording while nerves jumped in my belly. It had been a damn long time since I'd sung. I was much happier with the bass and the occasional backup vocal. But the song suited my mood.

The lyrics were a little too close, but I leaned into the acoustic notes Lindsey offered as Zane's manipulated electric guitar gave the song an extra layer of epic to match my darker, lower register.

Jamie's voice wasn't as pure as Lindsey's. It was more Joan Jett with a rich, silk overlay that set the people around us back a step. A hush fell over the crowd as the acoustic version of the song built, and we sang into the microphone together until we were forehead to forehead.

When the last notes of Lindsey's acoustic guitar floated out into the surprisingly quiet room, I finally opened my eyes.

Jamie slapped my chest, her face split with a wild smile. "Fuck. That was amazing."

I laughed, a little lighter now that some of the pain had been released into the song. It wasn't nearly as effective as Daisy's sweetness, but I finally believed I could make it through the rest of the show without ending up as a passed-out drunk.

Jamie popped up from the couch and stole the microphone. She slipped through the thirty or so people that had managed to snake around the security guards and stared right at Noah as she did a trust fall into the screaming fans.

They lifted her high, handing her over the crowd to surf through the general admission pit. She sang "I Love Rock and Roll" as she drifted toward the stage.

Noah growled and barked orders to his staff to keep people back and get some order.

I took a few selfies with fans before I made my way to the barrier to get back onto the stage.

Jamie had the crowd screaming along with her by the time she managed to get handed back up to Lindsey and Teagan's waiting grab.

Jamie ran to her tech to get her Warlock back. The claps and laughter from the crowd made the sing-along even longer.

Cooper's drums thundered.

Zane and Jamie dueled the guitar outro as Teagan and Lindsey clapped in time.

Finally, I reached them and accepted Vicki from Fred, my longtime tech. My beloved bass felt right in my hands, achy or not, and my bass line became the backbone and reminded me where I was supposed to be.

This was my home. My family. They always had my back.

The rest of the show went by in a jumble of jukebox favorites, deep cuts that only true fans would love, and ended with a "Black Magic" mashup into Post Malone's "Hollywood Bleeding" that we'd all been loving on through the tour.

Remembering where we came from—the little places we'd bled in to find our sound all those years ago—was always humbling. And when we finally finished the nearly three hour set with "Ruin", our biggest hit to date, we finally called it a night.

I didn't want to go.

I knew the minute I walked off the stage, I'd have to face the loneliness again.

Music was my savior, but eventually, the last note always faded away.

EIGHTEEN

"I NEED YOU TONIGHT."

"No, you need to not go. I'll come home and we'll watch *Steel Magnolias* and *Easy A* and cry until we laugh."

I stared at myself in the mirror on the back of the bathroom door in Ever's apartment. I didn't have a ton of body issues—and thank God for that, because I had a baker's dozen of other ones—but I was starting to sweat because of this outfit.

I turned sideways and smoothed a hand over my jumping stomach. I wasn't naked, but a lot of my legs were showing. The short velvet dress was backless, plunged low in front, and was short—did I mention short? The royal blue color brought out my eyes and was super soft to the touch.

Not that I wanted anyone to touch me tonight.

Liar. It's been a week and you're horny as fuck already.

That was neither here nor there. Besides, a night out with the girls didn't mean that I was looking for a hookup. I couldn't even imagine being with someone who wasn't Oz. Plus, there was that whole little problem of not getting nearly as turned on when I was with anyone else.

He'd broken me in too many ways to count.

Sighing, I glanced at my shoes. I'd finished off the outfit with chunky heels. I loved stilettos in theory, but since I usually wore sneakers for work most of the time, walking in them was a challenge. These were hard enough. They made my legs look longer though.

I tugged on one of the curls tumbling down from my updo. Ugh, I just wanted to put on my pajamas and hide in bed as I'd done for most of the last week. If it hadn't been for Teagan basically begging me to hit the club with them tonight before we headed to the next stop on the tour—someplace in Pennsylvania next week, before returning to MSG several days after that—I wouldn't have needed to plead with my heartless sister.

Who wasn't replying to me yet I could still hear her breathing, so I knew she was still on the line.

"Look, I'll do whatever you want. Clean your room—"

"You mean our room, since you're the sloppy one who gets shit everywhere?"

I couldn't argue that point. "Yes."

"Not good enough. Keep going."

"I'm your sister."

"You sure? I'm almost certain you're adopted. My sister wouldn't be so soft-hearted toward such an emotionally unavailable male."

"Who said I was?" I picked at my freshly done wine-colored nails then waved my hand to stop myself.

"The woe kitten I've lived with this whole week. I told you nothing good would come of you throwing yourself at him. If it was meant to be, he wouldn't have ignored you for six months."

Part of me wanted to say, *guess what, we fucked, and it was amazing.* Which I might have done had he not bailed on me while my thighs were still quaking.

She wouldn't be impressed on several levels. Definitely not about my recent lost virginity. I could hear her groan now.

Seriously, Daze? You waited for that jerk all these years?

I hadn't waited for him. That would've been ridiculous, considering the only place I'd seen him for years was on the pages of magazines or on websites.

That I bookmarked religiously in my browser.

It wasn't my fault I couldn't seem to stay in the zone when I got naked with other men—or even partially naked. The fact that just looking at Oz's picture gave me all kinds of dirty thoughts probably proved she wasn't entirely wrong. But the guy was hot.

And I hadn't thrown myself at him. Exactly. Actually, I'd nearly thrown myself *out* of his truck before he made me come.

I rubbed my face. How could the single best weekend of my life have so many awful moments mixed in with the incredible ones? The ultimate rollercoaster, that was what it would be like to be with Oz. The highest peaks and the most heartbreaking lows.

No wonder I'd decided I was staying off that ride. He'd nudged me out the door—okay, walked out it himself—but I hadn't tried to make him change his mind. I'd lived through enough train wrecks to get off the tracks.

All week, I'd had to dodge paparazzi, despite Noah hanging around more than made sense. I wasn't part of the band, and I didn't entirely grasp the threat against them anyway. Surely Noah had more important things to do than to randomly show up when I went to lunch near Ever's apartment before heading to work. Or jumping into my Uber when I traveled across town to visit my old salon and chat with some of my former coworkers.

Every time, he made it seem as if we were just "catching up", but I hadn't caught up with him that much since...ever. Like the whole of my life since he'd been in it.

Something weird was going on at Ripper Records, and the random stuff like the graffiti and maybe even the would-be robber at Oz's cabin seemed not random at all.

But *why* was the question no one was willing to answer—at least in front of me. I doubted Oz had gotten to the bottom of it yet either.

So, I supposed it was just as well Oz and I didn't get more involved. I had enough anxiety issues. How freaked out I'd been over the tabloid guy possibly following us had been bad enough, especially on the heels of getting freaking stabbed.

A shallow mark that was healing quite nicely without stitches, but still.

The tabloid types still shouted questions at me I didn't know how to answer. But Noah always seemed to be there at the right moment to herd me through the maze.

I wasn't built for dealing with that side of the business, and that wasn't even saying anything about the public in general. I didn't know how Oz handled it. He just signed whatever was shoved his way and strolled through the crush of fans as if it was normal to have complete strangers fall in love with you.

And when it came to that tabloid dude, seem to hate you on sight.

"Daze? You okay? You're not talking." Ever sighed. "All right, what I said was bitchy. Most of what I say about Oz is, but I don't want him to screw you up. And if a guy was ever designed to screw up a woman, it's Ozzy Taylor. Especially since you have a past."

The emphasis she put on the last word made me laugh. "We do, but that's exactly what it is. The stuff with Kerry happened a long time ago."

So long that sometimes I didn't realize it. Another reason I was forcing myself to go out tonight. I didn't want to have fun, especially when my heart felt as if it had been skewered. But I wanted some girlfriends. I *needed* them. If I said no to every invitation, I'd never have any. Teagan was nice, and so was Lindsey. Jamie was too, most of the time. Hopefully, she wouldn't hold a grudge about me telling her off before the fan club show.

Well, sort of. No one truly told Jamie off and lived to tell the tale unless she was in a benevolent mood.

The whole band was awesome, truthfully. One particular member excluded. Sure, they were the talent, and I was just the hair and makeup chick, but they didn't make that into a thing.

So, I wouldn't either.

At least I'd try not to. Right now, it felt as if everything was an issue. Especially the anxiety bubbling in my belly.

Even pulling my jacket hood over my head every time I stepped outside caused my heartbeat to quicken. Because someone—or a few someones—would be out there waiting to shout questions about Kerry and Oz that wounded me as much as a physical attack.

You two haven't been cozy all week. Is it already finished?

Are you still a user like your poor tragic friend?

Does Ozzy beat you like he beat that journalist?

Journalist, ha. There was a joke.

Ever sighed again. "You sure about that? You don't seem like you've let it all go. Then everything with Oz last weekend. Between his hotheaded bullshit and getting you stabbed—"

"He didn't *get* me stabbed. He intervened and saved me from getting more seriously hurt."

"If you say so."

"And considering I held Kerry's body as she was dying, I'd say I'm well aware of how long it's been," I snapped.

"Sorry." Ever let out a long breath. "I'm sorry I made you remember all that, sis."

I shut my eyes. No one seemed to get that being reminded of Kerry didn't make her any more real to me. She was with me every moment of every day. Sometimes she felt a little more present, the memories a bit closer, but some part of her always existed in my consciousness.

"No, *I'm* sorry. I know you keep getting confused and trying to big sister me, but guess what, Sara Lee, you'll never be the older and wiser one."

Ever groaned. "Not Sara Lee. I haven't heard that nickname in forever."

"Obviously, I was overdue."

She let out a laugh. "Fine, I'll come. I'll be off work in an hour. I have to cover for Mabel's yoga-genics class."

I had no idea what yoga-genics was, but if anyone would know, it was my exercise freak sister. My idea of working out was...

I pressed my thighs together. Yeah, I wasn't going there.

"Okay. Club Kulture. It's just us girls, and we have the VIP section tonight. Second level. Way in back. Give the bouncer Lindsey's name and the code Irish."

"Irish? Why?"

"Her dude's from Ireland. Guessing that's why."

"But it's only ladies' night? You sure about that?"

The first tendrils of unease curled inside me. "Teagan promised me. I'll see you in a bit."

Unshockingly, there were a couple of tabloid types lurking near the entrance to my sister's building when I emerged a bit later. I turned quickly and started walking north, trying my best to ignore the shouted questions and popping flashbulbs.

No big deal. You'll be out of the glare soon. They'll realize you and Oz are over and back to obscurity you'll go.

I glanced back as I ducked into an Uber. A tall guy in a black trench coat stood a few feet away, his gaze fixated on me.

When he started to speak, I shut the door.

I let out a sigh of relief as the driver swerved into traffic. And grabbed the bottle of hand sanitizer tucked in my minuscule purse, as if somehow I could obliterate the existence of the paparazzi by rubbing my hands raw.

Under an hour later, I found myself crammed in a huge circular booth with Teagan, Jamie, Lindsey, and Elle Crandall and her hulking husband, Mal Shawcross. That wasn't all. Our table also included Alexander Nash, Lindsey's man, and some himbo Jamie had picked up on her way in—her word, not mine. She was sitting on the guy's lap, and Lindsey was wrapped around Nash, and Elle and Mal were five seconds away from indecency as always.

I was growing more uncomfortable by the minute.

"You lied to me," I muttered to Teagan.

"Lie is a strong word. Besides, I didn't know the whole band was coming, I swear."

I clutched my blue lagoon drink, complete with little floating gummy fish. I'd wanted to have a drink like a regular twenty-something. Not to get hammered, just to be social. "Whole band?" I choked out. "Which band? Warning Sign? *That* band?"

Teagan looked at me as if I was slightly daffy. "My band. You know, Brooklyn Dawn?" She leaned forward to sniff my drink. "How much alcohol is in there anyway?"

"Not enough." I gulped half of it down and winced as the sweet liquor went straight to my head. I'd vowed to nurse one or two drinks all night, but if Oz was about to appear, I needed to pregame.

Once a user always a user, right? The only thing that changes is the drug of choice.

No. That wasn't the truth. I'd had maybe a handful of drinks over the past couple of years. I hadn't touched any sort of drug in even longer. Oz or no Oz, I could handle myself just fine.

Deliberately, I set the glass down. "So, the *whole* band?"

Teagan was still staring at me strangely. "I think so. Oh, crap, this is about Oz, isn't it? Men suck so hard."

"It's nothing. What about you? Are you seeing anyone?"

Teagan played with her cocktail napkin. "Well, no, but I was kind of hoping something would happen with Noah, since he's always hanging around lately. But he's all about you."

Jamie picked up her tall purple drink and plucked off the wedge of orange. She sucked half her drink down before tipping her head back to smile at her new male friend. "I could use another. Mind?"

"We're in VIP, babe. They'll handle it."

"I'm thirsty now. Please?"

"I was comfortable here, but I guess." He frowned and diverted his hand from where it had been happily placed two inches from the swell of her breast. She had on a revealing corset top with a cropped black leather jacket and huge hoop earrings. Total rockstar look.

"Awesome. Thanks!" She beamed at him and slid off his lap into the free space between us. "Hiya, Daisy."

"Hi." I took a breath. Even though I'd done her hair and makeup for the fan club show, we hadn't really spoken much since I'd told her off about Oz. The dressing rooms were pure chaos before a concert, and any conversations were usually drowned out by laughter and music and general revelry. "Um, about earlier this week—"

Jamie waved a hand, waiting to speak until her male companion slid out of the booth and ambled away, looking peevish. "Old news. What's this about you and Noah?"

"Not you too." I shook my head. "You do realize we're related, right? I mean, super distantly through marriage, but there's some sort of familial thing there."

Actually, I was surprised I hadn't seen Noah yet tonight. It was rare for me to make it out of my building lately without him swooping down as if he had a tracking device on me.

He *didn't* have a tracking device on me, did he? I wasn't sure I'd put it past him.

"Does Oz know that?" Jamie rested her chin on her palm. "Maybe you're trying to make him jealous."

I snorted. "Why would I bother? I saw the pictures of him and that blond. Then they were together at the fan club show." I'd tried very hard to ignore the photos, but it seemed as if news about Oz was everywhere lately. The worst part was she looked an awful lot like me, even if she dressed in a more utilitarian fashion.

The few pictures I'd seen hadn't been salacious. Not even close. Most of the time, they were getting in and out of vehicles. But the fact remained she was a female, and I'd never seen her around before this past week.

Maybe I'd broken his streak of not needing to have condoms strewn all over. After all, he'd purchased that industrial-sized box and only used one with me.

I grabbed my drink and took another long swallow. The kick of sugary sweetness from the coconut rum only slightly killed the ache in my chest.

It was Jamie's turn to snort. "You mean his bodyguard? That's Sarah. She's on Noah's team at Roth."

"Oh." I set down my glass. "Hey, want to see some naked pictures of him?"

Elle leaned across the table, her eyes wide. I didn't know her that well, but she'd always been really nice to me. "Naked pictures of who? And the answer is yes. Always yes."

"Hey there." Her husband Mal slung his hugely muscled, tattooed arm around her shoulders and hauled her back against his side. "You see enough nudity for five women."

"Yes, and I enjoy it greatly." She reached up to rub his bald head in a way that made me avert my gaze. "Even so, it never hurts to admire the scenery." She clasped her hands together and leaned forward, making Mal roll his eyes. "Let's see the goods."

"They aren't exactly naked. Only partially."

Lindsey laughed as she stole the piece of pineapple off the tiny sword in Jamie's drink. "Now you've ruined their night."

"Their backs are basically porn. Why I took the pictures in the first place."

Lindsey cocked a brow. "Now you're talking. Which 'their' are you referring to?"

"Noah. And um, Oz."

Jamie rolled her eyes. "Trust me, we've seen all of Oz enough times to be able to do a police sketch of his junk. He's inordinately proud of it."

"As he should be," I muttered, my skin flushing straight down to my waist. Or at least that was how it felt.

Obviously, I'd had enough to drink already. My tolerance seriously sucked now. That was the only explanation for why I'd mentioned those pictures. Then again, I'd tried the same thing as a kid on the playground, only I'd used Twizzlers to make friends instead of flashing exposed male muscles.

I shrugged and pulled out my phone. Whatever worked, I supposed.

It took me a second to scroll to the right pictures. I took a lot of photos in a normal week—how a shaft of light shone across a hardwood floor, a flower tilting toward the sun, the pattern of raindrops on a windowpane.

Then there were the concert shots. I had a ton of those too since I'd started working for Ripper Records.

But this week, I'd only taken a few. Looking for beauty in dark places only worked when you had enough strength left to see it. For the last little while, all I'd been able to see was gloom.

The sole shot I'd taken at the fan club show of Oz snagged my attention. He was singing with Jamie, his voice so deep and strong, their foreheads tipped together, their smiles so natural. They were clearly tight.

I was happy he had his band with him. He needed people more than he realized, even when he was trying to pretend he didn't need anyone.

Jamie leaned over and grinned. "Hey, we look pretty cute. Guessing you didn't take that one because of me."

"I was so glad he sang. He needs to. His voice is amazing."

Had he taken to heart what I'd said at the cabin about him singing more again? Maybe. Maybe I wasn't just a video vixen to him. Maybe my thoughts held some sway.

Jamie tipped her head against mine instead of Oz's. "Doesn't sound like you're over him."

"More like she wishes she was still under him." Teagan popped an olive in her mouth. "Sorry, he's still an asshole. But you know, needs."

Did I ever.

Landing on a picture of Oz and Noah mid-pull up took my breath away, and not because of Noah. The tattoo on Noah's back of a large hawk with its wings extended made me take another look. Somehow I'd scarcely noticed his ink the other day.

I'd had other preoccupations.

Oz's body might not mean much to Jamie—and I had to say, my jealous soul appreciated that—but to me, he was the most beautiful creature who'd ever lived. Miles of golden skin wrapped over bone and sinew and fear and loss disguised as fury. As tall as he was, he was still graceful, moving with the elegance of a panther. And mercy, his gorgeous hair framed a face carved by angels, sent to earth to torment women who weren't so innocent anymore.

Before I allowed myself to wallow, I slid my phone toward Teagan first. She snatched it, ignoring Elle's grabby hands.

"Ugh, see, he's so hot. When he carried me out of Elle's engagement party, I would've sworn there were sparks."

"You sure that wasn't from the head rush? Didn't you pass out?" Mal asked drily as Elle elbowed him in the belly.

"It was an emotional night. My best friend since birth, getting married. And to you!"

Elle exchanged a look with her husband. "We weren't actually friends since birth, Teag. Just since school."

"I'm just saying, it was a very emotional day."

"Right, that's why you were flashing all your assets at Noah. Because of your deep emotion at our wedding." Mal smirked. "Nice try."

Teagan flipped Mal the bird and kept scrolling, making noises that verged on the infamous scene in *When Harry Met Sally*. "God, I'd ride him bareback. I'd ride him so hard I'd break his spine. Look at his abs. Look at his *ass*."

I jabbed Teagan in the side as a familiar cluster of males approached. Too familiar. Cooper was in front, his jaw as immovable as granite, but Noah was right behind.

"Teagan!" I hissed.

She paid me no mind.

"He's built like a fucking stallion. And I bet he is a stallion. You know he has stamina. Like there's just no doubt. He can't be a two-pump chump. It's just not possible."

Jamie glanced up and choked on a laugh. "Um, Teag, seriously, shut up."

"Damn, look at that huge ass bird tattoo on his back. What is that? An eagle?"

"A hawk," Noah said smoothly, stopping beside the table.

Teagan let out a squeak and dropped my phone. It hit the floor with a loud crack.

"Oh, God, please let that just be the case. I can't afford a new iPhone right now."

"Nah, they're sturdy fuckers. Hang on." Surprising the hell out of me, long-legged, long-everything Jamie shimmied off the bench and under the table like a damn eel to retrieve my phone.

Only problem was, Noah had bent to do the same. The table shook and I wasn't sure if they were engaged in combat under there or making out, but after a minute, Jamie emerged victorious with the phone held high above her head and one hoop earring missing. "I intend to see these pix. Teagan was hogging the damn phone. Seriously, girl, you need to get some. Fast."

"Sounds like she knows who she wants it from. Right, Teag?" Cooper's voice was uncharacteristically hard.

Teagan ignored him. "So, Ricki, are you pregnant yet? How's it going there, shooter?" Teagan pointed at Mal. "You got any bullets in that gun?"

I didn't think I'd ever seen Mal flush before. His whole head turned red. "If I did, you'd probably better duck."

I was pretty sure that didn't mean what he'd intended, but who could blame him? He probably hadn't expected to be accused of fertility issues in front of a dozen people.

Elle stomped on Teagan's foot hard under the table. "No, thank you very much. We aren't even trying yet, you jerk. I am not mentioning anything to you ever again." She sniffed. "Also, no, you cannot have my Adam and Eve platinum club membership discount now. Go fish. I hope your girly bits dry up and fall off."

Teagan reeled back. "Harsh. Seriously harsh."

Lindsey coughed delicately into her hand. "So, has anyone seen any good movies lately?"

Cooper circled the booth to come stand behind us. He leaned over. "So, let's see those photos."

Teagan frowned and shoved him back. "These aren't for you."

"They aren't for you either, seems like. Sorry to break your heart."

It sounded to me as if Cooper was the one with the broken heart. And Noah was definitely not concerned with Teagan's latest verbal fumble. His focus was solely on Jamie as she tapped on the screen of my phone.

Jamie cocked her head while she scrolled through. "Hmm."

"Hmm?"

"Nice ass," was all she said as she dropped my blessedly intact phone in my lap.

"Whose?" Noah asked, his voice surprisingly sharp.

I blinked. Had Noah been drinking? Which, by the way, Teagan was now doing. She'd finished off my drink and snagged the rest of Jamie's, but she hadn't made eye contact with Noah yet.

He seemed to have other fish—uh, rockstars to fry at the moment.

Jamie flashed him a serene smile. "You'll never know, will you, tyrant?"

He crossed his arms over his bullish chest, pulling the seams of his shirt tight. "You slipped your guard again. Make that guards."

"See what I mean?" She relaxed in the booth and spread her arms wide on the back of the seat, thrusting out her breasts in a way I doubted was incidental. "Besides, why do I need one of your flunkies killing my game when I'm surrounded by all of these beautiful people?"

Noah's jaw flexed. "All of these 'beautiful people' have their guards on the premises."

"Exactly how many men do you think it takes to watch over me anyway?" Jamie picked at her nails. "I mean, I'm a lot of woman, but—"

"One," Noah grated out. "It takes just one to take care of you."

A hush fell over the table that for once didn't have a thing to do with Teagan's inappropriate comments.

"We have a guard?" Elle asked Mal. "Besides, who can Roth hire that's bigger than you?"

"Size isn't all that matters," Teagan said primly.

Jamie laughed, the sound higher than usual. Almost as if she'd lost some of her lung capacity. "You've brought up a good point. Is being a bodyguard only related to size, Noah?" Her usage of his actual name was like tossing a match onto a puddle of gasoline. "Or how you use it?"

He didn't say a word, just smoldered.

Mal threaded his hand through the ends of Elle's swingy blond hair. "Pretty sure I accidentally backed over our guard." His voice was still strained.

Jamie's date chose that moment to reappear, balancing two drinks and a bucket of what looked to be crispy wings. "Hey, baby, drink special."

Nash cleared his throat. "Oh, thank heavens for a deal."

Lindsey laughed, shaking her head at him. "*Shh.* Be nice."

There were now so many people crowded around the table I couldn't even take stock of them all, except I knew one of them was Oz. I could feel him breathing down my back in a not-so-figurative way.

Not my concern. There were already enough hormones flying around this booth. I was not going there with a table full of witnesses.

Between the band and the bodyguards and the assorted others who were streaming over to our section in the VIP area, my head was swimming. I was pretty sure I got a glimpse of Lila and her husband Nick, yet another rockstar and Elle's brother.

Bet he must've loved the pregnancy conversation if he was listening. I certainly hadn't enjoyed it much. *Hi, awkward.*

There were some of the members of Warning Sign to boot, as if there weren't enough bodies pressed into too small of a space.

My face grew warmer and the room tilted as I gripped the edge of the table. I wanted to get out—needed to—but Teagan's thigh was up against mine on one side and Jamie was on the other. Nowhere to go.

I jerked up, trying to stand, but before I could even ask Teagan to slide out, Jamie's date fumbled his drinks and Jamie's purple one went flying across the table, splashing me in sticky liquid. And then the glass rolled off the table and landed in my lap for a nanosecond before shattering to the floor.

"Oh my God, let me help you." Teagan finally shook herself out of her embarrassed stupor and grabbed for napkins, patting them all over me.

At my side, Jamie spewed curses and launched herself at Lindz, who scrambled back, but not fast enough. Jamie climbed up on the seat and pointed at her himbo. "Help Daisy clean up."

He sneered. "Who's Daisy? I don't know these people."

Noah stepped forward, moving through the newest surge of people toward our table. "You okay?"

"Look, he speaks! Always for our sweet Daisy."

Noah didn't acknowledge Jamie. Neither did anyone else.

I nodded, but the room revolved as Teagan rubbed napkins over me. Jamie's sticky drink had dripped into unpleasant places, including the cups of my strapless bra. "Ugh, this sucks. Your pretty dress. I hope this comes out. Ugh. Men." She shot a look at Jamie's date. "So useless."

Although I didn't disagree at the moment, I wasn't sure I could speak, so I sucked in a long, slow breath.

Calm down. You're fine. You know what this is.

Panic attack number twenty-five-thousand.

Jamie planted a stiletto-heeled boot on the back of the booth before she climbed up and jumped down into the next circular booth, surprising the table of people clustered there.

Shrieks.

Chaos.

I needed out.

My gaze swerved to the swarm of people—now scattering, thank God, either to help clean up or afraid where Jamie might land next, Spiderman-style. In the crowd, I caught sight of that dark-haired guy in the trench coat who'd been outside my Uber. He'd followed me. Was he a photographer? Or was he someone who wanted to hurt me?

I shoved at Teagan, my breaths coming short, and scrambled to get out of the booth. "Sorry, sorry, gotta—"

Then hands were beneath my armpits, hauling me from the seat. Plucking me up and out as if I wasn't squirming and fighting for my very life.

I reared my neck back and glimpsed Oz, which only made me fight that much harder. He didn't scare me physically, but he was absolutely a threat to me.

He set me down and gathered me close, his big arms enfolding me in a way that tossed a thick, soft blanket on my panic.

I appreciated the effort, except now I could feel the tears starting. Humiliated, frightened ones. I tried to breathe through it while I wrenched my neck, trying to see the guy in the coat. He was still there. Not running. Bold as fucking day.

"Who are you?" I shouted over the noise. Somehow even with Oz reaching in to grab me like a human crane, our huge group still hadn't quieted.

Until that very moment.

"Daisy." Oz's voice was even. Steady. He ran a hand down my back. "It's okay. He's okay."

I pushed him back and stared up at him. Normally, I wasn't all that intimidated by his size, which was crazy considering the enormous difference in our heights and weights. But right now, he might as well have been a giant speaking down at me from very far away. White noise buzzed in my ears as I struggled through the fight or flight response still cramping my muscles. "How would you know that?"

Oz looked away before rubbing a hand down his face. It was only then that I noticed the heavy lines and shadows near his eyes, visible even in the low light of the club. "Let's go outside."

Deliberately, I moved back. "No. We can talk right here." I didn't care who heard. Who saw.

I was tired of trying to put a pretty face on things, including my emotions. I was fucking raw and freaked out and had gone through too many changes in too short of a time.

And I was also tired of having feelings for a man who would never admit he had real ones for me. If he even did. Sometimes I thought he might, but if he didn't allow them to take root, did they matter?

It wasn't enough to care about someone if you didn't *want* to. If you acted as if acknowledging anything other than a desire to fuck them brainless was akin to eternal torture.

Fuck that. And fuck him too.

"Daze." He smoothed a hand down my bare arm, and I shrugged off the gesture. "Fine. He's just someone I hired. Nothing to worry about."

"Someone you hired?" I turned around and glared at the man in question, who held his ground without saying a damn thing. Typical male. "For what? Why would you hire someone to follow me—" When it clicked, I pivoted to stare up at Oz incredulously. "You actually had the balls to fuck me and leave then you *dared* to hire someone to do the job you couldn't do?"

Behind me, there were a few scattered laughs and muttered comments, but I didn't care. Let everyone listen. Oz could try to make me his dirty secret and ignore me like he'd ignored me for months, but I wasn't going to take it quietly.

Yes, I'd been the one to push it. I'd forced him to talk to me. I'd stolen his truck and invited myself to his cabin. So, yeah, I had some problems with boundaries too. But I hadn't run away. *He* had.

I expected a smart remark. Something to keep his bravado firmly intact. Instead, he just shifted his head, and the silver chain around his neck gleamed.

Kerry's arrowhead. That he was wearing it hit me square in the chest, even though he was wearing it for her. Had to be. I was just the keeper of the necklace until he was ready for it.

He would probably never be ready for me. For us. I just had to accept that before it ripped me open any more than it already had.

Tears blurred my eyes and I pushed past him, not listening to the calls of my name or the heavy footsteps that followed.

I moved through the densely packed bodies, hurrying down the stairs to the main level. Just as I reached the doors, my sister came through them, her expression going stark as she saw my face.

"Daze, wait. Daisy!"

But I didn't stop.

And I didn't look back.

NINETEEN

CLOSING MY EYES, I FISTED MY HANDS. I HADN'T EVEN WANTED TO come tonight. For good reason. Daisy and I being in the same place meant something would happen. We couldn't stay away from each other.

Well, correction. She could stay away from me, evidently, as she'd done just fine all week. She hadn't even offered to do my hair and makeup, although it was technically her job. I'd said no all along, but every week, she'd asked anyway—until this one.

Her metaphorical and very deserved middle finger hadn't gone unnoticed.

I wanted to go after her. It took literally everything inside me not to chase her down and try to explain.

I just didn't know how.

I'd hired someone to keep an eye on her. She was right. I'd paid money to do something I wouldn't. Namely to be at her side and make sure she was safe. I knew Noah was watching out for her too, but he was only one man and spread far too thin as it was. As far as I was concerned, there couldn't be enough people keeping Daisy protected.

They just couldn't be me.

"You."

I opened my eyes and met the dark, narrowed ones belonging to Everleigh Flannigan. I hadn't seen her in five years, and she'd sprouted up like a damn weed since the last time I'd been in her presence, but there was no disputing it. She was a serious looker now too. Tall, willowy, effortlessly pretty with long hair and tight jeans and cowboy boots.

And her expression proved if I made one wrong move, she would take me out.

"You don't look like your sister," I said, which was probably one of the stupidest things I'd ever said. At least this hour. There were a lot of contenders.

She placed her hands on her hips. "What did you say to her?"

"Which time?" I rubbed my suddenly throbbing temple.

Next time, I was just going to stay home. It wasn't as if I was in a partying mood. Even getting drunk didn't appeal. That seemed like a way out I didn't deserve. All I wanted was to sit alone in the dark and listen to Whitesnake—what the fuck—and marinate in my idiocy.

"Tonight, asshat. I ran into her running out of here. By the way, why are you here? She said the only reason she was coming was because you weren't going to be here."

You'd figure that if you walked out on someone for very valid reasons that took their well-being into account, you wouldn't ache like a motherfucker at hearing they didn't want to sit near you at a tea party. You'd think.

"I didn't know she was coming." In fact, I'd told myself I hoped she wouldn't.

Until I walked in and got a glimpse of her sunny hair and all the knots inside me tightened even more from wanting her.

"Right, because God forbid she has fun with the band, right? Look, I know you've always had a giant head, so this is probably beyond you, but couldn't you let her down easy? If you aren't interested, don't be a prick about it. Kerry loved her even if you don't understand the concept."

"The concept of love or loving Daisy? Because you'd be very surprised what I understand, and it's none of your business in any case."

Oh, look, my prick side had shown up for attendance.

Ever shook her head, causing her long dark hair to tumble over her shoulders. "She's my sister, and I'm pretty sure you get that concept even if all others elude you. Just seriously, next time you treat her like trash, think of Kerry."

"Forget Ker, I was thinking about *Daisy*. How she didn't need a life dealing with me getting thrown in jail when I got pissed at myself and did something crazy. Or when some asshole made comments about her and looked at her too long. She deserves someone who can be real and honest with her and give her back everything she has to offer. Someone who wouldn't make her fucking *cry*."

And I'd done it again tonight. The visible pain in her beautiful eyes had hit me like a gut punch. I'd told myself I was doing the right thing. Sure, it sucked now, but she would be better off in the long run.

I wasn't the boyfriend type. I definitely wasn't a husband or a father in the making. I got too in my head and dwelled on shit I shouldn't, and when I let it out, I tied her to the goddamn bed.

She'd been a virgin.

She liked it. You know she did. She's handled everything you dished out and came back for more.

It didn't matter. No wonder Kerry hadn't wanted us together. Clearly, Ever couldn't fathom the idea either. We didn't fit. Oh, we might for a while, but in the long run, we weren't suited. Daisy would be the one who paid the price if I didn't do the right thing for the first time in my godforsaken life.

Ever stared at me, her lips parting. "Wait, what happened between you two?"

"You don't know?"

Ever frowned. "I know my sister has some explaining to do, if I can even find her."

"I'll find her."

I turned toward the man who had inadvertently caused all of this. "Sean, she's already pissed enough at you."

His dark brow winged up. "Think you rang that bell, mate, not me."

"You were supposed to be unobtrusive, remember? Undetected. Christ, I paid you more for that."

"I tried, but she's jumpy. She kept looking back. Hard to tail someone without being in their sphere. Besides, why didn't you tell her you hired a guard for her? I thought you wanted her to have a measure of security, and the way to do that isn't to make her afraid all over again."

I gripped the back of my neck. He was so right. "She wasn't supposed to see you."

"I'm not a shapeshifter, mate. I have a physical form."

Ever snorted out a laugh. "Don't you realize the whole universe is supposed to do Oz's bidding? Especially once he pays you off." Slowly, she shook her head. "I should know. You even paid *me.*"

I pinched the bridge of my nose. I'd kind of blocked that out of my head. "I hoped you'd forgotten."

"You really thought I'd forget my sister's frenemy offering me a hundred bucks to babysit my own sister? When she's the older one?"

"It wasn't for babysitting," I muttered as that dark brow of Sean's climbed once again.

We'd met in college and had kept in contact since then. He'd been a foreign exchange student from London who returned after graduation and opened his own security firm, a fact I'd paid little mind to until my genius idea at the fan club show.

"No, you wanted me to stick close to her and make sure she was okay. Which might've been sweet if you hadn't been a royal dick to her at Kerry's funeral and probably every time since."

"Give him a break. He's hopelessly inept with the ladies. Has been ever since university." Sean tapped his chin. "I think he's gotten even worse."

I wanted to argue. But the results couldn't be disputed.

"Are you going to go find Daisy?" I demanded instead.

"I'll find my sister. As if she'd want to see either of you again."

"It would be more efficient if I went," Sean said, already moving away.

"Oh, more efficient for your paycheck? Too bad, boyo. She doesn't need to be any more upset."

"Sean, give me a call if you find her."

Neither of them paid me any mind. They continued to argue as they descended to the main area of the club and disappeared.

I rubbed my brow. Great. Now I had to face my band and pretend I had any interest in partying when at least half of them had heard Daisy call me out for fucking and dumping her. In pretty much exactly those words.

I'd go outside, get my bearings, deal with the shitstorm my life had become. And if any photographers happened to be lingering outside...

Nope. Not tonight. Tonight, you're going to work on not being a tabloid target.

I strode outside, waving off the couple of people who tried to approach me, especially of the female variety. I'd visited this club with the band a few times. Each of those times in the distant past, I'd found a gorgeous woman to go home with for the night.

Always only one. No repeats.

I never brought them to my place. Any of my places. They were my sanctuary, my private space. I didn't do entanglements.

Sean was right there. I didn't know how.

It wasn't as if I'd had many good examples of love relationships at home. My dad had split on my mom when Ker and I were young. My mom had tried dating once or twice after, but it had never gone anywhere. Men never wanted to stick around when they found out she had two snarky teens. One especially, who guarded his mother fiercely and had until the day she died.

At least for her, I'd managed to stick around.

I cut through the crowd, most of them laughing and dancing and have a fine as hell time. I didn't begrudge them their enjoyment. It was more I was pissed I was in this spot, when I'd done what I was sure would be best in the long run.

Okay, not sleeping with Daisy would've been the best thing, but I hadn't managed to do that.

I was back to being no better than a horny, messed-up twenty-three-year-old who had a stupid thing for his little sister's friend.

Shoving through the side exit door, I stepped out into an alley, already braced to deal with more photographers.

But the only one in the alley was Nick Crandall, one booted foot braced against the brick wall of the neighboring building, his head tipped back as he blew smoke circles up at the sky.

"Sometimes I amaze myself," he said after a moment.

Inwardly, I groaned. I'd wanted to duck back inside, but I was just screwy enough right now to be tempted to talk to him. I didn't know why. What good could it do me? I didn't want to go to fucking confession. I definitely had no desire to talk about Daisy.

I let the door thud closed behind me. "I'm amazed at you too. How did you get Lila to marry you?"

"A question I ask myself often."

"Here I figured you'd brag."

"Nah, trust me, I still can't believe it myself. And that's even acknowledging she's a hard ass who loves unnecessarily busting my balls. But I sorta enjoy it." He let out a steady stream of smoke. "She'll bust them again when she smells the smoke on me. I was supposed to quit."

"Fifty times ago?"

"Probably closer to a hundred by now. I was doing a lot better. Went months without touching one. I didn't even think about them that much either. Then this shit started happening again at Ripper." He lowered his head and narrowed his eyes with the veil of smoke still lingering in the air between us. "Hard to stand back while you're worried about protecting someone you love, isn't it?"

His question caught me like a fist around my windpipe.

"No," I managed.

He chuckled, long and low. "Need an oxygen tank, brother? I can have Li order you one as necessary equipment. But I'll warn you now—it isn't going to get better."

"It isn't?"

Great. Now I'd turned into a parrot.

"No. The targets keep changing. You figure out the love stuff, or at least learn not to freak at the idea. Then you have to deal with cooperation. Not just your rodeo anymore, although I hate the cowboy analogy. Then it gets even crazier and you're not only negotiating with your wife but with tiny hostage-takers who cry for candy and use your logic against you and you would die for, without question." He took a drag. "Now I need a drink."

I had to laugh. "I'm covered on some of those."

"That so?"

"Yeah, I'm not having kids. Probably not a wife either."

He coughed into his fist. "Right."

I frowned. "You don't know me."

"I know of you, and I also know what you're saying. Because I said the same things. The kid thing I was still trying to wrap my head around up until the very minute I found out Li was pregnant."

"Hmm."

"Yeah, hmm. For that matter, the wife thing took me time too. Although I got there faster than Li did. She was newly divorced. Has Daisy been married?"

I started to answer before I realized he was reeling me in. "No, she's just twenty-three—" I broke off and crossed my arms. "Bet you think you're slick."

"At times but educated guesses don't count. I saw that shitshow in there. She basically told your whole relationship in one *Jerry Springer* worthy soundbite, minus the crowd shouting *Jerry! Jerry!* Though in that case, they'd be shouting *Daisy,* because she went toe to toe with you."

"Where the hell were you hiding to hear all our business?"

"Son, I didn't have to hide. Daisy was loud. I came in with Li right after you guys. My sister invited me. Not that I need an invite, since Li gets invited everywhere." He blew smoke out of his nose. "Unless it's a Dragon Lady free zone, and then she tends to show up to those places too."

My lips twitched. "She'd have your balls to hear you calling her that."

"You kidding me? It's our foreplay. She knows she's a dragon lady, and she's fucking badass at it." He grinned and pitched out his cigarette. "You didn't ask why I amaze myself."

"Am I supposed to care?"

"No, you think it makes you more tough to act like a dick. I used to too. What it made me was bitter and alone. I amaze myself because I guessed you'd sneak out here to escape. Could've gone either way. You could've drank yourself stupid—well, stupider, since you've driven a good ways down that road already."

"Thanks."

He shrugged. "We've all been there. So, she was best friends with your sister?"

"You did not hear that in the club."

"No, I think Ricki told me. Someone did. You know how bands work. Everyone knows everyone's business and tells everyone else, like a game of drunken Telephone."

"Yeah." I scratched the back of my neck. "Used to be she was too young for me."

"Did she catch up?"

"No, but there's bigger issues now. Like my sister is dead."

"Did she kill her?"

The blunt question made me shut my eyes. "No."

"Did you kill her?"

"No, but we fought the day she died. I made her cry. I hurt her. And she died thinking I was mad at her, that I didn't love her."

"Jesus, man, we all fight. You know she knew you loved her. One fight doesn't change that."

I dug the heels of my hands into my eyes. They were burning, and I knew I was skating far too close to the edge tonight. "I was brutal to her."

"Like you were brutal to Daisy?"

"No." I let my hands drop. "I didn't say anything to her at all."

"For some people, that's an even worse cut." He pried out a battered pack of cigs from his jeans pocket and tapped one into his hand. "I'm supposed to quit this shit, because it doesn't help me trying to knock up Li. And that's like my number one job right now."

I blinked. Blinked again. "Huh?"

"Smoking can damage the swimmers. Need every one of them playing for the team to score."

My head throbbed harder. "You didn't want kids. You had a kid. Two kids?"

He nodded.

"Now you want more?"

He flicked his lighter and lit his cigarette, then took a deep drag as if he hadn't just finished one a minute ago. "Yeah. It's been a multi-year project."

"Ouch."

He scratched his scruffy jaw and let the hand with the cigarette dangle. "It fairly sucks. So, you know, be careful what you wish for and all that. I'd like to kick my ass for not wanting them before, if I somehow karmically screwed the pooch."

"Thanks for that imagery."

"Just saying. You might think being alone is so awesome, but if you change your mind and you really are really fucking alone, you won't be singing the same broke ass tune."

I stared down at my boots, catching myself scuffing the toe the same way I'd done as a kid. "It's not awesome."

"Damn straight it isn't."

"I mean, it's good when you don't know who you want. But when you have a good idea..." I exhaled. "Gimme one of those."

"Nope. Mine."

I laughed. "You're a contrary bastard."

"You haven't earned one yet."

"That so?" I asked, mimicking him from earlier. "What hoop do I have to jump through?"

"It's a big one."

I jerked a shoulder. "Bring it."

"Sure?"

"Jesus, Nick, it's a damn cigarette, not a Lambo."

"Stop disrespecting your sister."

"Say the fuck what?" I advanced on him. "I may be a first-class prick, but I never disrespected Kerry. Not once."

Nick held his ground. "No? You think it's showing a lot of respect for someone by behaving as if they aren't responsible for their own life? As if they couldn't possibly handle making their own choices without your almighty help?"

I fell back a step, then kept going and sagged against the opposite wall. "I just wanted to protect her."

"Yeah, I get it. But loving someone means giving them the space to decide for themselves, even if what they choose kills you."

Swallowing hard, I didn't reply.

"My sister nearly died a couple times. I didn't know if she'd OD or hook up with someone who beat her unconscious one night. Sometimes I pushed her out of my life because I couldn't deal, and I still regret that." He turned his head and released a steady stream of smoke. "She survived, and she's thriving, and I was her biggest supporter when she came through it. But I couldn't live her life for her. I couldn't stand in her shoes and make her choices."

"I get that."

"Do you? Do you get that you can't be Daisy's shield either, especially by proxy? You love someone, you risk them every. Goddamn. Minute. It's hard as hell. Because it matters. Because you're breathing, not lying dead in the street."

I choked out a laugh. "You tell it straight."

"Only way I can." He flicked away ashes. "My sister told me you didn't have any interest in her offer of friendship. Since everyone loves her and everyone hates me, gonna guess you don't want mine either. But if you do, you know how to reach me."

"I do?"

He stared at me, his eyes glowing from the flaming tip of his cigarette. "Lila, dumbass."

"Right." I rubbed my forehead with the side of my fist. "That name feels fitting right now. I fucked this shit up bad."

"Nothing you can't fix."

"How?" I shook my head. "Don't answer that. Weak moment. I don't want to fix it. I don't. She's better off. Kerry didn't want her near me."

"You know that for a fact? And even so, your sister couldn't make your choices either. Or Daisy's. That's not how this works." He smudged ashes off his fingers. "Gonna guess that if she loved both of you, she would've wanted you happy. Also, chicks love when everyone they care about pairs up. It's probably better than sex for them." He shuddered. "I think *The Bachelor* has warped young minds."

"*The Bachelor* is garbage."

"Some women love it. Not my Li, but she's a woman of exceptional taste."

I grinned. "Not always."

He flipped me off and took another drag. "You fix it by being honest."

"I don't think so."

"Of course you don't think so, baby Yoda, because you still think you are wiser than those of us who have gone before. Tell her the truth about how you feel, including how messed up you are about possibly hurting her down the line. So, you figured you'd be expedient and do it now."

"That's not—" I fisted my hands at my sides. "God, I really am a dick."

"Can't argue."

"But it's not just that. I'm nobody's prize, but my life isn't what she's used to. She'll have to deal with paparazzi, and I go off the handle.

Goddammit, I bruised her cheek when she tried to wake me up from a nightmare. I'm a fucking beast, and she's like sunshine. I don't want to put it out."

"Aww, that was so sweet. Try setting it to music and you'll have a top ten pop hit. The Bieber set will love it."

I ignored him. "Then there's what happened with Kerry. I don't really blame her for not saving her, because you're right, my sister made her own choices. I didn't save her either. But are we just thinking something's there that isn't, that has to do more with loving Kerry than—"

"Loving each other?"

"No. Absolutely not."

"You hadn't seen her in a while, right? Before she joined the tour."

"Yeah. Five years." I tucked my hands in my pockets. "She's the same, but different. Everything she was back then is just more now. She's stronger, funnier, smarter, sexier..."

"And you're in deep. The ship has a hole and it's taking on water and you don't have a bucket big enough to bail your ass out."

I frowned, but I couldn't really argue. "It can't work."

"Okay."

"I'm a huge guy. She's so small. I didn't mean to hurt her, but I still did."

Nick held up a hand. "If this is about to divert somewhere I would never want to go without a bottle of something 100-proof in me, do not go there."

I chuckled. "Not sexually. I had a crazy dream about my sister. Daisy tried to wake me up and I—"

"Strangled her?"

"Uh, no."

"Cold-cocked her?"

I exhaled. "Close enough."

"Did you drive her to the ER?"

"It wasn't that bad."

"Then why are we talking about it?"

"She had a bruise. She still has it. I see it every time I look at her even though she tries to hide it with makeup. It kills me, man."

"You hurt her accidentally. You didn't mean it, right?"

I shook my head.

"Dude, you need more therapy than you paid for tonight. But I won't hang up on your calls. Probably." He tossed aside his cigarette stub and ground it into the pavement with his boot. "Look, apologize. Talk about all the crazy crap floating through your head that you think passes for logic. Fuck her silly. Whatever her flavor of catnip, sprinkle that shit all over and let her roll in it."

An image of Daisy tied to my bed and whimpering flashed through my brain. It was a damn miracle I didn't spring a semi. I was actually too fucking depressed to get hard.

Who knew such a thing could even exist?

"If all fails, grovel."

That one I understood. "I've never groveled in my life."

"Welcome to the jungle, son." He patted my back as he passed me on his way to the side door. "You're about to become an expert at it."

"What about that cig?"

"Still haven't earned it yet," he said before the door slammed shut behind him.

My cell phone buzzed. I pulled it out and scanned the readout. Sean. "Where is she?"

"Hello to you, mate. I'm well. And yourself?"

I hissed out a breath. "Have you found her or not?"

"She's home with her onerous sister. I suspect they'll share a pint of Rocky Road and watch *The Vagina Monologues* and discuss why men are so ghastly."

Thank fuck she was home. That they both were, for that matter. I didn't need anything else on my conscience.

"Thanks for making sure they got home safely."

"For the younger one, making sure she's locked away is my civic duty. She threatened to mow me down. I'm not sure she should be on the loose."

Somehow I laughed. "Everleigh has always been a pit bull when it comes to her sister. Which is a good thing. Daisy deserves someone like that in her corner."

"Everyone does. Including you. Someday you'll grasp that. My invoice will arrive soon. Goodnight."

He ended the call before I could reply. Not that I had a damn thing to say.

TWENTY

One lock of hair over the other. Again and again.

I built the fishtail braid into Teagan's curls. She liked to do wild braids along the crown of her head but keep the rest of her hair free flowing. And I didn't mind keeping my braiding skills sharp. I never knew when a job would end.

Or when I couldn't take it anymore.

The pang of sadness was getting harder and harder to slog through. Seeing him in the hallways and at the afterparties was painful. Not that he came near me. Nope. He didn't dare get too close.

All those pesky emotions.

Oz didn't deal with them. I wished I could be the same. I wished I could turn all this off. Because it was so damn heavy. Like there was a sleeper sofa sitting on my chest all the freaking time.

I knew firsthand how heavy those bitches were. I'd just helped Ever bring one to the curb for the freebie vultures. After I'd crashed on it and filled the ugly green cushions with tears.

Those had been the last tears I would shed for him.

I didn't think I had any left anyway.

"Earth to Daisy."

"Huh?" I met Teagan's huge blue eyes in the mirror.

"I've been talking to you for five minutes. Did you hear a thing I said?"

I sighed. "No, sorry. I was concentrating."

"No." She grabbed my hand and pulled me around in front of her. "I'm not done—"

"It's tight enough you can go back."

I shoved the rat tail comb into my jar of Barbiside before she could drag me back in front of her again. "Did I pull too tight?"

"Yes." She laughed at my face. "God, you really are in a fog. It's fine. You always do braids tight. I'm used to it."

"You don't want it to come out."

"Price for beauty. And that I don't have sweaty looking hair." She shook out my hands that had been increasingly tightening on hers.

God, I was so pathetic. I was hanging onto her like a lifeline.

"Daisy, I'm worried about you. We all are."

"You're talking about me?" Okay, so maybe all the tears weren't gone. My eyes stung, but I tipped my head back so none would fall. I'd spent an hour doing my damn makeup before I had to show up at the venue.

We'd all fallen into a rhythm. Soundcheck with each of the instruments with their techs then the band members would show up in a rotating basis. That way I was able to get everyone in for hair and makeup before the show.

I even helped out with the Warning Sign ladies.

I'd rather stay busy anyway. It kept me from thinking—mostly.

"Hey. It's okay to be sad."

"I don't want to be."

Teagan yanked me in for a hug. And well, there went the no tears thing. I clung to her because it was exactly what I needed.

I was so used to doing everything on my own. It was just how it always was. Kerry had always been my only family to speak of. My parents hadn't ever been the hands-on kind of loving people you saw in Hallmark commercials. Intellectually, I knew no one really had that greeting card kind of life, but the two bands on this tour, as well as their crew, reminded me just how lonely I'd been.

And Oz had shown me so much more than I was ready for.

"I don't want to go."

"*Go?* Go where?" Teagan pushed me back. "What?"

I winced at her shriek-level voice. "Keep it down." I hadn't meant to say that out loud. *Crap.*

"No, no, no. You can't let him drive you away from us. We love you so much already. I know it's only been a few months, but you're family." She shook my shoulders. "Truly."

My eyes burned. "It's really hard to to see him every day."

"Right." Her cornflower blue eyes went pink with unshed tears. "I didn't think about that." It seemed as if a lightbulb went off over her head. "I mean, I sort of did, but I guess there's a reason people shouldn't hook up when they work together."

I twisted my fingers with hers in solidarity. Maybe she knew a little bit about what I was talking about. She had been unusually interested in Noah as of late.

"I can truly say it sucks. Times eleven." I sniffed and dabbed at the corners of my eyes. "I never should have gone after him."

"Hey, Teag. Almost done?"

My heart sunk at the voice in the doorway. I turned away and went to the sink to wash my hands and pull myself together.

How long had he been there? This was usually my safe space.

I'd been avoiding him as much as possible. I didn't even eat with the crew like I used to because I couldn't handle being in the room with him.

"Since when did you come in for hair and makeup?" Teagan's voice was cool.

I smiled a little to myself. Such a fierce little warrior. I would really miss that part. I hadn't called the salon to ask for my spot back, but the last time I'd gone to visit, they'd hinted we might be able to work something out. I'd left the door open just in case. If not, there was a place down the block from Ever's apartment that seemed promising.

Maybe I'd always known this would just be a limited-time oasis for me. Or maybe I was just closing a chapter in my life. A painful one.

The thought of moving on with someone other than Oz made everything go cold. How could anyone compare?

The water flowing over my hands started to sparkle. Dammit, I'd cried enough over this man. I wouldn't be doing it again. I'd promised myself. And I was the only one who could keep that promise.

"Since today."

He was going to pick today to sit in my chair? He just lived for torturing me, evidently.

I spared a glance for myself in the mirror. The little flowers I'd painstakingly painted just above my lid were still there in all their frosted peach and pearl glory. My eyes were a little red, but no worse than someone with allergies.

You can do this.

I turned off the water and turned around as I dried my hands. "Come back in fifteen minutes, or have a seat on the couch."

He crossed the room to stand before me. He'd obviously freshly showered and God, he smelled good. "Think I need a trim?"

"I've told you that several times. Probably a good eight inches."

He swallowed and his skin paled a little. I resisted the urge to give him a big shark-like smile.

"Change your mind?"

He lifted his chin, daring me. "Nope."

Damn him. He knew I wouldn't cut his gorgeous hair. I loved sinking my fingers into it. So thick and silky, but it had absolutely no bend unless the humidity was in the stratosphere.

Unless...

I grinned up at him.

His dark brows beetled. "What?"

"Nothing. Just have something special planned for you, that's all." I sidestepped him to gesture for Teagan to get back in my chair.

"I can stay," she said in a low voice as she sat down.

I twisted her to face the large lit mirror again. "Don't worry about me." I rescued the ends of her braid and quickly finished it off. I pinned it into a crown and teased her curls around her face, then added a bit of glitter spray for good measure.

Five minutes later, I was brushing my favorite pearl highlighter along the crest of her cheeks. Teagan had flawless skin and didn't need much, but a little sparkle never hurt anyone. I widened her eyes with a few well-placed lashes.

"I'm so glad you used cruelty free makeup. I swear, if Cooper sends me another link about animal testing for makeup, I'm going to kill him." She sighed and looked up when I told her to. "But I still sent a thousand bucks to a sanctuary who takes those poor animals in after they're retired."

"Aww, that's sweet." I used a dot of glue to add another little clump to the corner of her lash line. "Only place mink is cute is on those cute little furry faces."

"Amen, sister."

"Okay, let that dry for another minute, and we'll set your face. Then you're good to go."

"Finally," Oz muttered.

I ignored him. Which was difficult because I could feel his gaze on my ass. Damn him.

When I couldn't fuss with her face any longer, I unsnapped her cape. "Have a good show."

She hopped down and fluffed her hair as she took a closer look at herself. "You are a genius."

"Easy when you're so beautiful."

Teagan's cheeks reddened, and she rolled her eyes. She dragged me in for another hug. "Don't let him get to you."

I hugged her back. "I'll be fine."

I turned around to find Oz looming over me. Those sexy dark eyes still made my system go haywire, but dammit, I could ignore that. I *would* ignore that.

I was a freaking professional.

"Get in the chair, please."

He moved even closer. I wanted to step back, but I wouldn't give him the satisfaction. He thought he could control me and this situation. He was so very wrong.

"What do you want, Oz? You're the one who cut me loose, remember?"

His jaw did that clench thing. Ugh, why did he have to be so unbelievably seductive and intense? Actually, better question was why did that intensity get me off so much?

Maybe that was why I'd never been able to find another man to interest me. I had hidden, unexplored kinks. At least mostly unexplored.

Another thing I'd have to work on.

Find another dude who knew just how to drive me crazy—only this time, he would stick around when shit got hard.

Sure, that would be easy.

I crossed my arms over my black smock with hot pink kiss marks all over it. I was determined to keep my game face even if everything in me wanted to climb up his crazy-hot body and shake some sense into him.

Didn't he see how good we were together?

"Are you really going to leave the tour because of me?"

Great. He *had* been eavesdropping.

"No, I'm leaving because of me. Big difference. I deserve more, so I'm going to go find it." I walked around him to my arsenal of tools. I turned on every one of my curling irons. "Sit."

"You think you can order me around, sprite?"

"This is my domain. You don't like it, there's the door."

He held up his hands. "I'm at your disposal."

"I know you appreciate the 80s."

He met my gaze in the mirror. "I love the music, yes."

"You know I love David's hair." I held up my spiral curling iron. Sometimes I used it to enhance Lindsey's thick mane of naturally curly hair. Oz's stick-straight hair would require a bit more finesse and product.

"Jesus," he muttered.

"You can still go. No one's stopping you."

"I'm good."

I found the hair curling machine my friend at the salon had convinced me to buy. I held that up. "We'll start with this."

"What the fuck is that?"

"This is magic for straight hair like yours. We'll have you in ringlets in no time."

"If this curling process lands on Instagram, I'm going to take it out on your ass."

"My ass isn't your domain anymore." I snapped out a cape.

"I don't need that. I'll get too hot."

I shrugged. "So, no makeup then?"

His growl was his only answer. "You expect me to sit here and become your David Coverdale fantasy?"

"That's the plan. Problem?"

The glower was back.

I resisted the urge to giggle as I took my biggest brush out of the Barbiside. "Let's get to work, shall we?" I patted the brush dry and handed him the large curl machine. "Hold this for me?"

His expression of disgust was priceless.

"Mind if I put on some music? This will take a while." I tapped through my music app on my phone and found Whitesnake's self-titled album and propped it on one of my makeup cases.

The surge of dirty guitars boomed out of the little, but very effective, speakers on my phone. I returned to my spot behind him and eased all his hair over his shoulder to flow down his back. It was ridiculously glossy and perfect even if he hadn't had a haircut in probably a few years.

Only men.

I dragged the brush through his dark hair with long, slow strokes. His eyes closed as a grumbling moan vibrated through his chest.

Dear God, maybe this was a mistake.

As the album cycled into the next song, I had to bury my fingers in his hair to part it into sections to give him a healthy cut first. Which of course was the sexiest song on the album. Long, orchestral guitar solos with David Coverdale's signature groans.

I had to move to the front of Oz to make sure the ends were even.

He opened his long legs so I could reach him. His scent wrapped around me as "Still of the Night" ramped up. The drums thundered behind me, and Oz played with the ends of my hair.

Of course that activated my nipples since he was a damn homing beacon for them. Thank heavens for my smock. His gaze lowered to my chest, and a small smile kicked up the corner of his mouth.

Maybe it didn't hide that much.

I slapped his hand. "You want me to accidentally snip off all of this? Maybe really get your 80s look going?"

He dropped his hands into his lap and straightened his shoulders. And that so didn't help. He was already wearing his stage gear. The simple black vest strained against his pecs, leaving his golden skin mostly bare save for the trio of necklaces he wore.

My breath caught at the arrowhead he wore close to his heart. A little farther up was the simple silver cross that had also belonged to Kerry.

I was saved from yet another emotional onslaught of memories by Jamie's husky voice.

"I approve of your musical choices. The epicness of David Coverdale's voice cannot be beat." She cocked a hip against the doorjamb. She was decked out in her stage gear of jet black leather pants, boots, and a skimpy top. Her hair was still wet from her shower. "So, what's going on in here?"

I stepped back and cleared my throat. "Oz is letting me play with his hair."

She tipped down her mirrored aviators. "Kinky."

Oz sighed. "I don't really need your play-by-play, James."

"Oh, now you definitely do." She came farther into the room and picked up my phone to fast forward through the power ballad. "I appreciate John Sykes and his amazing guitar solos, but I'm looking for...ahh, there it is."

"Straight For the Heart" and the fast guitars and tumble of lyrics careened through the space. Jamie's throaty voice followed along with David's powerhouse style.

She tipped her head back. "Right there. No one does guitar solos like this dude."

"Vandenburg is just as righteous," Oz chimed in.

"That's true. Remember when he pulled out that bow to do that song? Ugh, what was that song?" She reached over for the phone again and rewound. "This one."

"Still of the Night" filled the room again.

Jamie groaned. "So fucking good. Think Lindz could pull this off?"

"She can sing anything," I said without thinking.

Jamie propped herself up on her elbows on the counter, her long legs eating up the small space. "That's true."

"Do I hear Whitesnake?" Zane popped his head around the corner.

"Yes, you fucking do." Jamie bumped the volume up on my phone. "The man is a legend. I'd still fuck the shit out of this dirty dude. Have you ever seen them live? He still picks girls out in the crowd. Practically has them creaming their panties, and he's what? Sixty-something?"

Zane leaned on the door. "Sixty-eight, I think. Maybe good old sixty-nine." He waggled his brows.

"Gramps can still get it done with some Viagra, I bet."

I flushed as I took the curling machine from Oz and moved behind him again. "You guys are just as good."

Jamie stood up straight, picking at the array of barrettes, hair ties, makeup, and little Troll dolls I had tucked along my makeup case at my station. She fluffed the bright pink hair on one of the dolls before setting it aside to hop up on the counter.

I fed the first lock of Oz's hair into the machine, and he yelped.

"Relax." I held his head firm. "Don't want me to accidentally fry your hair, do you?"

His eyes widened. "You wouldn't."

"Then sit still."

Jamie snorted and cycled through a few more songs.

Zane folded his arms. "Play 'Here I Go Again'."

She punched the song and put the phone down to mime a synthesizer. "So fucking good."

"I need my guitar." Zane dug out his phone. "Yeah, we've got time." He stuffed it back in his pocket and headed into the hall.

"Grab mine," Jamie called after him.

"On it," he called back.

She swung her legs with a saucy grin. "This is cozy."

I unfurled a long dark ringlet from the machine. Fuck, it actually worked. Hot damn. I gathered another piece and fed it into the little contraption.

Jamie craned her neck. "Curls, huh? What did you do besides fuck and dump her?"

I winced. Yay, club meltdown that had put all my business on display.

"Or is there more? Did he cheat already? Gotta make it up to her, huh, Oz?"

"I'd be doing a hell of a lot more than curling his hair if he cheated. Acid, perhaps?" I asked into the mirror, meeting his gaze.

"Fuck that."

"That you'd have to make it up to me?" My heart stilled in my chest.

"That I'd cheat. I don't fucking cheat."

"Funny, I thought it was that you didn't get serious with women."

Jamie whistled. "Damn. Burn." She picked through the candy stash I had in a jar and found a wrapped piece of gum and folded it into her mouth. "That forever shit is dangerous, Ozzy. That's why we keep it simple, right?"

Oz's nostrils flared. "Simple's long gone."

I swallowed and went back to my curls. I was saved from answering by Zane's return with two guitars and Lindsey.

"Hey guys. I could hear Whitesnake down the corridor over the mic check." She glanced at Oz and then at me with a laugh. "No shit." She came around next to me. "Whoa. Those are killer curls."

"Right?" I gently laid another curl against the dozen I had. "For such straight hair, it curls perfectly."

"Dear God," Oz muttered.

"Can you do that to my hair?" Jamie piped up.

"Yours is so fine, not sure it would work. We could use the crimper though. And some crazy braids."

"Yes." She lengthened out the s with a big grin. "A la Pat Benetar's vid." She did devil's horns with her fingers and belted out a few lines from "Love Is A Battlefield."

"I could rock a side pony."

Lindsey cracked up and dropped into the couch. She crossed her long legs. "I know what we're doing for Halloween."

"Yes!"

Jamie did the little shimmy from the famous video.

Zane held out a purple acoustic. "We're still doing Whitesnake, right?"

Jamie hopped down then snatched her guitar. "Of course. Just got distracted. Now that I have my girl, we can figure out a song."

The three of them bickered over which song to do. They all had their phones out to look up lyrics.

Jamie stole my phone and played "Still of the Night" half a dozen times before she cried defeat. "I will figure out that song."

"'Crying in the Rain'," Oz said over the three of them.

Jamie dropped to the floor cross-legged with her guitar in her lap. "Will anyone know that one but you, pal?"

Oz picked up a curl that slipped over his shoulder and closed his eyes. He took a long, slow breath as if he was in pain. "Just listen to it."

Jamie sighed and put the song on.

Lindsey flicked open her phone again and mouthed along with the words.

Oz gripped the armrests of my salon chair. I hid a smile behind his increasingly voluminous curls. I took out hairspray, and he swore.

I resisted the urge to cackle.

Lindsey started getting into it. She got up and stalked around the little room, her angel-bright hair flowing around her as she reached for the lower registers.

Damn, that girl had a crazy amount of range. I didn't know much about music beyond pure love and appreciation for the art. Watching it unfold around me was incredible.

Oz began tapping to the beat, his shoulders loosening as the guitar parts started coming together. He shouted out some key changes to Zane.

Zane looked up, his eyes hazy and unfocused. His sun-bleached hair had fallen forward while he concentrated. His long, elegant fingers danced up the fret board as he tried again and grinned wide when the notes finally matched the song that was pumping out.

Jamie carefully mimicked it before putting her own flourishes on the song. Finally, they turned off the original version, and it became something altogether different.

I'd done as much as I could from behind Oz. I had to make sure the front looked as good as the back and that meant facing him again.

Lindsey hit an off key. Instead of being embarrassed, she turned it into a yowl-off with Jamie as they melted into a fit of laughter.

Distracted, I couldn't help but laugh back at them. They were all having so much fun. It actually pained me to think about leaving.

Oz slid a hand under my smock and his long fingers found the cropped edge of the babydoll T-shirt I wore under it. The skin on skin contact fried my brain cells. Even the slightest touch and my body instantly thirsted for more. My nipples tightened, and my skin tingled.

He coasted his calloused finger pads over my midriff and around the back to grip my ass. I closed my eyes, dragging in a steadying breath before I pushed his hand away.

No matter how much I wanted to drag him closer, I wouldn't give in.

He was the one who'd thrown me away. Thrown *us* away.

Cooper burst into the room. "How come I wasn't invited?"

Jamie tipped her head back. "Because your voice is trash."

"Yeah, well, you sounded like a dying cat from the hallway."

Jamie held up a middle finger.

I backed up. "You're done."

Oz's dark gaze pinned me to the spot. "We're not done."

That was so not what we were talking about. "Jamie, it's your turn."

Before I could turn away, he circled my wrist with his long fingers. "I'm serious, sprite. We're not done."

Jamie jumped up from the floor. "Oh, sweet shit. Look at that." She spun the chair, oblivious to the growl emanating from Oz's chest. "You really are a dark-haired David Coverdale." Her voice lowered to a sultry tenor. "Can you do the accent?"

He just arched a brow at her.

"No fun. Get out of the chair, Whitesnake. It's my turn to get glammed up." She glanced down at the hand still holding onto my arm. "If you can tear yourself away."

Oz dropped my wrist, but I could still feel the burn from his touch. He stood and brushed my hair over my shoulder. "Make sure you come out and see us tonight."

I shrugged. "Maybe. You know, to see this version of the song."

He pulled down his leather vest and straightened the buckle of his belt. "That's not the only reason you'll be out there."

"Why don't you just slap your dick out between us, for fuck's sake," Jamie muttered.

"You don't get to see his dick." The words flew out of my mouth before I could catch them.

Oz didn't say a word, just toyed with his arrowhead necklace before he whistled his way out of the room.

"Get in the chair," I told Jamie.

"Do I have to have as much hairspray as he had?"

"More."

"Dammit." She plopped on the seat. "The price for art. Do I get that cape thingie?"

I sighed and pulled it out of the pocket on the back of the chair. "Yes."

She wiggled her butt on the seat to make herself more comfortable. "Make me Pat Benatar."

"You know that doesn't match the Whitesnake look."

She shrugged. "I know, but she's more badass."

I lifted a hank of her long, unbendable hair. "So, we're going to cut off your hair to your ears?"

"Bite your tongue!" She grabbed her hair out of my hand and tried to get out of the chair.

I gripped her shoulders and pulled her back into the seat. "Don't worry. You trust me, right?"

"I don't trust anyone but Lindz."

I met her gaze in the mirror. I didn't want to live that kind of life. Even if we were semi-joking. "Don't worry. I'd never cut your hair. It's almost as pretty as Oz's."

Jamie blew raspberries at me. "Typical. Men always get the good hair without trying."

"Ain't that the truth." I sighed. "But I'm still going to make you look badass."

"That's what I'm talking about."

I'd do my damn job because I was a professional.

Just a few more days and I could get him out of my system.

Probably.

TWENTY-ONE

I wrapped up the last bag of clippings. The entire band ended up finding ways to make themselves look like 80s rejects. Even Zane ended up with a Bruce Springsteen red rag sticking out of his back jeans pocket a la the "Born in the USA" era.

I'd managed to wrangle a picture and video of all of them for their Instagram and TikTok accounts. The whole thing had become a social media coup, according to their fan club president who sent me a private message on Instagram.

I was pretty sure her name was Bailey. The only thing she'd complained about was that we didn't post it early enough so the fans could dress up too.

The internet was weird.

But if this was going to be a bit of my legacy with the band, then I really couldn't complain.

I'd have to talk to Lila about finding a replacement for me. Luckily, after the next New York City show, they had a bit of a break. Only four weeks, but it was enough to give Noah time to vet someone.

I smiled as I bagged up the trash. The crowd was losing their minds tonight. Warning Sign put on a good show, as well. I could feel the lack of tension in the hallways. It was amazing how easily I'd learned the ebb and flow of life on the road.

I'd never been anywhere, really. Sure, I'd made my way through the five boroughs of New York, bouncing around salons and working for off Broadway plays. Beyond that, I'd kept to my home turf. Getting to see other parts of the United States with the band had been something I'd never regret. Not doing the European leg of the tour kind of sucked though.

But I couldn't deal with these yo-yo feelings for Oz. He'd made me want him—no, want wasn't a heavy enough word. Yearn might be better. Because I'd known since I was a teenager that he was different. That what I felt was bigger than a crush.

Even if I'd tried to deny it.

And now after being close to him...seeing what we could be and how easily he threw us away? No, I couldn't live with that smacking me in the face day in and day out.

Not if I was supposed to get over him.

Like that was a possibility.

I washed my hands and tried to block out another surge of screams from the arena. I dried my hands and moved to the counter full of makeup and hair accessory shrapnel. I slapped the eyeshadow palettes into their slots. I traveled light, but my gear had to be packed up for the trucks.

"Oh, man, do you hear that?"

I glanced over my shoulder. "Oh, hey. How was your show?"

"I thought it was killer until I heard the crowd out there." Elle leaned against the door. She'd changed out of her concert gear into a pair of ripped jeans and an old Eagles T-shirt. I'd added a pink rinse to her hair, giving it an ombre effect. She was forever asking me to do something crazy with her hair and loved letting me try new products on her.

Said it kept things with Mal exciting.

If they got any more exciting, their hotel room would go up in flames.

"I heard the crowd. They were just as pumped during your set."

"You're sweet. However, we didn't have an 80s party going on. Did you see what Jamie found in wardrobe?"

I laughed. "Who do you think sewed her into that jumpsuit?"

"No shit. Glorious. You are the best addition to this tour, girlfriend."

I looked down at the blush brushes I was gripping. "Thanks."

"Hey." She came farther inside. "You okay?"

"Yeah, just recovering from hurricane Jamie."

"Well, that requires some partying."

"I'm beat." I snapped the lid on my brush case.

"Nah. You just think you are." She hooked her arm through mine. "Come out into the pit with me."

"I definitely don't have that in me tonight."

"Come on. Look how cute you are? I need you to do that thing with your eyes on me for a photo shoot we have next week. Maybe I can have purple flowers though."

"It's a stamp. I'm sure we can figure it out."

"Whatever it is, it's cute. And you are giving off primetime vibes. This is not to be wasted." She tugged me toward the door. "Please? I really want to go out there but don't want to go by myself. And Mal is too conspicuous."

"And he said no."

"Well, that too. But seriously, he's no fun for these things. He's just growling at people to back away from him. It's way more fun with a pal."

I swallowed down a lump. Everyone was so friendly. It wasn't like the cutthroat salon where everyone was trying to outdo each other. Here it was more like a family. And dammit, I was going to miss it.

"Okay."

"That's what I'm saying." She bounced up and down on her heeled boots. "Come on. They're almost to the midpoint of the set. That's when they do the covers."

I let her drag me down the hall to the side stage. She pulled a pair of lanyards out of her back pocket with all-access passes. The security in the venues didn't always know all the actual band members. Some of Noah's team and other members from Roth Security had been peppered into the staff for the night, but it was a big arena to cover.

Before I could come up with another reason to back out, we were in the thick of it. Bodies pushing at us, the screams were almost as deafening as Jamie's guitars. The air was thick with heat, and the thrum of a collective mania that only seemed to infiltrate a pack of fans without chairs. Jostling, laughing, loving, frustration, elation, and obsession.

The way people watched the stage with an almost manic glee was heady.

I understood it.

This band owned the stage. Seasoned from their years of endless touring, yet the joy was still there. I'd seen plenty of concerts in my years on this planet. Bands who had become numb to the fans, some who only lost themselves in the music and ignored the crowd, still others who managed the two. But there were very few in my purview who were like Brooklyn Dawn.

Regardless of my feelings about Oz, there was no denying this was their element.

Cooper stood behind his kit, slamming on his skins. His usual stick tricks flying in the air as he bounced one, then the other up and caught them without losing the beat. He had a tie wrapped around his head—where he'd found one, I had no clue.

Knowing Cooper, it was probably from the lost and found box at the arena. The dude could scavenge like no one I knew before. And that included klepto Jamie.

Zane was standing back to back with Jamie. They were almost the same height, especially with Jamie's rare use of spiked heeled boots on stage. She was already an amazon with her endless length of leg. Tonight, she had on a jumpsuit that we'd managed to sew her into a la Def Leppard from the eighties. Of course, we'd Jamie-fied it, which meant she was wearing little more than a bandana across her breasts, and the buttons undone to her waist on the jumpsuit.

The girl did not like to be restricted.

Zane was crouched over his guitar, playing it near his knees. His back slick with sweat, a white T-shirt wagging behind him from his back pocket like a tail. He chased his own fingers up the fret board, playing the actual neck of the guitar in some intricate fashion that harmonized with Jamie's more murderous style.

Speak of the devil herself, Jamie was practically laying along Zane's back. Her wicked, angular black guitar stretched across her, creating a cross. Her fingers were a blur over the strings as "Black Magic" came to a fevered pitch.

Lindsey hung off her blinged out mic stand, her powerhouse voice matched only by the sparkle of her pink and silver dusted boots and matching catsuit. Her soft blond hair curtained her face as she reached down for some feat of her amazing range I couldn't fathom.

The crowd surged forward, dragging me and Elle along for the ride.

She caught my hand before I could float downstream in the flood of fans who kept moving in waves. She hauled me in and hung an arm around my neck.

"Wild," she screamed into my ear.

That was one word for it.

I wanted to stay more toward the right side of the stage, but Elle was determined to get to the other side. To Oz.

I wasn't ready, but I also couldn't stem the tide. I was going to get him live and Technicolor whether I wanted to or not. Finally, the song slid into a light strum of soothing notes. Guitar techs scrambled across the stage as the lights went dark. The harsher electric sounds layered with acoustic tones.

The lights came up, and Oz was in the spotlight, a glossy black acoustic in his arms, his usual bass swung around to lay across his back.

Annette.

The guitar he brought to the cabin.

The canyon scene on his guitar was as familiar as Oz's face. As the touch I longed for every night. Both the strength of it when we drowned in one another, and the tight hold when I lay in the wreckage of our aftermath.

The first time, he'd held me. He'd even held me the time in the truck. But the last time...

Loneliness seared through me as the song built, and Oz stepped to the microphone.

Lindsey stepped back, a guitar in her arms.

Teagan's orchestral keys were the first layer.

Cooper's monstrous drums chased her.

The song was so layered with sound, I couldn't catch it all. But it really didn't matter. I only had eyes for Oz now. His lips brushed the microphone as the low growl of his voice purred into the arena.

The crowd screamed behind me, surging forward to get to him.

Shouts of his name surrounded me, and signs and phone cameras lifted high to catch the rare moment where he sang lead. He didn't look up. He was buried in a wash of curls and silky brown hair, leather and strength. His voice was a brilliant tenor with the rasp of his ode to Coverdale.

The song built as he spoke of judgement day, the mistakes of the past, and love's healing embrace.

He lifted his gaze, his eyes skipping across the crowd until he found me. Intensity radiated off him as the guitars built and the drums slid back to echo Oz's voice like a heartbeat.

He never looked away from me.

The lyrics were *for* me.

For that moment, I wanted to believe it, even if reality would bleed back in soon enough.

The words were a painful confession as he dropped to his knees, his guitar an extension of him and his voice dripping with emotion.

Then the song slid into "Crying in the Rain" with Lindsey taking back the vocals as a howling Jamie sent out a battle cry into the arena. Jamie and Zane were on the floating stage, both buckled in and headbanging their way over the sea of faces.

The crowd went wild. Elle was screaming as she jumped up and down like the rest of the fans.

Then someone recognized her, and the screeching hit a fevered pitch as they realized someone famous was in the pit with them.

Instead of overwhelming Elle, they jumped and screamed with her as Lindsey kicked out a leg and owned the crowd. Running up and down the stage to get everyone to sing.

Oz gave the acoustic to his tech and pulled his bass back in front of him, but his gaze didn't leave mine as he slowly rose to his feet. His bass was thunder as sweat dripped down his arms, and he went back to being the steady support for the song.

While Lindsey shone like the diamond she was.

But it was all too much.

It had started off as harmless fun to try to remind myself I could manage to have Oz around me. To poke fun at him with his hair metal roots. Instead, I had an indelible vision of him singing for me, kneeling before me, pleading with me.

As the song wrapped up and moved into Brooklyn Dawn's version of "Barracuda", I backed away. I glanced at Elle, and she seemed to understand I had to go.

She nodded to me and was enveloped by the fans looking to party.

I had to get out of there.

The pain of what could have been was drowning me.

I could trust the emotion radiating off of Oz and on display for the fans. Because he gave me everything then closed it away, locking me out when the feelings got too big.

And I was so tired of pounding my fists on his doors.

I flashed my badge at the security team and slipped back to where I belonged. On the sidelines and in the safety of backstage.

Alone again.

TWENTY-TWO

AFTER THE MSG SHOW A FEW DAYS LATER, I DID WHAT I DID best.

Hole up and hide from the world.

Before I disappeared, I did not rip apart a hotel room futon or spray any unfortunate guests with champagne. I'd only done each of those things once last year. Maybe twice on the champagne one. To be fair, I'd thought they were on their way to party with us, but it turned out nope.

At least they hadn't tried to have me arrested. Unlike the photographer I'd attacked. He wasn't so benevolent. Day after tomorrow, I had an appearance ticket back in good ol' Lake George. If that went as well as my lawyer assured me it would, my next step would be to do some home DIY in the cabin, drink heavily, and pray to whatever deities still listened to me that Daisy would follow the treasure map I intended to leave her.

Okay, minus the drinking. I'd gone out with Coop the other night and had bypassed alcohol for a lime and Coke and a serious discussion about first, saving for retirement—Coop's suggestion—and second, how to get Daisy to believe I wasn't a worthless fucknut.

Coop hadn't been impressed with the couple of extra scratch-offs I'd saved in a jar as a retirement plan. Apparently, five-hundred didn't get you much in annuities these days.

Then he'd brought the hammer down and told me that I should probably make sure I *wasn't* a worthless fucknut, if I wanted to convince her.

Not drinking until I passed out was a good start.

I didn't always have a problem with alcohol. I'd gone weeks and months without touching much of the stuff. But around the anniversary every year, I tended to backslide. I couldn't do that anymore. My sister was gone, and I missed her every damn day. I always would. But self-destructing in her name was just an excuse.

I had to be better than that.

So, I'd started by cleaning out my cupboards in my apartment in the city. I'd ditched every form of alcohol I had, including the rubbing kind used for cuts. Sarah had watched me, saying nothing until that particular moment, when she had doubled over in laughter. I think it had tickled her far too much to imagine me consuming rubbing alcohol to see the valiant effort I was making.

"It's the point."

"There's alcohol in hand sanitizer too."

Didn't it just figure? "Fuck. Well, that will have to remain on the list. Daisy needs that."

And I needed her. More with every passing hour.

I'd hoped opening a vein at the show would at least soften Daisy toward me again. I was wrong. She'd split mid-concert, and I hadn't seen her since.

Sarah was keeping her distance for the most part. She stuck closer when I went out, especially as the date of my appearance ticket neared and the cockroaches—I'm sorry, tabloid journalists—had again emerged from underneath their kitchen sinks to cluster around my building. Or their holes in the earth, whichever.

She'd come in for a meal now and then during her shift, and I couldn't deny the company was better than whatever deafening music I put on to pretend I wasn't alone. Suddenly, that whole solitude thing didn't hold much interest for me.

In the silence, I found myself flipping through old photo albums. Looking at pictures I hadn't touched in years. Most of the books were caked in dust from living in a box at the back of my closet. I'd never been ready to see Kerry or my mom again. Why did I need to? They lived in my memories.

Turned out the pictures pulled something loose in me just the same. I'd been so much younger then. Chronologically, not that much.

In reality? Lifetimes.

Daisy had been in a bunch of the snapshots too. Her arm slung around my sister, their smiles huge and goofy like the young teens they'd been. In one, she and my mom were dancing in our small, rundown kitchen, probably to some soul classic favorite of my mom's. She'd listened to Marvin Gaye, Al Green, and Teddy Pendergrass from the time the sun came up until it went down. I'd always been too busy to pay attention to much in those days, but Daisy had slid seamlessly into our family.

She'd always taken care, when I'd been so fucking careless.

I flipped through the albums my mom had meticulously kept, laughing at some of the pictures, reminiscing with others, and needing to walk it off a few times when it came to the rest. My life was in those dusty books, and I'd fought so hard to lock it away so it didn't hurt anymore. But I'd locked away the good too. I'd shoved my mom and my sister into the darkness when seeing them again eased the ache in my chest, just a little.

The last page of the final album had a photo from the last month Kerry had been alive. Somehow it was of the three of us, but Kerry had been more off to the side. I'd had my arm around both of them and was smiling at the camera—shockingly—as was Kerry.

Daisy was smiling too. Up at me.

Her hand was on my chest, her face tilted up toward mine. I didn't know if I was seeing what I wanted to or if there was something there. If she'd felt for me then what that photo suggested.

If somehow, someway she still felt that way about me now.

I pulled it out from underneath the clear page protector, rubbing away the gummy film on the back from where it had been placed in the album. My sister's small, precise handwriting hit me like...well, like only my baby sister could do.

Daze and the love of her life. Oh, and me.

2015 was written in a heart.

God, I was an idiot.

Touching the arrowhead around my neck, I released a long breath. "I hear you. Finally."

I grabbed my wallet and slid the picture inside into the spot where I'd kept the generic family photo that came with the wallet, because I didn't have a family anymore.

But I did. They were gone physically, but they were a part of me. Daisy was a part of me.

If she'd still have me.

I forced myself to put the albums back in their box. Then I decided to take them out again and line them up on the shelf above my living room fireplace. I rarely turned it on because my resting body temperature was about a zillion. I admired them on that shelf for approximately two minutes before considering the heat could warp them—if I ever had someone over who liked to stay warm, say someone beautiful and sweet with a definite side of kickass.

Just in case, I moved them to the end table beside the couch and stacked them precariously until I found a better location.

All in due time. Right now, I had other matters to attend to.

I snatched my phone and hit speed dial for a number I'd never called. A number Lila had actually willingly provided.

Nick's voicemail picked up.

Not available or I don't like you. If I do, I'll call you back. Or better yet text. Who calls people anymore? For fuck's sake.

That was it. His entire voicemail greeting.

I couldn't decide if I was amused or annoyed. In the end, I just hung up. He would see that I'd called and could do as he chose.

Now what? I didn't know anyone who did jewelry shit. I'd bought something for a woman with stones in it exactly once, and she was my mother. I'd gotten her a bracelet from a school fair where she'd provided the cash. Pretty sure the stones had been glass, but she'd *oohed* and *aahed* over them just the same.

My cell buzzed in my hand, and I stared at it in shock. He'd actually called me back.

"Did your wife make you call me?"

"She's not the boss of me."

"Willing to bet she has ways of convincing you to do things."

"I'll never tell," he said in Brittany Murphy's creepy singsong voice from that old Michael Douglas movie, *Don't Say a Word*. "If you're calling for love life advice, the doctor is out. I used up all my reserves on you last time."

"No, I'm good there."

"That seems unlikely. Let me guess, did you decide to play the field until your nuts fall off?"

I sat on the arm of the couch. "Is this your idea of friendship? It's not entirely unlike mine with the guys in the band, except it didn't start from our first conversation. There was at least a breaking in period."

"All right, what do you want?"

"I need a decent jeweler."

"Ahh, my reputation precedes me."

"Your reputation for what? I mean, other than being an asshole, but not sure that applies here."

"I can still not help you."

"Fine, yes, your reputation about...something precedes you. Do you know of any good jewelers in the city?"

"I live in LA. Not sure you're aware of that."

"Right, but you spend time in New York sometimes, don't you? At Lila's parents' farm?"

"Happy Acres is nowhere near the city. However, you're in luck. My network is vast."

I had to smirk. "Naturally."

"What exactly do you need done?"

I told him without getting too specific. As expected, he was not impressed.

"Dude, this is for Daisy? You're not going too hard with trying to win her over."

"She doesn't want me for my diamonds."

"You have no diamonds."

"Exactly. Besides, this has special meaning for us. Trust me. You think that place can do it? In like," I checked the time on the phone, "Seventy-two hours or so? I can give him like another day or two if necessary."

"Oh, jeez, can you? He'll be overjoyed. Craftsmen need time, Osmond." I named a figure, and Nick cleared his throat. "I bet he can work you into the schedule. Let me make a call."

He hung up.

I waited for almost an hour, sitting in exactly that same spot. This idea was the cornerstone of my plan. Well, one of the cornerstones. The biggest one, since the plan was kind of flimsy.

My knowledge of romantic gestures sat at exactly zero. Cooper had given me a list of rom coms from his sister to watch, stuff with titles like chocolate in French. Supposedly, they would up my romance IQ.

She'd mentioned Daisy's *Pretty in Pink*, but even the title scared me off that one. I'd tried *Dirty Dancing*, because dirty, and I knew Swayze was a good actor. But the dirty parts were moderate, and there was far too much stuff about pickles on plates and putting Baby in a corner.

I still didn't feel any more up on this crap, so I was winging it. Maybe Daisy would want to watch some of those movies at a later time. I could probably tolerate them if I got to grope her during snack breaks.

He finally called back. "You're in. Get over there in fifteen. Ask for Lance." He rattled off an address.

I jumped up. "That's crosstown from me. Do you know this city? Do you know how long it takes to get anywhere?"

"Better get moving. Also, thanks for being so generous. I get a ten percent commission. Good luck." Yet again, he hung up without saying goodbye.

His wife did the same thing. No wonder they'd found each other.

I went into the kitchen. Sarah was paging through a magazine, looking bored senseless.

"Want to go on a recon mission?" It wasn't one, but I figured the term would make her happy.

She leaped up. "Sure. Wait, what kind of recon are *you* doing?"

"Well, not exactly any." I tossed her the keys to Priscilla. I couldn't let her drive Jenny. That honor belonged solely to Daisy, when I wasn't behind the wheel. But in this case, I was willing to test Sarah's supposed super skills. "This is for Daisy."

"Okay, I'm listening."

I filled her in on the way over, once we'd yet again sneaked out of a side exit. The traffic took far more than fifteen minutes, as predicted, but Sarah's skills truly were something to behold.

Once we arrived at the small, unobtrusive jewelry shop, I took a deep breath. "I'll be out soon."

I hoped.

The consultation took under fifteen minutes. Lance promised to have the piece couriered over to me by Monday, which was a couple of days past when I'd hoped but still better than I probably deserved. I thanked him profusely and left the store to ask Sarah to drive me to a place where I was guaranteed to receive a much cooler reception.

Ever opened her apartment door and immediately started to shut it again. "No."

"C'mon, Ever. Hear me out."

"How do you know my sister isn't here?"

"I don't. I was hoping."

"Hoping for which?"

I mopped my brow. I was actually sweating, and it wasn't only from the ten flights of stairs I'd just run up to burn off some energy. "I want to see her. I need to. But not yet. Where is she?"

Ever opened the door wide. The furniture had been shoved back, and a yoga mat took up half the room. "She got a temp job doing hair down the block, since her actual job is about to end. Her dream job gone forever, because of you and your wandering dick."

I half expected her to spit on the ground in disgust.

"My dick hasn't gone anywhere, I swear. And no, she won't be losing her dream job." I hoped. "Can I come in, please?"

Ever crossed her arms. "You have never said please to me before. Even when you were shoving money at me to take care of my own sister, as if I didn't do it for free. Although I had fun using your cash to sign you up for dating sites. Funny they never contacted you. Must've been because I said you had syphilis. And yes, I used your full real name."

"You did not."

She shrugged. "You'll never know."

"Look, I love your sister." I swallowed hard, amazed the words hadn't gotten stuck. "I want to be a good guy for her. I think I can be, with some help."

Ever didn't so much as blink. "Let me guess, now you're offering credit instead of cash?"

"What? No. I'm doing it myself. Mostly myself. I have ideas. They require a little assistance."

"Doesn't everything with you?"

"Ever, just let me in, and listen to me. If by the time I'm done with the plan, you still think it sucks—that *I* suck—I'll leave you alone."

"And find someone else to help you break my sister's heart? Which is already broken, thanks to you."

I didn't know what else to do, so I took out my wallet and the picture of us I'd stashed there. I handed it to Ever.

"Look at the back."

She studied the photo for a moment before turning it over. "Kerry," she murmured.

"Yeah. I didn't know. I swear, I didn't. It never occurred to me someone like Daisy could see me as...well, someone worthwhile. Someone she could love. Maybe. If she does. Or did." I scraped my hands through my hair. I hadn't bothered tying it back, and it was in full wild mode. "I haven't earned it yet, but that doesn't mean I won't. I'll die trying."

"Right, another escape." She handed back the picture. "Sounds like Croly Street Oz to me."

I had to laugh. "If you don't help me, if no one helps me, I'm still going to do this. I'm still going to try. I have to. My life without her was so dark and empty I didn't even know it."

"That makes no sense."

"I thought that was as good as it got. But it wasn't. It isn't. A few days with her and everything changed. Me most of all. I want more of them. I want a lifetime."

So, yeah, that was new.

Ever narrowed her eyes. "She doesn't even do yoga."

I didn't know the connection, but I wasn't about to ask.

She relented and let me inside. I asked her nicely about three times for her assistance, which she finally gave once I mentioned if this went well, maybe Daisy would want to live with me since I had a number of homes.

That was the closest Ever had ever come to being perky in my presence.

Sarah frowned when I got back in the Spyder a short time later. "How did it go?"

"That woman is a black belt in ball-busting, but I think she might help. She also really wants Daisy off her couch."

"You do realize offering a place to live for financial reasons hardly makes a woman's heart go pitter-patter. Nor is it wise in the long term."

I snapped on my belt as Sarah shot into traffic. "I want her to live with me because there's so much I've missed in five fucking years. Never mind all the shit I missed before that while she was standing in front of me."

"The rate of homicide goes up greatly in close quarters. Proceed carefully."

I grinned. "Hey, I've got a bodyguard, right?"

Then I thought of Noah. I kind of wanted to talk to him too, without this whole episode becoming too Lifetime movie of the week. I mean, Daisy wasn't being sent off to war.

If this didn't work, we'd both be fucked up, but we'd live. We'd get over it.

I opened up my wallet and gazed at that picture of us. No, I wouldn't get over it. I'd never gotten over her in five years, even if I hadn't been smart enough to realize I'd fallen in the first place.

"It has to work. If it doesn't, she's going to leave the tour, and she'll never give me another chance." I looked out the window at the blur of traffic. All those strangers rushing by, going home to someone.

I wanted that life. I wanted a home and a family. *My* family.

I wanted Daisy.

I could only hope she still wanted me too.

TWENTY-THREE

THIS WASN'T GOING TO WORK.

Monday afternoon, I juggled the phone against my ear as I tried in vain to search through the literal tower of post-it notes my predecessor at Lou's Beauty Emporium had used to keep notes on her customers. Most inefficient system ever, but who was I to judge? I'd just started here. Maybe it would all make sense in time.

Maybe I needed a lot more coffee.

"Mrs. Jensen, I swear, your hair had your typical rinse. I can go through percentages if you'd feel better. I followed Dee's numbers exactly."

"Dee always made sure the blue looked more silver. I don't want to look like a grandmother."

"Of course not." *Then skip the blue rinse.*

"Unfortunately, I have a number of customers right now, but I'd be happy to help you with those percentages once I, um, service them."

"Miss Daisy, I'm very displeased. Let me talk to your supervisor."

Wow, there was the way to start a new job.

"I'd be happy to let you speak to her, but she's currently unavailable. Can I have her call you back?" I didn't say Stacy was out back smoking and gossiping with the only other stylist currently working, leaving me to man the phones and deal with customers as they came in.

I wasn't elitist at all. A job was a job. But boy, it was a serious knock in the keister to come from working on the tour of a world-famous rock band to being dressed down at a place where I was basically scrambling for tips—scraps of tips at that.

Why had I threatened to give my notice again? Oh, right, because Osmond Taylor had used his massive penis like a mallet on that pesky organ in my chest.

"Surely there's someone I can speak to. I'm not happy at all with your attitude."

I gritted my teeth around a smile. She couldn't see me, but facial expressions conveyed over the line. Mine was wholly insincere, but I could only do so much. "I'm so sorry. I know this must be a very trying time," two of our other lines lit up, and I fumbled around the desk, looking for a plain pad of paper, not a freaking post-it note I'd have to keep track of, "but at Lou's Beauty Empire, we always stand by our work."

Accidentally, I bumped the coffee cup by my elbow—Stacy's, not mine—and hot coffee sloshed over my lap, drenching my bare legs. So much for wearing a skort on my first day. "Motherfucker!"

That was the end of my brief, colorful employment at Lou's Beauty Emporium. Which I only fully remembered the name of when I got my pink slip.

That was actually yellow, since post-its ruled the world.

I stomped back to the apartment, calling my sister on the way. She didn't answer. Well, actually, she did, in the form of a changed voicemail greeting that made me frown, hang up, and immediately call back.

I'm not home, but once you are, walk seven steps from the door, take a left, then another left, and look down. You know where to go.

I picked up the pace. Luckily, I'd chosen this salon for its proximity to Ever's place, so I didn't have far to go.

What the hell? It wasn't my birthday. She didn't know I'd gotten fired. Lila didn't even know officially that I was quitting, so I was just going to...not do that. There was no reason at all to be celebrating, other than I wasn't going to let Oz drive me away.

I'd lived without him for five years. I could live without him again. I had a whole soundtrack of women's anthems on my iPhone that proved men were only good for one thing.

It sucked that Oz was truly exceptional at that one thing, but I still had a vibrator and good fantasy fodder. Somehow getting off to him when he had no clue was poetic justice. Probably a little twisted, but hey, a spurned woman had to take the good with the bad.

Once I arrived at Ever's, I followed her directions to a T. I ended up in the small bathroom, staring down at a collection of Trinity's hair products and a used condom in the garbage can.

That had better not be my sister's. I was going to kick her ass. Why, I didn't even know. She was being responsible. It just wasn't fair she was getting some and I wasn't, although I probably wouldn't lead off with that in my speech.

Before I lit into my sister, I listened to the voicemail greeting again and realized I'd made a vital misstep.

Being with Oz had made me as directionally challenged as he was. Good thing he'd dumped me. Who knows where I would've ended up if we'd stayed together?

Sexually satiated, happily employed, and just happy period, but who was keeping score?

At least I hadn't given my notice. I was keeping my dream job and ditching the male baggage.

Yay vibrator.

I retraced my steps according to Ever's directions and frowned down at the chair in front of the window. The Mötley Crüe keychain made my heart kick hard, but this time, there were only two keys on the chain. One labeled J and one labeled D.

My head started to spin so I dropped my bag and sat down on the floor to wait for the ground to not feel like it was about to crumble beneath me.

J was for the truck. Oz's truck. He'd done this? But what was the D for?

I turned the truck key over. *Red tree.*

What the hell? I scrambled to my feet again and gripped the windowsill, bumping my forehead against the glass as I looked in both directions. Sure enough, Oz's truck sat in a spot just up the street, underneath a tree with oddly red leaves.

I'd never noticed that tree before, but now I would never forget it.

Damn Oz.

I picked up my bag again and ran into the bathroom to fuss with my hair. My makeup was still intact, and my hair was a little crazy from the humidity, but nothing a few spritzes from one of my magic sprays couldn't fix. I washed my hands a couple of times, just to buy myself a moment or two to settle.

To not jump out of my damn skin.

I hated that I missed him so much. That I craved him more than any drug I'd ever tried.

If any man could break me, it was Oz. He'd already tried to do it once.

Hell, twice. First at the funeral, then leaving me alone in bed.

Third time was *not* going to be the charm.

I debated changing my clothes before deciding that he was going to get me as I was. Sweaty, coffee-stained, mad, and uncomfortably horny. But the yearning side of me was already trying to poke out her head like a shoot through cracks in the sidewalk.

Just so I could get trod on again? Nope, not this time.

I slicked on my expensive red lipstick and tossed my bag over my shoulder. If he had something to say, I would hear him out, but I wasn't going to swoon at his feet. He was getting a full dose strength of the real Daisy.

On the way out the door, I went back for my vibrator. It was a new model, large enough I could probably use it as a weapon if need be.

I didn't know why I took it with me. Maybe as a reminder he'd been dismissed?

Possibly.

Most likely, I was not in the right frame of mind to have this conversation, what with having sticky thighs not from good sex, bad sex or any kind of sex at all, but from burnt coffee that had tried to get into my panties and had partially succeeded.

I slammed Ever's door behind me and sent her a quick text.

I don't know how he got you to do his bidding, but you can warn him I'm on my way.

TWENTY-FOUR

IT WAS ALMOST NIGHTFALL WHEN THE SOUND OF GRAVEL ROLLING
under the tires of my truck outside had me leaping to my feet. I rushed
around the place, quickly fluffing throw pillows and kicking my
discarded song pad under the sofa.

Fuck, I hoped I'd done enough.

The truck stopped. I watched Daisy climb out, wearing some short
skirt thing that left almost her entire legs bare. I swallowed and willed
the pike in my jeans to cooperate. She wasn't going to make this easy
on me.

She seemed to be talking to herself as she stomped up the steps.
She paused briefly beside the sign I'd fixed and hung so proudly,
mumbling again before reaching into her bag and pulling out
something pink.

Only when I opened the door to greet her did I realize the object
she was brandishing like a weapon was a large vibrator. Or dildo.
Whatever, it was a woman's preferred bedtime buddy.

"Hi?" It was all I managed before she poked it against the screen
door.

"You see this?"

"Yes?"

"You have been replaced. And before you ask if I've been drinking, no, I have not. I am perfectly sober. I just want you to realize that nothing you say can change what I have in my life now. I can afford to be much more choosy."

I didn't know if I wanted to laugh or call the furniture store to return everything I'd bought.

Clearing my throat, I crossed my arms. "You saw the sign?"

She snorted. "You crossed out Fisher's Rest and wrote Daisy's in black sharpie. Is that supposed to impress me?"

"It was not sharpie. It's black acrylic paint I had to get at the women's craft store."

"The *women's* craft store? Is that a new kind?" She pushed on the screen door. When it didn't open and I didn't invite her in, she jammed the key I'd given her into the lock. "Stand back."

I did as she asked so I didn't get knocked unconscious by the door. In her current mood, anything was possible.

She stepped inside without even looking at all my hard work and pitched the keys I'd given her across the room. "You know what happened to me today? I got fired."

"What? Lila fired you?"

"I don't work for Lila anymore, in case you've forgotten. Because I was stupid enough to give up on my dream job just because you're a giant oaf without a sense of compassion." She tossed the vibrator the same place the keys had gone.

For her sake, I hoped it had a soft landing.

"Do you have any clue what it was like for me to wake up alone after what we had together?"

I started to answer, then shook my head. "It was a mistake."

"A mistake. You took me to the highest heights I'd ever known and then you let me drop all alone. I read up on it, you know. And you did every part of it wrong except the orgasms."

"Read up on what?"

"The whole dominance and submission game you were playing.

Except it isn't a game. Real people have feelings, and they get hurt. Never mind physically. Do you even know about sub drop or aftercare? Do you even grasp those words? Because I didn't. I had no idea what you were introducing me to, but I loved it and I loved you, so I trusted you."

Her words were pingponging through my head too fast. I couldn't keep up. But one word echoed beyond all the rest.

Loved.

Past tense. It was too fucking late.

She shut her eyes, letting her bag drop at her feet. All at once, her exhaustion seemed to cave in on her, as if she'd driven up here on no sleep and nothing but anger to keep her going.

It took everything inside me not to reach for her. To pick her up and cradle her and love her the proper way I should have done long before this.

But I hadn't earned that right yet.

"I don't know any of those terms," I admitted. "I never studied anything. Never felt I had to. I'd never...there was some rough stuff a couple times in my past, but nothing like that. No one ever reacted like you, and I never reacted quite that way either. You pull something out of me."

She opened her eyes and surprised me with a tired smile. "Words? You so rarely say so many at one time."

"I don't have anything else to give you."

Her laughter was so weary. "I only wanted you. I didn't want any of this. Not keys and maps to make me think you actually want me here now. Not signs with paint from the *women's* craft store."

I was never going to live that one down.

She finally glanced around the room before letting out a long sigh. "Definitely not a *pink* couch." She walked over to it and sat down, relaxing into it as if she couldn't sit up straight any longer. "At least it's comfortable. Better than the other one. That was a mess."

"Thank God." I didn't sit beside her on the sofa. Instead, I sat on the plush purple armchair, which I was beginning to regret. "So, you like neutrals? I think that's what the guy called them. The boring colors. Brown and gray and tan."

"This place looks like Willy Wonka's now."

Yet another reference I didn't get. I would really have to start reading more.

Especially about this sub drop and aftercare stuff. I mean, I'd probably heard those terms before somewhere, but they weren't anything I'd ever thought about.

I'd certainly heard of safe words though, and what we'd done had definitely required one. I'd been so busy trying to drive her away for her own good that I could've seriously harmed her, far worse than a few quick spanks on her ass.

Leaning forward, I buried my face in my hands.

She didn't come over to soothe me. When I finally lifted my head again, she was just watching me from her spot a safe distance away.

"Are you okay?"

After a moment, she nodded. "I'm fine. You might've gone about it all wrong, but my biggest regret is that everything was so good."

"I never wanted to hurt you beyond—"

"Beyond what it would take to make me leave. Yeah, I got that. You just never expected me to like it. To want more." She leaned forward and it took all my willpower not to let my gaze drop to where her breasts strained against her snug top. "Or for me to be willing to let you go forever."

That killed my interest in her tits. Now I couldn't drag my focus from her face. "You're here. You came. You have to listen." I was on the verge of pleading. Begging if I had to. "I fucked up, Daze. I thought I was doing you a favor. Being honorable."

"You broke my heart. Again. I've let you do it twice now. I won't do it a third."

This time, I was the one who dropped to my knees. She didn't so much as blink as I walked across the new square-cut white shag rug on my knees until I was before her where she was seated on the couch. I didn't touch her. Just braced my hands on the sofa on either side of her and hoped like hell I wouldn't make this worse.

In the end, there was only one thing I could say.

"I love you," I murmured as tears filled her eyes.

She still didn't reach for me. Didn't say anything. Just waited.

"I found a picture of us the other day. My mom kept all those photo albums, you know? I think you helped her with some of them once."

Silently, she nodded.

"I hadn't looked at any of them since...well, not since Ker. I shoved them in a box and stuck them in my closet and pretended they didn't exist. Opening them again hurt so fucking bad. It hurt to see them. To miss them. But I didn't expect for it to feel good too. Like I was getting them back in some small way. I could see their smiles and their laughter and it was so much more tangible than my memories." I squeezed my eyes shut and prayed I didn't embarrass myself. "I can't hear her voice as well anymore in my head. I'm so scared I'm going to lose it. That then she'll be gone forever."

"Whose?" Daisy asked quietly. "Kerry's or your mom's?"

"My mom's especially. Kerry's I still hear, but only as screams when I sleep. The rest is all fuzzy." Admitting it made my throat ache. It seemed like another way I'd failed them. Who forgot what their own mother and sister sounded like?

Who had someone like Daisy in their life and nearly destroyed everything?

Me. I'd had so much good in my life, and I'd lost it.

Almost.

Because if there was any fucking chance for Daisy and I to figure this out, I was going to fight like hell. She was worth everything, and I was going to make sure I was worth her.

No matter how long it took.

"Which photo did you find?"

I took out my wallet and showed it to her. She smiled, the smile fading as she turned the picture over and read the words on the back. Then her gaze lifted to mine.

"Is that true?" I asked.

"What?"

"What Kerry wrote."

She ran the edge of her red fingernail along the back of the photo. "It was definitely 2015."

"Daisy."

"If you're asking if you're the love of my life, I don't know."

If she'd punched me dead in the face, it couldn't have hurt more. It was no less than I deserved, but still, I reeled from the blow.

"You're the only one I've ever had. The only one I ever wanted. But I don't know if you'll be the only one. I was willing to walk away from you and the job I adored to keep myself from hurting. Except it doesn't matter. I'll still feel as if I'm missing an arm when you're not around. I'll still wish I could hear you laugh and roll my eyes at your maneptitude."

"Thanks, Jame," I muttered.

"You're the most amazing man I've ever known. Strong and brave and funny and sweet when you aren't trying so hard to be a tough guy. Maybe a little lackluster when it comes to studying up on required subjects, but everyone has a few flaws."

"BDSM lite is a required subject? I like your idea of school." As quickly as the bravado came, it drained away.

Her eyes were raw and wet. And I didn't want to wear armor in front of her anymore.

I wanted—needed—her to understand.

"I didn't think Kerry wanted us together. You even said it yourself, she told you not to hit on me. But then I saw that photo and maybe it was just a joke or maybe it meant something more. It just felt like she was giving me permission."

"Permission to fuck me senseless?"

Only her slightly teasing tone allowed me to smile. "Permission to love you for the rest of my life."

"Don't." Her chin wobbled. "Don't say stuff you don't mean. Or even if you mean it, don't say stuff that won't matter when you get pissed at me and shut me out. Or when some guy sees my tits and you lose your mind and decide you're evil incarnate for punching him."

"I didn't think I was evil incarnate, exactly. Just not good enough for you."

"Yet suddenly you are? You buy a pink couch and a purple chair— which clash horribly by the way, someone needs to teach you color theory—and you buy—"

"Paint at the women's craft store, yes, get to the point."

"Throw pillows," she corrected, "and shag rugs and dear God, is that actually a picture of a unicorn over there?"

"Put your glasses on. It's a damn Palomino."

"I only need them to read, thank you very much. The light's just weird in here. New lamp too." She started to laugh, and then she started to cry.

I nearly begged again, except this time for her not to cry. I couldn't stand it. But I knew bottling up her emotions was far worse than letting them out.

I was living proof of that.

Without speaking, I moved up to sit beside her on my new ugly sofa. I drew her into my arms, prepared for her to shove me away or hit me or God only knows. But she just curled into me, getting my shirt damp from the flood of her tears. I stroked my hand down her hair and rested my chin on the top of her head, so incredibly grateful I'd even been allowed this much.

It was a long road ahead of us, and I was ready to walk every step.

"I don't need anything from you," I said after a while, once her tears had slowed. "I mean, promises or a commitment or anything."

She angled her head toward me. "You realize we actually haven't made up yet, right?"

"Yeah. I'm just saying. I won't rush you. I won't demand a timeline or words or anything other than what you want to give. I'll give you space." I collected one of her spent tears on my fingertip and rubbed it away, wishing I could make them all disappear. "Anything you want is yours."

"All I ever wanted was you."

I couldn't speak.

She sat up and cupped my cheeks. "All beardy again. Happens so quick. As if I'd never even been here." Her thumb touched the corner of my mouth. "Kerry said we could be good for each other."

"What?" Slowly, I met her eyes. "But you said—"

"The night before she died we went to one of the field parties. She didn't touch anything that night. I didn't either. She was thinking about after. You know, once she was gone."

I stared at her, not wanting to understand.

Horror crossed her face. "No, not like that. You know, California. She must've meant..." She fell silent. "That's what she meant, right?"

I pulled her in, holding on when she started to shake. When I shook right with her.

"I didn't see it. I didn't know." She pressed her wet face into my throat. "She was my best friend. I didn't see it."

Carefully, I brushed her hair back from her stricken eyes and red cheeks. "We don't know anything for sure. Nothing has changed. She made her own choices."

"We were supposed to help her. We didn't."

"We didn't know. We still don't. Combing over her words and trying to guess what was in her head is enough to make anyone crazy. All I know for sure is that she never wanted to hurt you." I dragged in a breath. "Or me."

"No. She thought we would have each other." Daisy dashed at her tears, but they were falling too fast for her to catch. "What if we never had? It would be like she'd died all over again. We couldn't even give her that much."

"Loving her isn't a reason for us to be together. No matter what she wanted."

Daisy's throat moved. "No. You're right."

"The reason for us is to be together is because you make me happy. I've never been happy like I was with you for those two days."

Her smile broke through her tears. "You get this is crazy, right? No one falls in love in a weekend."

"We probably did a long time before that. It just helped seeing you naked. Because damn, you used to be hot, but now? Holy shit."

She laughed and pushed away my face. I kissed the center of her palm.

"I've only used that vibrator once."

It was my turn to laugh. "I'm still jealous of it."

"I bought it to scale." She flushed prettily. "At least I think it's close. I never had a ruler handy."

I cocked a brow. "You're rather filthy." I slid my arms around her. "I love it. I love you."

It didn't make sense that the words were so easy to say now, when I hadn't said them to another living person in more than five years. But it was as if they'd been there all along.

When she was in front of me. When she was gone.

Days we'd spent together and all the ones I'd missed.

"I want to believe that. I want to be with you. But I don't think I can bear to wake up again and find you gone." She lowered her head, and I caught the tears falling off her chin. I was trying like hell not to join her. "I want to trust you, Oz. Give me a reason. Make me believe you," she begged.

"I don't know how." My voice broke. "I don't know what to say. Or do. Help me figure it out."

She looked at me steadily, her gaze as direct as a laser. "You know what to do."

"No." I shook my head. "I haven't read up on it yet."

She laughed so hard I thought she might crack a rib. She cupped my jaw, her eyes going soft with amusement. "I won't tell if you won't. We can make our own rules."

"I have handcuffs in the bedroom. The velvet kind. They're much better than bedsheets. That's gotta be a *don't* in the handbook."

She wet her lips. "Not sure. I didn't get to that part."

"I thought you could, you know, do it to me."

Her eyebrow arched. "Do what to you?"

"Handcuff me. If we got there. Not saying I'm expecting that, because I don't." I allowed myself just the briefest glance down her sinful body. "We aren't all about sex."

"Even though I'm so much hotter now?"

"Well, do you expect me to lie?"

"No. You're hotter too. Or else I'm just really horny." She rubbed against me, and my cock reared against my zipper. "No, definitely hotter."

I frowned and rubbed at the brown spot on her leg, then noticed more were on her skirt. "What happened to you?"

"I dropped coffee in my lap. It's a theme. At the club, Jamie's boyfriend of the hour splashed me with her drink."

"Maybe you just shouldn't wear clothes anymore."

"Not sure how that would help, but gotta say I think the idea has merit. Especially right now." She cocked her head. "Please tell me you didn't buy a pink bed. Or a Barbie one. Or whatever some salesperson convinced you was the way to a woman's heart."

My lips twitched. "No. Same bed. But I did stock three kinds of creamer. One was called Va-Va-Voom Vanilla."

She laughed, and I realized that I could be happy hearing just that sound for the rest of my life.

A little later, I added another sound to that list—her moaning beneath me as I secured the cuffs around her wrists.

"Okay?"

We were already both breathing hard, and I'd barely gotten her undressed. Turned out she didn't much care about using the cuffs on me right now.

My girl wanted to go first. And I'd put her first every day, always.

"I'm so okay." She looked down at herself, spread wide for me. So vulnerable and open. Putting herself into my hands.

I'd never been given a bigger gift. I wouldn't waste it.

I kissed my way down her body. Being as patient as I could. I filled my hands with her breasts, teasing the tight tips with my thumbs.

Rubbing my stubble over them as she whimpered and strained against her bonds.

She'd decided she didn't mind stubble burn. I'd probably let her shave me again though.

Later. Much later.

"Oz."

"Hmm?"

She arched as I dragged my knuckles over her clit. "Will you please fuck me now?"

"I'm trying to go slow." I slipped a finger inside her. Then two. Then three.

It still wasn't enough, so I turned my fingers, twisting them erotically inside her, and went for broke, nudging the blunt tip of my thumb against her ass.

"Don't," she gasped.

I looked up at her, instantly removing my hand.

"No, not that. God, do that. Four fingers. All of them. In me."

My cock lurched just from her dirty words as I did as requested. "As she wishes."

"God, your hand. The way you move it. Like you're holding me, cupping me like Vicki."

Even unable to breathe from her wetness slicking over my fingers and her pussy sucking me in, I had to laugh against her shoulder. "That sounds more wrong than it should. Maybe I should stop personifying my stuff."

"Maybe you should name something..." She tried to breathe as I worked her body, drawing everything from her she'd stored up for me. "After me."

I drew her lower lip between my teeth. "Who says I didn't already?"

Her eyes flashed open before she bowed up, rattling the cuffs and the velvet ropes attached to them as she tumbled over.

I took my fingers from her and licked them. Shamelessly. Drawing out the moment while she writhed beneath me, already wanting more. "My favorite fucking taste. All of you, all over me."

I didn't wait. Couldn't. I went to grab one of the condoms, but she kicked out at me. "No. Let's try it without." Trust shone in her eyes. "Along with everything else, I literally just had my fucking period."

Her absolute disgust at that fact made me laugh into her hair, spread like sunlight over my pillows. "It's still a risk."

"It is. You're right. We shouldn't do it." Her tone was unnecessarily sober, her version of making fun of me.

It was stupid. Crazy. Shit happened.

We weren't being smart. But right now, I just did not care.

I didn't argue with her again. I just parted her legs and sank home, letting out a groan of pure relief that she was surrounding me again.

Bare. Nothing between us but skin and sweat and trust.

And love. So much fucking love.

I tried to make it last. Stroke after stroke, I held on. Already riding that thin wire's edge.

"Please. Don't make me wait."

Fuck, she actually wanted me to come inside her. Those words were all it took to yank me right up to the brink.

"God, Daisy."

I emptied myself into her, dropping my brow to her breasts as I let go. She took me, shaking underneath me, around me. With me.

As one. Finally.

I couldn't get the cuffs off her fast enough. She curled into my arms, tangling her legs with mine as she pressed a kiss to my jaw. "Mmm, can we do that again?"

"Sure. How's tomorrow?"

She opened one sleepy eye. "You got plans tonight?"

I laughed and kissed her temple, pulling her on top of me. I couldn't get her close enough. Couldn't wrap her tightly enough in my arms.

"Oz. The door."

I was halfway asleep. Warm, sated, happier than I had any right to be. "I locked it before."

"Not that. Someone's at it."

Dimly, I heard a knock. Short, staccato. It reminded me of—

"Oh, fuck. I forgot." I sat up straight in bed, nearly knocking her off me. She squeaked and flailed, trying to keep from tumbling to the floor.

"What the hell, Oz?"

"Sorry, sorry." I grasped her arm and righted her on top of me. "You have to get dressed and get that."

"I do? Why?" She looked around frantically. "Where are my panties?"

A little sheepishly, I pointed upward to where they were hanging from the ceiling fan. "I'll just get those for you."

She giggled. "Nice aim."

Two minutes later, the relentless pounding on the door had not stopped, and we were both a semblance of dressed, me sans shirt. Daisy shot me a look over her shoulder before she threw open the door and let out a gasp.

Whether it was from the giant bouquet of pink tulips or the fact that Chuckles was holding them, looking as if he was hoping to be taken down by enemy fire, I could not say.

"Surprise." His tone could not have been any flatter.

"Oh!" She grabbed the vase from Noah and buried her face in the dozens of flowers. "Hey, look, more pink." She grinned at me from between the flowers, and I probably could have fallen in love with her again, right there.

I shrugged, feeling stupidly pleased with myself. "I've heard girls like it."

Hell, her vibrator was pink, right? I could've done worse.

"We do. We also love lace and dolls and women's—"

"Craft stores," I finished for her. "Have your fun, Flannigan."

"There's this too." Noah produced a square jeweler's box from inside his jacket pocket and handed it to Daisy, who nearly dropped the vase in her haste to accept it. "Have a good night, kids." He pointed at me. "You better remember what I said."

Then he was gone.

"Thanks. Bye, Noah!" Daisy set down the vase and ripped the top off the box. "What did he say?"

"All manner of threats. Good thing I have a bodyguard."

Daisy sucked in a breath as she peeled back the tissue. "Oh my God." Her hand went to her mouth before she withdrew the arrowhead carefully from its cushioned rest. "You—oh, it's so beautiful." She bit her lip as she traced the new stone inlaid where the turquoise had once been. "Rose quartz."

"You know stones?" My voice came out thick. "It's for love."

"Yes. And pleasure. And warm, positive energy." A tear escaped as she touched the edges of the piece. "Is this silver?"

"White gold. The chain too." Swallowing hard, I turned it over to show her the back of the necklace and the simple childish heart etched there, a replica of the one Kerry had done.

2015.

"When we started," I said in case she didn't get it. "But it was before then, wasn't it?"

"Yes." Her eyes met mine as she lifted up her hair with one hand. "Put it on me. Please."

I fastened the clasp around her neck and she closed her fingers around mine on the chain. "I love it." She rose up on her tiptoes to kiss me, slow and sweet. "I love you."

"Thank God." I cleared my throat. "One more thing in that box. I hope."

Eyes widening, she turned back to pull out the single folded sheet of paper.

You were going to be her savior
But you couldn't even save yourself
Burn the candle at both ends
Revel in the flames
Heat's too much
Need more

More
More
Like the burn licking against your skin
Swallow the match
Come back and do it again

I won't fall
Balanced on the tightrope
I'll do it for you
We can survive together
Thrive together
Just look away
Don't watch and see

Laugh in your face
It's just a game, silly
I like how it makes me feel
You can't save me
You won't save yourself
A savior in the dark is a coward in the light
And I'll take both of us down
Tonight

"So, that's not exactly a love song," I began.

Her head came up, her expression dazed. "You wrote this? It's incredible. Is it going to be on the album?"

"I don't know about that." I scratched the back of my neck. "You're the only one who's ever seen it so far."

"I'm honored. Truly. Will you sing it to me? And play Vicki?"

"Sure. You're not upset it's not, well, romantic?"

"Honestly, I thought it might be an ode to the color pink, so I'm actually overjoyed." She giggled as I pinched her hip.

"You wanted to know what's already named for you?" I grabbed her hand and brought it to my chest.

She gave me a sly smile. "Here I thought you'd say your dick."

"Hmm. In retrospect, maybe that would've been better. I'll learn as I go along." I drew her into my arms. "You own both. Lock, stock, and Daisy."

"Since we're confessing things, I didn't ever really quit the tour."

"What?"

"I planned to. It wasn't a stunt. But when I got fired today, I decided I wasn't going to lose the job I'd always dreamed of just because you were a cocktoast."

"Let me guess. Jamie's word?"

"Who else?" She shrugged. "But the band is becoming my family. Every last crazy one of them. Finally, I found my place. With them," she rubbed her thumb over my knuckles, "and with you."

I released a long, grateful breath. She'd given me a second chance.

Or maybe a fiftieth.

I wasn't going to waste it.

"I was a cocktoast. And a prick. And many other things you've probably called me before and since." I tipped up her chin with my finger. "Let me make it up to you for the next fifteen thousand days."

Slowly, she smiled. "You've got a deal."

EPILOGUE

Two weeks later

ANOTHER WEEK, ANOTHER BAND MEETING.

I was so fucking happy I didn't even mind.

Cooper poked the pad I was doodling on. "So, I'm guessing that dopey expression means your reconciliation went well? My sister said that French movie was good for sex tips. Which, gross, but I guess she was trying to help."

I grinned. "Sex is the one thing I actually didn't need help on."

That wasn't entirely true. But let's just say Daisy and I were doing our research together and making up for lost time.

She was probably still recovering right now.

"Doubtful, but Daisy has been humming every time we've seen her this week, so you must've at least found her clit." Jamie leaned across the table to slap my hand. "Good job, stud."

Even Jamie couldn't kill my mood today.

Everything was going so well. I hadn't sneaked out on Daisy this morning. I'd awakened her just to make her coffee and heat up a croissant—she liked those—and to tell her that I was absolutely not running away, I just had a band meeting and would be back afterward.

After I'd said it three times, she pushed me out the door and shut it in my face.

So, I guessed we were good there.

Lila walked into the meeting room of Ripper Records' New York corporate offices. And she wasn't alone.

Donovan Lewis strolled in after her, dressed all in black as he tended to be. The meaningless chatter came to a sudden halt as the door closed behind them.

I could've sworn I heard locks bolting shut around us.

"Good morning, Brooklyn Dawn." Lila's voice was clear and crisp, as it always was. But her face was unnaturally pale, and her eyes were stark.

I sat up straighter and exchanged a look with Cooper. He shrugged. He was as much in the dark as I was.

Fuck, it was back. I might've been in a love-drunk haze for the past two weeks, but whatever the *thing* was that surrounded us, it hadn't gone away.

Judging from Lila's expression and the presence of Donovan, it had only gotten worse.

"I know this is your break, but circumstances have arisen that made this meeting an imperative." Lila sat at the head of the table. Only then did I realize she didn't have her iPad with her for the first time in forever.

Donovan remained standing. "Lila received a letter this weekend. It was sent to her house."

We all glanced at each other.

"A letter?" Lindsey asked. "Saying what?"

"The gist was that the things that have occurred weren't accidents or random events, as we suspected." Donovan shifted his gaze to me. "Including what happened at your cabin. Are you still staying there?"

"No."

Fuck, Daisy. She was alone at my apartment after she'd made me call off Sean. I knew I shouldn't have listened to her. Bigger forces were at play than we realized.

Even with all our suspicions, we still hadn't fucking realized how dangerous this situation was.

I rose. "I've got to get home. Daisy's at my apartment."

"Sean's on her guard. She's fine."

"My Sean?"

"Yes, your Sean. He recently joined Roth's security team. We need everyone we can trust right now. He's been throughly vetted," Lila said to everyone else, as if any of them cared about Sean's credentials.

I was the one flipping out.

"Sit down, Osmond." Lila gave me a small smile that didn't reach her eyes. "She's fine. I promise you."

I sat.

"The letter came to my home," she said again as if we hadn't grasped the gravity of that. I hadn't in my worry for Daisy, that was for sure. "The layers of protection I have should have made that impossible. Not just that my location is so vital to hide, but Nick lives there too. With what happened before, we took every precaution." Her fingers shook before she clamped them together. "This should've never reached there."

Nick. Fuck. I couldn't imagine what he was going through right now. They had kids. And they were trying to have another.

"You're okay," I said quickly.

Our gazes connected, and she smiled again. "I'm fine. Thank you for asking. We're going to get through this." She shifted to look at everyone else in turn. "We're going to be all right."

"I asked Lila to step away." Donovan's voice was low and level. "She has other concerns than Ripper Records. She should be with them right now."

The band glanced at each other. For the second time today, real fear flooded me, the kind I didn't know what to do with.

"I said no."

I exhaled, and I was fairly certain everyone else did too. Lila was part of the bedrock of Ripper Records. She'd been our manager since the beginning.

"It's not happening. I've been here far too long. No one is chasing me away. Especially not some anonymous person with an axe to grind."

"Against me," Donovan said. "In case you were wondering, the attack is personal. We haven't isolated it yet. We're working on it, pulling threads. Following every lead."

"Who's working on it?" Cooper demanded. "Roth? Noah? Because correct me if I'm wrong, they've been handling this from the beginning, and look where we are."

"We're bringing in additional security support, but we have full faith Aidan Roth and his team will figure out who is responsible. That includes Noah. He remains in charge of the security force and will be bringing on more bodyguards. Quinn Alexander, for one, whom some of you may know as Faith from Hammered's husband. Keys," Lila said when Teagan frowned. She was still the new kid.

"Oh, right. Gotcha."

"Sean is on Daisy's detail, since she has been directly targeted—"

"What?" The word exploded from me.

"We have to assume it because of what occurred at your cabin," Lila said gently. "Most likely, the target was you because you're a member of this band or just on this label, period. But just in case."

I nodded, but I didn't fucking like it. Not one bit.

"Noah will be shifting to Teagan, due to the situation in her past. We can't take any chances right now." Lila looked at Teagan, who dropped her gaze to her hands. "Your ex probably doesn't have anything to do with this, but we just don't know. Anyone could be involved."

"Her ex?" Lindsey frowned. "What are you talking about? When she joined this band, we asked her if she had anything we had to worry about in her past. You said you didn't, Teagan."

Teagan didn't answer.

"Elle vouched for you," Jamie put in. "Did she lie for you too?" She slammed a hand on the table. "Fuck. As if we need this shit."

"I've got Teagan." Cooper cracked his knuckles. "She doesn't need Noah. I was in the same fucking unit as he was. Had the same training."

"We don't have time for pissing matches. Cooper, Noah has had additional security training you have not. Not to mention three little words called conflict of interest. You also have your own detail."

Cooper stood and walked out of the room, the door thudding shut heavily in his wake.

Teagan still hadn't lifted her head. She was the quietest I'd ever seen her.

Guess our bubbly Teagan had some secrets. Then again, who the fuck didn't?

"We were going to cancel the tour."

"No. Absolutely not." Lindsey's voice shot out like a whip. "There are too many dates left. We have so many people on our team to think of. We can't just leave them in the lurch without a job with no warning." She pulled her hair band off her wrist and yanked her hair back severely from her face. "They won't send us running like cowards."

"Retreat isn't always cowardly." Donovan crossed his arms. "Sometimes regrouping is the smartest move you can make."

"We don't need to regroup. We're doing fucking fine. Our ticket numbers are in the stratosphere. There's absolutely no reason to go into hiding right now."

"You might want to think about how you'd feel if you lost one of those members of your team you're so worried about, Miss York," Donovan said evenly. "It's happened before. We're going to make damn certain it doesn't happen again. Even if that means making hard choices."

Lindsey pressed her lips together until they were white. "No. Not yet. Surround us with security. Lock us in our homes. I don't care. But we can't cancel the tour. Not yet."

Lila nodded. "I'm inclined to agree. Oblivion will also be going on tour again soon, so that means we'll have two major tours to cover at one time." She curled her fingers into a fist. "Two members of my family will be on the road at once, along with my stepsons and my best friend. Margo has a new baby."

None of us spoke.

"Never mind all of you. You're my family too." Her gaze moved over each one of us. "Every single one of you."

"We love you too," Jamie said, causing more than one head to shift in her direction. She shrugged. "I can have feelings too."

"For a while, life is going to get harder. Things will change. But we will get through this if we all work together and watch out for each other." Lila paused. "You're all in agreement about remaining on the tour?"

One by one, we each nodded. Not knowing what we were risking by just doing our jobs.

The thing we loved more than anything else.

I rubbed my chest. Well, it had once been what I'd loved above all else. Not anymore. Now I had a new reason to want to live my life besides the screams of the crowd.

"So, that seals it." Lila glanced over her shoulder at Donovan. "It's go time."

We appreciate our readers so much!
If you loved the book please let your friends know.
If you're so inclined, we'd love a review on your favorite
book site.

Keeping Teagan safe - and in my bed - is all I want. But I may have underestimated the threat that's facing us...

Turn the page for a special sneak peek of
PLAY MINE - Brooklyn Dawn Book 3.

Teagan

PLAY MINE

I HURRIED UP THE DARK ALLEY, LOOKING OVER MY SHOULDER with every sharp click of my low-heeled boots on the concrete. It had been awhile since I'd been a flagrant trespasser.

Technically, I wasn't trespassing now either. This wasn't the first time I'd visited a venue after hours. It didn't really count as trespassing if you had a pass to get you in, did it? Doubtful. But I'd definitely sneaked out to Purgatory.

Not the actual realm between heaven and hell. I wasn't sure where to find that particular portal and wasn't in any hurry to know if that would be my ultimate fate.

Certainly not for my current transgression.

It wasn't as if I'd hidden behind trees and Dumpsters as I ran down the sidewalk or anything. No, I'd taken a perfectly respectable Uber crosstown to the club where my band would be performing tonight.

The driver had let me off down the street and I'd taken my time passing by a few interesting storefronts. At this time of night, it probably wasn't wise. I'd gotten too used to being shadowed by Noah Jordan, my bodyguard.

But I hadn't even needed to duck my bodyguard detail, since those restrictions eased slightly when we weren't traveling from show to show. Though I would have ducked, if said bodyguard had been, well, guarding my body.

A metaphor for sure, since Noah had no use for it other than making sure I stayed in one piece.

We were just coming back from a couple of weeks off. Starting tomorrow night, my life would get locked down even more. We'd been asked to curtail our extracurricular activities during this "troubling" time for Ripper Records—our manager Lila Crandall's phrase, not mine.

That wasn't much of an issue for me, since I was single and had been since....

Okay, yeah, not going back that far. My ex Pat was part of the distant past, and I didn't have time for trips down memory lane. I was coping okay with singledom.

Over the past few years, I'd even managed to go on some dates. I'd let friends set me up a couple times. Right before I'd gotten the Brooklyn Dawn gig, I'd even tried Tinder.

But I hadn't slept with anyone since Pat. Maybe I was destined to be alone forever. God knows my fruitless crush on Noah hadn't gone anywhere. I'd channeled halfhearted energy into getting him to notice me. He had not. So, I'd moved on.

Clearly, I didn't know how to do relationships right. I definitely didn't trust my choices. And somehow, even though it had been a couple of years since my ex, I still felt...stuck.

At least my adult toy collection was currently at its peak, both in quantity and quality. If I kept it up, I'd probably achieve that All-Star membership with my online shop of choice like my high school friend Elle, though to me she would always be Ricki.

Hey, a girl had to have goals.

I bumped into a trash receptacle and had to slap a hand over my mouth to keep from screaming. Guess I was more spooked than I'd realized. Then again, it was freaking late.

Quickly, I used my laminated access pass at the side entrance. The door was almost indistinguishable from the wall surrounding it. When the security light glowed green, I slipped inside and leaned back against the door, my heart beating way too hard.

I shuddered and wiped my sweaty palm on my night creeper-style black pants. For heaven's sake, I hadn't done anything illegal. I had a pass, and I was one of the performers tonight. I'd done this before at venues we'd played at, although it had been a while. But I was starting to remodel my place, and I'd temporarily put most of my instruments in storage. My stage piano was here, unused. So, why not?

This whole adventure was just proof that I was *not* cut out to be a bad girl. How had I managed to join one of the most successful rock bands in the entire world?

A question for the ages.

If I'd been smart, I would've been home in bed, pretending to sleep. Toy time optional.

Maybe I should try melatonin again, weird dreams and all. That had to be better than burning off excess energy by playing alone in shadowy clubs.

The security lights near the ceiling provided the only illumination. A hush had fallen over the place that didn't entirely seem natural, as if all the loud music and sounds of talking and laughter had been cut off like a cord pulled from an amp.

I gripped my throat and forced myself to keep moving. This was not the ideal environment for a chick who jumped at spotlight switches and startled every time someone dropped a guitar pick.

After hurrying up the hallway, I moved into the main area of the club, which contained a mix of booths and overturned chairs on tables. The long bar gleamed even in the low light off to one side, and in front, the wide expanse of stage beckoned.

I crept toward it and then climbed the short flight of stairs on the side. The floor was reflective black tiles, perfect for magnifying the lights. Normally, the stage would be empty, but we'd arranged to have some of our equipment brought in around closing time so we would be ready to go for an early-ish band meeting and then rehearsal. At least two was early for me.

Once upon a time, I'd been a morning person, back when I'd temped as a legal assistant from nine to five while Pat went to his shared office space and worked on his art in a safe, non-judgmental space. I'd never understood how our empty townhouse had been unsafe or judging him, but in retrospect, I hadn't understood a lot about him.

I took a steadying breath and moved toward the curved bench placed in front of my keyboard. In the arenas, I used my designer pink Steinway Grand piano, a gift from my far too sweet parents for joining the band. At smaller venues like this one, I made do with a portable piano rig.

But my special riveted padded bench came with me everywhere.

I slid a loving hand across the leather, molded precisely to my own shape after many hours of rehearsal and shows, then sat down and ran through a quick set of scales. Limbering up my fingers as an athlete would, warming them so that I could do the tricks I saved for my own personal concerts. Hand over hand, occasionally even behind my back. Fun stuff that amused me and had no place in Brooklyn Dawn shows.

In a band full of big personalities, I was happy to just play a support role, quietly and competently. Well, mostly quietly, except when I'd had a little too much tequila.

I rolled my achy, tense shoulders and forced myself not to look out into the empty audience. Already I was going to that place in my mind where I imagined a crowd listening to me as I played. The sound of the notes rang out so clear and true, luring me to play one of my favorites. "Moonlight Sonata" was a moody, desolate piece, at least to me. But instead of helping me relax as it usually did, the nerves buzzing along my spine only grew.

It's just thoughts of Pat crowding in. And hello, middle of the night, weirdo.

My hands moved without me telling them to, which was a good thing since my mind was racing in concert with my heart. But the music eased me even as I glanced around, half expecting to catch a movement out of the corner of my eye.

Maybe Coop had followed me. He was my closest friend in the band and we hung out often. At least we had before the latest Ripper Records chaos had opened up a rift between us.

He didn't make a habit of lurking around my place when I hadn't invited him over, but lately, he was fairly obsessed with keeping an eye on me. That was a less worrisome thought than thinking someone *else* could be here with me.

Nah. That was just nerves talking. Much better to focus on my fingers gliding across the keys as I played Gershwin's "Rhapsody in Blue" than to work myself into a frenzy over nothing.

Hadn't I sneaked out tonight for the thrill of pretending to play for a crowd of my own? Now I was freaking out about shadows.

Think about Coop. Just Coop.

A smile curved my mouth. He wasn't a hardship to think about. No one could make me laugh like he did. Every now and then he called me "little redhead girl" after Charlie Brown's crush. I didn't even know where he'd picked that up, but he teased me with it when I poked at him about his love of peanut butter and banana sandwiches—gross—or his solitary ways to relax. He loved to go on long hikes anytime our bus was parked and we weren't needed for band stuff. Mostly because I wanted to hike with him. Silence between us was so easy and natural.

Or it had been before.

Things between us had been strained since Lila told us about the threatening letter she'd received at home and a little—very little—about my aggressive ex had come out. Coop had been hurt I hadn't gone to confession about my past relationship, but I hated talking about Pat. Or thinking about him. I also didn't like remembering the woman I'd been then.

And worse, wondering if I could become her again with someone else.

I'd been so shocked Lila had found out about Pat that only fragments of the ominous letter remained in my memory. Someone had a score to settle with Ripper Records, and that meant we were in the crosshairs as much as anyone else since we were in the middle of a big cross-country tour.

Lindsey, our lead singer and one of the de facto leaders of the band, hadn't wanted to cancel any dates, never mind the tour itself. Why would she? We were selling out venues left and right. If we didn't meet our commitments, our crew and all the various people part of the Brooklyn Dawn juggernaut would be out of a job for however long this threat remained. Not to mention disappointing the fans.

Nope, the show must go on. Period. As a band, we all agreed on that.

But doing shows and even innocuous stuff like riding in style in our tricked out tour buses wasn't the same right now. Nothing was. Not when we had bodyguards lurking around us at every turn when we were on the road.

And it wasn't just us. We were on a double header ticket with Warning Sign, Ricki's band, and they had the same deal. As would Oblivion when their world tour began later in the year, along with some of Ripper's other larger acts. Lila's husband Nick was a guitarist in Oblivion, and the letter had been delivered to their home, so naturally, Oblivion would get a lion's share of the security budget. Their bodyguards probably would have bodyguards by the time their planes were wheels up.

So much of our world was in flux right now. I didn't doubt the nameless specter hanging over our heads had something to do with my recent inability to sleep. I could only blame the full moon for my insomnia so many days of the month.

I stumbled over the keys, losing my place. I blew out a breath and tipped my head back, focusing on the few lights still on above the stage until they swam and shimmered.

Keep it together.

With effort, I shifted my gaze toward the main section of the club and imagined fans filling the seats, standing behind the booths, lining up along the bar. I willed my fingers to play the opening notes of one of Brooklyn Dawn's biggest hits to date, "No Escape."

Almost without realizing it, I began to sing along with the music, strengthening my voice as it faltered. As it wobbled and caught. But I kept going. This particular song was difficult for me. Too much of my past was held prisoner in lyrics and a melody I hadn't written yet felt down to my marrow.

he told me he was poison
 I didn't listen
 he swore he was no good
 but I saw only stars

in his eyes
 in my heart

I got off on the lust
 and the need
 oh, how he needed me
 it was hard to see
 that the stars were blinding me

cracks in the sidewalk
 make me fall
 poison in my blood
 taste it all

but i know when you call again
 there's no escape

no escape for me

A sharp, high-pitched sound like feedback screeched through the empty club, and I jumped, banging on the keys.

I almost took a header off the damn bench, just as I had at Ricki's engagement party. I'd met Noah that night. He'd helped me up and carried me out of there like a white knight. Of course I'd developed a little hero worship toward him. A little crush.

No one to help you now.

Breathing hard, nearly panting from panic, I gripped the edge of the bench and ducked my head as if I could make myself small enough to avoid detection.

Just an equipment malfunction. Maybe you imagined it. It might just be—

My cell phone blared shrilly in the pocket of my thin jacket. I swallowed a whimper as I fumbled for it, dragging it into my lap to make the noise stop.

The name on the readout made my hand shake.

Patrick Krell.

What were the chances he'd call me when I'd been thinking about him on and off all night? I didn't know why. We hadn't talked since... God, I didn't even know. They'd never found him to serve the restraining order I'd put in place after the break-in. In time, it had expired. I hadn't heard from him in years so I hadn't sought to get it renewed.

Now I was trembling, unsure what the hell to do, and he was on my phone.

I dismissed the call and forced myself to take a steadying breath. Then another. I shoved my phone in my back pocket so I wasn't tempted to look at it and slowly rose to my feet, wishing I had a weapon. I had a small, illegal bottle of pepper spray in my purse at home. Why hadn't I brought it with me?

Stupid. My life was a series of bad choices. I sincerely hoped this wouldn't become another one.

I glanced around. Nothing seemed out of place. I didn't hear anything. Could I have imagined the noise? I was certainly skittish enough tonight.

Swallowing hard, I reached up to redo my hasty topknot and huffed a few loose curls out of my eyes. I was freezing, my typical fear response. Didn't matter that it was the middle of June or that I'd worn a thin jacket in deference to the late night breeze. The air conditioning was pumping in the club, and my fight or flight response added a layer of goosebumps.

I really wanted to run. I wasn't supposed to be here anyway. Maybe someone who wasn't supposed to still be here had stuck around. Hell, someone could have followed me.

Or I could be having one hell of a waking dream-slash-nightmare.

Whatever the reason, I wasn't going to be able to relieve some stress by playing my heart out for a crowd that didn't exist.

And I also couldn't just back up and run away. I'd done that far too often. If there was a threat here, I'd deal with it.

I rushed to Cooper's drum riser and felt around behind his kit. He kept a spare set of sticks in a pouch there. It wasn't a traditional weapon, but if I had to nail someone between the eyes with a pair of walnut sticks, I would. Better to be prepared.

The best defense is being pissed off at needing a good offense.

I slipped the sticks out of their protective sleeve and gripped one in each hand as I approached the open doorway to the area behind the stage. I wasn't helpless. Not anymore. I had a gun at home and I knew how to use it. I'd taken Krav Maga. As small and petite as I was, I wouldn't be someone's victim again.

Even if I was shivering inside and out.

It was dark enough backstage to make my belly twist like wet ropes, frayed against the skin. I wanted to turn around. My feet seemed stuck to the floor. But I tightened my hold on Coop's sticks, letting their solid weight in my hands remind me that I wasn't some defenseless bird.

Coop himself had reminded me more than once that a man had many weak spots. His instep. His eyes. And hell, no one could dispute the power of a swift knee to the junk.

I would use whichever of those tactics I needed to. If I was lucky, I wouldn't have to use any of them and would walk out of here feeling strong.

Okay, so maybe I'd cool it with the late night solo club practice sessions. I could buy a portable keyboard to use at home until the renos were done and I could get my precious instruments back out of storage.

A sudden creak had me fumbling on the wall for a light switch. Shit, there had to be one in here. Another sound came from behind me and I whirled, shoulders braced, only to see more endless dark. I swung my arms out, suddenly claustrophobic, the darkness that enveloped me as solid as a wall.

Can't see. Can't breathe. Can't think.

Something clattered to the floor, pelting my feet. I barely felt the pain as I bolted out of there.

I ran across the stage and stumbled down the side steps then raced down the hallway to the side exit. It was locked from the inside and I slammed my fists on the glass, rattling the door in the frame. I didn't consider myself terribly strong, but I was so freaked out that I was pretty sure I could have broken the door with the power of my mind.

Glancing around frantically, my gaze landed on the "in case of fire" glass box attached to the wall. I didn't know what it was called or if it even worked the same way as it had when I was in school, but I yanked on the lever and pulling out the handled blade inside.

I didn't think. Didn't give my frenetic mind a chance to reason my way out of this. I just whacked at the door until the glass broke and alarms blared and I could shove my arm through the broken glass and wave my pass over the sensor.

The lock unsnicked and I burst into the alley, gasping for breath as if I'd run miles. My gaze pingponged around the narrow space until I oriented myself enough to glimpse the street at the opposite end. A yellow cab was chugging by and I sprinted toward it, shouting like an idiot over the still-screaming alarm as I flagged down the cabbie.

The older man stopped the car and rolled down his passenger window, his forehead puckered with a frown. "Hey, lady, you okay?"

"No. I'm not. I need a ride. Please."

"Okay, okay, lady. Where to?"

Biting my lip, I hesitated. I'd never been to Cooper's place. Now that I thought about it, that didn't make much sense. We were tight. He was my best friend other than Ricki, and she was so busy with her own band and her husband and probably endless baby practice that we rarely saw each other lately.

But Cooper and I were in close quarters all the time. Onstage, on the bus, and otherwise. Through strain and weirdness and late nights of bad diner food and stupid jokes I doubted anyone else would get.

He was my center.

The sound of sirens got my mouth going even as my brain rebelled. I couldn't run away. I'd caused property destruction. It didn't matter I hadn't meant to.

God, I hated being the woman who ran to a man. I'd promised myself I never would do that again. But everything felt like it was on the line. My safety. My life. My position in the band.

And no one had a cooler head during times of crisis—self-created or not—than Coop.

I rattled off Cooper's address and didn't quite understand the cabbie's wolf whistle. I mean, yeah, Coop lived on the Upper West Side near Central Park, and no, he wasn't hurting for cash. None of us were, but he'd been with the band far longer than I had. Just...whoa. The cabbie looked seriously dazzled.

Being impressed with Coop's digs was the last thing on my mind. I was so overwhelmed and afraid I'd lose my spot in the band—never mind the property damage I'd have to pay for and possible criminal charges—that I couldn't do anything but press my flaming hot face against the cool windowpane.

The car was muggy. Stifling. The AC didn't seem to even reach the back, although that could've been my terror keeping my temperature in overdrive and my heart racing.

Go me for changing it up from being perpetually freezing during times of stress.

And flights from justice. God.

By the time we reached Coop's building, I was practically numb. I juggled the sticks I still clutched and shoved money at the cabbie, far more than I should have. He tried to hand some back, probably thinking I needed it more than he did.

I didn't check out the huge spear of a building climbing toward a sky now edging toward dawn, the balance teetering between the darkest part of the night and the hope of another sunrise. My opulent surroundings only registered after I passed through an elaborate security setup with a pair of unsmiling guards into a foyer so white and gleaming I was nearly blinded.

I wasn't in my comfortably rundown brownstone anymore.

The cool-eyed older man behind the desk eyed me like he would a discarded condom wrapper. "Good evening. Welcome to The Edgemont. Do you have business in this building?"

Suddenly, I wasn't at all sure I did. I didn't have a spot with anyone. Certainly not *here*.

Now Available

For more information go to www.quinnandelliott.com

OBLIVION WORLD CHARACTER CHART

BEWARE...SPOILERS APLENTY IN THIS CHARACTER CHART. READ AT YOUR OWN RISK!

Aidan Roth: Roth Defense CEO and head security detail for Warning Sign
Brother of Marcus

Alexander Nash: Record producer
*Involved with Lindsey York, best friend to Kyle Brady *, friends with Logan King*

Angel Martin: Singer

Ava Templeton: Blogger, runs Hammered website and blog, writing book on Hammered
Sister of Callie

Beckett Manning: Owns Happy Acres Orchard
Brother of Zoe, Hayes, and Justin

Bent: security for J Town, JoEllen Foundation

Callie Templeton: Photographer
Married to Owen Blackwell, mother of Lily, sister of Ava

Chloe Adams: Waitress
Married to Michael Shawcross, mother of Axl (bio-father Snake Scotsman*), and Hope

Cole Riggs: Bodyguard for Roth Defense

Cooper Dallas: Brooklyn Dawn drummer
Involved with Teagan Daly, brother of Jenny Dallas

Daisy Flannigan: Stylist
Involved with Oz Taylor, sister of Everleigh Flannigan, best friend to Kerry Taylor *

Darcy: Brooklyn Dawn stage manager

Deacon McCoy: Oblivion bass guitarist
Married to Harper Pruitt, father of Alexa Grace, co-founder of Oblivion

Denver Casey (nee: Casey Lewis): Tour bus driver for Rebel Rage and Warning Sign
Married to Ryan Waters, niece of Donovan Lewis

Dex Munroe: Ripper Records executive, manager for Hammered and Warning Sign

Donovan Lewis: Ripper Records CEO
Uncle of Denver Casey

Ethan Haywood: Professor at UCLA

Involved with Molly McIntire and Luc Moreau, best friends with Lauren Bryant

Evie Pierce: MMA fighter
Involved with Johnny Cage, sister of Sutton, friends with Lindsey York and Jamison DuCaine

Everleigh Flannigan: Student
Sister of Daisy Flannigan

Faith 'Keys' Keystone: Hammered keyboardist
Married to Quinn Alexander

Felicity Hudson: Waitress
Involved with Myles Vaughn, sister of Robin

Flynn Sheppard: Solo country rock artist
Friends with Luc Moreau, Ian Kagan, and Rory Ferguson

Fred Ronson: Owns Happy Acres
Married to Laverne, father of Lila, step-grandfather of Michael and Malachi Shawcross, grandfather of Charlie and Avery

Gray Duffy: Oblivion rhythm guitarist
Married to Jazz Edwards, father of Dylan Edward, and Briana

Harper Pruitt: Tour chef
Married to Deacon McCoy, mother of Alexa Grace, sister of Randy *, best friends with Jazz Edwards

Hayes Manning: Owns Happy Acres Orchard
Brother of Zoe, Beckett, and Justin

Hudson Wyatt: Hammered drummer, former Formula
1 racecar driver
Involved with Piper Lockwood, best friends with Hunter Jordan

Hunter Jordan: Hammered lead singer
*Married to Kennedy McManus, brother of Noah, best friends with
Hudson Wyatt and Reed 'Bats' Mason*

Ian Kagan: Solo artist
*Engaged to Zoe Manning, father of Elvis, brother of Simon, best friends
with Rory Ferguson, friends with Flynn Sheppard and Kellan McGuire*

Indiana West: Hammered band manager

Isabella Grace: Bookstore owner in Winchester Falls
Married to Logan King, mother of Nichole, and Jared

Ivy Beck: Waitress at the Rusty Spoon and owns Rolling Cones ice
cream truck
*Married to Rory Ferguson, mother of Rhiannon, sister of August, and
Caleb, best friends with Kinleigh Scott, friends with Maggie Kelly and
Zoe Manning*

Jamison DuCaine: Brooklyn Dawn lead guitarist
Best friends with Lindsey York, friends with Evie Pierce

Jazz Edwards: Oblivion drummer
*Married to Gray Duffy, mother of Dylan, and Briana, sister of Molly
McIntire, best friends with Harper Pruitt*

Jenny Dallas:
Sister of Cooper Dallas

Johnny Cage: Rebel Rage lead singer and solo artist
Involved with Evie Pierce

Jonas Decker: Owns Purgatory

Juliet Reece: Warning Sign guitarist
Married to Tristan Eves, involved with Randy Pruitt*, father of Joshua Randall, sister of Margo

Justin Manning: Owns Happy Acres Orchard
Brother of Zoe, Beckett, and Hayes

Kellan McGuire: Lead singer of Wilder Mind, solo artist
Married to Maggie Kelly, father of Wolf, brother of Bethany, friends with Rory Ferguson, Ian Kagan, and Myles Vaughn
Kennedy McManus: Publicist for Hammered
Married to Hunter Jordan

Kyle Brady *: Former drummer and current studio technician
Best friends with Alexander Nash

Lauren 'Lo' Bryant: Author and occasional Warning Sign pianist
Married to West Reynolds, best friends with Ethan Haywood

Laverne Ronson: Owns Happy Acres Orchard
Married to Fred, mother of Lila, step-grandmother of Michael and Malachi Shawcross, grandmother of Charlie and Avery

Lila Ronson Shawcross: Ripper Records executive and Oblivion's manager
Married to Nick Crandall, mother of Charlie and Avery, stepmother of Michael and Malachi Shawcross, cousin of Zoe, Beckett, Hayes, and Justin Manning, best friends with Margo Reece

Lindsey York: Brooklyn Dawn lead singer
Involved with Alexander Nash, best friends with Jamison DuCaine, friends with Evie Pierce

Logan King: All the King's Men lead singer
Married to Isabella Grace, father of Nichole, and Jared, friends with Alexander Nash

Luc Moreau: Warning Sign co-lead singer
Involved with Molly McIntire and Ethan Haywood, brother of Katie, Kira, and Dean, former lead singer for The Grunge, friends with Flynn Sheppard

Maggie Kelly:
Married to Kellan McGuire, mother of Wolf, best friends with Kendra Russo, friends with Ivy Beck and Zoe Manning

Malachi Shawcross: Warning Sign drummer, former racecar driver
Married to Elle 'Ricki' Crandall, brother of Michael

Marcus Roth: Roth Defense CEO
Brother of Aidan

Margo Reece: Oblivion violinist
Married to Simon Kagan, mother of Raine Lila, sister of Juliet, best friends with Lila Ronson Shawcross

Michael Shawcross: Warning Sign guitarist
Married to Chloe Adams, father of Hope, stepfather of Axl, brother of Malachi, best friends with West Reynolds and Ryan Waters

Molly McIntire: Warning Sign co-lead singer

Involved with Ethan Haywood and Luc Moreau, sister of Jazz

Myles Vaughn: Former Wilder Mind pianist and solo artist
Involved with Felicity Hudson, friends with Kellan McGuire

Nick Crandall: Oblivion lead guitarist
Married to Lila Ronson Shawcross, father of Charlie and Avery, twin brother of Ricki 'Elle', best friends with Simon Kagan, co-founder of Oblivion

Noah Jordan: Roth Defense specialist
Brother to Hunter, best friends with Quinn Alexander

Owen Blackwell: Hammered bass guitarist
Married to Callie Templeton, father of Lily

(Osmond) Oz Taylor: Brooklyn Dawn bass guitarist
Involved with Daisy Flannigan, brother of Kerry Taylor *

Piper Lockwood: Owns Rosie & Hank's Pussy Palace Café
Involved with Hudson Wyatt

Quinn Alexander: Roth Defense specialist, former Navy Seal
Married to Faith Keystone, best friends with Noah Jordan

Randy Pruitt*: Warning Sign roadie/lead lighting technician
Involved with Juliet Reece and Tristan Eves, father of Joshua Randall, brother of Harper

Reed 'Bats' Mason: Hammered lead guitarist
Best friends with Hunter Jordan and Zachary Kane

Ricki 'Elle' Crandall: Warning Sign guitarist

Married to Malachi Shawcross, twin sister of Nick Crandall

Roman: Clothing designer

Rory Ferguson: Record producer/rhythm guitarist
Married to Ivy Beck, father of Rhiannon, brother of Thomas and Maureen, best friends with Ian Kagan, friends with Flynn Sheppard and Kellan McGuire

Ryan Waters: Warning Sign jack-of-all-trades
Married to Denver Casey, best friends with Michael Shawcross and West Reynolds

Sabrina Price: Ripper Records executive who manages Ian Kagan and Brooklyn Dawn

Sarah Webster: Bodyguard with Roth Defense

Sean Reagan: Roth Defense Consultant
Friends with Oz Taylor

Simon Kagan: Oblivion lead singer
Married to Margo Reece, father of Raine Lila, brother of Ian, best friends with Nick Crandall, co-founder of Oblivion

Teagan Daly: Brooklyn Dawn keyboardist
Involved with Cooper Dallas, high school friend of Ricki 'Elle' Crandall

Tristan Eves: Head chef at The Hollow
Married to Juliet Reece, involved with Randy Pruitt*, father of Joshua Randall, best friends with Hunter Jordan

Victoria Sheer: Actress/Model

Involved with Reed Mason, ex-girlfriend of Hunter Jordan

West Reynolds: Warning Sign keyboardist
Married to Lauren Bryant, father of Chloe (isn't in her life), brother of Raven, best friends with Michael Shawcross and Ryan Waters

William 'Snake' Scotsman*: Oblivion ex-drummer
Father of Axl with Chloe Adams, co-founder of Oblivion

Zachary Kane: Hammered rhythm guitarist
Best friends with Reed 'Bats' Mason

Zane Landry: Brooklyn Dawn rhythm guitarist

Zoe Manning: Artist/photographer
Engaged to Ian Kagan, mother of Elvis, sister of Beckett, Hayes, and Justin, cousin of Lila Ronson Shawcross Crandall, friends with Ivy Beck and Maggie Kelly

*denotes deceased

as of 11/18/2020

BROOKLYN DAWN

BROOKLYN DAWN

Play Dirty

Play Fast

Play Mine

Play Hard

Coming Soon

Play Rough

FIND MORE OF OUR HOT ALPHA ROCKERS AT

www.quinnandelliott.com

QUINN AND ELLIOTT

Rockers Reading Order

Lost in Oblivion

Winchester Falls

Found in Oblivion

Hammered

Rock Revenge

Brooklyn Dawn

Other Series

The Boss

Tapped Out

Love Required

Boys of Fall

If you'd like more information about us please visit

www.quinnandelliott.com

CRESCENT COVE

Have My Baby

Claim My Baby

Who's The Daddy

Pit Stop: Baby

Baby Daddy Wanted

Rockstar Baby

Daddy in Disguise

My Ex's Baby

Daddy Undercover

Wrong Bed Baby

CRESCENT COVE STANDALONES

CEO Daddy

CRESCENT COVE BITES

Fireman Daddy

Mistletoe Baby

For more information about our books visit

www.tarynquinn.com

ALSO BY TARYN QUINN

For more information about our books visit

www.tarynquinn.com

ABOUT THE AUTHORS

USA Today bestselling author **Cari Quinn** likes music and men, so she figured why not write about both? When she's not writing, she's screaming at men's college basketball games on TV, playing her music too loud or causing trouble. Sometimes simultaneously.

USA Today bestselling author **Taryn Elliott** is obsessed with rock stars, men, and her unending playlists—maximizing these things seemed like a very good idea. When she's not writing, you can probably find her surrounded by planner supplies trying to organize her life.

They decided to combine forces and found that hey...this writing deal is even more awesome when you collaborate with your best friend.

And so the Oblivion World was born.

Want to know more?
www.quinnandelliott.com
taryncari@quinnandelliott.com

www.ingramcontent.com/pod-product-compliance
Lightning Source LLC
Chambersburg PA
CBHW072115250626
47159CB00007B/2454